Eugenia

EUGENIA

A FICTIONAL SKETCH OF FUTURE CUSTOMS

~A CRITICAL EDITION~

Eduardo Urzaiz

edited and translated by

Sarah A. Buck Kachaluba and *Aaron Dziubinskyj*

The University of Wisconsin Press

Publication of this volume has been made possible, in part, through support from the Brittingham Fund.

The University of Wisconsin Press
1930 Monroe Street, 3rd Floor
Madison, Wisconsin 53711-2059
uwpress.wisc.edu

3 Henrietta Street, Covent Garden
London WC2E 8LU, United Kingdom
eurospanbookstore.com

Originally published as *Eugenia: Esbozo novelesco de costumbres futuras*, © 1919 by Talleres gráficos A. Manzanilla, Mérida, Mexico

Printed in the United States of America

This book may be available in a digital edition

Library of Congress Cataloging-in-Publication Data

Urzáiz Rodríguez, Eduardo, 1876–1955, author.
[Eugenia. English]
Eugenia : a fictional sketch of future customs / Eduardo Urzaiz; edited and translated by Sarah A. Buck Kachaluba and Aaron Dziubinskyj. — Critical edition.
pages   cm
Originally published as: Eugenia: esbozo novelesco de costumbres futuras, ©1919, by Talleres gráficos A. Manzanilla, Mérida, Mexico.
Includes bibliographical references and index.
ISBN 978-0-299-30684-7 (pbk.: alk. paper)
I. Buck Kachaluba, Sarah A., editor, translator.
II. Dziubinskyj, Aaron, editor, translator.   III. Title.
PQ7297.U78E813   2016
863'.62—dc23
2015010204

For *JP* and *August*
                    —Sarah
For *Rosalía* and *Mathias*
                    —Aaron

Contents

Acknowledgments

Much like *Eugenia* itself, this work began as a dream. It then became a work in progress for a long time. I happened across a copy of *Eugenia* in an old bookstore on Donceles, in the historic *centro* district of Mexico City, in 1998 or 1999. It caught my eye because I had run across Urzaiz in my research on Yucatecan women's activism and the Yucatecan birth control campaign discussed in the essay "Social and Biological Reproduction in *Eugenia*." I mentioned the novel in this context in my dissertation and in an article published in *Signos Históricos* and hoped that someday I would figure out a way to develop it into a larger project. Early words of encouragement from Gabriela Cano helped this seed to germinate; she commented that the passage on Urzaiz was one of the "perlas" (pearls) in my *Signos Históricos* essay on Mother's Day and Pronatalism in post-revolutionary Mexico. The project developed further when I presented on *Eugenia* at the 2005 Berkshire's Women's History conference at which friends and colleagues gave me helpful feedback and encouragement both at my session and in less formal conversations beyond. By this time I had a more developed vision of a translated, critical edition of the novel with at least one and possibly more essays introducing, contextualizing, and examining the work.

Ten years later, after two cross-country moves (one from New Mexico to Florida and another from Florida to California), the transition from history professor to academic librarian, and a baby (who is now eight), the book has become a reality. This would not have happened without the support of my husband, JP, and my son, August; my coauthor Aaron Dziubinskyj; many other colleagues, friends, and extended family (listed below); and the University of Wisconsin Press.

The beginning of the critical apparatus for this book came from the paper that I presented at the Berkshire women's history conference and an article published by Aaron in *Science Fiction Studies* but the bulk of the manuscript—the translation and the critical essays—were written during my tenure as Humanities Librarian at Florida State University. I was incredibly fortunate in my work at FSU Libraries to have the history department treat me as one of their own. This work is much stronger because of the feedback I received through participation in two works-in-progress seminars, close readings by a few friends and colleagues, and multiple discussions over coffee or meals on campus and beyond. In the FSU Department of History Charles (Chuck) Upchurch, who was my grad school companion at Rutgers, helped me understand aspects of the overlap between physical (for example endocrinological) and psychiatric/psychological theories related to gender identity and sexuality at the turn of the century and pointed me to important early readings in this area before I had a coherent draft to give to anyone to read. Darrin McMahon closely read my earliest draft of the critical apparatus of this project. I gave this to Darrin as he was preparing to head off for a year's sabbatical in Germany since he would be unable to attend the works-in-progress seminar where I was presenting it. His response, advice, and encouragement on what eventually became three separate essays, as well as the project as a whole, has contributed to significant organizational changes in the book and clarifications in the historical context and arguments presented therein.

At the first works-in-progress seminar at which history colleagues graciously read my work, Chuck Upchurch and Alex Aviña pushed me on the question of whether to consider *Eugenia* a utopia or a dystopia. Chuck encouraged me to emphasize one or the other while Alex suggested attributing Urzaiz's ambivalence to the Mexican revolutionary and postrevolutionary context. Robinson Herrera and Will Hanley were also very receptive to the project. Robinson suggested doing an abridged version if I felt that not all passages were as interesting as others (Aaron and I unanimously felt it was worth translating it in its entirety, but this suggestion helped me to start what seemed to be a daunting project).

At a second works-in-progress session, Darrin McMahon and George Williamson offered needed clarifications, references, and suggestions in intellectual history to an early draft of the chapter on eugenics. George even prepared a written summary of these suggestions. Kurt Piehler and Chuck Upchurch highlighted the significance of Mexican eugenic experiments and the importance of bringing Mexico and Latin America into global discussions of these and other issues as they were shocked (as US and British historians, respectively) that such things were happening in Mexico. And Frederick (Fritz) Davis pointed me to important developments in and readings on the history of evolutionary science. Darrin, George, Fritz, and Michael Ruse reread a revised draft of the eugenics chapter and gave me very helpful suggestions for the final version. I also sat in on Darrin and George's twentieth-century intellectual history course in the spring of 2014, which helped me understand Sigmund Freud and Friedrich Nietzsche's influence on Urzaiz in particular, and the broader intellectual context in which Urzaiz was writing more generally.

Colleagues at FSU Libraries, particularly Gloria Colvin, Jessica Evans Brady, Marcia Gorin, Renaine Julian, Kyung Kim, Jillyann Sánchez, Abby Scheel, and Trip Wyckoff and others in Modern Languages, especially Silvia Valisa, Juan Carlos Galeano, José Gomariz, and Dana and Christian Weber, and History, including Andrew Frank, Jennifer Koslow, and Suzy Sinke, were also encouraging. As a scholar at FSU I can now join many other faculty members in thanking FSU Libraries Interlibrary Loan department (who I also love as my colleagues) for quickly getting the books and articles I needed to complete this as well. I have been incredibly grateful to Velma Smith, who heads the department, for moving boulders to get my research materials and for her personal warmth and encouragement.

Paul Eiss was very receptive to this project when I ran into him at LASA in 2013 (after not seeing him for at least ten years), and he is the one who connected me to Doña Candelaria (Candida) Souza de Fernández, who provided very helpful insights on Urzaiz's character, interests, and possible motivations in writing *Eugenia*. Maritza Arrigunaga Coello, archivist emeritus at the University of Texas–Arlington, sent me two copies of the *Catálogo de las fotocopias de los Documentos y Periódicos Yucatecos en la Biblioteca de la Universidad de Texas en Arlington* so that I could identify newspapers to search for reviews of *Eugenia*, facilitated my acquisition of the *Revista de Yucatán* through ILL, and went above and beyond meeting my requests by alerting me to the Universidad Nacional Autónoma de México's new edition of *Eugenia* in 2006 and related articles.

I am grateful to Roy Ziegler, to whom I reported for many years, for his consistent support of this project and Dean Julia Zimmerman, who advocated on my behalf for Professional Development Leave that allowed me to spend six weeks in Mérida, Yucatán, in the summer of 2014, during which I was able to do follow-up research on Urzaiz and *Eugenia*, including interviews with Urzaiz's mentee and colleague, Doña Candida Souza. This was also made possible by a grant from FSU's Council on Research and Creativity, which funded travel to Yucatán to work on *Eugenia* as well as an ongoing digitization project involving oral histories that I began in 2000.

My travel to Mexico was also facilitated by Julian Hernández, who loaned me an unlocked cell phone to use in Mexico. Julian and his family (including his son, Josiah, who is a good friend of my son, August) join my dear friend Inés

Ortiz Yam and her extended family (grandmother, Emma, with whom I lived in 2000 while doing dissertation work in Yucatán; mother, Concha, who provided me with a house that I could rent in the summer of 2015; brother, Antonio, and sister-in-law, Deysi, who arranged for August to attend school for a month with their daughter Mariana, and took August home with them three days a week to play with their three children, Mariana, Ana Sofia, and Toñito, so that I had the freedom to do my work until 5 p.m.) in supporting my attempts to provide August with a study-abroad experience at age six and to learn Spanish so that he too can love Mexico as I have. While August and I were in Mérida, Inés and her husband, José Luis, and their daughter, María Inés (who was not yet one year old), and other members of the family mentioned above invited us to multiple get-togethers exposing August to many aspects of Mexican life and making us feel truly at home.

Mark Wasserman has supported this project and all of my scholarly endeavors since I became his graduate student in 1995. My parents, Katherine Hillier and Edward Loranger and Paul and Gloria Buck; my siblings, Abby and Jay Reynolds and Jonathan Buck and Christine Hunter; and my parents-in-law, Everett and Rita Whittaker and Ann Marie Kachaluba, have also encouraged me and celebrated my successes on this and other projects. My mother read initial drafts of the entire translation, corrected awkward phrases, and offered alternative words that worked better in several places. Mark Cobb and Melissa Bruhn's interest in this project (and willingness to let me babble on about it) has also meant a lot to me.

Working with Aaron has been truly a pleasure. I cannot imagine a more perfect work partnership. I approached Aaron about translating and writing a critical edition after reading his article in *Science Fiction Studies*. Early on we discussed possible formats for the book, the work balance, and technicalities such as the listing of our names and who would be given credit for what. From this initial conversation we agreed that it was to be our work, done together. That is exactly what it has been. Aaron completed the initial translations; I read multiple drafts and suggested changes. I wrote the initial drafts of the introduction and the essays "Social and Biological Reproduction in *Eugenia*" and "*Eugenia* and Eugenics." Aaron drafted the final essay, "*Eugenia*'s Literary Genesis and Genealogy." We carefully read one another's essays as they went through multiple drafts on which we wrote extensive comments. We had many phone conversations, which were always a pleasure. We talked about minor and major arguments in our essays and book, drew comparisons to current events—including those related to two American political election cycles. We compared notes on our boys—two weeks apart in birthday—and learned a little bit about one another's spouses. I will miss working with Aaron but perhaps we can come up with another joint project down the road.

The University of Wisconsin Press has also been a joy to work with. From the moment I met her at LASA 2013, Gwen Walker has been interested, supportive, and proactive in making this book a reality. Carla Marolt has done a masterful job coordinating the book's cover design, based largely on the 1919 original. The entire editorial staff, including Gwen and Carla, as well as Adam Mehring, Sheila McMahon, and Michelle Wing, corrected errors and asked insightful, substantive questions about the content that led to needed clarifications and revision. Two anonymous readers had both encouraging and constructively critical comments on the first draft of the introduction and three translated chapters, and Andrea Bell and Cristina Rivera Garza provided equally enthusiastic and probing feedback on the full manuscript. Ron Numbers asked very insightful questions about the draft of "*Eugenia* and Eugenics" submitted with the complete manuscript, forcing us to significantly clarify our thinking and improve our writing therein. The book is far better for all of the input we have received from colleagues approached by the press and ourselves.

Above all, I am grateful to JP and August for all the ways they supported this labor and I hope they will enjoy reading at least the fictional portion of this work as much as I have enjoyed producing it. I am thankful to JP for cooking so often, driving the 2.5 hours to Destin to spend Saturdays at the beach, helping me think of alternative words for the translation, and learning more about Eduardo Urzaiz and Mexican eugenics than he probably wanted to. I appreciate the many times that August entertained himself at home and in the car so that I could—passage by passage—complete this work. I thank both of them for helping to keep our household afloat and operating relatively smoothly and for understanding that housework is not, nor ever will be, my strong suit. I dedicate this work to them.

SARAH

This work has been germinating for many, many years. I had put it on the shelf and was about to move on to other projects when Sarah contacted me out of the blue in the fall of 2011 asking me if I would like to collaborate with her on a critical translation of *Eugenia*. Had it not been for Sarah, this book would have never happened. Our collaboration has grown over the years, and I have come to know and respect her as a tremendously generous and intelligent colleague. I have learned much from Sarah about research and translation, and combining those to create a scholarly work that we hope will be enjoyed by a wide readership.

There are many people who have helped to make this project a possibility. Sarah has eloquently recognized and thanked the numerous scholars and colleagues to whom I am indebted for all of their contributions on many different levels. In addition, I would like to thank Miguel Ángel Fernández-Delgado, who first introduced me to *Eugenia*, and for his scholarship that has been invaluable to the field of Latin American science fiction. I am also extremely grateful to Andrea Bell, Rachel Haywood Ferreira, and Dale Knickerbocker, all of whom I met while attending conferences held by the International Association for the Fantastic in the Arts. At different points in my career they have served as chair of the international division of the International Association for the Fantastic in the Arts, and thus read my papers, attended my presentations, and offered much-needed advice and criticism. I have considered each to be solid mentors and colleagues throughout the years.

I would like to thank Art Evans, scholar, colleague at DePauw University, mentor, friend, and editor and publisher of *Science Fiction Studies*. He gave me my first professional break by publishing a couple of my articles, including an early version of my scholarship on *Eugenia*. With his wealth of experience and research, Art has always been a great inspiration.

Finally, I would like to thank my wife, Rosalía, who encouraged and supported me throughout this project; my parents, Andy and Marta; and of course, my son, Mathias, whose youthful insights and inquisitiveness have given me perspective and kept me grounded throughout this project.

AARON

Note on Translation

Throughout *Eugenia*, Urzaiz's language is at once playful, ironic, descriptive, and imaginative. One might expect this from an early twentieth-century Mexican intellectual who worked primarily in the medical profession but also dabbled in art and literary scholarship. Urzaiz's Villautopia is a futuristic place that can only be painted in words, and thus the author had to rely on what he knew, as well as what he dreamed and imagined as he projected his vision some three hundred years into the future. Many of the words that Urzaiz uses to describe the futuristic apparatus and concepts are likely of his own invention, thus, one of the challenging aspects for me as principal translator of his novel was in finding a balance between what I thought Urzaiz was attempting to describe with his early twentieth-century Spanish, while at the same time respecting his unique voice and literary style. He is at once eloquent and cruel in his language, especially with respect to Celiana, as the reader will discover. Urzaiz also writes with scientific precision, such as when he describes the *cannabis indica* cigarette that Celiana smokes. Rather than translate this as "joint," we decided to let Urzaiz's terminology speak for itself. Likewise, the author demonstrates an ironic sense of humor, such as with the character known as "Miajitas," whose name might best be translated as "A Few Crumbs." As a final example, the term *tocofobia*, which might be described as a fear of childbirth, really has no English translation that captures the nuance of this concept. The origin and context of *tocofobia* is described in the essay "*Eugenia* and Eugenics." In terms of grammar, Urzaiz did not use quotation marks in his novel but rather em dashes to indicate when people speak. While this is a fairly common practice in non-English texts, we decided to use quotation marks here to make it easier for the English-language reader. He also uses ellipses throughout, within paragraphs or at the ends of chapters, and we have also maintained this characteristic of the novel.

Sarah was extremely helpful in cleaning up my translations so that this work reads as smoothly as possible for the modern-day reader in English. If there are any passages that appear clunky or awkward, it is because they are equally so in Spanish. In general, though, we have attempted to capture the tone and intent that Urzaiz set out to convey in *Eugenia*. As one of the reviewers of our manuscript observed, we have managed to keep the somewhat solemn tone of Urzaiz's early twentieth-century Spanish without diminishing its intensity and speed. Another reviewer noted that we did an excellent job at preserving the lofty, slightly antiquated feel of the original Spanish while avoiding ungainly words and phrasing. In the end, we hope that all readers will enjoy this translation of *Eugenia*, as much for the story that it depicts as for the intensity and antiquated feel of Urzaiz's language.

Aaron Dziubinskyj

Eduardo Urzaiz's Eugenia

A Critical Introduction

*I*n the prologue to his novel *Eugenia*, Eduardo Urzaiz writes, "I too dream often! And in my dreams, dear reader, I contemplate a humanity that is almost happy, free at last from the shackles and prejudices with which today's humanity willingly complicates and embitters life. The simple love story that unfolds in this attempt at a novel has served me only as an excuse to conjure up a vision— even if pale and imprecise—of that future humanity of my hopes and dreams."[1]

Written in 1919, the "simple love story" created by Urzaiz is set within the futuristic community of "Villautopia," the capital of a subconfederation of Central America in the twenty-third century. In Villautopia, Urzaiz imagines a political-economic order that is free of the past social plagues of war, poverty, neglect, or other social ills that his own early twentieth-century community (of Mérida, Yucatán, Mexico) was trying to eradicate. He portrays a society that embraces an ethic of free love and relies on a publicly regulated reproductive apparatus through which selected breeders create biologically desirable off-spring who are raised in state facilities until they are old enough to choose their own, nonnuclear families.[2] In devising such a system, Urzaiz demonstrates an apparent utopian vision of eugenics, a corpus of ideas and practices compelling to people throughout the world during this period. Thus, in many ways, Villa-utopia tells the story of the triumphant conquest of modernity achieved by the supreme reign of technology, as humans gain control of economic, political, social, and biological reproduction.

Villautopia's very name; Urzaiz's narrative of technological, modernizing achievement; and Urzaiz's self-stated goal to "conjure up a vision . . . of that future humanity of [his] hopes and dreams" suggest that the novel is a utopia. Yet some of the social dynamics that Urzaiz describes challenge his vision of a perfect society, indicating that Villautopia has not found answers for some of the more difficult aspects of the human condition. Thus, it can be argued that within the utopian narrative of *Eugenia* there are elements of a dystopian menace that appear to be of a spiritual or moral character. Dystopian "literature," as M. Keith Booker has explained, "situates itself in direct opposition to utopian thought, warning against the potential negative consequences of arrant utopianism."[3] The dystopian characteristics of Villautopia necessarily challenge traditional notions of utopian societies and force the reader to resolve for him or herself those aspects of the human condition that are contrary to Urzaiz's "utopian" vision for a future humanity. One issue in particular—how humans bond together in relationships of love and family—constitutes a major, unresolved tension at the core of the novel.

Villautopia is characterized by the replacement of the nuclear family (composed of blood relatives brought together through biological reproduction and institutionalized by marriage) with family groups based on affinities of character, originating in and rooted by the commitment to "free love" and a state-regulated reproductive system. But by the end of the novel, two of the main characters, who are selected breeders for the state, live by themselves and conceive a child. It is unclear what will happen next, and the author leaves it up to the reader to decide by ending the novel long before the baby is born. On the one hand, the father describes the state's reproductive apparatus to the mother, explaining that if the couple wants to, they can rely on the state to help birth and raise the child. On the other, the novel presents no other example of a couple living by themselves (without other adults), and conceiving, let alone giving birth to and raising, a child. Yet these characters appear to be very much in love and it seems logical that they may wish to remain living only with one another and with the child they are expecting (as well as others who may come in the future). This second scenario can be understood as indicating the possibility of actions contrary to the utopian vision of Villautopia.

The question of whether to encourage or even to allow the survival of the nuclear family is central to the narrative of *Eugenia* and raises additional physiological and psychological questions that fascinated Urzaiz and remain unanswered in the world of Villautopia. Such questions include: first, the degree to which human reproduction is a "natural" and even "divine" process or one that can or should be technologically manipulated; and second, whether there is a necessary connection between the biological process and practice of reproduction, the emotional or psychological experience of love, and the sociological formation of families.

Such questions define and haunt the novel, and the fact that they remain unanswered—or, rather, answered in contradictory ways, preventing Urzaiz from offering a clear vision or argument—suggests that rather than being defined *only* as a utopia, *Eugenia* might *also* be characterized as a dystopia. Or, as Miguel Ángel Fernández Delgado has observed, in *Eugenia*, love crumbles under the weight of science to the degree that Urzaiz's initial utopian vision "disintegrates into a dystopian nightmare by the end of the novel."[4] And it may well be that this disintegration is Urzaiz's intent all along. He may be arguing, through this tactic, that natural laws, including the emotional drive to love, reproduce, and create a family with one's chosen love, should not be ignored or suppressed in the face of scientific modernization.

Whether one defines *Eugenia* as a utopia and/or a dystopia, one should read *Eugenia* as a pioneering work of speculative science fiction that anticipates a future when the distinction between shaping social organization and enforcing scientific dogma will be clouded by humanity's obsession with controlled human reproduction as a means to fabricate an ideal society. The subtitle of Urzaiz's novel is *A Fictional Sketch of Future Customs*. The speculative vision in *Eugenia* is in a sense a meditation on the influence of hard science on human behavior and foreshadows the eventual dystopian unraveling of the novel. The juxtaposition of themes suggested in the title and subtitle (eugenics as a scientific project vs. the ideal or dream of a social utopia that incorporates eugenic ideas and principles) draws attention to the dual dimension of the work's structure. The prologue sets up the novel as a kind of daydream, a vision that the author has had in which he contemplates a society that is free from "the shackles and prejudices with which today's humanity willingly complicates and embitters life."[5] Urzaiz defends this utopian vision from those who might attack him as mad by reasoning that "I have known and still know insane people who write with such beauty and reason, that I would be neither surprised nor offended if my work were classified as such."[6] This seemingly eccentric stance is accepted by Urzaiz as a kind of sublime philosophy, understood only by those whose worldview is unorthodox, or insane, and expressed to the rest of the world through literature. Urzaiz's allusions to his work with the sick, insane, and other groups also evoke a tragic vision of humanity in the prologue that permeates the entire novel. Between his eccentricity and this sense of tragedy, perhaps Urzaiz is providing a clue to reading *Eugenia*, in that if it is merely a daydream or an insane vision of the future, then the novel is not to be taken too seriously and that perhaps humanity's efforts to achieve progress—in revolutionary Mexico and other regional and temporal contexts—were to some degree futile. This reading of *Eugenia* is corroborated by Urzaiz's regular contribution of stories of a parochial nature to a magazine column in which he poked fun at priests, nuns, and monks, as well as religious fanatics. This did not sit well with some in Mérida's conservative society. His enemies, especially those who never forgave him for his support of higher education for women, accused Urzaiz of being an atheist, heretic, and of commiserating with the devil.

In his preface to the third edition of *Eugenia*, Leopoldo Peniche Vallado writes that "in its time, *Eugenia* upset the critics and the public and was, perhaps, the work by Dr. Urzaiz that most contributed to people viewing him as having an undesirable reputation and regarding him with the precautionary distrust reserved for eccentrics and the unbalanced."[7] In fact, Peniche Vallado acknowledges that Urzaiz "anticipated popular consensus" when he announced in the prologue: "I am certain that many individuals, those who consider themselves the only legitimate heirs of common sense, will scandalously cry out, 'But this is the work of a madman!' after reading my book."[8]

In contrast to Urzaiz's critics and enemies, to those who knew him well he was a harmless, freethinking agnostic of strong convictions who respected the beliefs of others. Urzaiz, then, invites his readers to contemplate the social implications of his novel as a dreamlike vision that is firmly grounded in scientific discourse. Hence, *Eugenia* is a speculative novel that asks the reader to question the motives of revolutionary science as the foundation for a utopian worldview and new model of social order that privileges the will of the collective over the needs of the individual.

A Biographical Sketch of Eduardo Urzaiz

Dr. Eduardo Urzaiz de Rodríguez (1876–1955) is fondly and widely remembered in Mérida, Yucatán. He was born in Guanabacoa, Cuba (now a suburb of Havana), but as Carlos Peniche Ponce, editor of a recent edition of *Eugenia*, has stated, Urzaiz eventually became "totally *yucateco*," having lived in Mérida since the age of fourteen.[9] By all accounts he was an energetic, creative, artistic, professional, progressive, charismatic, friendly, and charming character, working as a normal-school teacher, gynecologist, and obstetrician. He also studied art and literature, and produced drawings, paintings, and literary criticism as well as fiction. Finally, he was a serious student of psychiatry, although he was never certified as a psychiatrist.[10] In addition to his prolific, creative, varied career, he and his wife, Doña Rosita Jiménez, had a busy and complete home life, raising fourteen children and often housing and supporting other family members or close friends as well.[11]

Urzaiz's parents, Fernando Urzaiz Arritola and Gertrudis Rodríguez Ramírez, were both Cuban creoles.[12] According to Urzaiz's biographer and son, Carlos Urzaiz Jiménez, Eduardo Urzaiz's father enjoyed "fortune and

Eduardo Urzaiz in 1904, during his visit to New York to study psychiatry. At that time, he was twenty-eight years old. Reprinted by permission from Carlos Urzaiz Jiménez, *Oficio de mentor: Biografía del Dr. Eduardo Urzáiz Rodríguez* (Mérida, Yucatán: Ediciones de la Universidad Autónoma de Yucatán, 1996).

Eduardo Urzaiz (*front, second from left*) flanked by his colleagues Clodomiro González Ortiz and Efraín Moguel Montes de Oca, as well as his students, on a morning in 1952. Reprinted by permission from Carlos Urzaiz Jiménez, *Oficio de mentor: Biografía del Dr. Eduardo Urzáiz Rodríguez* (Mérida, Yucatán: Ediciones de la Universidad Autónoma de Yucatán, 1996).

esteem" in their native community of Guanabacoa.[13] In spite of this, Urzaiz Jiménez explains, Urzaiz's mother homeschooled her children because she felt that late nineteenth-century Cuban public education was lacking and private education was prohibitively expensive for those of the middle classes.[14]

The family moved to the La Víbora neighborhood in Havana and later to the Yucatán. According to Urzaiz Jiménez, the exact circumstances for the move to Mexico are unknown, but in general, it is clear that the main motive was economic. Eduardo Urzaiz's father was a "highly educated and literate poet of great sensibility," but it was a challenge for him to support his family and although he had studied business in France he could not maintain the hardware business that he had inherited.[15] Thus, he welcomed the offer from his brother-in-law, a stamp (tax) collector in Mérida, to pay the cost of his passage to Mérida and employ him as his bookkeeper.[16]

When the family arrived in Yucatán in 1890, the Mexican state and federal governments both viewed public schooling as a critical component of Mexican economic development and national identity formation. Between 1857 (when Mexico's liberal constitution separated church and state) and 1880, most primary schools were managed by municipalities or private individuals and corporations, including churches, but after 1880, state governments became increasingly involved in the administration of public primary schools. Such control, however, "depended on the state governor's commitment to education and his resources."[17] The extent of this commitment "could range from the establishment of normal (teachers' training) schools to the creation of incipient inspection systems, from oversight of local educational expenditures to their subsidization," as well as "the appointment of teachers by governors' prefects, or *jefes políticos*."[18] Consequently, by 1900, most Mexican states had teacher-training schools that supported primary public schooling, at least one public preparatory school for boys, and Catholic and sometimes Protestant schools, which all opened avenues of mobility to middle-class males.[19] Urzaiz and his brothers served as examples of middle-class males who benefitted from the opportunities presented by Yucatán's public schools. Urzaiz's success in public school led him into teaching, educational administration, and ultimately into a career as an obstetrician-gynecologist and university professor and administrator.

Urzaiz also enjoyed extracurricular study beyond the parameters of public school. For example, he studied oil painting with the artist Juan Gamboa Guzmán, cultivating a lifelong interest in art and the practice of drawing and painting.[20] In particular, he enjoyed drawing cartoons, which appeared in magazines including *Pimienta y mostaza* (1892–94 and 1902–3) and *La Campana* (1907–14). He also published drawings and cartoons about current Yucatecan events using the pseudonym Claudio Meex. The most notable of these were published in the *Diario del Sureste*. Many of these essays were reproduced in a two-volume collection called *Reconstrucción de hechos*.[21]

Urzaiz was also a prolific writer, publishing works of literary analysis, biography, and translation, as well as pedagogical and medical textbooks and articles and other narratives "demonstrating the advances of science and letters in social and political spheres."[22] He could often be found teaching or narrating in the public spaces of Mérida, including on his ride home on the public bus, making him "one of the most well-known characters" who lived in mid-twentieth-century Mérida.[23] His good friend and admirer, Dr. Luis Peniche Vallado, writes that "for more than half a century, he was a guide for youth . . . recognized by everyone, even his enemies, for his . . . civic virtues . . . versatile culture, and over all, his incredible goodness."[24]

Urzaiz began his working years as a professor at a teachers' training college (normal school), following his graduation in 1894 at the age of eighteen. After several difficult years facing the limitations of putting pedagogical theory into practice with rooms of students ranging in abilities and interest, he enrolled in medical school in 1897, and in 1902, he received his medical degree with a specialization in surgery from Yucatán's School of Medicine and Surgery, writing a thesis on mental disequilibrium.[25] After three years spent living and working in the nearby city of Izamal, he received a scholarship from the Yucatecan government to study psychiatry and obstetrics in New York in 1904.[26] Although he does not tell us when they met or married, Urzaiz's son and biographer, Carlos Urzaiz Jiménez, states that in 1904 Urzaiz (who was twenty-eight years old) "moved with his young wife [Urzaiz Jiménez's mother] to the 'metropóli de acero' [iron metropolis] and from there imported the rich reserve of his knowledge in psychiatry which he disseminated widely in our School of Medicine."[27]

Following his return to the Yucatán in 1907, Urzaiz asked the governor of the state to create professorships in both psychiatry and obstetrics at the state's medical school.[28] As there was no one else with such a strong interest in psychiatry, Urzaiz became the university's first professor in this area, a position he held until his death, thereby "initiating all [of Yucatán's] doctors in the mysteries of mental illness" for almost fifty years.[29] He later became a professor of histology as well, but his focus remained obstetrics.[30] As professor of obstetrics, he trained many in the art of assisting birth and also modernized the "treatment of difficult births," especially by training students in the safe practice of the cesarean birth in Yucatán.[31] According to the archivist Maritza Arrigunaga, in the course of his career Urzaiz delivered a good part of Mérida's population.[32]

Urzaiz also played an instrumental role in shaping Yucatán's two major medical institutions: the Ayala Asylum (for the treatment of the mentally ill) and the O'Horan Hospital. He helped found the asylum, becoming its first director in 1906, managing services for mentally ill women especially, and his leadership there ensured the introduction of important changes "in the concept of mental illness and its therapeutic management . . . in accordance with scientific advancements . . . humanizing the treatment of the patients."[33] In 1912 Urzaiz became head of maternity services at the O'Horan Hospital. He was also a founding member of the Yucatecan Society of Obstetrics and Gynecology and served twice as its president.[34]

Urzaiz's work as a health and educational administrator converged with revolutionary and postrevolutionary reform projects led by the Yucatecan governors Salvador Alvarado (1915–18) and Felipe Carrillo Puerto (1922–24).[35] One of Urzaiz's earliest contributions to Yucatecan revolutionary reform was his involvement in two congresses on pedagogy, held in 1915 and 1916, at which Urzaiz defended rationalist schools and female and male coeducation at all scholastic levels.[36]

During the 1920s and following decades, Urzaiz continued to cooperate with Yucatecan governors to promote education at all levels in the state of Yucatán. He did this by teaching at the secondary and university level for his entire life and by holding many positions of authority for the state related to his expertise as a teacher and doctor. Some of his positions included teaching at and serving as director of the Escuela Normal de Profesores (Normal School of Teachers); teaching as professor of artistic anatomy at the Escuela de Bellas Artes (School of Fine Arts); serving as the head of the section of pedagogy for the Ateneo Peninsular (Peninsular Scientific and Artistic Association), of which he was a founding member; serving as medical inspector; directing the Escuela Normal Mixta (Coeducational Teachers' College) in 1920; and teaching religion at the "Rodolfo Menéndez de la Peña" Teachers' College in 1935.[37]

In 1920, Urzaiz was one of Yucatán's delegates to a national educational conference in Mexico City, which must have been related to his acquisition of the directorship of the state of Yucatán's department of education in 1921 (a role he would again fill from 1930 to 1935). During these years (1920 and 1921), Urzaiz convinced the Mexican intellectual and statesman José Vasconcelos, later known as the author of the racial manifesto *La raza cósmica* (*The Cosmic Race*, 1925), who was, in those years, the national minister of education, to grant funds for the establishment of the Universidad Nacional del Sureste (National University of the Southeast) in 1922.[38] In relation to his role in creating the university, Urzaiz became its first rector.[39] Urzaiz was also involved in the new university as a professor, since the medical school became incorporated as one of the university's faculties in 1922. Urzaiz served as the director of the Faculty of Medicine between 1944 and 1946.

Urzaiz also played an instrumental role in the creation of the state of Yucatán's first secondary school, which opened in 1930 and allowed nonprivileged students to continue their studies beyond sixth grade.[40] By 1931, the demand for admission was already greater than the school could accommodate, leading to the opening of more secondary schools in the following years. Consequently, by 1955, more than ten secondary schools existed in the state of Yucatán.[41]

Luis Peniche Vallado describes Urzaiz's work as an educator and founder of educational institutions as the realization of one of his "most precious desires, . . . to advance the culture of [Yucatán's] proletariat class," thereby expressing his "great love" for the people, and in particular, students and youth.[42] Peniche Vallado's assertion that Urzaiz cared deeply about social uplift helps to situate Urzaiz's work, including the writing of *Eugenia,* within the local and national context of the Mexican Revolution and the postrevolutionary period that followed.

Urzaiz's novel was published in 1919, in Mérida, Yucatán, a key site of revolutionary battles, debates, and experimentation, and a vigorous center of postrevolutionary reform.[43] *Eugenia* does not argue for militaristic revolution as an arbiter of change or explicitly suggest that the Mexican Revolution would produce the radically altered society described in his novel. In fact, the literary scholar Robert McKee Irwin points out that "although the novel was published in 1919, there is no mention of the Mexican Revolution anywhere in it."[44] Nonetheless, it is important to understand the revolutionary and postrevolutionary context in which Urzaiz wrote for several reasons. First, this was the world in which Urzaiz lived and which provided fodder for his ideas and defined his work, lifestyle, and leisure. Second, Urzaiz contributed in many ways to Yucatán's revolutionary and postrevolutionary project. Third, centered as it is on the creation of an imaginary world, Urzaiz's novel reveals much about the ideals of Urzaiz and the real world in which he lived: revolutionary and postrevolutionary Yucatán. Thus, one way to read *Eugenia* is as an attempt to portray the successful (if the novel is to be read as a utopia) or unsuccessful (if the novel is to be read as a dystopia) resolution of the major social issues with which Yucatán's revolutionary and postrevolutionary adherents struggled. These include efforts to build new political administrative systems; bring about economic restructuring through labor organizing and land reform; transform public schooling; carry out hygienic and medical campaigns to improve public health; address racial inequalities and ideologies; transform gender roles, sexual mores, and family structures; and resolve the division and battle between the

Catholic Church and secular, revolutionary state. What might facilitate or further complicate how we read *Eugenia* is to ask what Urzaiz had to personally gain or lose if his novel was read as a utopian or dystopian resolution to those major social issues.

Revolutionary and Postrevolutionary Yucatán, Mexico

The military phase of the Mexican Revolution (1910–17) was a complicated civil war involving various factions, of which the most prominent were peasants seeking land and political reformers seeking a new legislative and government order. Pressures brought by both factions ushered a new group of reform-oriented, middle-class leaders into power, who replaced the oligarchy of land-owners that had dominated local, regional, and national politics in the second half of the nineteenth century, particularly during the period in which Porfirio Díaz served as president (1876–1911).

This new class of leaders, which included the Yucatecan governors Salvador Alvarado (1915–18) and Felipe Carrillo Puerto (1922–24), was explicit about the need to reconstruct, rebuild, and modernize Mexico, transforming it into a "civilized" country. Most revolutionary programs shared some core characteristics. They were anticlerical, vigorously enforcing national decrees to seize church land and outlaw religious schools, aiming to disempower the church and thereby grant the state more social, political, and economic control. They aimed to foment economic development and to some degree encourage socioeconomic equality, through the state's mediation of the ownership and distribution of key resources, such as land. Such economic initiatives experimented with capitalist, socialist, and anarchist strategies and policies. They launched massive educational campaigns, seeking to promote revolutionary politics; teach Spanish language and cultural rituals to all Mexicans to forge a unified national culture; encourage modern hygienic and medical, agricultural, and industrial practices; and define desirable gender roles and family structures.[45]

The state of Yucatán constituted one of a number of regions that served as "laboratories" of the revolution.[46] Yucatán's dynamism as a center of revolutionary experimentation centered on the gubernatorial administration of Salvador Alvarado (1915–18), who was appointed military commander and governor of the state by Mexico's revolutionary commander and first postrevolutionary president, Venustiano Carranza, in 1915. Alvarado demonstrated his commitment to the ideals and goals of Mexico's new revolutionary class of leaders in several ways. First, he introduced a program to revitalize Yucatán's henequen industry for the benefit of Yucatecans and Mexicans, through land reform, the

organization of peasants and workers into leagues and syndicates, and the creation of a state monopoly of henequen harvesting and export.[47] He matched
this political-economic restructuring with a social reform project that sought to
reeducate, "defanaticize" (secularize and remove attachments to Catholic
mores and superstitions), and sober up Yucatecans, turning them into modern,
conscious citizens as well as effective economic producers.[48] In fact, Yucatán
was "the first state in Mexico to organize rural schools under the national law
for rudimentary education."[49]

As part of his general program of political, economic, and social reform,
Alvarado took several steps to give women more freedom and increase women's
public roles. Alvarado and other revolutionary Yucatecan and Mexican leaders'
interest in women's roles and rights makes a focus on gender an interesting way
to examine the tendencies of the Mexican Revolution and postrevolutionary
reform. In this book, initiatives related to gender, sexuality, and family are used
as a focus for examining the revolutionary and postrevolutionary context in
which *Eugenia* was written. Such issues are explored most directly in the essay
"Social and Biological Reproduction in *Eugenia*."

Alvarado's work in the realm of women's issues included the organization
of two feminist congresses in 1916;[50] the introduction of coeducation to the
Yucatán and the preparation of women for political participation as well as a
variety of careers;[51] the implementation of new divorce and family laws introduced at the national level by President Venustiano Carranza;[52] calls to improve
the working conditions of female domestic servants;[53] support for the creation
of women's organizations that fought alcoholism, drug use, and prostitution;
the creation of cooperative kitchens to feed working women and their children;
administration of milk programs for poor children; and promotion of literacy
and education for women about home economics and hygiene.[54]

Alvarado and other members of Mexico's new group of revolutionary,
middle-class governors embraced a complex mixture of proletarian sympathies
and middle-class sensibilities, joining anarchist and socialist discourses expressing zealous and idealistic desires to uplift urban and especially rural
workers—indigenous campesinos—with calls for the emergence of a new revolutionary middle-class leadership.[55] Consequently, such leaders glorified "the
proletariat"—by which they meant urban working-class Mexicans and rural
indigenous campesinos—as innocent and pure models of future citizenry, at
the same time that they frequently refused to examine or to value proletarian
culture and lifestyles.

Anarchism played an important role in Alvarado's and other early Mexican
revolutionaries' reformist orientations. This was because, as John Hart has
demonstrated, preceding, during, and immediately following the revolution,

anarchist ideology predominated in Mexican social-political experiments. In the late nineteenth century, foreign immigrants, especially from Spain, introduced the ideas of anarchist philosophers such as Pierre-Joseph Proudhon and Mikhail Bakunin to Mexico, thereby nudging workers to embrace anarchist thought in its various manifestations of mutualism, cooperativism, and finally anarcho-syndicalism.[56] Throughout Mexico (including in the Yucatán), anarchists established *casas del obrero* (houses of the worker), rationalist schools, and libraries. Mexican state and federal revolutionary governments recognized anarchists as a force to be contended with and vacillated between support, repression, and cooptation of organized labor.

As Gilbert Joseph has aptly put it, Alvarado was driven by a belief that "his state socialism provided a detailed blueprint for state capitalism via a populist brand of bourgeois revolution."[57] In the process of turning his vision into a Yucatecan reality, Alvarado not only created new political and economic structures and organizations but also introduced new social, political, and economic ideologies, through a mixture of anarcho-syndicalist, socialist, and capitalist influences, to peninsular culture.[58]

Conclusion

Urzaiz's involvement in developments in the medical profession at a broad level and in the disciplines of obstetrics-gynecology and psychiatry more specifically; his interest in related changes in gender roles and relationships, sexual behavior, and ideas about sexual difference and sexuality; and his eugenic-driven desire to "improve the race" are evident in *Eugenia*. His interest in such themes is connected to his role as an activist professional in postrevolutionary Yucatán. Through his work as a medical doctor (focusing on obstetrics-gynecology and psychiatry, the two medical disciplines most closely linked to the study of sexuality), Urzaiz articulates a desire to improve women's lives and challenge conventional gender roles and relationships. In such work, he engages explicitly with Marxist, Darwinian, and eugenic discourses.

While Urzaiz's immediate context was postrevolutionary Yucatán, Mexico, communities throughout the world were struggling with the same issues Urzaiz explored in *Eugenia* during the same years (the 1910s and 1920s): gender roles and sexual behaviors related to new socioeconomic structures and new ideas about scientific and sociological human development. Using *Eugenia* as a means to engage in such international debates, Urzaiz designs a partially socialist welfare state regulating human reproduction in order to promote eugenic principles and a society that rejects the nuclear family and embraces free love.

At the same time, despite exploring such issues through utopian and dystopian frameworks, which suggest the articulation of arguments about the way things should and should not be, *Eugenia* ultimately demonstrates an inability to resolve the tensions embedded within the complex themes Urzaiz explores. Thus, *Eugenia* leaves its reader with a sense of ambivalence, particularly regarding two central themes: women's liberation and relationships of love and family (both directly related to sexual behavior and reproduction).

On the one hand, in *Eugenia* men and women can both be seducers, and women's occupational and career opportunities are generally equal to men's. On the other hand, Urzaiz continues to promote the idea that maternalism especially, and parentalism and nurture more generally, are essentially feminine characteristics and qualities, whereas autonomy, individualism, and "selfishness" are essentially male ones. This is the primary reason why women continue to serve as nannies to newborns and young children, even though men have replaced women as "incubators" or "gestators."

Relatedly, there is absolutely no reference to homosexuality or homosexuals in *Eugenia*. It is presumed that everyone is clearly male or female and conforms to all idealized gendered and sexual characteristics associated with these different sexes.

Finally, Urzaiz's vision depends on the control of women for the achievement of eugenic, reproductive ideals. Women are impregnated, and then the embryos are extracted, taking away women's power as reproducers. In effect, the control of sex, gender, and reproduction through prescribed gender and sexual roles and through a closely regulated reproductive apparatus makes possible the control of race and the ascension to the modern and civilized.[59]

Eugenia also sends contradictory messages about the shift from the nuclear family to unions characterized by "free love." After describing families formed through an ethic of "free love," Urzaiz challenges this model when two selected breeders run away from society and the state to live by themselves and, possibly, form their own nuclear family. This act also challenges the contradictory defense of traditional gender roles described above, for ultimately, the male partner in this union is unable to "distinguish between mere carnal possession, instinctive and mechanical," which he planned to use in taking lovers for the purposes of reproduction, and "the pure and idealistic affection of a heart in love," which he expected to continue to hold for his longtime lover, considering that he ends up abandoning this love for a new partner.[60]

At the end of the novel, it is unclear whether this pair of selected breeders' decision to live by themselves while they wait for the birth of their child is a self-conscious attempt on the part of Urzaiz to write a dystopia or whether it reflects unresolved complexities in the themes of emotion, mental health,

gendered and sexual behavior, and reproduction that *Eugenia* explores. However, it is Urzaiz's exposure of the complexities of human emotion, as both a
cause and a product of individual human development, that challenges what
would otherwise be a tidy utopia designed by a strict biological division of male
and female identities and characteristics and human technological regulation
of every aspect of human life, including the highly complex process of reproduction formerly left to the laws of nature. Thus, it seems that this is Urzaiz's
intention all along: to write a dystopia warning of the harmful results of extreme,
utopic scientific, modernizing reform. Biological control of gender difference is
required for the eugenic strategies of reproduction promoted in the novel. But
ultimately, this biological control threatens to destroy core aspects of human
experience: human emotion and the psyche.

In addition to presenting an English translation of *Eugenia*, this book offers
an examination of the key issues outlined above in three additional essays. The
first, "Social and Biological Reproduction in *Eugenia*," uses gender, family, and
sexuality as rich avenues to discuss the actual historical context informing
Urzaiz's vision of the future. It outlines, in detail, postrevolutionary Mexican
reforms in family law (including important changes in divorce legislation), the
arguments made by Yucatecan contemporaries of Urzaiz who were proponents
of "free love," an early 1920s campaign to introduce birth control to Yucatecan
campesinos (of Mayan descent) and working-class citizens of Mérida (in which
Urzaiz played an important role), and a reactionary, pronatalist, counter-
campaign to introduce Mother's Day to Yucatán and Mexico on a national
scale. It also identifies key actors in such historical processes, including representatives of the government and revolutionary reformers, such as feminists,
teachers, healthcare and welfare workers, and points to some ways that such
changes impacted ordinary Yucatecans.

Next, "*Eugenia* and Eugenics" examines eugenics—which functioned as a
point of intersection for developments in physical and mental health and social
and "scientific" ideas about race for much of the twentieth century—as it
manifested itself globally and in Mexico. It considers the ways that eugenics
helped to legitimate psychiatry, psychology, and sexology as medical professions,
and anthropology and criminology as social scientific disciplines, and the ways
that eugenic ideas and arguments informed population debates involving those
favoring Malthusian arguments justifying population decline, as well as those
favoring pronatalist arguments for population increase.[61] As this essay shows,
Eugenia illustrates an awareness of all of these trends in Mexico, as Urzaiz
envisions a state-regulated reproductive apparatus that not only relies on selected
breeders to further eugenic goals but also introduces male pregnancy as the

remedy for an extreme depopulation crisis produced by "Malthusianism" and a female (psychological) fear of childbirth. This essay explores the ways that Urzaiz draws on such practices and ideas in *Eugenia* to put forth utopian and dystopian visions of the possible consequences of social changes happening in the years following the Mexican Revolution.

Finally, "*Eugenia*'s Literary Genesis and Genealogy" examines *Eugenia*'s relationship to a long tradition of speculative and utopian literature and science fiction. This essay offers a closer examination of the definitions of and relationship between utopian and dystopian literature and explores ways that *Eugenia* combines aspects of both. It asks how consciously Urzaiz draws upon previous and contemporary examples of related and similar literature and analyzes his uses of historical and current medical, scientific, social, and intellectual knowledge and practices in the novel. This essay also considers *Eugenia* as a work of literature by exploring how the (un)reliable narrator influences the reading of the novel and how Urzaiz uses various literary conventions to establish a relationship with the reader.

NOTES

1. Eduardo Urzaiz, *Eugenia: Esbozo novelesco de costumbres futuras* (Mérida, Yucatán: Talleres gráficos A. Manzanilla, 1919); Eduard Urzaiz, *Eugenia: A Fictional Sketch of Future Customs*, A Critical Edition, ed. and trans. Sarah A. Buck Kachaluba and Aaron Dziubinskyj (Madison: University of Wisconsin Press, 2016), 3. All page numbers cited refer to the English translation.

2. "Free love" could mean many things in the early twentieth century. For example, the historian George Robb writes that "despite its bohemian associations," in turn-of-the-century Britain, "free love might mean nothing more than freedom to marry as one's fancy dictated" (George Robb, "The Way of All Flesh: Degeneration, Eugenics, and the Gospel of Free Love," *Journal of the History of Sexuality* 6, no. 4 [1996]: 593). In contrast, *Eugenia* suggests that for Urzaiz, free love meant sexual and platonic unions arranged outside of the institution of marriage and the nuclear family.

3. M. Keith Booker, *Dystopian Literature: A Theory and Research Guide* (Westport, CT: Greenwood Press, 1994), 3. Indeed, the literary scholars Robert McKee Irwin and Miguel Ángel Fernández Delgado identify *Eugenia* as a dystopia. Although Irwin describes Villautopia as a "utopian futuristic world" (*Mexican Masculinities* [Minneapolis: University of Minnesota Press, 2003], 147), he also calls *Eugenia* a "futuristic dystopia" (148). Similarly, Fernández Delgado describes Villautopia as a "utopic vision of the future" that "disintegrates into a dystopian nightmare" ("Eduardo Urzaiz Rodríguez [1876–1955]," in *Latin American Science Fiction Writers: An A to Z Guide*, ed. Darrell B. Lockhart

[Westport, CT: Greenwood Press, 2004], 205). *Eugenia* also shares characteristics with some better-known examples of contemporary fiction that literary scholars have identified as dystopian, such as Yevgeny Ivanovich Zamyatin's *We* (1924) and Aldous Huxley's *Brave New World* (1932).

4. Fernández Delgado, "Eduardo Urzaiz Rodríguez," 205.

5. Urzaiz, *Eugenia*, 3.

6. Ibid.

7. Leopoldo Peniche Vallado, "El mensaje de *Eugenia*," preface to the 1955 edition, Eduardo Urzaiz, *Eugenia: Esbozo novelesco de costumbres futuras* (Mérida, Yucatán: Universidad Autónoma de Yucatán, 2002), 22. This translation of Peniche Vallado is from Rachel Haywood Ferreira, *The Emergence of Latin American Science Fiction* (Middletown, CT: Wesleyan University Press, 2011), 67.

8. Ibid.

9. Urzaiz was born in Guanabacoa on March 19, 1876. See Carlos Peniche Ponce, "Introducción," in Eduardo Urzaiz, *Eugenia: Esbozo novelesco de costumbres futuras* (Mérida, Yucatán: Universidad Nacional Autónoma de México, 2006), viii; Carlos Peniche Ponce, "La infertilidad femenina en 'Eugenia,' de Eduardo Urzaiz," *Proceso* 1571 (December 10, 2006): 80; and Ramón López Rodríguez, "El Doctor Eduardo Urzaiz Rodríguez: Su vida y su obra," *Gaceta Preparatoriana: Vocero Estudiantil de la Universidad Nacional del Sureste* 2, no. 12 (March 1955): 1.

10. Peniche Ponce, "Introducción," vii, and "La infertilidad femenina," 80.

11. Candelaria Souza de Fernández, "Prólogo," in Carlos Urzaiz Jiménez, *Oficio de mentor: Biografía del Dr. Eduardo Urzaiz Rodríguez* (Mérida, Yucatán: Ediciones de la Universidad Autónoma de Yucatán, 1996), 11.

12. Cuban creoles are of Spanish origin but born in Cuba.

13. Urzaiz Jiménez, *Oficio de mentor*, 17.

14. Ibid.

15. Ibid., 18.

16. Ibid.

17. Mary Kay Vaughan, "Education: 1889–1940," in *Encyclopedia of Mexico: History, Society, and Culture*, vol. 1, ed. Michael Werner (Chicago: Fitzroy Dearborn, 1997), 441–42.

18. Ibid.

19. Ibid., 442–43.

20. Urzaiz studied painting with Gamboa Guzmán between 1891 and 1892, roughly a year after his arrival in Yucatán, when Urzaiz was fifteen and sixteen years old (López Rodríguez, "El Doctor Eduardo Urzaiz Rodríguez," 13).

21. This collection was republished as Claudio Meex, *Reconstrucción de hechos: Anécdotas yucatecas ilustradas* (Mérida, Yucatán: Ediciones de la Universidad Autónoma de Yucatán, 1992). See also Santiago Burgos Nuñez, "El Doctor Eduardo Urzaiz Rodríguez: Literato," *Gaceta Preparatoriana: Vocero Estudiantil de la Universidad Nacional del Sureste* 2, no. 12 (March 1955): 11; Peniche Ponce, "Introducción," viii, and "La infertilidad femenina," 80.

22. Peniche Ponce, "Introducción," viii, and "La infertilidad femenina," 80. In addition to *Eugenia*, Urzaiz published the following titles: *Antropología* and *Biología* for students of the Normal School (Rubén Cámara-Vallejos and Marco Palma Solís, "Eduardo Urzaiz Rodríguez: Universitario ejemplar en medicina, psiquiatría, educación, artes y cultura," *Revista Biomédica* 25, no. 2 [May–August 2014]: 106); *Conferencias sobre biología* (Mérida, Yucatán: Talleres gráficos de "La revista de Yucatán," 1922); *Conferencias sobre historia de las religiones* (Mérida, Yucatán: Imp. y Lin. El Porvenir, 1935), which, according to Burgos Nuñez, was related to Urzaiz's teaching of this subject at the Escuela Normal "Rodolfo Menéndez de la Peña" in 1935 ("El Doctor Eduardo Urzaiz Rodríguez," 11); *Estudio psicológico sobre el espíritu varonil de Sor Juana Inés de la Cruz* (cited in Cámara-Vallejos and Palma Solís, "Eduardo Urzaiz Rodríguez," 106); *Conferencias sobre sociología* (cited in López Rodríguez, "El Doctor Eduardo Urzaiz Rodríguez," 13); *La emigración cubana en Yucatán* (Mérida, Yucatán: Editorial Club del Libro, 1949); *Del imperio a la revolución: 1865–1910* (Mérida, Yucatán: n.p., 1946); *Don Quijote de la Mancha ante la psiquiatría* (republished as *Don Quijote de la Mancha ante la psiquiatría: Tomado del Boletín de la Universidad Nacional del Sureste* [Mérida, Yucatán: Universidad Autónoma de Yucatán, 2002]); *España es la misma* (cited in Peniche Ponce, "Introducción," xi, and Peniche Ponce, "La infertilidad femenina," 80); a Spanish translation of Henry Wadsworth Longfellow's *Evangeline*, *Evangelina: Una historia de la Acadia* (Mérida, Yucatán: Talleres gráficas del sudeste, n.d.); *Exégesis Cervantina* (Mérida, Yucatán: Universidad de Yucatán, 1950); *La familia, cruz del apóstol* (Mérida, Yucatán: Universidad Nacional del Sureste, 1953), which, according to Burgos Nuñez, was about Martí and published in 1953, on the occasion of the one hundredth anniversary of Martí's birth ("El Doctor Eduardo Urzaiz Rodríguez," 11); "Historia de la educación pública y privada desde 1911" and "Historia de dibujo, la pintura y la escultura," both published in the *Enciclopedia Yucatense*, vol. 4 (Mexico City: Gobierno de Estado, 1945); *Los hormones sexuales* (1922, republished as *Los hormones sexuales: Tomado del Boletín de la Universidad Nacional del Sureste* [Mérida, Yucatán: Universidad Autónoma de Yucatán, 2002]); *Manual práctico de psiquiatría* (Mérida, Yucatán: n.p., 1936); *Nociones de antropología pedagógica* (cited in López Rodríguez, "El Doctor Eduardo Urzaiz Rodríguez," 13); *Petite Chose* (republished as *Petite Chose* [Mérida, Yucatán: Universidad Autónoma de Yucatán, 2002]); *El pintor Juan Gamboa Guzmán* (republished as *Juan Gamboa Guzmán* [Merida, Yucatán: Universidad Autónoma de Yucatán, 2002]); *El porvenir del caballo* (republished as *El porvenir del caballo* [Mérida, Yucatán: Universidad Autónoma de Yucatán, 2002]); "Psiquiatría" for medical students (cited in Cámara-Vallejos and Palma Solís, "Eduardo Urzaiz Rodríguez," 106); *¿Quién fue José Martí?* (Mérida, Yucatán: Comité pro-centenario de Martí en Yucatán, 1953); *La racha espiritualista contemporánea* (cited in Peniche Ponce, "Introducción," xi, and "La infertilidad femenina," 80); *Reconstrucción de hechos*, authored and illustrated with the pseudonym Claudio Meex, republished as *Reconstrucción de hechos: Anécdotas yucatecas ilustradas* (Mérida, Yucatán: Ediciones de la Universidad Autónoma de Yucatán, 1992); *Las tribulaciones del maestro Buendía* (cited in Peniche Ponce, "Introducción," xi, and "La infertilidad femenina," 80); and *Vidas tronchadas o Los dramas de la obstetricia* (cited in López Rodríguez, "El Doctor Eduardo Urzaiz Rodríguez," 13).

23. Peniche Ponce, "Introducción," viii.

24. Luis Peniche Vallado, "La enseñanza secundaria en Yucatán, obra del Dr. Urzaiz," *Gaceta Preparatoriana: Vocero Estudiantil de la Universidad Nacional del Sureste* 2, no. 12 (March 1955): 3.

25. *Oficio de mentor*, authored by Urzaiz's son Carlos Urzaiz Jiménez, offers a thorough and sensitive look at Urzaiz's career path and significant insight into Urzaiz's character. See, for example, Urzaiz Jiménez's discussion of his father's experiences as a normal school teacher (pp. 20–25).

26. López Rodríguez, "El Doctor Eduardo Urzaiz Rodríguez," 13. In 1902, the Yucatán's medical school was the Escuela Especial de Medicina, Cirugía y Farmacia. This school had evolved from the Escuela de Medicina, founded by decree on June 10, 1833, with a four-year course of study resulting in a diploma, followed by a two-year hospital practice, resulting in the bachelor's degree of medicine. After three years of practice, the "title of Doctor was awarded." In 1859, "the grade of bachelor was changed and in 1862 the students obtained the degree of graduate in medicine. On June 30, 1869, the Escuela Especial de Medicina, Cirugía y Farmacia . . . was created with a six-year-long course" and on September 22, 1884, a decree "determined the degree to be Doctor in Medicine. When the Universidad Nacional del Sureste was created on March 1, 1922, the school became a faculty of this university" (Arturo Erosa-Barbachano, "Historia de la Escuela de Medicina de Mérida, Yucatán, México," *Revista Biomédica* 8, no. 4 [October–December 1997]: 267).

27. Urzaiz Jiménez, *Oficio de mentor*, 34.

28. López Rodríguez, "El Doctor Eduardo Urzaiz Rodríguez," 13.

29. Conrado Menéndez Díaz, "El Dr. Eduardo Urzaiz Rodríguez: Maestro universitario," *Gaceta Preparatoriana: Vocero Estudiantil de la Universidad Nacional del Sureste* 2, no. 12 (March 1955): 10.

30. Ibid. Histology is "the study of the microscopic structure of tissues" (*Oxford English Reference Dictionary*, 2nd ed., s.v. "histology").

31. Menéndez Díaz, "El Dr. Eduardo Urzaiz Rodríguez," 10. In *Oficio de mentor*, Urzaiz Jiménez discusses his father's importance and popularity as a medical instructor who allowed his students to practice surgical procedures including the caesarean (pp. 49–51) and his father's pioneering work and publications on how the caesarean could be used to save mothers and children in risky birth situations (pp. 51–60).

32. Arrigunaga's exact quote—"He was indeed a great character. I think he helped to deliver half of Mérida's population"—was made in an e-mail communication on January 19, 2007. It is included as evidence of Urzaiz's legendary status in Mérida. A native of Yucatán, Arrigunaga spent many years as an archivist at the University of Texas–Arlington, where she was involved in important projects to microfilm Yucatecan library materials. She is well versed in Yucatecan history as well as its contemporary society.

33. Cámara-Vallejos and Palma Solís, "Eduardo Urzaiz Rodríguez," 103. This relatively recent article (Spring 2014) provides a very useful biographical sketch of Urzaiz and includes illustrative anecdotes from his life.

34. "Hospital O'Horan" and "Asilo Ayala," in Instituto Nacional de Estudios Históricos de la Revolución Mexicana (INEHRM), *Diccionario histórico y biográfico de la Revolución Mexicana*, CD ROM, 1994.

35. In this study, the terms "revolution" and "revolutionary" refer to the period in which various factions battled in a civil war that has become known as the Mexican Revolution (1910–17). Likewise, the term "postrevolutionary" refers to the decades after the revolutionary battles had ceased, in which social reform programs motivated by revolutionary ideas were initiated and fleshed out. Until the early 1990s, the postrevolutionary period generally referred to the 1920s and 1930s, ending in 1940, as Mexico's presidential election that year purportedly marked a "turn to the right" from the socialist, populist sexenio of Lázaro Cárdenas to the capitalist initiation of export-driven development that took off in the context of World War II under Manuel Ávila Camacho. Since the 1990s, historians have examined grassroots and state-supported programs (some of which supported one another) that extended postrevolutionary reform as well as the revolutionary state-building project beyond the 1930s. For an introduction to much of this newer literature, see Susie Porter, "The Apogee of Revolution, 1934–1946," in *A Companion to Mexican History and Culture*, ed. William H. Beezley (Malden, MA: Wiley-Blackwell, 2011), 453–67.

For a useful critique of the decision to use the term "revolution" to refer to the 1910–17 period of war only and the term "postrevolutionary" to refer to the decades that followed, see William Beezley, "Reflections on the Historiography of Twentieth-Century Mexico," *History Compass* 5, no. 3 (2007): 963–74. In this review of recent literature on the revolutionary and postrevolutionary periods, Beezley questions the existence of a separate "postrevolutionary" period at all, arguing that "the revolution did not end in 1920" for "only with teleological blinders (that is looking ahead to the authoritarian success of the Partido Revolucionario Institucional from 1972 to 2000) can one say that a new stable [revolutionary] regime had been established in 1920" (ibid., 964). Furthermore, Beezley writes, "violence was endemic throughout the country during the 1920s and the 1930s" and "the nation witnessed if not an unparalleled era of assassination, . . . a time at least equal to the decade from 1910 to 1920" (the years in which the military revolution [1910–17] took place) (ibid., 965).

36. López Rodríguez, "El Doctor Eduardo Urzaiz Rodríguez," 13; Gilbert Joseph, *Revolution from Without: Yucatán, Mexico, and the United States, 1880–1924* (Durham, NC: Duke University Press, 1995), 214. Rationalist schools "linked the educational process with the socialist notion of class struggle" (Joseph, *Revolution from Without*, 214). They "called for an end to all rewards and punishments, examinations, diplomas, and titles and . . . emphasiz[ed] . . . knowledge that could be acquired from manual work in the fields, shops, laboratories, and work areas of the schools themselves. Furthermore, all . . . would be 'based on liberty,' that is to say, off-limits to priests and other religious personnel and co-educational" (ibid., 215). They were established by Spanish exiles throughout Spanish America in the early twentieth century (see John Mason Hart, *Anarchism and the Mexican Working Class, 1860–1931* [Austin: University of Texas Press, 1978], 113).

37. López Rodríguez, "El Doctor Eduardo Urzaiz Rodríguez," 13. Salvador Alvarado created the Asociación Científica y Artística Ateneo Peninsular in 1915 to bring together progressive intellectuals to foment the reorientation of literary, artistic, and scientific expression ("Asociación Científica y Artística Ateneo Peninsular," in INEHRM, *Diccionario histórico y biográfico de la Revolución Mexicana*). Regarding teaching religion, see Burgos Nuñez, "El Doctor Eduardo Urzaiz Rodríguez," 11.

38. Erosa-Barbachano, "Historia de la Escuela de Medicina de Mérida, Yucatán, México," 267. The Universidad Nacional del Sureste became the Universidad de Yucatán on November 5, 1938.

39. López Rodríguez, "El Doctor Eduardo Urzaíz Rodríguez," 13.

40. Peniche Vallado, "La enseñanza secundaria en Yucatán, obra del Dr. Urzaiz," 3.

41. Ibid., 15.

42. Ibid.

43. For now classic historiographical essays on the regional history of the Mexican revolutionary period, see Carlos Martínez Assad, *El laboratorio de la revolución* (Mexico City: Siglo Veintiuno Editores, 1979); Mark T. Gilderhaus, "Many Mexicos: Traditions and Innovations in Recent Historiography," *Latin American Research Review* 22, no. 1 (1987): 204–13; Paul Vanderwood, "Building Blocs but Yet No Building: Regional History and the Mexican Revolution," *Mexican Studies/Estudios Mexicanos* 3, no. 2 (1987): 421–32; Carlos Martínez Assad, ed., *Balance y perspectivas de los studios regionales en México* (Mexico City: UNAM, 1990); Thomas Benjamin and Mark Wasserman, eds., *Provinces of the Revolution: Essays on Regional Mexican History, 1910–1929* (Albuquerque: University of New Mexico Press, 1990); and Eric Van Young, *Mexico's Regions: Comparative History and Development* (San Diego: Center for U.S.–Mexican Studies, 1992).

A few classic regional and microhistories of the revolutionary era from the same historiographical period include Joseph, *Revolution from Without*; Romana Falcón, *El agrarismo en Veracruz: La etapa radical (1928–1935)* (Mexico City: El Colegio de México, 1977); and Heather Fowler Salamini, *Agrarian Radicalism in Veracruz, 1920–1938* (Lincoln: University of Nebraska Press, 1978).

In the past thirty years, new generations of historians have continued to look to the provincial and even the local level to complicate understandings of the Mexican Revolution and postrevolutionary period. In addition, such recent histories have given significant attention to the class, race, and gender dimensions of the struggles and experiences it involved. According to a review essay by Mark Wasserman, "the major innovations in the historiography of the Mexican Revolution over the past three decades lie in four linked areas." Historians of this generation have revealed: (1) "that we can understand the revolution only if we explore what occurred at the state and local levels"; (2) "that the *clases populares* not only were the cannon fodder of the conflict but shaped it as well[,] . . . [that] the revolution itself was very much the work of subaltern classes . . . [and] . . . [that] whether it succeeded or not, [the revolution] was the product of workers and peasants"; (3) "that the initial protests and subsequent long period of violence did not arise from strictly economic and political factors; instead, there was a strong cultural element"; and (4) that "gender [has played a] . . . crucial role . . . in shaping the discourse and structure, if not the events, of the revolution" (Mark Wasserman, "You Can Teach an Old Revolutionary Historiography New Tricks: Regions, Popular Movements, Culture, and Gender in Mexico, 1820–1940," *Latin American Research Review* 43, no. 2 [2008]: 260–61).

Recent studies of the revolution and the postrevolutionary period in the Yucatán revealing all of these characteristics (a focus on the state and/or local communities; the participation and agency of the popular classes, popular culture, and gender and alternative periodizations; and uses of the terms "revolution"/ "revolutionary" and "postrevolution"/ "postrevolutionary") include Ben Fallaw, *Cárdenas Compromised: The Failure of Reform in Postrevolutionary Yucatán* (Durham, NC: Duke University Press, 2001); Sarah A. Buck, "Activists and Mothers: Feminist and Maternalist Politics in Mexico, 1923–1953" (PhD diss., Rutgers University, 2002); Jocelyn Olcott, *Revolutionary Women in Postrevolutionary Mexico* (Durham, NC: Duke University Press, 2005); Stephanie J. Smith, *Gender and the Mexican Revolution: Yucatán Women and the Realities of Patriarchy* (Chapel Hill: University of North Carolina Press, 2006); and Paul K. Eiss, *In the Name of El Pueblo: Place, Community, and the Politics of History in Yucatán* (Durham, NC: Duke University Press, 2010).

Moving beyond Yucatán, two anthologies provide superb introductions into work on women and gender throughout Mexico during the revolution and in the immediate decades following: Jocelyn Olcott, Mary Kay Vaughan, and Gabriela Cano, eds., *Sex in Revolution: Gender, Politics, and Power in Modern Mexico*, foreword by Carlos Monsiváis (Durham, NC: Duke University Press, 2006); and Stephanie Mitchell and Patience A. Schell, eds., *The Women's Revolution in Mexico: 1910–1953* (New York: Rowman & Littlefield, 2007). In addition, Mary Kay Vaughan and Stephen E. Lewis, eds., *The Eagle and the Virgin: Nation and Cultural Revolution in Mexico, 1920–1940* (Durham, NC: Duke University Press, 2006), and William H. Beezley's and Susie Porter's contributions to William H. Beezley, ed., *A Companion to Mexican History and Culture* (Malden, MA: Wiley-Blackwell, 2011)—Beezley, "Creating a Revolutionary Culture: Vasconcelos, Indians, Anthropologists, and Calendar Girls," 420–38; and Porter, "The Apogee of Revolution, 1934–1946," 453–67—point to much of the cultural and social history that has filled in important holes on what many have called the "postrevolutionary" period.

44. Irwin, *Mexican Masculinities*, 148.

45. Mary Kay Vaughan, *Cultural Politics in Revolution: Teachers, Peasants, and Schools in Mexico, 1930–1940* (Tucson: University of Arizona Press, 1997).

46. I take the term "laboratories of the Revolution" from Benjamin and Wasserman, *Provinces of the Revolution*. The creation and development of such laboratories involved dialogue and movement back and forth between national government authorities in central Mexico and regional authorities (some local and some implanted from the outside) in the provinces. Gilbert Joseph in particular has depicted the state of Yucatán as a "laboratory of the Revolution" in which programs that became implemented in national policy were first tested and worked out on the regional level (Joseph, *Revolution from Without*).

47. Henequen, a fiber extracted from the agave cactus, was used to make a strong and effective binder twine. Henequen became a very successful cash crop, and during the nineteenth century, it converted Yucatán into a mono-crop, export-driven economy. For a thorough and compelling study on the rise and characteristics of this industry and the society that sustained it, see Allen Wells, *Yucatán's Gilded Age: Haciendas, Henequen, and International Harvester, 1860–1915* (Albuquerque: University of New Mexico Press, 1985).

48. For overviews of Alvarado's governorship, see Joseph, *Revolution from Without*, 71–95, and Jaime Orosa Díaz, *Breve historia de Yucatán* (Mérida, Yucatán: Universidad de Yucatán, 1981), 117–20. For an excellent discussion of vanguard initiatives in education in Yucatán, sponsored by Alvarado and others, see Paul K. Eiss, "Deconstructing Indians, Reconstructing *Patria*: Indigenous Education in Yucatán from the *Porfiriato* to the Mexican Revolution," *Journal of Latin American Anthropology* 9, no. 1 (2004): 119–50.

49. Eiss, "Deconstructing Indians," 124.

50. Feminist demands raised at these conferences included calls to broaden women's educational opportunities and claims for women's right to vote. For further discussion, see *El primer congreso feminista de Yucatán: Anales de esa memorable asamblea* (Mérida, Yucatán: Talleres Atenzo Popular, 1916); Anna Macías, "Felipe Carrillo Puerto and Women's Liberation in Mexico," in *Latin American Women: Historical Perspectives*, ed. Asunción Lavrin (Westport, CT: Greenwood Press, 1978), 294; Anna Macías, *Against All Odds: The Feminist Movement in Mexico to 1940* (Westport, CT: Greenwood Press, 1982), 70–78; Shirlene Ann Soto, *The Mexican Woman: A Study of Her Participation in the Revolution, 1910–1940* (Palo Alto, CA: R&E Research Associates, 1979), 52–55; Shirlene Ann Soto, *Emergence of the Modern Mexican Woman: Her Participation in the Revolution and Struggle for Equality, 1910–1940* (Denver: Arden Press, 1990), 67–68 and 73–80; Gabriela Cano, "Revolución, feminismo y ciudadanía en México (1915–1940)," in *Historia de las mujeres en Occidente*, ed. Georges Duby and Michelle Perrot (Madrid: Taurus, 1993), 301–11; Emma Pérez, "Feminism-in-Nationalism: The Gendered Subaltern at the Yucatecan Feminist Congress of 1916," in *Between Woman and Nation: Nationalisms, Transnational Feminisms, and the State*, ed. Caren Kaplen, Norma Alarcón, and Minoo Moallem (Durham, NC: Duke University Press, 1999), 219–39; Laura Orellana Trinidad, "'La mujer del porvenir': Raíces intelectuales y alcances del pensamiento feminista de Hermila Galindo, 1915–1919," *Signos Históricos* 5 (2001): 109–35; and Olcott, *Revolutionary Women in Postrevolutionary Mexico*, 28–32.

51. Macías, *Against All Odds*, 68–69, 78–79.

52. See article 2 of the *Plan de Guadalupe* of March 26, 1913. This divorce law appeared in Yucatecan legislation in 1915 (*Diario Oficial*, May 27, 1915). See also the federal Ley de Relaciones Familiares (1917), which became law in the Yucatán through the Código Civil del Estado de Yucatán (Mérida, Yucatán: Gobierno del Estado, 1918). The federal and Yucatecan divorce laws are discussed at more length in the essay "Social and Biological Reproduction in *Eugenia*."

53. Macías, "Felipe Carrillo Puerto and Women's Liberation in Mexico," 287–88.

54. Soto, *Emergence of the Modern Mexican Woman*, 71–72; Macías, *Against All Odds*, 92; Macías, "Felipe Carrillo Puerto and Women's Liberation in Mexico," 287–88; Joseph, *Revolution from Without*, 105; Piedad Peniche, "Las ligas feministas en la revolución," *Unicornio* (1996): 8–9; Gabriela Cano, "Congresos feministas en la historia de Mexico," *FEM* 11, no. 58 (1987): 24–26; and Ana Lau, "Una experiencia feminista en Yucatán, 1922–1924," *FEM* 8, no. 30 (1983): 12–14.

55. The word "campesino" literally means "people of the field." It is generally translated as "peasant." Christopher Boyer argues that some revolutionaries went so far as to use terms defining rural Mexicans as workers (*trabajadores*) rather than peasants (campesinos). This semantic difference related to the fact that terms such as "'indigenous people' or . . . 'members of rural communities' seemed to conjure up images of a passive, backward, and ignorant rural multitude, whereas mobilized *workers* might band together, fight for their rights, and actively transform society along more equitable and modern lines" (Christopher Boyer, *Becoming Campesinos: Politics, Identity, and Agrarian Struggle in Postrevolutionary Michoacán, 1920–1935* [Stanford, CA: Stanford University Press, 2003], 84).

56. Hart, *Anarchism and the Mexican Working Class*, 15.

57. This was the subject of volume 3 of Alvarado's 1919 book *La reconstrucción de México* (Joseph, *Revolution from Without*, 101).

58. Joseph, *Revolution from Without*, 101.

59. Robert McKee Irwin offers a different interpretation of Urzaiz's representation of gender roles. He argues that *Eugenia* seems "more concerned with feminism" and is characterized by "a paranoia that women's advances into the workplace [would] result in the annihilation of the institution of motherhood" than in the broader implications of the Mexican Revolution (Irwin, *Mexican Masculinities*, 148). According to Irwin, *Eugenia* is one of several examples of popular Latin American literature of the 1920s and 1930s that reveals "a paranoia about gender that resulted in both the popularization of the virile literature of the revolution and also the emergence of a pop literature that explored gender anxiety, but that was ignored by Mexico's literary establishment because it did not address class issues so much as gender issues and therefore was not considered serious. Enlisting pop genres such as science fiction, this minor literature competed with the novel of the revolution, but without the benefit of sanctions from the cultural elite of the day, it never had the chance to be incorporated into Mexico's literary canons and nowadays has been forgotten" (Irwin, *Mexican Masculinities*, 146).

60. Urzaiz, *Eugenia*, 50.

61. Malthusianism refers to the British preacher and economist Thomas Malthus's warnings that without intervention, humans' natural propensity to reproduce would result in unsustainable population growth exhausting the resources to support society and resulting in poverty and violence.

Eugenia

⌐ *Prologue* ⌐

¡ANCHE IO SOGNO SPESSO![1]

I too dream often! And in my dreams, dear reader, I contemplate a humanity that is almost happy, free at last from the shackles and prejudices with which today's humanity willingly complicates and embitters life.

The simple love story that unfolds in this attempt at a novel has served me only as an excuse to conjure up a vision—even if pale and imprecise—of that future humanity of my hopes and dreams.

I am certain that many individuals, those who consider themselves the only legitimate heirs of common sense, will scandalously cry out, "But this is the work of a madman!" after reading my book.

I am a doctor of madmen, and it would not seem strange that, in the fourteen long years that I have dealt with them on a daily basis, something of their deliriums and habits would have been passed on to me. Naturally I believe myself to be sane and in my right mind. And in addition, I have known and still know insane people who write with such beauty and reason, that I would be neither surprised nor offended if my work were classified as such.

After all, the very concepts of "sane" and "insane" are relative, since they depend on which side of the fence the one who judges or classifies them is standing. At least it was understood to be such by that Spanish friar who, in the

---

1. "I too dream often!" (Italian).

3

seventeenth century, wrote a book entitled: "On Whether They Are Crazy or We Are."[2]

You, therefore, benevolent or critical reader, can judge me as you see fit. I am left with the option—and naturally take refuge in it—of using the same yardstick on you that you use to measure me.

---

2. Although we have been unable to find any such title, it is interesting to note the possible connection to Fray Manuel Antonio de Rivas (ca. 1707–?), a Spanish Franciscan who worked as a "definidor" or governor in Mérida. Antonio de Rivas collected and read books banned by the Church, and held unorthodox Christian views. Such polemical behavior caught the attention of the Inquisition, which brought him to trial for heresy in 1775. While it is known that Fray Rivas wrote many pamphlets on varying topics as well as denouncements of his fellow friars and of the Church, his best-known work, considered by many scholars to be the first example of science fiction in Spanish America, is *Syzygies and Lunar Quadratures Aligned to the Meridian of Mérida of the Yucatán by an Anctitone or Inhabitant of the Moon, and Addressed to the Scholar Don Ambrosio de Echevarria, Reciter of Funeral Kyries in the Parish of Jesus of Said City, and Presently Teacher of Logarithm in the Town of Mama of the Yucatán Peninsula, in the Year of the Lord 1775* (ca. 1772). See Aaron Dziubinskyj, "The Birth of Science Fiction in Spanish America," *Science Fiction Studies* 30, no. 1 (2003): 21–32.

⇐ 1 ⇒

𝒫assing through the crystal panes of the luxurious window, the sun's rays took on hues of red, yellow, and green. They rested for a moment on the whiteness of the sheets and, rising with a slow, steady motion, they reached Ernesto's face. Still half asleep, he opened his eyes as he felt their warm touch. Blinded by the excessive light, he quickly closed his eyes and lay on his back a bit longer, enjoying the rare pleasure of not thinking about anything, a short reprieve from the never-ending exertion of the intellect that is only possible during the brief moments that come just before or right after sleep.

After a long stretch that made every joint in his body creak, the young man felt around for the button on the wall next to the bed. There it was. At the touch of his finger an invisible bell rang out ten deep chimes, followed by two sharp chimes: ten fifteen. It was late! Surely Federico, Consuelo, and Miguel were already out and about. As for Celiana, the tireless worker that she was, she must have gotten out of bed early, being careful not to wake her lover, since the spot on the pillow where her head had rested was already cold. She was probably upstairs, in the study, and at that hour, must have already prepared the outline for her afternoon lecture at the Athenaeum.

Removing the silk kimono that covered him, Ernesto forced himself out of bed and moved slowly toward the corner of the bedroom where, hidden by a sliding curtain, the dresser and hydrotherapeutic equipment were. Refreshed by a short automatic vibrating massage and a cold shower, he emerged as agile and quick as if he had returned from some extraterrestrial world where muscular exertion and fatigue were completely unknown.

Ernesto shaved, combed his hair, and splashed on some cologne, but he was still naked as he admired himself for a moment, with an innermost satisfaction, in the large moon-shaped mirror that hung on the front wall. He could forgive himself this touch of vanity since his body was worthy of admiration. Taller

than average, his proportions were exact, displaying the perfect muscular tone and the harmonious robustness of Doryphorus of Polyclitus, while his facial features greatly resembled those of Mercury of Praxiteles, but with that expression of high intellect that human physiognomy has acquired after many centuries of civilization.[3] Add to all that the warm glow of healthy skin, perfect, silky and unblemished by superfluous hair, and you will have an idea of what Ernesto was like at twenty-three: a figure worthy of posing for a Greek sculptor and a good example of what progress in hygiene had achieved from a humanity that, hundreds of years before, is known all too well to have been rachitic, toxic, and sickly.

Ernesto, who—let it be said once and for all—had no job nor any other responsibilities, quickly put on a simple outfit, in accordance with his social status and the fashion of the time, and prepared to leave. His plan consisted in, at least for the time being, a ride around the outskirts of the city on his aerocycle. Because it was late he didn't eat breakfast so that he could join his friends for lunch later at the Circle; afterward, they might enjoy lighthearted intellectual exchange. As always, he would eat dinner at home, and during the brief, daily soirée, a pleasant and intimate occasion for everyone, evening plans would be discussed. Most of the time, everyone would participate in the chosen activity together, unless it got late while they were talking and they decided instead to just stay in. Ernesto began to feel bothered by the monotony of his life and a little ashamed by how useless it was becoming compared with the lives of his friends, who all worked not only for their own benefit, but for his as well.

With hat in hand, Ernesto was finally leaving to get his aerocycle when he noticed an official sealed envelope that he apparently had not seen before on the marble stand. Celiana must have gotten it early and, discreet as always, in spite of their intimate lifestyle, left it there without opening it so that he would

---

3. Polyclitus was one of the best-known Greek sculptors of the classical period, with the *Doryphorus*, or *Spear-Bearer*, being his most important work. His *Canon*, perhaps based on this sculpture, is a treatise in which Polyclitus describes his principles for the mathematically balanced proportions of the human form in art. His chiastic style is represented in *Doryphorus*, which "shows the male figure standing on his right leg with his left relaxed; his right arm hangs limp and his left is flexed to hold the spear" (Andrew Stewart, "Polyclitus," in *The Oxford Classical Dictionary*, 4th ed., ed. Simon Hornblower and Antony Spawforth [Oxford: Oxford University Press, 2012], 1176). Mercury refers to *Hermes Holding the Infant Dionysus* by the Athenian sculptor Praxiteles, known for his great attention to the surface finish of his statues (as Hermes is Mercurius in the Roman pantheon) (Andrew Stewart, "Praxiteles," in Hornblower and Spawforth, *The Oxford Classical Dictionary*, 1205).

see it when he woke up. Very intrigued by the Government's stamp, Ernesto
broke the seal and read:

[handwritten margin notes: He's perfect / So he's gonna / be breeding]

To C. Ernesto R. del Lazo.
    You are hereby informed that, in recognition of your robustness, health,
beauty, and other favorable conditions, the Superior Government, at the proposal of this Bureau, has considered it appropriate to name you Official Breeder
of the Species, for the present year and with the compensation indicated by the
Bureau's established budget.

[handwritten margin notes: Thanks Miss / so celianal requested / this too for him b/c / she's tired of him / or Miguel cuz / Ernesto is jobless]

                                                Health and Longevity.
                              Director of the Institute of Eugenics
                              Dr. Remigio Pérez Serrato.
              Villautopia, Sub-Confederation of Central America,
                                                March 2, 2218.

    The young man was overtaken by mixed thoughts after reading this letter.
Clearly the flattery of seeing his merits as a perfect specimen officially recognized
fed his vanity a little, and the opportunity of no longer being a burden to his
friends, Celiana in particular, pleased him. . . . Yet could it have been she who,
growing weary of Ernesto, requested this appointment in order to rid herself of
him? For a moment the thought of this left a bitter taste of jealous despair in his
mouth. . . . But no, thinking it over, the hypothesis was inadmissible. Celiana
hadn't changed in the least and, after five years of living together, she continued
to be the same passionate lover, at the same time protective and maternal, that
she was in the first days of their love. . . . It must have been the work of Miguel,
in whom Ernesto must have noted more than once a certain false appearance
of ironic reproach toward the idle uselessness of his life.

    Could he, on the other hand, remain impartial in the midst of the promis-
cuity that would be required by his new responsibilities in dealing with different
women and keep intact his faith for the one who had been his teacher in life, his
first and, until now, only love? Their love was a tranquil one, certainly, without
great raptures or anxieties, almost filial and with a hint of respect and gratitude,
but all that would have been enough to make Ernesto happy for a long time.
Among so many women, might one come along who would bring a touch of
poetry or a shaking off of tragedy to his existence, the call to unleash the passionate storm that all young people unconsciously desire in order to brighten, even
just a little, the gray monotony of life?

    Analyzing his position with respect to Celiana, Ernesto's thoughts shifted to
the past, which began to parade across his imagination with a cinematographic

They met whm Ernesto was
10 and celiana was 25...
(She was his teacher)

clarity. And so vivid and exact was his internal vision, that the young man's hand relaxed over the edge of the couch, and without realizing it, he let the letter fall to the floor, while his eyes took on a wandering expression as if he were daydreaming.

He saw himself thirteen years earlier in primary school, having just arrived from the farm-seedbed where his first years had elapsed in complete freedom. He was at that time a turbulent little boy of ten, full of health, who, like Rousseau's Emile, did not know his left hand from his right.[4]

Celiana, then a beautiful young woman of twenty-five, was Ernesto's first teacher. She tenderly sweetened the restlessness of his character and, when she had gained the necessary influence over him, gave him the gifts of reading and writing, in a few sessions of hypnotic suggestion, expertly spaced out over the course of one month. By the same process, which had come to replace all of the bothersome pedagogy of the past, she instilled in him an elementary knowledge of arithmetic and geometry.

Ernesto recalled with delight his school and the joyful years that he spent there. The luxuriant and fresh avenues were reborn in his imagination with intense color, along with the abundant amusement parks, the great reservoir, the bustling activity of the workshops and the gentle calm of the laboratories, the rich living zoological collection, the orchards, the farm, the gardens. . . . There, in close and constant contact with nature and with life itself, he had acquired knowledge of natural phenomena and indispensable practical skills. And the memory of those cheerful games with his classmates and of the delightful lectures by which the instructors expanded his scientific notions, rapidly solidifying them by means of short hypnotic sessions, pleased him so much.

How happy those times were, gone never to return and which, perhaps because they were in the past, appealed to him more than the present ones! It was then that his association with those that today would form his familial group started. Consuelo and Federico, approximately his same age, were already in love. They had been his classmates and such was the harmony between their

4. Emile was the protagonist of Jean-Jacques Rousseau's *Émile, or On Education* (*L'Émile ou de l'éducation*), first published in 1762; see "Rousseau, Jean Jacques (1712–1778)," in *Encyclopedia of European Social History*, ed. Peter N. Stearns (Detroit: Scribner, 2001), 6:303. In this work Rousseau uses the development of the fictional Emile from infant to adult as a means to explore the deeper political and philosophical aspects of the relationship between the individual and society (Jean-Jacques Rousseau, *Émile, or Education*, trans. Barbara Foxley (New York: E. P. Dutton, 1930).

personalities, Consuelo's and Federico's being gentle and tranquil, and Ernesto's burning and dominating, that the three turned out to complement each other and therefore became inseparable.

During that time Ernesto also met Miguel, who was then Celiana's lover and came to the school to meet her every afternoon. It was clear that at first Ernesto hated Miguel a great deal. After all, Ernesto did feel an affectionate and absorbing love for his charming teacher, which his precocious temperament instinctively turned sexual and in which was reborn, after several generations of absence from humanity, a purely jealous tendency. He never would have believed that later—the love between Celiana and Miguel converted into frank, loyal, and lasting friendship—Ernesto would come to love Miguel with the same fraternal tenderness with which, by then, Consuelo and Federico loved him.

Ernesto remembered later that terrible crisis of puberty, which briefly alleviated the turbulence of his games and filled him with wandering anxieties and unmentionable desires. The fresh color of his face and the youthful tonicity of his muscles gone, he turned sullen and solitary. He would have fallen hopelessly into a state of neurosis if Celiana—always she—had not reached out a lifesaving hand to him. Like Madame Warens to Jean-Jacques, she opened for him the gates to the garden of Eros and was for him a complete woman: mother, teacher, sister, friend, and lover.[5] And she was all of these to the degree that, in five years, his heart had not so much as sighed for other loves, nor had the countless beautiful girls that he would encounter along the way ignited the spark of desire in him.

And could it be possible that that love, still sufficiently intense to completely fill his sentimental aspirations and the physical needs of his powerful masculine youth, had begun to decay in Celiana? At that age when a woman reaches the peak of her passion's strength, and after not having found through multiple trials the absolute ideal, she had made him the target of all her love. Moreover, who knew? Female emotions were and had always been so complex! . . . . Again the

5. Madame Louise Eléonore, Baronne de Warens, took Rousseau in when he was fifteen years old, becoming his patron and giving him the education he lacked. Although she (at age twenty-nine) was fourteen years older than he, eventually she also became his lover, fulfilling his hungry spirit and need for love. They lived together off and on for thirteen years. See "Rousseau, Jean Jacques (1712–1778)," 6:302, and Jean-Jacques Rousseau, *The Confessions of Jean-Jacques Rousseau*, trans. W. Conyngham Mallory (New York: Tudor Publishing, 1928).

enamored young man felt the ancestral yeast of jealousy ferment in the depths of his being. And out of this fermentation came the doubt that paralyzed his resilient willpower, until then so impulsive and quick in all of its decisions.

Ernesto admitted, in theory, the convenience of accepting the appointment; if until now he hadn't worried about earning money, it had been out of a lack of ambition—more than mere laziness—or perhaps, necessity. If he or his friends had needed anything, Ernesto would have put to use long ago that overflowing energy that he demonstrated in athletics into finding a job.

And he could use the money. At the end of the year, he would collect at once all of his salary and use it partly to settle his debt of gratitude toward Celiana by giving her the pleasure of traveling to Europe, an unrealized dream that she had confessed to him on more than one occasion.

But as long as Ernesto didn't clearly see the reasons for his lover's intervention in that matter—if there was even a matter—as long as Celiana could not prove her total innocence, he couldn't be certain. The best thing to do was to wait until Celiana, or perhaps Miguel, disclosed their intentions, which wouldn't take long, since neither cared much for secrets.

And, after all, this wasn't a case of blowing such an insignificant issue way out of proportion. . . . With the superficiality characteristic of the times—which resulted from the complete refinement of civilization—Ernesto laughed to himself at his momentary hesitation. He stuck the letter of appointment in his pocket and left with his usual carefree and happy attitude.

he live w his friends
+ lover
rent free, had no reason
to get a job

~ 2 ~

Celona POV

$\mathcal{T}$he study was located on the third floor of the chalet. It was a vast room with a sloping ceiling covered completely with crystals, and a large sliding glass door with a balcony that opened toward the east. A system of running gray silk curtains could be adjusted at will in order to take advantage of direct or indirect sunlight. The walls, of a uniform pearl tone, were decorated with Miguel's artwork, landscapes and nudes of ideal beauty, which showed an absolute mastery of the cubist technique and a rich and precise vision of color. In one corner of the study a marble Venus showed off the caste eurhythmy of its form. On an ebony easel was a large canvas covered with angry shapes, upon which a stormy sky and agitated sea began to take shape.

From the balcony one could make out the picturesque surroundings of the city. A multitude of white aristocratic villas dotted the intense greenness of the tropical countryside and a wide avenue flanked by tall buildings and shaded by thick evergreens extended toward the south until it was out of view. The asphalt, freshly covered by dew, glittered and a hurried crowd already occupied the revolving sidewalks.

In the bright calm of the morning, the sky had a clear blue tint of pure cobalt, upon which massive aeroships, full of passengers, regularly traced their bulky outlines as they headed toward the neighboring ports. In the distance, the vibration of sirens that sounded as the ships took off resembled the soft, steady moan of an Aeolian harp, their dark outlines rapidly growing until they were suddenly nothing more than points, barely visible for an instant.[6] The

6. Aeolus was the Greek god of the winds. The Aeolian harp is a wooden box with strings stretched lengthwise across the bridges at both ends and is played by the wind moving over the strings (Michael Garagin, "Aeolus," in *The Oxford Classical Dictionary*, 2nd ed., ed. N. G. L. Hammond and H. H. Scullard (Oxford: Clarendon Press, 1970), 15.

elegant neo-Mayan architecture of the central hangar from which they left towered above a large quadrangular pyramid of stone.[7] At the truncated apex of the triangular roof, an enormous golden bronze eagle, with its wings spread as if preparing to rise up in flight, seemed to glow with fire in the sun's rays.

Sitting in front of a large desk covered with books and papers in disarray, Celiana lifted her hands from the keyboard of the tiny typewriter upon which she had been typing. She spun her chair around until she was facing the window, lit a *cannabis indica* cigarette perfumed with the essence of ambergris, threw back her elegant head, and contemplated with delight the verdant vastness of the heavens.

Celiana was truly beautiful in a disturbing and unique way: tall, slender, and full figured, even if her breasts were not very pronounced. Her complexion was white and unpolished; her lips were fleshy and fiery. Her eyes were large and luminous, as if consumed by an internal fever, and intensely black, just like her short curly mop of hair and thin eyebrows, perfect outlines that extended toward her temples and almost came together above the bridge of her Greek nose. Her forehead was high and spacious, her arms admirable and she had hands that, just like her feet upon which she wore lightweight sandals, were as transparent as porcelain and graciously emerged from her loose, sensibly cut lilac robe detailed with a black pattern along the hem and square collar.

Paying close attention, a keen observer might notice a slight squint in Celiana's eyes, three fine wrinkles on her forehead, and a few gray threads in her hair. Next to the total whiteness of her face, her teeth, large and fine, appeared to be yellowing like old ivory.

Her work that morning had been fruitful and her afternoon lecture was planned. As every Saturday, the tickets would sell out and the public would cram into the Athenaeum, as anxious to gaze at the beautiful speaker as to hear her succulent and flowing words, to which the serious and sweet pitch of her voice leant tremendous power of suggestion.

For the past five years, since her passion for Ernesto became public, requiring that she leave the teaching profession, Celiana had devoted herself to giving

7. Neo-Mayan or Mayan Revival architecture was a movement in the 1920s and 1930s that, as its name implies, drew inspiration from the pre-Columbian indigenous civilizations of Mesoamerica as well as art deco. Two manifestations of this style in Mérida are the Casa del Pueblo (inaugurated in 1928) and the Parque de las Américas (built in the early 1940s). See Marjorie I. Ingle, *The Mayan Revival Style: Art Deco Mayan Fantasy* (Albuquerque: University of New Mexico Press, 1989), for a discussion of this movement in Mexico and beyond.

→ Job!

lectures on sociology and history, her favorite areas of study. As she gave one successful talk after another, her fame began to spread beyond the borders of her homeland. The financial reward was not insignificant either, more than providing for her needs and fancies. *→ why Ernesto is jobless*

    With her next lecture already outlined, Celiana mentally filled in the details and cleverly sketched out some rather convincing phrases whose impact would win applause. She planned to follow the evolution of the family step by step over the past three centuries. She would demonstrate the causes that were responsible for slowly weakening the physiological fabric of that institution, previously so solid, until it disappeared. She would narrate how, as religious prejudices gradually faded and the legal system became simplified, human couples eventually formed and dissolved freely. She would review how the problem of unwanted offspring seemed to be insurmountable for a long time, since, although children had ceased to be a burden for their parents as the state took on the responsibility for their support and education, women increasingly avoided the challenging physiological role that nature assigned them. The depopulation of nations took on alarming proportions. Surely humanity would have died out had a way to use human eggs as soon as they were fertilized not been discovered, a brilliant discovery that took all the dreaded consequences out of love.

    Now on familiar, and therefore solid, ground, Celiana would delight in laying out the enchanting images of that happy time in which she had been lucky enough to live. With love free from all obligations, reproduction of the species was supervised by the State and regulated by science. Instead of the traditional family, bound by imaginary blood ties, the *group* had appeared, based on affinity of character, shared pleasures, and aspirations, making it, by nature, truly indissoluble. This was for Celiana the ideal sign of human sociability, the only one possible at this stage of civilization.

like in "Brave new world" book

    What family in the past enjoyed such a close and truly harmonious bond as that which prevailed—for example—in the group that she formed with Ernesto, Consuelo, Federico, and Miguel? *→ They are a Family!*

    Celiana inhaled with delight the smoke from her cigarette and, with the gentle influence of the indigenous alkaloid to enhance the bliss of the moment, her thoughts turned to the past and she relived the painful *via crucis* of her first youth.

    From primary school on, Celiana's intense cerebral constitution revealed itself as an insatiable and almost morbid thirst for knowledge, which had required her instructors to cautiously space out the hypnotic sessions in which it was transmitted to her, fearful of reaching the point of true imbalance. And because

Nuclear Family Notion = Dissolved

People who weren't
deemed "perfect" had to
undergo forced sterilization
(Celiana did) bc of
this

of her excessive intellectual curiosity, and in spite of the lushness with which her body developed, she would have to later undergo the sophisticated, although innocuous, surgical procedure that sterilized girls incapable of producing perfectly healthy and adjusted offspring. This was a simple tubal ligation that, without altering the mechanism of internal secretions and preserving other sexual functions, prevented only conception. Severing the epididymis, the same result was obtained in boys who were not considered perfect examples of the human species. Because of procedures like these, at that time commonly practiced throughout the civilized world, a reliable check against the advances of degeneration had been achieved.

Like almost every other woman of her time who preserved the ancestral instinct of motherhood, Celiana became a teacher and for ten years she found that this profession provided her with ample freedom and satisfied her desire to love children, the weak, and those in need of protection and guidance. But her maternal instinct was an unusual force and, left unfulfilled by her love for everyone else's children, it grew more intense, focusing on an increasingly small and selected number of people. In centuries past, such a woman would have made an excellent mother.

Celiana felt with the same force the internal necessity of another kind of love, complementary to her maternal instincts. She longed to completely surrender her body and her soul to another—still vague in the limbos of her virginal imagination—who was at the same time dominating and submissive, a tyrant and a comrade, in whom the demands of her flesh, her artistic ideals, and the expansive power of her intelligence would find complete satisfaction.

Determined to conquer this noble ideal, each attempt was a new failure that wilted in Celiana's spirit the rose of some illusion and left in her memory the bitterness of defeat. Had she not met Ernesto in the twilight of her youthfulness, she surely would have died for a sentimental life. Her fresh nature, blooming body, and generous heart were wasted on the perverse and sadistic attentions of a prematurely old man, who quickly dried out her romantic illusions and made her useless for love for a long time. When she was able, through an enormous display of willpower, to free herself from him, she thought that she hated men forever. What good would it do to remember each one of her lovers? There wasn't one who wouldn't take another turn at her optimism, or drive the wooden stake of a new ingratitude into her chest.

Celiana admired Miguel first for his artistic independence, and then she loved him for his eternally good mood, his charming ugliness, and the transparent frankness of his character. But Miguel was inconsistency personified, and after mutual and useless attempts to take each other seriously, their love ended in a burst of laughter and a familiar handshake. A three-week love affair that ended in a fraternal friendship that would last for the rest of their lives!

Later new lovers and new disappointments. . . . Until at last Ernesto, her favorite student, became a man. And she who had initiated him in all of the sciences also wanted to initiate him in love. When he caught on, Celiana realized that she had found what she had been searching for in vain for so long: the ideal lover, servant and master, at once dominant and submissive.

Consuelo and Federico, those adorable kids who sprinkled about them the contagious happiness of their idyllic love and the silvery notes of their laughter, couldn't live without Ernesto and, because he cared about them, Celiana, who already loved them, loved them even more. Ernesto himself was well liked by everyone, and now even by Miguel. The truly ideal group had been established: Celiana was the intellect at the center of the system; Ernesto, the sum of all of their affections; Consuelo and Federico were the sun's rays, the poetry of the home; and Miguel was the sure and loyal friend, the councilor who resolved difficult cases with his admirable practical sense and his ample life experience. Economic well-being greased the axles of this simple mechanism and facilitated its fluid operation. What seed of hatred or discord would have had enough force to alter or interrupt its course? . . . .

The chime of a clock striking eleven brought Celiana out of her sweet trance, reminding her that she had agreed to eat lunch at the Universal Casino with some wise foreign tourists. She threw her papers together, put away her notes, and went down to get dressed.

— 3 —

Miguel is the one
who schemed the reproduction
Ernesto thing

Ernesto was wrong to assume that his lover was an accomplice in the innocent appointment that had him so perplexed. It was Miguel who called upon his friendship with Dr. Pérez Serrato in order to arrange it and who personally placed the official letter on the nightstand early that morning after Celiana had already gotten out of bed.

A trained artist and a bohemian in spirit, Miguel was a typical product of his time. From his long and numerous trips and his forty-five intensely lived years, he had gained immense life experience that he almost always took comically. His pencil wielded a political and social force, and on more than one occasion one of his cartoons was enough to damage that type of false prestige obtained by who knows what maneuvers. His extremely elegant conversation was a continuous flow of brilliant paradox and penetrating wittiness.

Art
?
love

Sterilized since his youth, Miguel never found love to be anything more than a pleasant pastime, whose emotions did not penetrate any deeper than his skin. For him, the only thing worthy of adoration was art. Outside of that, Miguel had no serious feelings other than the fraternal affection he felt equally for Celiana, Ernesto, Consuelo, and Federico.

Physically he was of a kind and attractive ugliness, like that of certain strange animals. Tall, thin, and very dark in complexion, he was bald and had a sharp face. Because of the penetrating look of his bright brown eyes and the ironic smile of his thin and hairless lips, he reminded one somewhat of Voltaire. Partly out of laziness and his carefree nature and partly out of *snobbishness*, he went everywhere wearing his artist's smock and never took off a large wide-brimmed hat of an indistinguishable color.

For the same reason that Miguel loved Ernesto in an almost paternalistic way, it hurt him to see the best years of Ernesto's splendid youth spent doing nothing, and he was embarrassed by the deliberate nature of Ernesto's parasitic life, which among some of Miguel's friends had already become something of an annoying joke. When a young man, considered worthy to perpetuate the species, took on the responsibility of fully developing his reproductive faculties, he contracted with the State to provide the community with a certain number of offspring, a duty that had come to be as unavoidable as military service had once been.

Ernesto appeared to have forgotten that sacred duty, and Celiana, having been asked to remind him of this, did not do it, most certainly out of the consuming selfishness of her love. Miguel thought that it was his turn to take some initiative in the matter and for some time had been looking for a way to do it without offending the sensibilities of the two lovers or allowing for twisted interpretations of the unselfish honesty of their intentions. Certain that Ernesto, with his unclouded intelligence and sound judgment, would easily come back to reason, Miguel decided to raise the issue naturally and without warning, but now he wanted to have a frank conversation with Ernesto, something that he would have been better off doing in the first place.

With this goal in mind, and with no doubt that he would find Ernesto there, he headed toward the great *restaurant* that was attached to the Youth Center where Ernesto ate lunch almost every day with his comrades. This was the community's fashionable lunch venue frequented especially by the detached, *state-sponsored* youth of both sexes. On the splendid fifth-floor terrace, the joyful after-dinner conversations lasted well into the night.

Arriving at the first landing of the staircase, Miguel already noticed the loud laughter and animated conversation. Once on the terrace he could only stop to contemplate for a moment, with the eyes of an artist, the lively scene. Small, faint clouds of blue cigarette smoke danced about, fading into the foliage of climbing plants that became the roof above the terrace. The sun's rays passed through the leaves and were dispersed by crystal glasses and bottles and became fleeting rainbows in the tiny drops of four large fountains, whose chilled water was ready to preserve the room's pleasant and humid coolness.

Dressed in light Greek-style togas, split open over the left thigh and also leaving the right shoulder and arm exposed, with their hair tied up high and wearing sandals, young, busy waitresses ran from one side to the other, bringing trays of liquor or refreshments, between pinches and flirtatious remarks. Hidden among the foliage, in Eastern fashion, an orchestra played sweetly.

The artist's entrance was greeted with applause and shows of joy. He was called to from all directions at once. In one gathering of artists, a lively lad, soprano voiced and wearing a large bow tie, argued heatedly with an eccentric old man who sported long whiskers and white flowing hair under a red velvet hat. Seeing Miguel, the young man stood up shouting: "Save me, indisputable teacher! You arrived just in time to be our arbitrator; this one" — and he pointed to the old man — "maintains that pointillism is and will always be an irreplaceable technique. And in vain I waste my valuable breath that his fossil-ized brain might understand that there is no truer technique than that of the microscopic polyhedron, carried out in the three basic colors."

"As art critics," Miguel said, laughing, "you both are as brutal today as those in the twentieth century; you speak of techniques and methods as if these were all that mattered, and you forget or can't see with your blind eyes the part that deals with the soul: nature's own vision that the true artist places in his work. The impressionable public, which doesn't pay attention to technique, always critiques better than you two, and has the final say in who can and cannot paint."

Afterward, some consulted Miguel on sports. Further on, others tried to get his opinion on whether the legs of ballerina X were or were not superior to the bust of coupletist Z. He always responded with a joke, a witty observation, or cheerful statement. And, going from table to table, sharing smiles and hand-shakes, he finally arrived at the gathering in which Ernesto was explaining for the twentieth time the adventures of his victory in the last aviation competition. On his aerocycle equipped with a colloidal nitroglycerin engine, he had com-pleted the "Villautopia — Havana — Villautopia" run in barely forty minutes, and he didn't tire of telling the story, nor did his admirers tire of hearing about it. Welcomed with kind gestures, the painter sat in the chair that those good boys offered him and he ordered an ice cream.

Naturally, Ernesto knew that his friend had come there only to speak with him, and even suspected just what it was he wanted to talk about. So, taking advantage of a pause in the conversation, Miguel suggested that they leave together. They would take a walk and, before returning home for dinner, they would pick up Consuelo and Federico at the entrance to the novelties work-shop where both worked.

They had already gotten up when something interrupted their departure for a moment, turning their attention to the general uproar. It turned out that an eccentric character named Miajitas had just come in. He was bad-mannered and opportunistic and passed himself off as a champion of the workers and carried on on their behalf, filling their ears with the strange firework display of crude speeches in which he prophesied, in a not-too-distant future, the arrival of a more perfect social and economic equality. As always, his entrance in that elegant center was greeted with taunts and wisecracks.

Miajitas was, in spite of all of this, pleasant. Short and very plump, he radiated health and little shame. He was dressed as a worker and, while others typically carried an umbrella that was never opened, Miajitas was always weighed down with a new hammer that, in his hands, became a symbol, since he had not given a single blow with it. Everyone, including himself, had forgotten his real name, that is, if anyone ever knew it. A funny incident resulted in the nickname by which he was known. It was said that, when he was very young, he arrived at a restaurant at the exact moment that several of his friends were feasting; they invited him to join them but he declined, claiming to have already eaten. "However," he added, "to not seem ungrateful, I'll eat some 'crumbs.' . . . ." And such was the amount of crumbs that he ate that from that point on he was called "Miajitas" ("A Few Crumbs").

"Welcome!" someone said upon seeing him appear, "the false Spartacus, who comes to merrily drink with the privileged that those at the bottom have sweated to make!"

"No sirs," he replied. "I have not come for that but rather to exercise a sacred right; given that those on the bottom have fed me, I have come to demand from you, who call yourselves the *ones on top*, that you buy me coffee and pay me a bonus. It serves you well that I lack everything; and if the poor share with me the piece of bread that they earn with their work, I repay them fully with the sweet honey of my eloquence, which, in their tormented lives of wanting but never attaining, creates the golden mirage of an illusion, intangible, it's true, but for that very reason even more beautiful and seductive. What do you, who consume so much without producing anything, give them, you who get by on your good looks, supported by a man or a woman, like ladies' men? In spite of the countless evolutions and revolutions that humanity has suffered through, you continue to be as parasitic as your ancestors from semibarbaric centuries. Seeds of mistletoe, I curse you a thousand and one times!"

Exalted by his own words and without avoiding the laughter that followed his proclamations, Miajitas adopted a declamatory tone and continued. "Laugh and enjoy, reincarnated Nebuchadnezzars, but hurry and do so, because the tragic end of your festivity is nigh!"[8]

The welcomed arrival of drinks and the gratifying job of sipping them slowly, for a second appeased the oratorical impulses of that humbug, who,

8. Nebuchadnezzar was a king of the Neo-Babylonian Empire who reigned ca. 605 BC–562 BC. He is credited with the construction of the Hanging Gardens of Babylon and the destruction of Jerusalem's temple (Timothy Darvill, "Nebuchadnezzar," in *The Concise Oxford Dictionary of Archaeology*, 2nd ed. [New York: Oxford University Press, 2008], 305–6).

now with a more relaxed and familiar tone, began to expound on some more serious news items that the international press had addressed and which none of those present had paid attention to, if indeed any one of them was aware of anything newsworthy.

A conflict had arisen over the price of sugar between the sugar workers' labor unions and several governments. If an agreement wasn't reached soon, it was almost inevitable that the relations between the great Confederation of the Americas and the Euro-Asian Confederation would break.

It was true that wars were no longer orgies of blood and killing, as they had been in the past. No other weapons were brandished than the closing of ports and the cessation of all commercial exchange. But even so the consequences were not any less terrible. The lack of exports resulted in the general stoppage of factories, importation and misery, even more so now that no place on Earth could feed its citizens with only the fruits of its own land.

His oratorical spirit refreshed, Miajitas resumed his sermon: "May the equalizing war," he said, "come sooner rather than later. I am happy and I await it anxiously. If those last wars of the twentieth and twenty-first centuries resulted in universal disarmament and the dismantling of nations, if they con- tributed to the establishment of this lauded economic equilibrium that we enjoy today, then the war that approaches—and it will be awful, I tell you—will bring about absolute equality, as much with respect to social order as to economic order, a noble ideal to which I have dedicated the best years of my existence. Yes, ladies and gentlemen, I am happy that war is coming. And I am happy, most of all for you, who will find out what it is like to live only on bread and synthetic albumin; you will be forced to work and maybe then you will be regenerated. . . ."

As if to calm the fire of his enthusiasm, Miajitas ordered an ice cream, and then an absinthe, and afterward some pastries. And even though the size of his audience diminished little by little, as long as someone remained to pay for him, he continued stuffing himself; the capacity of his stomach, for liquids and solids, was proportional to the untiring movement of his tongue.

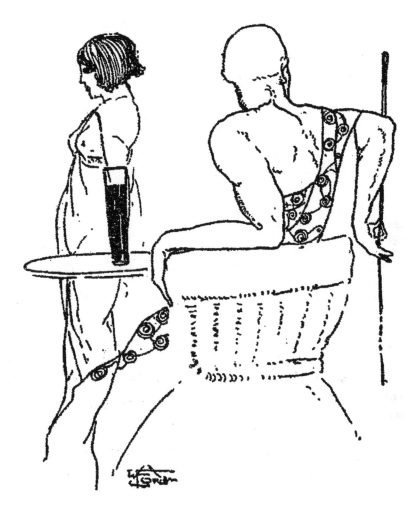

~ 4 ~

Quickly tiring of listening to such foolishness, Ernesto and Miguel were not the last to leave the terrace of the Circle. Miajitas had no sense of grace.

Once in the street, they did not want to take the aerotrolley. Nor did they need to, since, like all concentric streets in the city, the one on which the Youth Circle stood was abundant with moving sidewalks. They stepped up onto one and soon were in front of the large archway that gave way to Occidental Park, at the very end of the street.

Occidental Park was the largest and most frequented park in Villautopia, and at that hour of the day, in the quiet serenity of the afternoon, it had an enchanted feel. The blue of the sky became more and more pale and, toward the west, several small stratus clouds began to darken to a pink and greenish tint. Almost grazing the tops of the thick trees, countless aerocycles and aerocarriages flew by, carrying young men and women who greeted each other in passing. Children ran along the wide avenues while sweethearts looked for a safe place to cuddle in the thick brush.

Overcome by the soothing effect that the atmosphere of immense parks has always had on the nervous system, Miguel and Ernesto walked in silence for a while, neither one wanting to be the first to broach the difficult topic that had them both bothered. They wound up sitting on a bench, under an awning of flowers, and admired the sunset that now burned with a brilliant warmth.

"Why are you so quiet, Miguel?" Ernesto finally said with a slight tone of reproach. "Do you have such a low opinion of me that you don't dare to speak to me with your usual candor?"

The painful, sincere tone of the young man melted away the ice of his growing hesitation, and the explanation came on its own. Miguel spoke with his characteristic frankness and clarity, and Ernesto, convinced by the straightforwardness of his friend's gaze, promised to no longer delay fulfilling his duty to the State. He only wanted to know if it was Celiana who had been the first to think about reminding him.

Miguel masked his jealous suspicions. "I assure you," he said, "that she knows nothing about this, and I thought it fitting that it be you who lets her know. I understand well," he added, "that your scruples come from the deep honor of your character, for which many look up to you, it's true. You yourself, Ernesto, fear getting caught up in the heat of new lovers and forgetting how grateful you are to Celiana. But know that eternal fidelity is a beautiful utopia. When spring causes new flowers to bud and burst open, no one takes notice of the ones that dried up the previous spring. What foolish person ever thought of objecting to a falling star, the metamorphosis of an insect, or the budding of a plant? The natural law of the human heart is also the continual exchanging of old loves that wear out for new loves that bloom. And whoever chooses to go against this law will only cause their own misfortune and contribute to that of others, since simulated love is more tragic than oblivion and more painful even than hate itself.

"If some day your affection for Celiana should be extinguished or transformed, the efforts of either of you to stop it would be useless. And no matter how hard you tried you both would be miserable. I believe that she has enough emotional capacity to adapt her love to all of the nuances and changes that yours might have gone through over the years. But if I am wrong, if she isn't so strong, if she is not capable of such multiple displays of love, all the worse it will be for her and for everyone."

Miguel stopped talking, and Ernesto, convinced, had nothing to say. The contagious sadness of that painful afternoon crept into their spirits and they felt overcome by—they didn't know how to describe it—an unusual melancholy or strange premonition.

At a turn in one of the paths of the park, Consuelo and Federico suddenly appeared. They came joined at the waist, laughing happily. Having finished earlier than normal that day, they too had wanted to take a walk before dinner. Spotting their friends, they ran toward them and Consuelo kissed them both as if she were a six-year-old girl.

Between outbursts of laughter and expressions of excitement, Consuelo and Federico described the funny incident that had just happened to them. From behind a thicket of plants they had surprised Don Fabio Cerillas in animated and very suspicious conversation with a colorful, dolled-up old woman.[9] Don Fabio, although young, was a serious and stern moralist, editor of a neo-Theosophic newspaper, and through his columns and soporific background articles, he became an apologist for chastity and he always went about praising "the pure and rigid traditions of our ancestors."[10]

According to Consuelo, the comical faces that those lovebirds made after being surprised was enough to make anyone burst out laughing.

There are those in the world who carry their own ambience with them, their own little atmosphere in which, without intending to, they engulf those around them. Thus, some people instill in us respect or fear without cause. Others leave in their wake a trail of sadness, an impulse of hate, or the feeling of a coming misfortune. Those two young people, Consuelo and Federico, always cheerful and full of glee, wandered the world as if engulfed in a halo of happiness, leaving behind them a trail of laughter.

They both were graceful and slender and appeared to be much younger than their age. With her large dark-blue eyes, small red mouth, tiny and very white teeth, narrow hips, almost childlike breasts, delicate ankles, and extraordinarily tiny hands and feet, Consuelo resembled one of Watteau's pastor girls.[11] Federico had very clear, green eyes; his hair, also curly, formed a golden

9. "Don," and its counterpart for addressing women, "Doña," is a title of respect in the Spanish-speaking world. While the expression doesn't have an exact translation into English, it would fall between "Mr." and "Honorable."

10. In a later passage in *Eugenia*, Urzaiz defines neo-Theosophy as "nothing more than ancient Theosophy, stripped of the Oriental myths and the remnants of Buddhism of other times, and reduced to a philosophical doctrine that recognized the existence of a Supreme Being, the immortality of the soul and its evolution toward superior worlds and planes through a series of reincarnations" (*Eugenia*, 73). Theosophy was an important spiritualist movement of the nineteenth century that combined many European occult movements, including Neoplatonism, gnosticism, kabbala, hermeticism, freemasonry, and esotericism into "a supra-confessional, universalistic, 'primitive' and 'world' religion, . . . contrast[ing] with the orthodoxies of Judaism and the Christian churches," as well as an alternative nonreligious truth that some claimed to find in science, and specifically in "'materialistic' Darwinism" ("Theosophical/Anthroposophical Society," in *The Brill Dictionary of Religion*, ed. Kocku von Stuckrad [Leiden: Brill, 2006], 1884).

11. Jean-Antoine Watteau (1684–1721) was a French painter credited with inventing the fête galante genre, which features scenes of bucolic and idyllic charm with an air of frivolity (Marc Jordan, "Watteau, Jean-Antoine," in *The Oxford Companion to Western Art* [New York: Oxford University Press, 2001], 791–92).

tuft at the top of his head; above his upper lip and about his rounded face grew an innocent and almost colorless fuzz.

One would have thought that they were brother and sister, and they practically were. They had been raised together without ever being separated. As infants they slept in the same crib. In school, they always played and did their homework together. Like Daphne and Chloe, as adolescents they bathed together and, again like Daphne and Chloe, discovered on their own, in the freedom of the countryside, that sacred mystery.[12] Any possibility for unwelcomed consequences of their love having already been eliminated, their mutual and serene fondness, solid and without passionate torments, was the greatest raison d'être of those two lives, the only motive of their actions and the sum total of their ambitions. Not even the faintest cloud blurred the polished glass of such a romance. If Federico ever felt the fleeting flap of the wing of temptation or gave in to a strange request, his companion, if she learned of it, didn't feel it any more than she would have if he ate some sweet treat in the street and had forgotten to bring her a piece.

Swept up by the sincere joy of his young friends, Ernesto forgot his heavy worries. They appeared as three small children, running and playing along the park's avenues.

Contemplating that frolicking, Miguel thought that, much to his sorrow and in spite of his skepticism, a quasi-paternal fondness had planted in his chest much more solid roots than he could have ever imagined. With age he was turning sentimental without realizing it; these young people with their sibling love and Celiana with her sincere camaraderie had given him a domestic warmth that he never would have enjoyed in his carefree and nomadic youth and that now, as old age came ever closer, he began to need.

When the four of them—looking for their favorite spot for a delicious dinner and pleasant conversation afterward—boarded the aerotrolley to return home, the burning sunset had already been extinguished and in the sky, now almost black, the first stars began to flicker.

---

12. *The Pastoral Story of Daphnis and Chloe*, by the second-century AD Greek writer Longus, depicts the coming-of-age of the two orphans who are raised by shepherds on the Isle of Lesbos and eventually fall in love (Ewen Bowie, "Longus," in *The Oxford Classical Dictionary*, 4th ed., ed. Simon Hornblower and Antony Spawforth [Oxford: Oxford University Press, 2012], 858).

MIGVEL

⌐ 5 ⌐

$\mathcal{D}$r. Remigio Pérez Serrato, Director of Villautopia's Institute of Eugenics, was one of those uncontrollable talkers who, when no one else was around to listen, spoke to themselves or to their office furniture.

Since the inexhaustible flood of his learned discourse had a hypnotic quality, finding an attentive listener was especially rewarding for him.

That day was particularly satisfying, since propitious luck had given him an exclusive audience with two important Hottentot doctors who, sent on a scientific mission by their government, came to study ways to introduce into their country effective means to prevent the evolutionary stagnation of their race.[13]

When Ernesto, carrying Miguel's business card, arrived at the doctor's office to announce that he would accept his appointment as Official Breeder and to inquire about his subsequent responsibilities, the African doctors were already there. Dr. Remigio was pleased, and made formal introductions:

"Mister Ernesto del Lazo, one of our most distinguished breeders; the wise Doctors Booker T. Kuzubé and Lincoln Mandínguez, worthy representatives of medical science in Hottentot. . . ."

---

13. The Hottentots originally inhabited southern Africa and belong to the Khoisan speaking peoples. "Hottentot" is a pejorative word meaning "savage" or "barbarian." Modern anthropologists prefer the term "Khoikhoi" (men of men), the people's own name for themselves ("Khoikhoi," in *The World Book Encyclopedia*, vol. 11, *J–K* [Chicago: World Book, 2002], 309). That Urzaiz chooses the more derogatory term to refer to the black doctors suggests that his thinking was greatly influenced by the racist tendencies often associated with eugenics. One of the main preoccupations of eugenics was the stagnation of genetic evolution caused by uncontrolled reproduction among individuals shown to be genetically inferior, which would lead to the eventual degeneration of the human race.

Ernesto greeted them with a bow. Smiling, the Africans displayed their
pearly rows of formidable cannibal-like teeth. One young and the other old,
they both were ugly, thick-lipped, and had a comical air of frightened curiosity
about them. They spoke perfect English and their gestures were animated.
They wore long black frock coats and very tall hats in the shape of a truncated
cone, which they kept pulled over their ears as a sign of respect. The elder, with
his long white beard, looked like a domesticated chimpanzee.[14]

Around sixty years of age, tall and stout, Dr. Pérez Serrato wore his long,
straight white hair combed back. His round pale face, cleanly shaven, his thick
black eyebrows above bovine eyes, made him closely resemble in appearance
another illustrious doctor of antiquity, the celebrated Charcot.[15]

His purple silk robe, nobly wrapped about the abdomen, and a felt beret of
the same color, likened him to a bishop and emphasized the majestic elegance
of his outward appearance. On his chest he boasted the traditional red button
of the Legion of Honor, an insignia that, without a doubt, the Africans also
flaunted on the lapels of their respective coats.

To properly indoctrinate his visitors before showing them the departments
of that vast institution that was his responsibility, and, above all, to take complete
advantage of their audience, Dr. Remigio began the conversation with a discussion of the earliest origins of eugenics. Had it been possible, he would have
begun with prehistoric times.

"You should remember, distinguished colleagues," he began, "that even
toward the middle of the twentieth century, even though mankind believed that
it had reached the height of civilization, humans continued to reproduce in
exactly the same way as any other mammal. Close to three hundred years ago,
an illustrious fellow Earthling, whose statue you must have seen at the entrance
of this building and whose name need not be spoken, since the entire world
knows it, demonstrated through experiment that the ovum of a mammal, once
fertilized, can develop in the peritoneal cavity of another individual of the same

14. Racist patterns of thought were an inherent part of eugenics. Even the most
educated and informed scientists of the early part of the twentieth century, including
Urzaiz, would have found it difficult to avoid making such dehumanizing observations.

15. Jean-Martin Charcot was a founder of modern neurology and one of France's
most celebrated medical teachers and clinicians. His reputation as an extraordinarily
gifted teacher attracted students from all over the world. Sigmund Freud was his student
in 1885; Charcot was also a pioneer in using hypnosis as a means to discover an organic
basis for hysteria.

species, even if that individual is of the male gender.[16] He started by observing ectopic gestations and, naturally, conducted his first trials on laboratory animals.[17] The challenge remained in modifying, or to put it another way, feminizing the body of the male animal, and when he achieved this, thanks to intravenous and intraperitoneal injections of ovarian extract, the main problem was practically resolved. The entire scientific world was moved by admiration when, in the great Rockefeller Institute of New York, in the presence of notable doctors from many different countries, our fellow sage opened the stomach of a male guinea pig and took from it five perfectly formed and lively little guinea piglets.[18]

"Similar experiments were later conducted on the human species, with remarkable success; but many years passed before such experiments became something more than scientific curiosities.[19] Secular prejudices opposed the general application of this procedure, and that brilliant innovator, regarded today among the greatest benefactors of Humanity, died almost forgotten and without knowing the absolute and radical transformation that his discovery had on the ways of civilized societies, changing the fundamentals of morality, the economic conditions of nations and international relations.[20] Thanks to him, today we consider ourselves completely different from other living beings and advanced beyond the physiological animalism of our ancestors.[21]

16. Urzaiz may have been referring to Walter Heape, who in 1890 conducted an experiment in which he transferred two fertilized ova from a female Angora rabbit to the uterus of a female Belgian hare; see Heape's article "Preliminary Note on the Transplantation and Growth of Mammalian Ova within a Uterine Foster-Mother," *Proceedings of the Royal Society of London*, no. 48 (1890): 457–58.

17. Urzaiz is possibly referring to Albert Brachet, who grew rabbit embryos in serum in 1913; see J. B. S. Haldane, *Daedalus; or, Science and the Future; A Paper Read to the Heretics, Cambridge, on February 4th, 1923*, 6th ed. (London: K. Paul, Trench, Trubner, 1925), 59.

18. For relatively recent academic examinations of the Rockefeller Institute's medical and public health interventions in early twentieth-century Mexico, see Anne-Emmanuelle Birn, *Marriage of Convenience: Rockefeller International Health and Revolutionary Mexico* (Rochester, NY: University of Rochester Press, 2006), and Heather L. McCrea, *Diseased Relations: Epidemics, Public Health, and State-Building in Yucatán, Mexico, 1847–1924* (Albuquerque: University of New Mexico Press, 2010).

19. In *Daedalus*, published in 1925, Haldane predicted that in 1951 "Dupont and Schwarz" would produce the first ectogenetic child (63).

20. This is a utopian statement on the potential for eugenics as a vehicle for the universal transformation of humanity.

21. The scientist to whom Doctor Pérez Serrato is referring is most likely a fabrication, a composite of the real scientists that we have identified.

"But at last the day came when governments had to resort to these methods of artificial reproduction and establish special institutions where such projects could be carried out on a large scale, as the only way to stop the depopulation of the earth, which would have occurred had the social conditions of the centuries from which we emerged been allowed to continue.

"It is certain that in the end multiple circumstances converged, the nature of which I am unable to grasp even now due to their extreme complexity. But it seems that the most salient advantages of the happy state of affairs of contemporary societies are these: governments regulate the production of children in such a way that the human population never exceeds the Earth's natural resources, they maintain economic equilibrium, they carry out in an efficient manner the scientific selection of the human species, and they thereby avoid all possibilities for degeneration."

Serrato, seeing a new opportunity appear, did not want to waste it. Rather, he tried to take it as far as he could. Satisfied with the patience his listeners had shown throughout his first oratorical deluge, he allowed himself to give them a brief pause; he rubbed his hands together, coughed lightly, and continued:

"Because of the intrinsic conditions of that deficient and incomplete civilization of past centuries that today we consider semibarbaric, the human species had voluntarily submitted itself to natural selection which, in other animal species, occurs by means of the struggle for life and the triumph of the strongest or the best adapted to the environment. In the societies of yesteryear, the most intelligent, most astute, or the richest triumphed, and since they were generally also the worst off physically, that meant that the species degenerated at an alarming rate.

"It is certain that the most advanced nations of that time tried to the best of their abilities to undertake artificial selection. Out of these trials eugenics was born, but this science, which today, perfectly regulated, has achieved maximum development and constitutes the principal responsibility of governments, had to be limited by purely mitigating measures, and its results were all but absurd."

Ernesto, understanding that this introduction would last a while, made a superhuman effort not to yawn, since all that was being said interested him very little. The blacks appeared to be hypnotized. The doctor continued:

"The advances in aseptic surgery have permitted the sterilization of both men and women, without changing in the least the complicated synergy and dynamism of internal secretions and fluids. This procedure, the salvation of the species, was initially performed on naturally born or reoffending criminals, on the insane and the mentally disturbed, and on those with certain incurable diseases like epilepsy and tuberculosis.[22]

"Later, a few individuals of both sexes began to sterilize themselves voluntarily to avoid the economic responsibilities of fatherhood or the physiological responsibilities of motherhood. Now that fatherhood has ceased to be a burden for men, poor or rich, and motherhood does not last beyond conception, the government has reproduction under its immediate care and vigilance. All individuals who are physically or mentally inferior or deficient are sterilized, and only those who are perfect species and capable of producing ideal offspring are left with their full genetic faculties. And we must not forget that for these individuals this distinction implies the obligation to give to the community a certain number of children, a duty that has become as unavoidable today as military service, popular elections, or suffrage had been in the past.

"The selection of ideal breeders begins from the time they are in primary school. Before puberty and after a detailed examination, both medical and psychological, it is decided which children are to be sterilized and which are not. We prefer the purely muscular type and systematically discard the cerebral of both sexes, since experience has shown these to be poor breeders; in the event there is a scarcity, respiratory males may be used, as long as they are paired later with digestive women.[23]

"With your permission, we will begin our visit with the statistics department. There you will see for yourselves that each year the number of children sterilized

22. Programs of sterilization were widespread throughout Europe, and even in some parts of the United States. It was believed that by sterilizing such people, these traits would eventually rid themselves from the gene pool.

23. In a 1927 article in *The American Naturalist*, Professor R. Bennett Bean explains that early twentieth-century European medical researchers and practitioners, including A. Chaillou, L. MacAuliffe, and Sigaud, identified four human types: respiratory, digestive, cerebral, and muscular. This categorical scheme was different from an earlier Greek one, developed by Hippocrates and expanded upon by Aristotle, Galen, and the School of Salerno, which used the amount of moisture in the body to identify humans as yellowbile, phlegm, black bile, or blood. The newer scheme took facial shape, cranial measurements (such as the distance from the chin to the forehead), and the size of body parts—including outer components such as limbs, as well as inner parts such as organs and glands—into account in making its assignments of type. See R. Bennett Bean, "Human Types in Relation to Medicine," *The American Naturalist* 61, no. 673 (March–April 1927): 160–72.

diminishes; the day will come when the procedure is performed only when the excess of inhabitants requires the restriction in the number of births.

"Since these measures have put a stop to the degeneration of Humanity, the populations of prisons, mental asylums, and hospitals for the terminally ill have been reduced to almost zero. And if we further take into account that the economic conditions of the working classes have notably improved and that today we don't hesitate in applying euthanasia on those condemned to spend the rest of their lives, or a large part of it, in a state of unconsciousness or among incurable sufferings, it will be easy to understand that such institutions, which before constituted an extremely heavy responsibility for the state, are no longer needed and the numerous funds that they consumed are now appropriately applied to more urgent needs."

Having had enough of the long-winded dissertations of the doctor, Ernesto didn't wait for him to repeat the invitation and he stood up as if ready to begin the tour. The blacks imitated him; given the ease with which those of their race had for sleeping anywhere at any time, these unfortunate two had done all that they could to stay awake. Dr. Serrato could do nothing but give in and moved to the front to lead them; he would soon have the chance to indulge himself in every department that they would visit.

Crossing the secretary's office, adjacent to the Director's office, the Secretary General—a neatly dressed little old man—and more than thirty subordinate employees stood up upon seeing their boss. While the young female typists exchanged smiles and cheerful comments about the exotic costumes of the blacks, the illustrious guide explained the complicated function of that office, detailing how things were classified, how work was distributed, how applications were reviewed, and how the communications from the various institutions with which that office worked were filed and answered.

The Department of Statistics, where they arrived next, occupied three vast rooms with high ceilings and excellent lighting. More than one hundred employees, mostly women, worked there. The visitors were introduced to a middle-aged woman, tall, dry, with her hair shaved short like a man's, who served as head of that important department. Very proper in her manners, she gave meticulous reports on the state of the affairs that fell under her responsibility.

In well-organized and carefully kept-up-to-date books, it was easy to verify the truthfulness and exactness of the previous claims of the Director. So far that year, only three thousand five hundred boys and close to two thousand girls had been sterilized, barely one tenth of all those that had reached the required age for the procedure, and less than one twentieth of the population of the schools in Villautopia. These statistics predicted that within a few years they would have a splendid crop of breeders. They left that department feeling satisfied and carrying some figures from the *Bulletin of Statistics*, the departmental publication.

After crossing a beautiful garden, Dr. Serrato stopped his visitors in front of a large operating room, deserted at the moment since it was not a day for performing surgery.

"This pavilion," he explained, "is only used for sterilizing males. The other operations are performed in special pavilions that we will visit later. On Wednesday and Saturday mornings we perform operations. If you would like to attend them, dear colleagues, you will have the opportunity to admire the skill of our surgeons."

Continuing on, the dignified Director became absorbed in minor details of a technical nature—(it all sounded very foreign to Ernesto)—that related to the surgical procedures and the antiseptic precautions, thanks to which the operation was so innocuous and safe, that for years not a single accident had been reported.

Leaving the patients and suffering Hottentots as bait for the doctor's inexhaustible loquaciousness, Ernesto withdrew himself from the lecture and internally gathered the profound, almost overwhelming sensation that emanated from that enormous circular room, completely white, with its walls and floor of lustrous porcelain, and in which ten surgeons could work simultaneously; the immense amphitheater, in the shape of a horseshoe, could accommodate more than three thousand students. Light flooded in through the crystal dome of the ceiling, causing the nickel bars of the operating tables to shine, which for Ernesto, as for all those outside of the medical profession, gave the impression of infernal torture machines.

Before leaving that pavilion, they visited its various areas: the anesthesia room, the splendid and well-equipped arsenal, the sterilized water service, and the large autoclaves for disinfecting the surgical instruments and the materials for recuperation.

They had to cross another section of garden to reach the rooms where children who had been recently operated on rested for a maximum of five days. Very clean, bright, and well ventilated, the appearance of the white beds lined up in a row was cheerful and soothing. It was time for the first snack and the nurses, dressed in white, ran around hastily, attending to the impatient uproar of the little ones. There were close to five hundred, both male and female, distributed throughout six great pavilions. In the beautiful park next to the pavilion, the convalescent children went for walks in groups or played in the shade of the lush trees and flowered surroundings. The visitors were surprised to learn that in less than two weeks, those children would be well enough to return to their classes.

After the inevitable presentation, the department's on-duty night intern joined the group. He was Dr. Suárez, a kind young man, with a black beard and an intelligent gaze. He stayed with them for the remainder of their visit.

The tour continued without the terrible verbosity of the wise Director of the institution letting up for a moment as he explained everything with a luxury of superfluous details and references of a pedantic and inopportune erudition. At times he became aggressive, taking anyone of his listeners—whoever was closest—and shaking him by the collar for a moment or pinning him against the wall, monopolizing him and crushing him under a barrage of comments.

Next they arrived at another pavilion that was also deserted at that hour. It consisted of three rooms: a small waiting room, coquettishly furnished and with its own entrance from the street, and two small operating rooms, with their respective tables. These rooms were separated by a partition of opaque crystal. The entire pavilion had a certain air of discreet mystery about it, of gallantry and subterfuge, which greatly intrigued Ernesto.

"Here," Dr. Serrato rushed to say, "we perform the removal of the ovum, the *prise*, as we say, and its grafting to the foster uterus. The women come here on their own at the right moment, which they know how to recognize perfectly well, and they return soon after. The operation, though delicate, is very simple. It comes down to delicately removing the fertilized egg when it has started to attach itself to the mucous of the uterus. For this procedure we use this ingenious spoon." And he held one up that he took from a glass case.

"In the adjoined room," he continued, "the incubator, having been feminized, and in whose abdomen another surgeon has already made an incision, awaits. The egg is deposited into the peritoneal cavity as if it were a grain of wheat in a furrow, and, if the operation is successful—these days it is rare not to be so—exactly two hundred and eighty-one days later we perform a laparotomy and remove a perfectly developed and lively child.[24] With progress in aseptic surgery, the dangers of these cesarean sections have become almost nonexistent.

---

24. In the 1897 follow-up article to his 1890 "Preliminary Note on the Transplantation and Growth of Mammalian Ova within a Uterine Foster-Mother," Walter Heape outlined the procedure used to transfer fertilized ova from one female rabbit to another: Walter Further Heape, "Note on the Transplantation and Growth of Mammalian Ova with a Uterine Foster Mother," *Proceedings of the Royal Society of London*, no. 62 (1897): 457–58. It seems likely that Heape's article inspired Urzaiz in his descriptions of male pregnancy and delivery via the caesarean in *Eugenia*, as the procedures described by

We have one gestator who has been operated on successfully ten or twelve times. I should warn you that, during the removal of the ovum and its grafting to the host uterus, it is crucial to keep the room at a constant temperature, which is approximately equal to that of the human body so that the elements aren't exposed to the smallest change or alteration. This makes the job of the surgeons quite arduous and requires that we have a sufficient number of surgeons on hand and rotate them so that they don't work more than two days in a row.

"Now," he continued, "I am going to show you our institution's most intriguing department: the rooms occupied by the incubators and the pavilion where the laparotomies or surgical deliveries take place. If you still aren't tired, afterward we will visit the nursing rooms and the Department of Infancy."

Surrounded by a beautiful and open park, which they had to cross in order to enter, the building designated for the incubators consisted of several dormitories with large windows and beds aligned in rows. There was also a large banquet hall, a magnificent spa, a dining hall, a library, and a billiards hall. A small and elegant theater stood at one end of the park. Lunchtime had not yet arrived and the self-sacrificing gestators of future humankind, who numbered approximately six hundred, wandered about the various rooms. Some read novels or newspapers in the library, since they were prohibited from any serious reading. One played the piano while others played cards, chess, or billiards. No small number of them strolled along the avenues of the park, read, or conversed under the shade of the trees, or participated in nonviolent sports, suitable for their condition and favorable for a good gestation. They were not permitted to smoke. The oldest of them—who would have believed it!—knitted, crocheted, or sewed tiny shirts and exquisite hats. The ages of these subjects ranged from eighteen to forty-five, and all were fat, lucid, and had a healthy complexion, with an air of blissful satisfaction about them.

Greeted with displays of friendly camaraderie, the doctor smiled at everyone and joked with several of them.

Seeing the comical manner with which those most advanced in their pregnancies crossed their hands upon the abdominal sphere, the youngest of the blacks couldn't contain an inopportune moment of laughter that caused him to shed tears the size of garbanzo beans that nearly drowned him. Dr. Serrato blushed slightly, and Ernesto needed all the strength of his will to not compete

---

Heape and Urzaiz are quite similar. See the essay "*Eugenia*'s Literary Genesis and Genealogy" in this volume for a more detailed comparison of *Eugenia* and Heape's texts.

with the black man. At last he was able to calm himself, thanks to the stern stares and strong expressions of his companion.

"Don't you think, Doctor," Ernesto asked the intern, "that the condition of these sorry-looking men is no less sad and difficult than it was before for women, and that this curiously artificial state will be nothing but an affront to their condition as men and even to their human dignity?"

"Each century has their ethic, my friend," replied the young doctor. "Furthermore, the State rewards splendidly the services of these worthy subjects; the life they lead here couldn't be more comfortable and, as my worthy boss said before, the final operation is free from danger."

"You can be sure," the Director, who didn't allow anyone else to speak for very long at a time, interjected, "that the job of incubator is really one of the best paid and, therefore, one of the most desired. We always have more applications than we need, and therefore we don't accept just anyone. The incubator must be someone perfectly healthy and stable, both physically and mentally. He must be a purely digestive type, of excellent character and good habits, and must not smoke or drink alcohol. It is also necessary to know and analyze his heredity and ancestry.

"Of course from the time they are children, gestators have been prohibited from acting as breeders, and before each graft, it is necessary to give them a series of intravenous and intraperitoneal injections of ovarian extract in order to alter the dynamism of their internal secretions and their humoral conditions. In this way they are suitable to develop the eggs, and they have been, in a word, feminized. During the gestational period all erotic impulses in them disappear and, in time, their effectiveness and their inclinations are definitively altered. They become aficionados of feminine pastimes and occupations.

"It is rare for one of them to not enjoy the responsibility, and we have veterans. A few days ago, in fact, we lost our 'dean of incubators' after twelve happy laparotomies. Before his thirteenth gestation, we wanted him to retire, which he was entitled to do. He had already turned forty-eight and had twenty years of service, and besides, he was obese and had incipient cardiac adiposis. But, stubborn and spoiled, he begged us to let him serve, 'just one more time.'. . . . We had the unfortunate weakness of giving in to his pleading and, at the moment of birth, he remained anesthetized. . . . Poor Manuelón! Poor unselfish friend! Humanity should be grateful to you and tenderly remember your heroic name, obscure and ignored. Of course, gentlemen, his posthumous delivery was not wasted and is now a beautiful boy."

The nursery, or Department of Infancy, which they visited after leaving the Department of Incubators, had a truly charming appearance capable of instilling optimistic ideas in even the most recalcitrant spirit. More than two thousand infants were divided by age into three chambers that, clean, lighted, and ventilated, left nothing to be desired. The first chamber, for newborns, boasted in one corner a large scale for weighing, and in another a modern autoclave with bottles, numbered and lined up, ready to serve. The infants stirred in their elegant white cribs, and their faces, deep in the unconsciousness of their first sleep, were as round and brightly colored as ripe apples. Next to each crib was a clinical report with the name of the child, the child's assigned classification number, and charts that graphically showed the child's increase in weight and height. The nurses watched over each crib, attentive to the child's needs, as solicitous and tender as real mothers.

In the second chamber, three- to six-month-old infants were carried around or rested in their cribs, rattling little bells and, smiling, showing off their pink gums, where from time to time the first incisors emerged. The children in the third chamber crawled or took their first steps between laughs and falls. In the exquisite garden that surrounded the pavilion, the older ones noisily ran and played under the care of nannies, almost all of whom where young and pretty.

What healthy joy there was in their adorable children's faces! What maternal diligence on the part of the nannies! That splendid blooming of life and health alone was enough to justify whatever violence and immorality there might have been in the measures that Humanity had deemed necessary in order to stop its degeneration and demise and firmly continue its evolutionary journey toward an ideal of perfection. Not one of these infants displayed the sad vision of disease or emaciation, so frequent in the past centuries.

"Since the birth of a child nowadays," said Dr. Suárez, "is the result of scientific deliberation and comes after a rigorous selection, today, unlike in the past, when the fruit of an impetuous instinct was rarely desired, all those born reach complete and total development. One can say that infant mortality, that horrible and absurd thing that caused desperation in our ancestors, has completely disappeared."

It was just before two in the afternoon when they left the Department of Infancy; Dr. Pérez Serrato didn't want to free his prisoners, and since chattiness doesn't give way to politeness, he made Ernesto, the two blacks, and the intern eat lunch with him in his splendid private residence, situated within the grounds of the Institute. It was not possible to refuse without committing a sinful faux pas. On the other hand, the prospects of a good lunch seemed quite alluring, in that opportune moment, as far from the city as they were and with the exercise they had done. Later they would continue their visit. There was still much to see of the departments of the great Institute of Eugenics, the true pride of Villautopia.

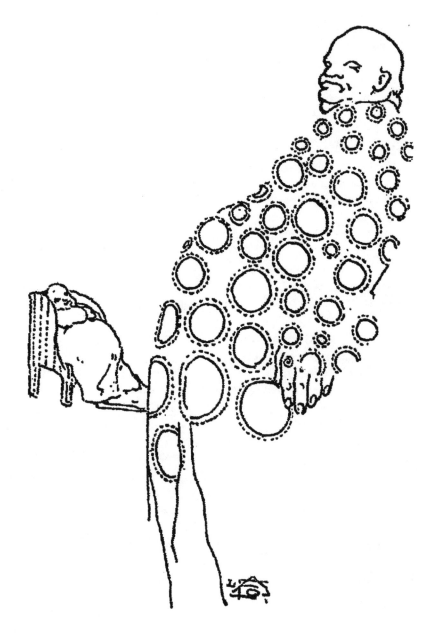

~ 6 ~

*T*he illustrious Dr. Remigio Pérez Serrato did not live alone. Moreover, the family group that he had created for himself was quite heterogeneous and original. It was made up of a man somewhat older than him, a matron of around forty-five years of age, and a beautiful young woman of twenty. The old man, also a doctor, was Don Teodosio Reyes. He had been Don Remigio's classmate and partner in crime, and since his youth he had distinguished himself by the patience with which he listened to Remigio, by the infrequency with which he interrupted him, and by demonstrating seeming immunity to Remigio's dissertations.

These invaluable characteristics had reached a complete state of perfection with age, given that poor Teodosio was hemiplegic, aphasic, and an insomniac. What an ideal audience! Remigio never failed to go to bed without chatting for a few hours with the invalid Teodosio, who listened and nodded his head once in a while. When he finally closed his eyes, his friend covered him gently, turned off the lights, and tiptoed out of the room. The day that Teodosio no longer opened his eyes, Remigio would miss him greatly.

Isabel was the older woman's name, a very presentable middle-aged woman with traces of an autumnal beauty that in its prime must have been first class. She was the last lover of the Doctor, not bad looking either in his younger days. Together they had exhausted every burning coal in their hearts, and when the fire had burned out with the chilling breeze of the passing years, there remained the embers of mutual respect, a certain compatibility of their characters, and the force of habit that kept them together. It's also true that the good woman had learned to listen and keep quiet, a quality that her partner appreciated above all others. Isabel was not the type to put up a fight and would fall asleep quickly. And for some subject matters, a sleeping audience is not a bad thing in the absence of an alert one and, at any rate, is always better than a

couch or a table. How many illustrious speakers have 95 percent of the audi-
torium asleep before their talk is even half over, and in spite of it continue their
flavorful speech until the end!

The young woman displayed that rare type of beauty in which harmony is
the dominant feature: harmony of lines, of proportion, and of color. No part of
that adorable body was bigger or smaller than that prescribed by aesthetics.
Nothing stood out for being lacking or excessive. The rosy tint of her skin, the
burning red of her lips, her large black eyes, and the light brown tone of her
silky hair, along with the whiteness of her loose gown, resulted in the most
perfect chromatic composition. Harmonious as well in movement, without
even trying, each and every one of her poses formed a perfectly academic
posture. Her name was Rosaura, but from the time she was very young Don
Remigio had christened her with the name Athanasia, which for him represented the beauty of its etymological meaning (without death, immortal) and
also reminded him of the circumstances through which she came under his
care. She was his real daughter, since in his younger days and in his capacity as
a healthy and strong man, he had fulfilled his quota as a reproducer. He was a
surgeon in the same Institute for which he now served as Director, when the
young Rosaura came into the world and, for scientific interest and out of paternal
pride, he got used to frequently visiting his offspring and took pleasure in closely
following their development. She was his favorite child, for her unique beauty,
the spitting image of her mother, a woman with whom he had been madly in
love and who had abandoned him early on, leaving him with the bitterness of
unfulfilled love. When the little girl became gravely ill, Don Remigio arduously
fought to save her from death's grip, something that he managed to do just
when it seemed humanly impossible. The zeal of the battle and the happiness
of the great triumph caused the paternal love in Don Remigio to be reborn
with all the selfish force of the past. Ever since then he called the girl Athanasia
and later, upon the completion of her education, he took her to live with him.

Dr. Pérez Serrato narrated this episode with his usual amount of abundance,
which gave way to a more general conversation, since Ernesto was curious to
know what in reality, and given the social organization of the time, were the
standard manifestations of paternal love, a feeling that in the past appeared to
be so profound and consuming.

"In men and women of three hundred years ago," the doctor said, regaining
the tone of a majestic lecturer, "the feeling of parenthood was as blind and as
instinctive as it was in any member of the animal kingdom. With their selfishness
and poorly understood affections, parents often twisted the vocation of their

children, falsified their character, and plotted the unhappiness of their complete existence. Rarely parents were able to see the educational mission that society bestowed upon them through to its fruition. And this is a truth so evident that it was recognized by a few philosophers from those times as well as pedagogues as ancient as Froebel.[25]

"Given that today the support and education of all children are functions of the State, which carries them out in a scientific and rational manner, offspring do not constitute a burden to anyone, poor or rich. But the instinctive part of paternal love has not completely disappeared. Nor can it disappear, being like a law of nature that has noticeable manifestations even among plant life.

"It doesn't show, however, with the same intensity in all subjects nor does it have the same form in one gender or the other. Since woman was freed from the physiological yoke of gestation—in the way that you all already know—her love for children has become more general and less selfish. Those women in whom the instinct of motherhood still thrives find ample room to act on it by caring for and raising small children. All of the mistresses and babysitters in our Institute are mothers by heart. And in many cases, so are fertile women, real mothers, who stay on to care for their children, but after a period of time, spread the treasure of their love equally among their own children as well as those of others, given that all children are and always will be adorable in their own right.

"The cerebral and educated woman of today generally looks for a more elevated way to externalize and objectify her affection and becomes a teacher. And it is worth noting that the most self-sacrificing mentors are sterile women. Of course, now as before, there are frivolous women that abide by the pleasurable aspects of love, without ulterior motives, which, on the other hand, do not bear for them the awful social consequences of past centuries.

"Man has always been, and continues to be, more selfish. Many—if not all—are like a tree that does not know where the wind carries the pollen of its flowers. And don't deny that men were like this in the past, in those patriarchal times that our sappy moralists and sentimental poets so long for. Others— that are also more often than not sterile—dedicate themselves to the teaching

25. Friedrich Wilhelm August Froebel was a German pedagogue who laid the foundation for modern education based on the recognition that children have unique needs and capabilities. He created the concept of the "kindergarten" and also coined the word now used in German and English.

profession out of their love for children and youth, and thus they come to identify themselves with some of their favorite students, and often end up forming with them the family groups best unified by the commonality of aspirations and cultural similarities.

"Some reproducers, albeit few, closely follow the development of their offspring and take pleasure and pride in seeing their aptitudes, inclinations, and characters perpetuated in them. On occasion, they find true kinship with some of their children and have them join their group. Because of the male ego, in the majority of cases—mine is an example—a daughter is chosen to fill the need that men have for the care and affection of a female, once we get to that age when we can no longer aspire to be loved for our looks."

The younger of the Negroes then asked if, out of female curiosity or out of atavistic regression to primitive instinct, women ever asked to be allowed to carry the fetus throughout the gestational period.

"No, dear colleague. At least I'm not aware of a single case. And besides, I'm fairly certain that, as a result of all the years that we have been interrupting the process of gestation, the human uterus has changed and has become unable to carry the fetus to term, and it's possible that for this reason it would miscarry the product of conception."

"And what do the women in your country think about this, Doctor?" asked Athanasia curiously, directing her inquiry toward the young African.

"Miss, the social state of our country is quite imperfect and lags behind by at least three centuries. We have only read about artificial extra-uterine pregnancies and we do not yet perform them. The poor women in our country still resign themselves to their harsh destiny, but educated and wealthy women already are horrified by it and use any means necessary to avoid it. Our current government—may enlightened reason preserve it—is democratic and progressive and tries to lighten the burden of offspring, setting up pensions for those who have many children, and educating, feeding, and clothing all children. But these measures are merely mitigating and are frighteningly ineffective against the advancing depopulation.

"In order to avoid the evolutionary stagnation in which our country finds itself, we have tried to mix with superior races. But, given the excellent economic conditions of the white nations, and even of the most advanced nations of Africa itself, so few are the incentives that we can offer to immigrants, that the project has not been able to reach a level of prestige. We are fully convinced that our only hope is the implementation of the system that has yielded such good results here and in all advanced countries. And we are thinking of doing this upon our return, if our government—may enlightened reason preserve it—give us some effective help. And we are not blind, Miss, to the rough and tenacious effort that it will cost us, given that our wretched country is still weighed down by a multitude of religious and social prejudices."

At this point in the conversation it was announced as welcome news that lunch was ready and everyone retired to the luxurious dining room and sat around the table, splendidly set for sure.

What followed was the initial period of all banquets, that ceremonious moment in which appetites supersede sociability, and tongues remain silent while the jaws actively work. Once the zeal of this first task "à la spoon" passes, tongues slowly begin to regain their mobility, at least in the intervals between swallowing. Dr. Pérez Serrato's tongue was the first to loosen up. But Ernesto—sidestepping the Hottentots—found a way to separate himself in an intimate and animated conversation with those sitting next to him, the one-of-a-kind Athanasia and the friendly intern. Doña Isabel ate in silence, without diligently attending to the guests. From his wheelchair, the old paralytic nodded in agreement at the pompous reasoning of his friend.

Athanasia studied medicine. Ernesto quickly figured out that she and the young Suárez loved and understood each other. Both were voluntary reproducers and from them he learned all he wanted about their charge. For now, Ernesto didn't need to do anything more than introduce himself to a woman—whose name and address the two gave him—who carried out the duties of the superintendent of the official reproducers. She would be in charge of matching him to potential future collaborators, from which he could freely choose. During his year of mandatory service, he should produce at least twenty children. Afterward he could stay on as a volunteer until he reached the age of fifty, when it would then be necessary to sterilize him. Ernesto also found out that he would have to give up smoking and alcohol. He would have to show up at the end of each month to sign the payroll and collect his salary or let it accumulate and draw the entire amount at the end of the year. The kind informants already had fulfilled their "service."

Once lunch was over and the after-meal conversation had subsided, the tour resumed with the areas of the vast institution that had yet to be seen.

Made up of a system of individual pavilions, the Villautopia Institute of Eugenics, situated on the outskirts of the city, sat on an extensive plot of land of several kilometers. In order to more comfortably survey the Institute, the group moved about in a light vehicle with a compressed sulfuric-ether engine. They spent the rest of the afternoon in the vehicle, visiting and admiring the large kitchens, supply warehouses, administrative offices, the large bacteriology and industrial chemistry laboratory, the synthetic albumin factory, and finally the stables and pastures where the beautiful herds of goats and she-donkeys, whose milk was used to nurse the babies, roamed.

It was getting dark when Ernesto embarked on his trip home, unsure if he was happy or satisfied. He felt a kind of inexplicable anxiety about meeting up with his friends and it seemed to him as if he had been away from them for a long time.

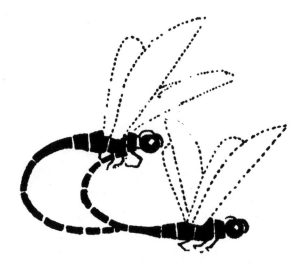

~ 7 ~

*A*lthough she found the exactness of scientific language to be useful for describing the elevated ideas of research and of meditation, Celiana had never been able to use it to express her most intimate feelings. Shame weighed heavy in her soul and, rather than allow herself to be vulnerable to the clarity of a lyric poem or sentimental prose, she ran from her feelings. Moreover, when the delicate curiosity of her nerves, stretched by pleasure or lacerated by pain, vibrated excessively, she urgently experienced the need to objectify to a certain extent the state of her spirit in order to not explode in a hysterical crisis of tears. And it was then that music became her salvation, suitable to translate the most delicate nuances of her feelings, with its universal and eternal language that, within its own vagueness, is the key to enormous strength of expression.

The piano was Celiana's favorite instrument and, ever since she overcame the technical difficulties of playing, she never played other people's music. She played only for herself, always improvising.

It was the first night of her abandonment. Ernesto was at a dance, held for the sole purpose of matching him up with his future collaborators. Federico and Consuelo had gone to the theater with Miguel and, given that Celiana declined the offer to go with them, they didn't insist, understanding that their friend's pain was of the type that requires being alone.

Now, in the nighttime tranquility of the nearly dark room, the piano played sweetly. Through the open window the garden could be seen, completely bathed in the white light of the full moon and the penetrating aroma of the spikenards.

A melancholic prelude echoed with such a smooth ease that it evoked the flow of a stream between its flowering edges, the sailing of a swan across a lake, or the path of a tranquil life without ambition. . . . The melodic thread was suddenly broken by a violent, almost out of tune musical phrase that suggested

45

a rough and sudden movement, the fear of something unexpected. A succession of rapid scales and brilliant arpeggios followed, alternating with more serious chords, simulating a conversation in which a lively and impassioned argument clashed with the extraordinary and logical reasoning of a strong will, unwavering and persuasive. Celiana then returned to the original song, accelerating its rhythm until arriving at an allegro vivace that, in brilliant phrases, first expressed fear, then the violent rebellion of a wounded heart and, finally, unbearable pain immune to any thought of solace. And the final movement, the leitmotif, gradually sweetened, as if softened by tears, and repeated itself with the tenacious insistence of a firm idea, becoming in the andante a painful and resigned moan, that slowly extinguished itself, without knowing if it faded away in time or space.

That music, full of grief and not requiring elaborate and challenging techniques nor technical ability, reproduced with frightening exactness the internal drama of a destroyed soul, the tragic failure of a happiness that believed itself to be everlasting and safe from all danger. What now passed from the nerves to the fingers, and from these to the gentle keys and sensitive strings of the piano, was the reawakening of what Celiana felt the night before when, in the sweet intimacy of the nuptial hours, Ernesto told her about accepting the official appointment that he had received, and about his visit to the Institute of Eugenics.

At first it was a big shock, which shattered her will and nullified her conscience. Later, she felt the impulse to protest, to show with unyielding logic, the inviolability of her right, to defend that right with the ferociousness of a wounded lioness. . . . And finally she succumbed to the difficult conviction of her inevitable and fatal defeat. This was a cruel sorrow against which she struggled by exploding into tears, beating, prostrating, and dragging herself, begging, on her knees. But all of this happened deep within her being, without complaint or recrimination, in the bravery of a never-ending and terrifying silence. Even so she still had the tormented, martyred strength to smile at that ingrate and jokingly conceal the timid and belated scruples of that boyish lover who, frightened and kind, was ready to turn his back on her at the slightest sign on her part.

But now, as she felt with a kind of serene cruelty the bloody depths of her own wound, she diagnosed it as unstoppable and mortal and understood that her happiness was on its deathbed.

Sadness is the agony of all love. This is even more true when the sprouts of new feelings are discovered among the very ashes of a love affair's corpse, giving the appearance that one is in the midst of a dusk that will submerge one into the pitch blackness of night, but that, because of its very condition of night, carries within it the promise of a new dawn. On the other hand, there is no comfort for the heart that feels and declares itself incapable of any type of recovery. Upon this heart the sun has set completely, followed by an eternal night without a dawn. There is no pain that compares to a passionate woman who sees a love affair through to the end, that for her must necessarily be the last one, because the end of this love affair coincides with the appearance of the light creases at the corners of her lips, the lines of her forehead, the sad sagging of her breasts, and the slow whitening of her hair, all evidence of the passing of the relentless years.

Any kind of protest against the pain of that which is inevitable is useless. At any rate, it only relieves the complaining a little bit without any purpose. Celiana found a happy musical outlet for that sorrow, and the piano sobbed—at first quietly, as if embarrassed—a harmonious moan that expressed the authenticity of her bitterness over and over in different keys. It was like a parasitic idea that, within the horror of the insane asylum, makes an insane person cry out the same phrase day and night.

By force of repetition, Celiana's thoughts faded away, her music losing in expression what it gained in tenderness and, caught up in its own harmony, it finally turned into a melancholic song, amorphous and pain-relieving, slowly working its soothing properties on the irritated nerves of its artist.

And as the nervous storm calmed, Celiana's mind regained all of its strength of inhibition and its clear sense of justice, and she overcame the very notion that the end of her love fantasy was logical, natural, and necessary. What right did she have, spoiler of so many passionate sprees, to forever monopolize the virgin heart of that boy? Celiana didn't need to create any illusions for herself. Whenever Ernesto tasted the honey of other lovers, the spells of a twilight beauty such as hers surely would not be capable of successfully achieving victory over those of other women in full bloom. Convinced of her inferiority, Celiana saw her defeat as inevitable and naturally resigned herself to the fight; if her morality admitted the sacrifice, her aesthetic sensibility didn't tolerate ridicule.

She still found, in the total balance of her life, that happiness was in her favor; the absoluteness and completeness of those five years that Ernesto had belonged to her in body and soul was already more than enough to sweeten an entire life of bitterness and suffering. And by shedding the last remains of selfishness and vulgar jealousy, Celiana's love felt invulnerable, absolute, polymorphic, and susceptible to adapting in all ways, capable of all renunciations and sacrifices. If Ernesto felt a lukewarm and brotherly attachment toward her, or if he even kept some sweet memory of their love, she would be the self-sacrificing friend, the loving mother, able to wipe away the tears he shed over other women and stop his heart from being hurt. Even more, as long as she did not completely belong to him, did not feel him close, Celiana found herself ready to tolerate anything, from deceit and indifference, to coldness and hate itself. . . .

The piano played again. But now the notes expressed the calm of total resignation, the sweet tranquility of a triumph forcefully achieved through heroism. Later, feeling their own greatness, the notes flaunted a sense of pride and ended in a magnificent tune, a great hymn in the vein of Tabor of a soul redeemed from utter vileness, superior in the numbness of stoicism to the pain of torture.

This fair homage gave way to its own superiority, the melancholy overshadowing the notes of the song. But the melancholy was now sweet and resigned, suggestive of a state of peace, as if yearning for something that was painful, because it remembered something good and pleasurable that had been lost, because in that place Celiana could enjoy and relive those moments. . . .

When Miguel got back from the theater with his young companions, Celiana was still playing. But the shrewd assessment of her loyal friend concluded that inner balance—pure logic and justice—had already been reestablished in that higher spirit.

Ernesto arrived a bit later, around daybreak, and he found his family happily having dinner. He noticed the same serene smile as always on his lover's face, welcome, frank, and loving, without any visible darkness or any hint of the storm that had just passed. On the other hand, Ernesto, suspicious and worried and not prone to charades, poorly pretended and strained to show happiness and tried to appear, although his falseness betrayed him, to be in a good mood. Noticing this, Celiana felt sorry with him and for him.

— 8 —

There is no doubt that the solution to any problem, including a matter of the heart, depends mostly on how it is posed. In life there are difficult situations, extremely complicated matters, which naturally are presented with such mathematical and clear facts that any tangled mess, at first seemingly inextricable, unravels by itself or with a little effort and a bit of patience. On the other hand, simple and even trivial matters are sometimes unresolvable. That's because to resolve them, a single stern and trustworthy word would do, but it is precisely that word that nobody wants to speak, that word that forms in everyone's head and stops before reaching the lips.

Such was the situation that an incident—almost insignificant, given the habits of that period—had given rise to in Celiana and Ernesto's relationship, only by having happened in an atmosphere of mutual distrust. Very delicate and subtle scruples, born out of the very purity of their affection, had created a serious problem that was nothing more than a triviality. Having a premonition of a possible end, that love, until then so serene and unsuspecting in its run, slowed down as if frightened before the faint shadow of distrust, like a spirited and nervous colt that jumps a fence or a ditch without hesitation, but then trembles and bucks before a piece of paper thrown in the middle of the road, or the shadow of a few branches blowing in the wind.

Although seemingly nothing had really changed with the essence of their love, in those dealings, always so caring and cordial, little by little a courteous reservation, cold and conventional, began to percolate. But only the lovers themselves knew what was going on. Anyone would have thought that they were as close as ever, and even Miguel, such a wise and good observer, thought that their conflicts had been happily resolved.

For more than a month Ernesto had been conscientiously carrying out his duty as an official breeder and, from the beginning, had managed to clearly distinguish between mere carnal possession, instinctive and mechanical, and the pure and idealistic affection of a heart in love. This is a dualism of subtlety, well tried for everyone else, that men have been instituting with ease for years, but that only a few highly superior women have been able to comprehend.

And not even in the land of physical delights had young Ernesto found until then anything that would make him forget or slight those of his dear Celiana. For her own part, she had never considered requiring absolute physical fidelity from her lover and found herself ready to handle all rejection and pardons. And yet, the happy synergy of those two wills, before so agreeable, was broken beyond repair, and in the thought of each of the lovers there was now a deep reserve that the other did not dare or want to penetrate. It was as if an ice-cold tear had divided their souls, and a glacial wind had caused it to slowly grow in size and strength.

Locked in her room, under the pretext of some imaginary work, Celiana thought deeply about that anomalous state of her spirit and tortured herself in vain without finding any answers, at times looking in the realm of logic, at others trying to find it through simple sentimental impulse.

Then she felt the need to relieve most of her sorrows, in the fullness of confession and under the protection of a dear friend, and she found comfort in an affectionate and sincere word, and, if it were possible, in a straightforward and clear sign.

For Miguel problems of love had little to no importance, so Celiana naturally removed him from her list of confidants, fearful of his biting ironies. Instead, she thought about one of her former teachers, for whom she felt true veneration and from whom in days gone by she had sought advice in those difficult moments of her life.

This was Don Luis Gil, an old man as kind and good-natured as he was illustrious, a distinguished man of letters, a wise teacher, a notable historian and a strong debater. Everyone knew him as "the Professor"; because that's what he truly had been, during the best years of his life, and because, with his instructive and elegant lectures, his penetrating advice and the manner of his choice and accurate prose, that's what he continued to be for those who ventured, with a degree of uncertainty, into the vast field of learning in which there had never been boundaries nor enclosures. With an open letter, an editorial critique or a prologue for one of his works, many crude romantics had gained reputations as lyricists and had even achieved degrees of eminence, and many a dreaming courtesan was elevated to the rank of superfluous muse. What a shame to take them away from such activities in exchange for a place at a department store counter, or household chores!

It's true that at times that which the protective hand of the Professor took out of limbo didn't lack any real merit. And on more than one occasion it happened that the protégé became arrogant, like a child taking his first steps, and put up a power struggle with the Professor himself. Thus, for example, it was Don Gil who first discovered and encouraged Celiana's cheerful literary tendencies, which had so splendidly blossomed over the years. And in the years of her apprenticeship, Celiana, a woman of independent and ample judgment and of highly advanced ideas, used the forum of the press to carry out brilliant confrontations with her old teacher who, due to the natural effects of age but without his realizing it, was becoming a de facto conservative. Of course, this all happened within the strict guidelines of courtesy and without jeopardizing in the least the honest friendship that they held.

Don Luis lived completely alone and had a silly policy about not receiving guests in his house. So in order to speak with him, one had to go looking for him at a nightly social gathering, which he rarely missed and for which he was the president ex officio for life.

This curious and heterogeneous literary, scientific, and philosophical discussion group met every night on the first two or three benches that sat on the east edge of the main plaza of Villautopia, in front of the great neo-Theosophic temple. And as the small monoplanes for hire that people of Villautopia called *volingos* impatiently paced back and forth in the magnificent esplanade as they waited for a fare, there they discussed with crystal-clear frankness anything and everything. The members of that group had been coming from one generation to the next, and for more than three centuries they had kept up a kind of elite literary circle in which reputations were made or broken. This was the oldest and most distinguished of the many discussion groups that set up shop in the middle of the park during certain hours, and there were more than a few, since those comfortable iron benches disposed to the shade of the ancient and abundant laurel trees seemed to constantly attract transients looking for conversation or a place to rest. So in the mornings, a group of carefree old men gathered on the benches to enjoy the warm sunshine, talking fondly about the past. Later, as high tea approached, the restless throng of joggers and shady businessmen turned the benches into a temporary stock exchange or marketplace. At night it was rare not to see an incoming wave of people from outside, bewildered by the massive movement of the capital city and the friendly gang of bohemian poets and bickering students, as well as a privileged group of students—the crème de la crème—that gossiped over the parade of elegant young women or discussed fashion or sports, the only topics that they knew anything about.

Moved by the desire to confess her suffering to the Professor, Celiana set out for the park one night. Aware of his habits, she went as early as she could, in order to find him alone. In spite of her efforts, when she arrived he was already in the company of three of the most assiduous members of the discussion group, and they were no strangers to her. One of them, Matías Urrea, blind in one eye, a doctor, and sharp-tongued, with the pretensions of a man of letters, an eternal arguer and acute defender of the most daring paradoxes, was engaged in heated argument with Don Luis, and the shouts and interjections of both of them could be heard from half a block away. The other two members of the group were a young and handsome blond lad, Nicasio Castillo, also a doctor, who in his spare time penned elegant sonnets in the same way that others twirl a walking stick; and a certain Don Pedro, a broker and businessman, who, to this day, no one knows why he attended that literary discussion group so regularly and punctually. With nods of the head these two agreed with the Professor's reasoning.

When Celiana arrived, the fighting temporarily ceased and the men gallantly stood up. Don Luis went to meet her and kissed her hand, a kiss that Celiana returned on his forehead, venerably, as though she were his daughter. As one can see from this act, the kiss, an instinctive show of affection, capable of adapting to all the variations and modes of this feeling, had not vanished from social customs, in spite of all that was said against it by a few foolish hygienists of past centuries. On the contrary, with humanity having become less hypocritical, the kiss in this manner was generally considered a savory greeting, given that kissing between friends of the opposite sex was seen as the most natural and innocent thing in the world.

Celiana was no stranger to meetings of men of letters, and her presence, therefore, did not impede the heated discussion from resuming. They were arguing over an aspect of sociology, a topic much to her liking. A sharp and educated woman above all else, Celiana, distracted by the debate, soon forgot about her emotional worries and even bravely joined in.

The argument started upon mention of the alarming news of the imminent breaking off of relations between the great Pan American Confederation and the integrated nations of the old Continent. Everyone agreed that a rather grave situation was just around the corner. The impending war, purely commercial and diplomatic, with its closing of ports, its general strikes and factory shutdowns, would not be any less horrible than the armed conflicts of the past, with their bloody land, sea, and air battles, in which men died by the millions.

But—in the end—Don Luis declared himself an admirer in favor of the social organization of the past centuries and attributed all the blame for the possible conflict to the weakness of the current governments, which were merely administrative.

"We no longer have," he said, "government, in the complete sense of the word. No longer are there armies or navies to keep the continent in balance. Lost is the concept of countries with borders, and therefore, the beautiful feeling of patriotism is also dead. What will now be the ideal for which we spill our blood or sacrifice our lives?"

"None, Professor," replied Urrea sharply, "nor is one needed. Our precious blood was not created to be shed, nor is there any human or divine ideal that would authorize or justify the sacrifice of even one life. . . . Patriotism! National honor! The sacred flag! These were the convenient crutches of our great-grandparents; those were the excuses with which they concealed their great collective crimes. Do you think it was beautiful to kill and die for such abstractions, that it was noble to sacrifice everything so that a crown could pass from the head of William to the temple of George, that it was fair to bloody the entire territory of a country in order to clarify whether a deserted island or a few leagues of uncultivated land should belong to us or to our neighbor? Well I, for my part, congratulate myself for having come to the world in this blessed moment in time in which such aberrations no longer exist for the shame of civilization.

"With respect to feelings of patriotism," Urrea continued, "it hasn't exactly disappeared. It's true that it has changed considerably, but in the sense of becoming more extensive and less selfish, losing whatever it had of farce and conventionalism.

"In those happy times for which you yearn, dear Professor, there already was a kind of dualism about patriotic love, which the hack reporters and other commonplace cultivators expressed by dividing the country into *large* and *small* entities. The *large nation* (*patria grande*) was something conventional and theoretical that was invoked with great fuss every time the masses, the disenfranchised, or the pariahs were forced to sacrifice themselves on the altars of pride for an ambitious government or a few intriguing politicians. For the people of today, the *large nation* is the entire world, Humanity, and of course our love for it also has a theoretical element and is very conventional and could, with some difficulty, lead us toward sacrificing ourselves. But from one concept or conventionalism to the other, the one before us naturally is more ample and beautiful than that of the past and has the further advantage of not being stained by injustice or exploitation."

Urrea went on. "The love for the *small nation* (*patria chica*)—for the region and territory or land and soil—has always been natural and instinctive and remains complete. Today, as in the past, for each of us, there is a corner of the earth where the water is more crystalline, the sky bluer, the flowers more aromatic and the women more beautiful. When we are far away from this place, it is as though we are still bound to it by an invisible rope through which its heartbeat is transmitted to us. And when the coldness of old age, that which comes before death, begins to penetrate our bones, we long to return there, because we suppose that that land, trampled by our feet as children, will shelter our bodies with more love than any other place. And notice that this favorite place of the heart has not been nor is exactly that in which we were born, but rather that place where one spends time between the second infancy and the first adolescence, that fertile period in life in which one's personality is outlined and one's character is defined, when the rosebush of first loves blossoms and lasting affections and friendships are made."

"Bravo!" shouted Don Luis, clapping his hands together. "Not bad, Urrea. You deny the beauty of love for one's country, and then right away you paint it with phrases so poetic that they are worthy of being put into verse by our friend Nicasio." Then he burst out laughing, such that Don Pedro and the poet alluded to naturally joined in.

"Laugh, laugh as much as you like," pushed back the somewhat bothered one-eyed Urrea. "Make fun of my lyricisms and even put them to music, if you wish. But you can't deny that it is only natural and spontaneous for a man to feel love toward the place where he is respected and lives happily and freely, and for which he has fond memories. For his betterment and prosperity I understand that he might sacrifice everything in the world that can be sacrificed. Beyond this, the rest is empty rhetoric, verbiage without substance."

"But you can't deny, dear Doctor," replied Don Luis, "that patriotism, such as it was understood by our ancestors, was a beautiful feeling worthy of admiration and respect. Are you daring to deny that in that great European war at the beginning of the twentieth century, the Belgians, the French, and the North Americans, driven by this feeling, carried out acts of heroism that bordered on the sublime?"

"What an example! . . . . ," replied Urrea. "For me, Professor, the hysterical patriotism of the French and of the Belgians only made idiots of them for England and Germany, who were the true cause of that destruction due to their similar aspirations for world commercial dominance. As for the North Americans, theirs was a patriotism of a compound interest, of which nothing can be said. But I am glad that you have brought up this historical conflict, precisely because with it began the series of what we might call general wars."

"Would you be so kind as to explain to us why they are called such?" asked Don Pedro.

"It's very simple," chimed in Celiana in support of the Doctor. "In the past, commercial exchange was so reduced that two nations could be tearing each other apart over a period of five whole years without changing in any way the world balance. The last such event was the Russo-Japanese War, which broke out between the years of 1904 and 1905, if I am not mistaken, and was quickly resolved with a few formidable battles."

Celiana continued, "It seemed then that, because of the enormous development that was driven by reparations from material destruction, wars would no longer last very long nor end in any other way. But then came the European conflict that the Professor mentioned earlier, and with it could be seen the beginning of this phenomenon that our friend Urrea has astutely called the *generalization of war*. Discord appeared in an insidious and unexpected way, precisely when the balance of power seemed as stable as ever, and didn't take long to expand to the entire continent. This became the justification for Germany's longing for world domination and for England's sneaky ambitions. It stirred up the unexpected heroism of the Belgians, exalted to the point of insanity the romantic patriotism and the urge for revenge in the French, and in such a way managed to change the world balance of power, by interrupting commercial relations, so that the day came when, for the weak nations, it was much more difficult to stay neutral than to allow themselves to be drawn in and take part in the struggle. Finally, the United States, the most powerful nation in the Americas at the time, saw itself materially obligated to intervene in the matter and, with its enormous material resources, brought about the triumph of the coalition forces against Germany. But that victory was very short-lived and more apparent than real."

After hearing Celiana's elegant and erudite explanation, Dr. Urrea enthusiastically stood up and exclaimed, "Bravo, my dear friend, exactly right and well said! I can only congratulate myself for having an opinion that agrees with your highly authoritative one. But let me add that it wasn't only the allied cannons or the American gold that triumphed. German imperialism and military might came to fall on their own, because of the logical evolution of events. This was at first a political war, as they all are, but at a certain moment, it changed appearance and became a purely social war. Society in those days was organized around injustice and enormous differences. Societies were drowned by the calamities inherent in all wars, making them more sensitive, awakening the legitimate egalitarian hopes of the many and the protest against the privileges of the few. The old scaffolding, built on secular prejudices and propped up by fantastic and deceptive appearances, wobbled, shaken by the vindictive wave. And if it didn't fall completely, it became damaged and on the brink of ruin. The official end of the war, the signing of peace, was an unimportant event. It left unresolved, but firmly planted, the tremendous social dilemma. Thus it can be said that the only positive outcome of that ferocious battle was the step that Humanity took toward erasing national borders, socializing wealth, and promoting economic equilibrium.

"It's true," Urrea continued, "that these ideals did not yet come to fruition, but the first light of day of that triumph was already noticeable, and that day was only postponed for a very near future. The arrangement that was agreed on, by force of mountains of gold and rivers of blood, with its hypocritical concessions and sneaky reticence, was like a lovely puff pastry filled with dynamite, over which false gods, in whose honor so many lives were sacrificed, wobbled in their altars."

"And could our distinguished colleague," interrupted Castillo with impertinence, "speak less of symbolism and with more clarity and tell us to which false gods you are referring?"

Urrea replied. "Thank you for the piece of advice, dear colleague. The false deities that I allude to are named Patriotism and Democracy, and both entered a period of decadence at that time, the unfortunate discredit into which a miraculous saint falls and is quickly left without any worshipers. . . . And forgive me if I am still resorting to symbolism.

"Patriotism failed, in spite of reaching a height never before reached. Precisely because of this people began to see clearly and realize that, then as always and perhaps more than ever, the sacrifices were of the people, the heroism was of the people, and the profit went to a few powerful.

"That hungry and haggard democracy," continued Urrea, "born in the middle of the eighteenth century and that, naturally, came into the twentieth century weakened, also failed. And it couldn't have been any other way, since its strongest champions were England, the great exploiter of weak nations, oppressor of inferior races, always ready to put the blame on someone else; France, the aristocratic republic par excellence, which became reverent with its button-down coats and its titles of nobility standing behind aristocratic names; and the United States, that conglomerate of merchants where, until he was regarded as a citizen himself, the worker was owned by the boss, where the negro was treated worse than an animal and where even the government itself was ruled by money."

Urrea went on. "Out of the frozen steppes of Russia, trampled by the boots of tyranny, rose up a red radiance, that was of both fire and the light of dawn, and the fearful sound of something terrible was heard advancing like an avalanche, threatening to level the entire world. In the face of universalist Communism, a synthesis of the hopes of the true nation and the masses, the roles got mixed up and Democracy became Reaction. Democracy collapsed, terrified, but it soon calmed itself and, still feeling strong, was compelled by instinct to conform to the position in which it found itself and pressed to defend itself to victory or death.

"And still it seemed that Democracy had triumphed once again. It replaced social order with its consecrated prejudices, with all of its irritating inequalities, with all of its sanctioned oppression. But the privileged no longer lived peacefully alongside the growing nonconformity of the deprived. A new equilibrium arose, no longer European, but of the world, but it was the typical example of unstable equilibrium. It led to peace, but it was a peace armed to the teeth and ready to split apart at the first boom of a firing cannon, even if it were by accident.

"Naturally, it wasn't long before war broke out again, and then began the series of bigger armed outbreaks, truly universal, that we saw lasting until the middle of the twenty-first century. During this time there wasn't a country, big or small, weak or powerful, European, Asian, or American, that didn't take an active part in the fight."

Urrea continued. "Misery, hunger, epidemics, the lack of trade and the halting of industry, more than the war itself, weighed heavy on Humanity to the point that weapons fell to the ground by themselves, when the soldiers came to realize that they themselves were part of the masses, when there was no one left who wanted to fight, nor barely anyone who had the material strength to do so. On the other hand, there were a few, a very few, who still believed in the ideals for which they killed and died. Thus, because of the very power of those events, universal disarmament was achieved and national boundaries were effectively erased.

"Free from the enormous costs of maintaining an army, without the desire of domination or the fear of being looted, the people regrouped according to the natural geographic divisions of the land. Wealth, industry, and agriculture were socialized, trade was nationalized, and governments could limit themselves to administrative roles, the only ones that they were logically and necessarily fit for.

"For very complex causes worthy of a detailed study—some of those causes being derived from the events already described and others being concomitant or coincidental—the economy also became a function of the State, and thus soon achieved the stability that we enjoy today."

Dr. Urrea was tirelessly talkative. He was ready to explain the evolution of the phenomenon to which he had already referred and, as he was ready to assume that the others wouldn't completely agree with his appraisal, surely they would take up on the topic of the economy a new discussion as colorful as the last one. Tired, Celiana didn't want to wait for it and took advantage of the one-eyed Urrea's brief pause, perhaps to gather his thoughts, to take her leave.

It had just struck ten o'clock, and from the Academy of Fine Arts, housed in one of the large buildings that surrounded the courtyard, cheerful groups of students began to leave. Celiana walked in that direction, with the intention of finding Miguel, who was a professor of said Academy, and joining him on his way back home.

The others continued chatting, and surely dragged the discussion out into the late hours of the night, as they did almost every day of the year.

~ 9 ~

Celiana returned to those meetings in the main courtyard several nights in a row, without fulfilling her wish to find the Professor free from the irritating company of his talkative little friends. Their continuous arguments became so unbearable for her that she would take leave just as they'd barely begun, making up some excuse about an urgent matter that she needed to attend to, and sometimes, without even bothering to do that; an inexplicable shyness prevented her from pulling the Professor aside for a moment, so that she might ask him to talk alone. Fed up, Celiana soon stopped trying altogether.

Meanwhile time, that infallible panacea for all kinds of pains, had started to work its sedative spell on Celiana and, pushing her imagination a bit, she could consider herself happy up to a certain point. She saw Ernesto less and less, given that he now spent days at a time away from the house. But later, when he returned, he tried so hard to please her and lavished her with attention and such delicate caresses that Celiana did all that she could to not acknowledge the forced and artificial nature of Ernesto's ends; she purposely closed her eyes to the evidence in order to not see that it was only gratitude that kept her lover at her side.

The difference between this pale imitation of happiness and the complete and absolute happiness of before, turned out to be huge; but Celiana, resigned, gave in to being satisfied as long as things remained as they now were. She confided only in her piano, that faithful and old confidant, in the long hours of abandonment and loneliness of her nights and in the intimate bitterness that broken dreams caused her. Stoic in her pain, Celiana put all her effort in hiding it from her friends and in always pretending to be happy and satisfied. Her struggles did not go unnoticed by the clear insight of Miguel, who watched Celiana with compassionate and brotherly interest; but who, always discreet, respecting the sublime modesty of her delicate soul, was very careful in dealing with the matter.

On the other hand, Celiana's work on the weekly lectures that she continued to give at the Athenaeum became more and more intense and productive; in addition, her collaboration, which was handsomely rewarded, was often sought by numerous local and foreign literary and scientific journals. This growing cerebral activity also temporarily kept her mind off her love problems and became a diversion for her sorrows, becoming almost a comfort.

It wasn't exactly jealousy that made her suffer; in the social order of the period, this was an anachronistic feeling that Celiana, because of her age and her history, was perhaps the least qualified to have. But since the beginning of the matter Ernesto had acted with indescribable reserve and a lack of sincerity that was completely unfair and hurt Celiana to the core. He who before didn't have a thought, emotion, or intention that she was not the first to find out about was now stubbornly sparse in sharing his thoughts and impressions and he didn't say one word about how he spent his days or his plans for the future. That spirit that Celiana had created with such care and affection, in the image and likeness of Ernesto's, and that had been so transparent in the mutual understanding of their lives, now made that understanding completely impenetrable; those eyes that before she had been used to penetrating to their depths, no longer gave in to her tender gaze. Instead, they rejected her, as if they needed to ask her forgiveness for something. And this delusion, this sadness of seeing just how little the man who she held in such high esteem and in her affections was morally worth, was in reality the dart that burst that generous feminine heart. A superior spirit, a woman of her time, high above callousness and selfishness, Celiana would have eventually felt a sublime and detached pleasure seeing Ernesto happy, even if that happiness was due to the love of other women. What better use for the inexhaustible treasure of maternal love that she still felt in her chest, than by dedicating it for the rest of her life to the children of her soul mate? But Ernesto apparently did not think she was capable of such self-denial or couldn't see or understand it.

In spite of it all, time would have slowly softened Celiana's pain, which would have eventually reached a tolerable state of calm and melancholy resignation. But, by the laws of nature, all things that begin, in whatever sense, tend to follow through to the end. So, it wasn't logical to hope that, once the retreat of that love had begun, it would stop at the point where it now was.

Celiana herself understood this and, at times, hoped that the ending would come as soon as possible, with that lapse in logic that makes us prefer catastrophe to the anxiety of waiting for it to happen. And this ending wasn't far off; in spite of her efforts not to notice it, she soon realized that her lover's straying was growing: his absences were longer and more frequent, his kindness was more exaggerated and conventional, and his caresses were more forced. With intense pain, almost with shame, Celiana could at the same time appreciate the point to which the promiscuity required of his carnal responsibility had killed Ernesto's amorous idealism and awoken the depths of crude lewdness of his primitive nature. Ernesto, previously so calm and indifferent to the most splendid beauty, when he hadn't known any other love but that of Celiana, now seemed to desire every woman who walked by him and he stared at each with a rude fixation, as if he was undressing her with his eyes.

A scene with seemingly little importance, a detail that would have gone unnoticed to the disinterested or casual observer, was the drop that overflowed the chalice of bitterness that Celiana fought in vain not to drink. One night, Consuelo, being fussy or maybe just tired, didn't want to go out with Miguel and Federico; she and Celiana stayed in by themselves, one reading and the other playing the piano late into the night. Around midnight Ernesto, who had been away for close to a week, entered. Upon seeing him, Consuelo ran to Ernesto with childish and sincere joy and greeted him with a kiss on the cheek, a natural and innocent act that she had been used to since she was a little girl. Celiana, appearing to have not noticed that the young man had arrived while she continued playing the piano, saw how he cunningly turned the fraternal kiss toward that tempting mouth with such insistence that the girlish Consuelo, surprised and blushing, abruptly pulled herself away. So sharp was the pain that this embarrassing scene caused Celiana, that when Ernesto, still confused and not quite calm, approached her with exaggerated shows of affection, it took enormous willpower to not callously shun him. How bitterly Celiana later cried, heartbroken, over the final blow to her dying illusion, while he slept at her side, satisfied with pleasure!

At the pain of a lost ideal, a feeling of depression brought on by the failure of a favorite work congealed within her. Who could have imagined that her soul mate, her favorite pupil, her own creation, could fall to such despicable vileness? And if she could no longer respect him, could she at least also stop loving him?! But no; that love had roots so deep within her heart that Celiana couldn't tear it out without also ripping out her heart and her life. Broken again, and in such a cruel way, was the balance that with such hard work had started to return to her soul, that the days of bitter hesitation came back for Celiana. She began to torture herself in vain again, looking for a formula or a solution for such an intolerable situation.

Celiana began to feel anxious again for someone to confide in; but, whom? Miguel? She didn't dare. Perhaps Consuelo? No; she didn't have the right to rattle the beautiful serenity of that girlish soul, ignorant of such problems and complications.

So she planted once again in her mind, and now with the almost pathological characteristics of obsession, the desire to speak of her personal matters with her old friend Don Luis. Celiana came to believe that that kind old man had the key to her tranquility and that in the much-longed-for conversation with him he would necessarily say the magic words that would snap her back to happiness.

Certain that it would be useless to try to find him alone in his discussion group, Celiana resigned herself to putting up with the entire deluge of speeches and arguments and decided to stay the night in the courtyard until the moment when the group disbanded, so that she could get the Professor to formally commit to a visit.

⌐ *10* ⌐

Such was her streak of bad luck that Celiana chose a night in which the discussion group was more crowded than ever and, it might be said, in full forum mode. Participants included Don Luis, with the inseparable Don Pedro as the mediator, and Urrea and Castillo, as well as two other doctors: Dr. Reyes de la Barrera, who competed with Castillo in composing sonnets, and Dr. Arjonilla, wealthy, obese, and always smiling, who was retired from the professional army and served as manager of an important agricultural business, advisor to a bank, and editor of a periodical dedicated to agriculture. In addition, Ramón Répide, an engineer and a very distinguished and kind man, pal of the one-eyed Urrea and just as much a vehement and paradoxical arguer, and an eccentric figure whom they called Centellas and who was, as always, ungroomed and not wearing a tie, were present. It wasn't clear if Centellas was a nickname or a last name. "Centellas" was also the name of a small periodical, which the man by the same name edited and owned, and with which Centellas had beautifully solved the problem of his subsistence. The group also counted two poets and a poetess in attendance. The poetess was celebrated, while the men, still unpublished and unknown, went looking for the Professor's support. Rounding out the group of regulars were two newspaper reporters and a schoolteacher. Finally, accidentally forming part of the meeting was that known opportunist, nicknamed Miajitas, who claimed to be apostle and prophet of universal economic equality based on vagrancy. His presence had turned the discussion toward this interesting topic.

When Celiana arrived, the engineer Répide had the floor and was saying—
"Omitting that you, Miajitas, are a known fraud and have made a modus vivendi out of your boring talk of economic equality, I admit that the present balance is still open to perfection. But one can't ignore that this problem is fundamentally solved, especially when one compares the present situation with the irritating inequality of past times."

"As for me," said Don Luis, "the development of economic stability, as imperfect as it may seem, is Humanity's greatest achievement in recent centuries, and I firmly believe that it is next to impossible to progress any further with respect to this topic. Absolute economic equality, in addition to being utopic, would end up being highly unjust, since not all men have the same abilities or equal capacity to produce. In our present society there are still poor and rich, but these words no longer indicate the radical or large differences they did before."

"The social organization of our time," chimed in Dr. Urrea, "has turned out to be almost perfect compared to the populations in antiquity. Remember that less than three centuries ago, economic imbalance was truly frightening. The majority of people lived in want, many lacked even the most necessary things, and a few, very few, were the lucky privileged. The rich of that time monopolized enormous excesses, far more than they could consume during their lifetimes. And so it was that after their death, various generations of their descendants lived in idleness off of these excesses. And, at times, unhappy with enjoying that unjust legacy, the heirs grew their inheritance even more, such that the gap between rich and poor continued to grow, as the privileged acquired even more of the community's surplus resources. No one can deny that this was simply criminal. In the struggle for life, all beings have the right to conquer the portion of organic material that they need to subsist, even at the expense of another's life. But none, not even man himself, is allowed to hoard that which is needed to sustain life in such quantities that future generations can subsist without any effort.

"As the Professor has stated very well," continued Dr. Urrea, "society still has rich and poor, but the rich of today are simply gifted individuals that possess sufficient abilities to amply provide themselves with all necessities, as well as to enjoy the luxury of a surplus. Today we call *poor* those who, out of laziness, lack of ambition, or scarcity of faculties, don't earn enough to allow themselves whims and delicacies. But every man or woman, capable of carrying out any job, no matter how humble or hidden their work may be, can at least count on compensation sufficient enough to meet their basic needs. Understand that included among these needs are things that were considered secondary in other times, since the progress of industry has notably lowered the cost of living and, in the logical and simple organization of modern society, man finds himself free from some of the burdens that ruled his life the most in the past, such as offspring.

"When an individual manages to produce wealth greater than what he can spend in the course of his lifetime, this excess of production, upon his death, passes to the Treasury and increases the funds earmarked for public services.

But this is an exceptional case that only happens when dealing with a great inventor, a financial genius, or someone of artistic noteworthiness. Let's not forget that those colossal fortunes of multimillionaires from past times were always acquired through large-scale exploitation of the work of others.

"Today, with the nationalization of trade and the socialization of industry and agriculture, the fruits of labor are divided equally so that those relying on their brute strength or their intelligence receive proportional shares. With the suppression of inheritance and prohibition of legacies, no one may enjoy the estate accumulated by someone else, and no healthy, normal, and strong man may live without working."

"Unless," objected Centellas, "he or she has the good fortune of finding someone to voluntarily support him or her, as happens with the vainglorious and *kept* members of our youth who some have taken to calling golden, and who, as you all know, constitute a legion."

"In different stages of the zoological scale," said Urrea, "one observes examples of parasitism. As such, the fact that isolated cases of it occur in the human species does nothing to change the equation of economic stability that, as our friend Répide states, can be considered to be fundamentally resolved today. It is true that in our social environment there still exist young people of one sex or the other who live off of their physical attributes and let themselves be kept by individuals of the opposite sex, who can allow themselves that luxury, in the same manner that they could keep purebred dogs or race horses. But this thing that today, in certain social circles, is seen as one of so many fleeting and unimportant foolhardy acts of young people, is in reality something that has been left over from the depraved customs of the past. Of course it is quite attenuated because today, in the absolute equality of rights that both sexes enjoy, the *excessive gluttony* (of the vainglorious and their lovers) becomes one of many experimental practices that one undertakes in the search for happiness and the definitive order of life. In past centuries, if this way of living was considered shameful for a man, it was not so for a woman. Whether married or prostituted, it was simply woman's true condition in the majority of cases.

"But we should not forget, gentlemen," continued Urrea, "that humanity's progress is undefined. Perhaps universal social and economic equality, which for now seems to us to be unobtainable, will no longer be so in the more or less far-off future, when men are not so different from each other in aptitudes and merits—something that advances in artificial selection achieved in every civilized nation allow us to consider a possibility.

"The current stability appears to us to be quite simple because it was here when we were born, but not that long ago our ancestors regarded it as the most absurd of utopias. In order for it to slowly establish itself, all of that arduous evolution that followed the last wars of the twenty-first century, if I am not mistaken, was necessary. Right, Professor?"

"Exactly," replied Don Luis. "The factors that intervened in the achievement of stability were many and complicated, for sure. It seems to me that the coincidence, or better said, the path itself of the evolutionary process, caused those factors to group themselves in such a way that they worked simultaneously and in solidarity at the propitious moment.

"When, due to the tired and worn out state of the warring nations," continued Luis, "the armies were disarmed and national borders were erased, the socialization of industries and of agriculture, which had already existed— although imperfect—was made more effective, and trade became a branch of Public Administration, eliminating the abusive intermediary merchant between producer and consumer.

"Once governments noticed how much of these sources of wealth they were legitimately entitled to, and at the same time, found themselves free from the huge expense that maintaining naval and land forces incurred, they made themselves the administrators of the communal treasury and found that they could more than provide for all public services, including the obligation of supporting all those who were unable to work, such as children, the handicapped, and the elderly.

"In the face of the necessity to rapidly repopulate the land," Don Luis continued, "and in light of growing Malthusianism on the part of men and *tocofobia* on the part of women, it was necessary to scientifically regulate the reproduction of the human species and adopt an artificial system, currently in use by every nation that stands at the vanguard of civilization. At the same time, legacies and inheritance remained prohibited."

"Excuse me, Professor. What is *tocofobia*?" asked Centellas.

"Fear of childbirth, my friend. From *tocos* we get 'childbirth,' and from *fobé*, 'fear.'[26] How little you independent journalists understand of Greek

---

26. According to the psychiatrists Manjeet Singh Bhatia and Anurag Jhanjee, the term "tocofobia" (*tokophobia* in German and *tocophobie* in French) was first used to describe an extreme fear of childbirth by O. Knauer in 1897 (O. Knauer, *Urber puerperale Psychosen, fur practische Aerzte* [Berlin: S. Karger, 1897]; see Manjeet Singh Bhatia and Anurag Jhanjee, "Tokophobia: A Dread of Pregnancy," *Industrial Psychiatry Journal* 21, no. 2 [July–December 2012]: 158).

etymology!" said Dr. Castillo, who until then had remained silent, perhaps mentally composing a sonnet.

"It seems to me, dear Professor," Répide said, "that in the enumeration of the determinant factors of economic stability, you have left out the most important one of all. Neither the nationalization of trade and the socialization of industry, nor the elimination of inheritance and the regulation of offspring, nor universal disarmament and the disappearance of national borders, were able to produce the coveted stability while the pernicious custom of man to save and hoard money remained. Oh, to save, the origin of greed, the source of so many crimes! The day when a man hoarded a penny for the first time, stealing it from his neighbor, was when he committed the first original sin."

"Agreed, my dear friend. But the disappearance of personal economies is a secondary phenomenon, a consequence of the factors enumerated by the Professor," said Dr. Reyes de la Barrera, coming to the Professor's aid.

"Not at all, Doctor," replied the engineer. "This horrible vice was so rooted in the minds of mankind in the past that, in spite of no longer having the need for it, they would have continued to hoard for the morbid pleasure of saving, out of a pathological love for the metal that they themselves called villainous. The custom of saving disappeared only when circulating currency stopped having intrinsic value.

"Here we also see working admirably the simultaneity of causes that someone pointed out a moment ago," he continued. "Because of the excessive length of the last wars that humanity supported, misery hit such a level that when the administrative governments came about many of them found they had nothing to administer. While commercial trade was reestablishing itself, industries were reorganizing and agriculture was going through a rebirth, and these governments felt obligated to hand out large sums of paper currency, almost without any guarantee. The public took charge of depreciating that paper more and more, and minted coins became a luxury good for exportation. Then a curious thing happened. Those who, at all costs, wanted and were obligated to economize, considered themselves obligated to repay the coins, thus supporting many who, from this kind of brokerage, had created a profitable business. Those who did not have anything left over to save or who were not accustomed to doing so, spent beyond their means. Thus, since almost everyone bought without haggling over the price, every business prospered, everything for sale sold and every event overflowed with spectators. Everyone lived more or less well, although as one would expect there were many who complained about the situation.

"When the sources of wealth were reorganized and paper currency went back, as it should, to being guaranteed by metal monetary reserves, governments caught on that circulating currency should continue as it had been, without real value. Today the minted coin is held in reserve as a guarantee for paper currency and is used for large transactions that we would call international. In this way the economy is exclusively a function of the State and personal savings have disappeared, allowing for economic stability to become a reality.

"Presently only an abnormal and unbalanced being would think of hoarding money, knowing that he can't leave it to his descendants nor would they need it; knowing that, if through an accident or sickness or by arriving at an advanced age, he becomes unable to work, he will find all that he might need in the State institutions. And we are not referring to the leftover scraps of bread that the former public welfare system gave as a handout, but all the necessities or excesses that the most sickly person or the most capricious elderly person might demand."

The noisy eruption of some approaching newsboys announcing some breaking news caused everyone to stop the discussion so that they could get one of the newspapers. Since all of the papers were sold out, someone read one out loud. It contained up-to-date, and most certainly, gratifying news; it appeared that the highly debated topic of sugar prices had reached a friendly accord, and with it the fears of a rupture in the sugar cartel that they had been talking about disappeared.

Because the attention to the topic of debate had been interrupted, the discussion turned first to the point of the already resolved conflict over sugar prices, and later, mainly jokingly, to a variety of topics.

Soon afterward the mass exodus of the *tertulia* began. Firm in her motives, Celiana stayed there until the last one left. Then, saying that she felt like walking, she offered to accompany the Professor to his house.

"Well, well," said the old man, when during the walk Celiana insisted on talking at length and alone.

"Are we a little embarrassed? When I saw you so devoted to our *tertulia*, I imagined that something was going on in that little heart. Mine understands so little about love these days that it is almost fossilized. But to humor you, I will go to your house tomorrow so that you can tell me everything that you want to, and be assured that because my wish is to help you, no one will beat me there."

At the door to the house of the wise Professor, they said good night fondly and, retiring to her own home, Celiana felt that personal satisfaction associated with achieving something that one has sought for some time.

↜ 11 ↝

The next morning, Celiana awoke with a vague anxiety and a strange malaise. Without a doubt the continual suffering of the last few months began to wreak havoc on her body. Her mouth had a bitter taste and she had a deafening pain in the back of her neck. Far from comforting her, sleep seemed to make Celiana more tired. The idea of dying soon seemed like an acceptable solution, and the feeling of being slightly out of sorts almost cheered her up.

But at the same time, a childish impatience made Celiana wish that time would speed up, so that she could meet with the Professor sooner rather than later. In the catastrophic distortion of her illusions, she placed on that meeting an expectation as unjustified as the hope that a shipwrecked swimmer, about to die, feels when he grabs ahold of a piece of wood so fragile that it can't support his weight. Long accustomed to self-observation and analysis of her thoughts and feelings, Celiana clearly realized how childishly morbid her wish was.

After briefly contemplating with sadness the pillow that lacked its usual impression of that adorable head, and her lover's empty place on the large bed, Celiana got up laboriously and languidly and went to give her sore body the gift of a shower. When she returned to the dresser to comb her hair, the moon-shaped mirror accentuated with raw frankness the lines on her face left by her extreme inner turmoil. The sparkle and feverish passion in her eyes had now become intense dark shadows. The slight wrinkles of her forehead had become more pronounced. A stereotypical painful grin stretched across the corner of her mouth, and in the ebony of her hair, silver strands multiplied with alarming exuberance. Suddenly and without warning, as if she had all of a sudden reached the end of her rope, Celiana was tempted to dye her hair or tear out those insolent gray hairs, to restore her soft skin with powders, to color her faded lips. . . .

Almost irritated with herself, she moved away from the mirror. She threw on a simple robe and went up to the study, guided by the force of habit, and also by the idea of using her work to make the time she had to wait feel shorter.

Celiana opened the window and, feeling the caress of the fresh morning air, she also felt a passing sense of relief that those cheerful early hours of the morning always bring all types of pain, physical as much as emotional ones, no matter how serious. A person in such agony, if he hasn't died by dawn and manages to see the light of daybreak, feels better and hopes to live for another day.

It had rained during the night. The foliage shined with an emerald brilliance. Defeated by the sun's rays, the haze lifted in faint tufts. The birds were singing and the aroma of damp earth pleasantly filled one's lungs.

Feeling a little better, Celiana sat at her desk and looked through her notes. She had several projects pending, among others an article for an important New York magazine that had advertised her work with great praise, publishing her picture and biographical sketch as a way to move the project along. She had been thinking that the article would be a study of neo-Theosophy, an idealist doctrine, more philosophical than religious, into which all other religions had been recast. The study would examine the origins of religious sentiments and follow the evolution of beliefs across time.

Celiana wrote with surprising ease. In general, she would outline her ideas in her head and develop them naturally, typing them out on her typewriter with straightforward inspiration and complete control of language. Seldom did she have to erase or correct her work. But today she noticed an unusual difficulty in organizing her ideas. She felt them come in a mad rush, confused and poorly differentiated. For a long period of time she felt tortured by her useless efforts, the almost physical pain of true mental exercise.

Finally, Celiana's fingers ran across the typewriter with their accustomed speed. But soon the writer noticed that she was confused and that her main idea had escaped her, lost among quick and superficial associations. She stopped and read:

"In its run on earth, Humanity has needed to fix its sight on the one point that marks its path. It has needed an ideal and, when that has been lost, it has had to feel its way, slipping every once in a while. And so great is this need for an ideal that having a false one ends up being less bad than not having one at all. When Rome believed in the gods of Numa Pompilius, she was ruler of the world.[27] Afterward, when the mythological deities abandoned Olympus, and

---

27. Numa Pompilius (715–673 BC) was the second king of Rome. He is credited with establishing "much of the basic framework of Roman public religion through his institution of cults, rituals, priesthoods, and calendar reforms" (Andrew Drummond,

Christianity had not yet taken over the human conscience, the Roman state fell into the worst extremes of corruption and complete decadence.

"Two or three centuries ago societies found themselves in a similar situation. Faith had died, and nothing had come to replace it. Thus, that civilization, so decadent, carried in its bosom innumerable elements of death and decay. With great selfishness, excessive ambition, hate and jealousy, the men of those times made life complicated and bitter.

"A cold breeze of skepticism dried up the fountain of ideals for that generation and, moving into the realm of thought, changed at its very essence the concept of beauty and put its stamp on the arts, the means by which this concept was articulated. Because of this, artistic creations from that period are, for the most part, weak and ignoble. Beauty was not seen in the harmonic force of life but rather in the strange and extravagant, abnormal and morbid. Music strove to create strange and unheard rhythms that made one's nerves vibrate like strings about to snap. The visual arts, of form and color, spurned nature's eternal and unique model, lumping together different natural domains, giving the uncertain lines of a mollusk or vegetative foliage to the human figure and to all work produced in this medium, the tinges and contours of beings created by the mind in a state of delirium. Poetry idealized the straying of reason, and the horrors of doubt and hallucinations of drunkenness, disorder, neurosis, degeneration, and poetic form ran from clarity as though it were a vice, seeking out combinations of weird cadence and enigmatic meaning.

"Our present era is a revival. In customs as in the Arts, we have renounced complication and lies, conventionality and falseness. Having abandoned all ideals of an afterlife, today's Humanity places its ideals in the intelligent and healthy enjoyment of life, in living life to its fullest, in an atmosphere of justice and mutual respect. In love, today's men and women tend to be free of the atavistic chain of jealousy and passion, which turned what never should have been anything other than a paradise into a hell for our ancestors, since it is and always has been for the birds." . . . .

And here Celiana stopped reading and thought that, much to her regret and disgrace, she was one of those beings tied by hereditary chains to the pain of loving pathologically and abnormally. By some supreme power, she distanced herself from that thought, stopped analyzing herself as though she were part of the study, and continued reading:

"Pompilius, Numa," in *The Oxford Classical Dictionary*, 4th ed., ed. Simon Hornblower and Antony Spawforth [Oxford: Oxford University Press, 2012], 1181).

"As with nations, individuals need their lives to have some purpose, an ideal, and, when they lack this, their existence continuously vacillates and their mind is at the mercy of all impulses and is condemned to instability.

"There exist men of truly superior intelligence, in whom doubt is the source of truth, and once in possession of this, use it to point the compass to all of their aspirations. So, when they have run the full circle of the sciences, looking in vain in nature's book for their link to the divine and the relationship between the finite and the infinite, they end up convincing themselves that only matter is immortal and eternal in its polymorphism. Faced with this unsolvable problem, these men bravely confront the ghost of nothingness and resolve to be an integral part—consciously or subconsciously—of the great universal everything.

"Other men—who each day become less and less in number—find the purpose of life to be too miserable and don't resign themselves to fulfilling the limits of their desires here on earth, but seek to complement their aspirations in the hope for an afterlife. This fear of nothing, this desire for the continuity of the conscious 'I,' is the only raison d'être for religious sentiment, in its most pure and acceptable form.

"Finally, there are barely noticeable intelligences in which doubt is made eternal. Men who possess this form of intelligence arrive at the end of their lives with the question posed but unresolved." . . . .

Stopping here, Celiana's thoughts again drifted to her own situation, causing her to drop the analysis of her written paragraphs in order to analyze herself. Celiana was a materialist by conviction. If she had ever longed for the immortality of the soul, she had never found a logical basis for such a belief. And if at other times the hope for an afterlife would have eased her sorrows, this idea was now horrifying to her. Eternity of consciousness would be for Celiana the eternity of suffering. So of all the purposes and motives of human life, only love seemed to be worthy of consideration to her, and, without Ernesto's love, the final, irreplaceable ideal of her life, she could not conceive of happiness in life or in the afterlife. How attractive and soothing she found the idea of sleeping in the unconsciousness of an eternal dream to be, after so many nights of insomnia caused by the torture of an obsession! If the use of euthanasia for those suffering incurable physical pain had come to be considered legal and merciful, why not allow its voluntary use for those whose soul has been destroyed by moral suffering, as incurable as physical suffering, and perhaps even more dreadful? Why deny those who are fed up with life the right to detach themselves from it? . . . .

Celiana brushed her hand across her forehead as if to wipe away those gloomy thoughts. She lit up a marijuana cigarette, inhaled with pleasure, and, when she had finished it, fell into a brief and light state of drowsiness. . . . Oh, how she longed for euthanasia! To do it, all she would have to do is force herself a little to overdose on that treacherous alkaloid.

For now, the immediate effect had been achieved. Celiana's brain, responding to the impact of the drug, remembered its creative potential. She got ready to continue the article she had started.

Having already discussed the origin of religious sentiment in its abstract form, Celiana now needed to explain how in the past, some men—undoubtedly intelligent—redirected this feeling into fear in order to dominate the masses, thereby creating religion. She would then narrate how these religions popped up over the centuries, and copied and modified myths—generally written for children—more or less infusing them with symbolism in order to keep up with the period, but always maintaining a common tendency to exploit and enslave consciences.

Finally, Celiana would talk about how in present times, morality had been adjusted according to the laws of nature, so that man could no longer admit to being exploited, oppressed, or enslaved, and external and regimented religions were now impossible. The only thing left standing was the eternal and unresolved argument between the materialists and the spiritualists. Those who felt anguished by this ideal took refuge in neo-Theosophy, which was nothing more than ancient Theosophy, stripped of the Oriental myths and the remnants of Buddhism of other times, and reduced to a philosophical doctrine that recognized the existence of a Supreme Being, the immortality of the soul, and its evolution toward superior worlds and planes through a series of reincarnations.

Before giving shape to those thoughts, Celiana reread carefully with a critical eye the paragraphs that she had previously written, and she found them to be detestable. They contained ideas that could be useful, but on the whole they were disjointed, confused, childish, and deep down they were pretentious and forced in their form. . . .

Decidedly, Celiana was not in the mood to write articles, and even less so about such abstract topics. She stopped the project and tore up all that she had composed. To get it out of the way, she would just send the journal in New York any one of the works, purely literary, that she had in unedited form, or recycle one of her lectures. Playing the piano, she would wait for the Professor, who surely wouldn't be long in arriving.

And, as everything eventually runs its course, the old man showed up as expected. The conversation was long and warm, and it sincerely lifted the worries that Celiana had long kept bottled up. Celiana shared the feelings buried in the bloody depths of her shattered bosom, described her bitter sorrows, and explained her weak hopes for solace. The Professor listened to Celiana with sympathetic interest and even though he thought her situation was completely vulgar and not to be taken so seriously, he let loose beautiful words of encouragement and lavished her with pearls of wisdom and experience and wise opinions and advice. But overall, the unhappily enamored Celiana merely took away the sad conviction that in matters of passion, all outside intervention ends up being excessive, every word of comfort is commonplace, and every piece of advice is useless vulgarity, even if it comes from the most illustrious of wise men or the most sincere and dearest of friends.

For every enamored, eternal, and unwavering couple, the melodic note is always the same and only the accompanying harmony changes. But every love-struck individual firmly believes that he loves, suffers, and enjoys in a way that is different from others. Thus Celiana, after that much-anticipated conversation, unfairly and selfishly concluded that her old and wise friend did not understand at all the sublime heights of her affection and that in his cultivated and powerful intelligence were the beginnings of the inevitable process of senile decline.

～ 12 ～

The news that the European governments and American sugar-producing trade unions had resolved their difficulties regarding the pricing of that indispensable staple caused great merriment throughout the world. This attractive triumph for diplomacy dispelled fears of a terrible conflict just when it seemed imminent and almost inevitable. To properly commemorate the news, Villa-utopians held splendid parties that lasted for days.

The members of the organizing commission for the festivities wanted to give them a congenial and original touch, making them re-creations of community celebrations of past times. Thus, in addition to the indispensable aviation contests, of which the people of that period were such big fans, there was an impressive historical mounted procession, a civilian parade, free performances in all the theaters, fireworks, open-air concerts with Venetian-style lighting in all the parks, and bullfights with horsemen in the plazas.

Along the same lines, the city council celebrated solemn and elegant Flower Games, which were attended by jesters wearing provincial jousting costumes and the queen and ladies of her court wearing period dress.[28] The distinguished Don Luis Gil played the role of master of ceremonies with enthusiasm and elegance that no one would have expected from his many years. The ruddy

28. The flower games (*juegos florales*) were cultural, art, and literary festivals held in communities throughout Latin America in the late nineteenth and early twentieth centuries. For example, a 1918 *Revista de Yucatán* article described how, as Mérida's "admired bard, Mr. Mediz Bolio, chairman of the third Flower Games . . . read one of his best prose compositions," the "Spanishness of his soul" became more and more pronounced in his language and performance ("La Criada de Moliere," *La Revista de Yucatán*, October 5, 1918, 3).

and inspired Dr. Castillo won the "natural flower" contest with a sonnet that was truly ornate. His colleague and rival, Reyes de la Barrera, who received only an honorable mention, gave in to his demons and, without exercising prudence, cursed the panel of judges. The arguments between the two poets turned sour to such a degree that it took all the efforts of their fellow members of the plaza discussion group and all of the conciliatory authority of the Professor to stop the two from settling their differences in the field of honor, which was significant because neither was of the violent type.

But all of the chroniclers and gossip columnists of that time were unanimous in declaring that the culminating moment—the *clou*, as they used to say—of the said festivities was the great gala that was held during the last day in the vast ballrooms and enchanting gardens of the Institute of Eugenics. It didn't go unnoticed that the illustrious Dr. Pérez Serrato put into organizing that soirée, as he did with everything, the stubborn efficiency of his organizational ability!

In other times it might have seemed strange that an institution of such seriousness and importance as the Villautopia Institute of Eugenics would have occupied itself with something as paltry as organizing a ball. But at that time it wasn't so strange nor unwonted, since the Institute celebrated at least one every month.

Furthermore, in that epoch in which Humanity had once and for all renounced all hypocrisies and conventionalisms, everything was given a true purpose and place. And what better place for a gala than the Institute that oversaw the perpetuity of the species and was responsible for increasing the population?

The dance had always been a more or less hidden and idealized exercise of the struggle of love, or of courtship, which is the obligatory first step of coupling in all animal species. To come up with this ritual, first savage man, and later civilized man, did no more than put this instinctive act to music. The jealous male pursues the female while the playful female dodges the male in order to excite him more, running away from him in the evolution of a mating dance, or simulating polished flirtations in the form of a rigadoon.[29] Finally she allows herself to be swept up in the twirls of a waltz or surrenders to the voluptuous turns of a dance. . . .

In antiquity, when women were forbidden from participating in any experimental exercise of an amorous nature, this ritual was carried out under the

---

29. A rigadoon is "a lively jumping quickstep for one couple" (*The American Heritage College Dictionary*, 3rd ed., s.v. "rigadoon").

watchful and stern eye of older people so that, under no circumstances, would it go beyond just that. This resulted in one of the many variations of the torments of Tantalus.[30] But it couldn't have been any other way, given that the essential test of feminine virtue was in conserving intact that unpierced pearl of Arab folklore, as a gift for the sultan or to sell it in public auction to the Jewish merchant who would pay a vast fortune in gold for it.[31]

In the plain reign of free love, in complete equality of rights for women and men, the dance demonstrated its character as a sexual aperitif, with such crude forwardness that it would have caused the white skin of our hypocritical and formalist great-grandparents to turn red. Older people, depending on the weather, either stayed at home in front of the fireplace or chatted and took in the cool breeze in parks or drugstore doorways. Young couples would surrender to the delightfulness of the dance, free of any outside vigilance. Who would be shocked or surprised to see them steal away into the foliage of the gardens during intermissions or to leave the dance hall altogether at the height of the festivities?

Thus it was that Villautopia's Institute of Eugenics held monthly galas so that official reproducers of both sexes could get to know each other and, via that pleasant ambiance, could be stimulated into carrying out their responsibilities to the species.

But this time it wasn't about the standard monthly ball but rather an extraordinary festival, for which no expense or preparation was spared and to which numerous people from outside the institution had been invited.

30. Tantalus was a legendary king of Sipylus who "belongs to the group of archetypal violators of the laws laid down by Zeus for the conduct of human society. . . . Tantalus suffers eternal and condign punishment, 'tantalized' by having to stand in a pool which drains away when he tries to drink, with fruit dangling before his eyes which are whisked away as soon as he reaches for them" (Alan H. Griffiths, "Tantalus," in *The Oxford Classical Dictionary*, 4th ed., ed. Simon Hornblower and Antony Spawforth [Oxford: Oxford University Press, 2012], 1430).

31. This passage refers to the practice of displaying a nuptial sheet demonstrating blood to prove that the wife was a virgin. "Virginity, especially in unmarried girls, is of at least some concern in most cultures around the world. . . . Where virginity is required, a girl must often prove that she was a virgin on her wedding night. Such tests of virginity require that a newly married couple produce a blood-stained article of bedding or clothing" (Gwen J. Broude, "Sexual Attitudes and Practices," in *Encyclopedia of Sex and Gender: Men and Women in the World's Cultures*, vol. 1, ed. Carol R. Ember and Melvin Ember [New York: Kluwer Academic/Plenum Publishers, 2004], 180).

It must have been ten o'clock at night when Ernesto arrived at the ball-room, accompanied by his friends Consuelo and Federico. Having already played the overture, the orchestra, unseen as was the custom of the day, played a waltz.

Decorated with wreaths of natural flowers and an extravagance of lighting, the ballrooms had a dazzling feel. But the preferred spot of couples was the garden, full of aromas and calm. A large quantity of blue electric lightbulbs, artfully hung between the leaves of the trees, projected a soft and moonlike light.

Putting aside the fashion etiquette of the past, harsh black colors and un-aesthetic coattails had disappeared from masculine apparel. Young men now wore suits of light material and clear color tones. For women, style required Greek tunics, slit above the left thigh and leaving the right shoulder and breast exposed.

Those guests who no longer danced because of their age formed lively cliques under the trees, pleasantly contemplating with nostalgia, and not without envy, the squandering of beauty, joy, and youth.

Since Ernesto's job required that he live in that environment of purely physiological love, a profound change, explainable and natural, had come over him. When the shock and surprise of the first few days faded, his innate sexual appetite revealed itself in an insatiable yearning for pleasure. His masculine beauty and vigorous physical conditioning made Ernesto the object of desire of all of the fertile young women, who physically fought over him. A large number of his offspring were already gestating in the peritoneum of the human incuba-tors, a number that soon would surpass what was required by law.

It's clear that these amorous relationships, as fast as they were effective, didn't settle in Ernesto's heart nor did they affect in any way the sentimental part of his being. But it can't be denied that they suited his personality and temperament better than that sterile fondness that he used to have for Celiana. And if at first Ernesto could believe that the growing coldness toward his former lover came from the lack of frankness with which they both responded to their respective change in positions, now he understood that his situation was more and more fake and that sooner or later they would have to call it off once and for all. He felt ashamed for having lived for five years in idleness and as a parasite, kept by that woman like a lap dog. Turned into the embodiment of remorse, the woman that he loved so much was becoming almost repulsive to him. Ernesto understood Celiana's resigned sadness to be a constant and unspoken reproach, which made it more and more difficult for him to comply with the obligation, imposed on him by chivalry and gratitude, of pretending to love her. Poor Celiana! In spite of her enormous gift and keen insight, she was far from comprehending her young lover's state of mind. If she only knew how he really was, she surely would have been quick to release him from any responsibility to her, even if it cost her her own life.

In the turns of the waltz, Ernesto crossed paths several times with the young Dr. Suárez, who danced with Athanasia, the beautiful daughter of the Institute's Director. Greeting him with a smile, the likable intern, with whom Ernesto was already a close friend, signaled that they needed to talk. As soon as the number ended, the two friends met and, arm-in-arm, headed for the garden.

"I've been looking for you for a while," said the doctor. "It's important that you know that tonight a precious young woman who has just been named an official reproducer will make her first public appearance. Her name is Eugenia and I guarantee you that she is a delicacy, an authentic innocent, and a splendid thing of beauty. Since she still is not aware of the responsibilities of her role, you will understand that there are more than four young men already lined up and determined to give her her first practical lessons. But I want you, the pearl of our reproducers, the pride of the house, to be the zephyr in charge of opening the petals of that rosebud."

"Thank you, my friend," said Ernesto. "It doesn't seem like a bad idea. But what motives are behind your Galeotti-like move?[32]

"You are a true ingrate! My motives are, in the first place, the duty I have as an employee of this establishment to make sure that its goals are carried out, and second, the fondness that I feel for you and now understand that you don't deserve. I feel like letting her be carried off by any one of those good-for-nothings that have descended upon her like flies on honey," replied Suárez.

"And why haven't you, Mephistophelian Doctor, stepped up as the first bidder in the auction of this valuable jewel?" asked Ernesto.

"You know good and well that I am not a hypocrite. As a staff employee I have been around that girl for a few days now, and naturally I haven't stopped making advances. But since she is so innocent and doesn't hide her reactions, from the beginning I understood that I don't suit her, that I'm not her type. Besides, I've completed my term of service and these initiations by law fall on you all, those who are on active duty. But it won't be hard for me to serve again in the future, as I'm still in good shape. . . . Enough of this bickering already.

32. Henri Guillaume Galeotti (1814–58) was a French-Belgian botanist and geologist of Italian parentage born in Paris. He specialized in the study of cacti and spent several years in Mexico carrying out botanical and geological research.

Let's go so that I can introduce her to you." . . . . And grabbing Ernesto by the arm, Suárez crossed the ballroom with him.

The intern's praises of the young woman were no exaggeration. A harmony of figure and proportions, youthful freshness and perfect health, all joined to make Eugenia an admirable example of the human species, a prototype of feminine beauty. There in a remote village in the interior of the region, in full and constant contact with nature, that lush flower of flesh had developed. The notoriety of her perfection reached the ears of Dr. Pérez Serrato, and, because the jealous Director was always on the hunt for such jewels, he used every bit of his influence and didn't rest until he could count Eugenia among the personnel at the Institute under his charge.

Now almost hiding in a corner of the ballroom, in the amazement of that sumptuous party, hounded by a swarm of annoying ladies' men, the poor girl, lacking social experience, couldn't manage to do anything but blush and laugh nervously. Making out the familiar face of Dr. Suárez, she raised her eyes in a signal for help. But by chance or by destiny's decree, her gaze crossed with that of Ernesto, which caused a mutual bewilderment. Confused and embarrassed like a schoolboy, he could barely stutter a few senseless words when the young intern made the usual introductions. Even more confused, Eugenia was only able to muster a smile and a soft murmur.

But that gaze, smile, and murmur were more eloquent than a million words for Ernesto. Like Romeo when he met the daughter of the elder Capulet, at that moment he had a complete revelation and precise intuition about what first, absolute, and complete love was. One might say that Ernesto was born at that moment, that he had never lived before and that the past didn't exist for him. Where had the memory of Celiana and their former love gone? Where had the recent sensations of the last few months gone?

One would have seen Ernesto in a tight spot if someone had asked him if Eugenia was blonde or brunette. What color were her eyes? He wouldn't have been able to tell. Ernesto only knew that, surely tired of avoiding the stares of those annoying ladies' men, her eyes had met his with the calm and sincere happiness of one who, after an extended period, finally found a longed-for shelter, or of one who catches a glimpse of sunlight after a storm.

A force from above, or their will, kept them there and, while neither he nor she did anything but stare at each other and keep quiet, the other suitors, aware of or jealous of Ernesto's success, dropped out little by little. Dr. Suárez, having fulfilled his mission of introducing the couple and assured that they had the necessary affinity to make things happen on their own, carefully slipped away.

Alone, Ernesto and Eugenia still did not talk to each other. Nor did they have a reason to. All of the cells in their bodies, feeling themselves complementary, were already tending toward each other with a force superior to all reason and all conscious will. The orchestra began to play a *danza* and, as if obeying an unspoken rule, they stood up to dance. Without asking permission or telling the story of their lives, as if they already knew each other from long ago, had never been apart, nor should ever separate again.

Everyone respected that spontaneous union and they approved of it as a consummated and fatal fact. And, since nobody tried to intervene, isolated from all those who surrounded them, Ernesto and Eugenia continued dancing together the rest of the night, already so absorbed in each other that it seemed as if, for them, the universe didn't exist beyond the circle formed by their intertwined arms. . . .

The gala ended as dawn approached, and they left the ballroom together.

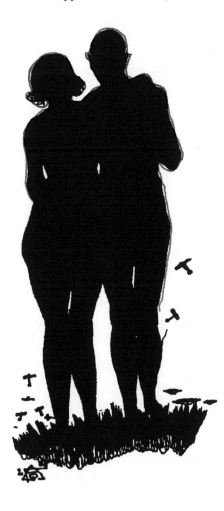

~ *13* ~

*C*eliana had gone twenty days without seeing her lover, though the time had weighed upon her as if it had been twenty years. Progressive emaciation, paleness, and slovenliness were quickly eating away the last vestiges of her autumnal beauty. She was a cadaver galvanized by hope. The only thing that kept her going was the yearning to see Ernesto again, to embrace him for a moment in her arms. And while she understood just how irrational this illusion had become, she willfully clung to these cravings like a dying person. From that horrible struggle between the proof of her abandonment and her inability to accept it sprung the Dantesque storm in which that wretched and bleeding heart of a sentimental woman flailed about.

Celiana no longer wrote or studied. Having lost the sole purpose of her existence, her brain, once so powerful and fertile, had lost all creative impetus. She barely thought about anything at all, and if ever out of habit she sat at the piano, her fingers mechanically ran up and down the keys, and no longer did she feel that suggestive music that with such clarity had previously expressed the nuances of her state of mind. Now it was a simple melody, without expression, almost childlike, monotonously repeating the joyful musical phrase with which she anesthetized her pain on that memorable night of her first abandonment. And playing it for hours at a time, Celiana conjured up the image of a mother who, with her favorite song, keeps rocking the cold body of a dead child.

Without the strength to keep pretending, she no longer tried to hide her pain from her friends. They in turn nursed her like a sick mother and fulfilled her smallest whims. They didn't even try to intervene in her now abusive use of those toxic marijuana cigarettes that were now, in a powerful way, activating the destructive work of her suffering, instead of providing a period of rest from her tortured existence.

Miguel watched Celiana with brotherly interest and, having reached the limits of his ability to resolve the situation, thought that perhaps an ultimate, definitive disappointment, signifying the bloody eradication of all hope, could exercise the healthy effect of a surgical operation on her sick brain and give her back her lost equilibrium. Out of gratitude, at the least, Ernesto should clarify his intentions with respect to Celiana. If he wasn't brave enough to talk to her with frankness and loyalty, he should write her a letter of farewell.

The painter was aware of his young friend's love affair in all its details. He knew that ever since the night of the ball, Ernesto and Eugenia had not been apart and had made a love nest in a chalet on the outskirts of the city. He should go there to remind Ernesto of his sacred duty and demand it of him if necessary.

Miguel acted prudently by resolving to take the first step in the matter, since Ernesto would not do so on his own. Completely absorbed in the absolute love that was the essence of their new life, Ernesto and Eugenia lived out their romance with the joyful recklessness of a pair of nightingales in the springtime. Without a single memory of the past nor a thought for the future, they seemed afflicted with total amnesia.

Sometimes after waking up in the morning, Ernesto would blissfully gaze upon his lover, asleep next to him, fully displaying—due to her breeding—her youthful delights. Gently kissing her and rising with infinite precautions not to wake her, he remembered a time when it was he who stayed in bed, while another woman took care to not wake him as she got out of bed and kissed him with identical tenderness. As if all that were now in the remote past, Ernesto vaguely remembered that he very much had loved that woman, and something deep in the honorable depths of his drowsy conscience fought to tell him that he had acted without tact or regard when he abandoned Celiana without so much as a word of good-bye. . . .

But then, realizing that she was alone in the bed, Eugenia woke up, and facing the brightness of those eyes that anxiously looked for him and the glorious poetry of that smile, the entire past vanished for Ernesto. And because the memory of an unhappy Celiana was a part of that past, she vanished as well. For the lucky lover, nothing existed that wasn't the here and now. And the here and now was Eugenia offering him the delicacy of her burning lips. He ran to kiss them with insatiable desire, each time with a thousand times more vigor, and they didn't do anything else all day nor most of the night.

For such happy and satisfyingly busy lovers, time passed without the usual divisions with which man marked its eternal and relentless movement.

One morning, Ernesto happened to be looking at the calendar and noticed that it still showed the unforgettable date when he had first met his darling

Eugenia. He had to check it against that of the day's newspaper to realize that twenty days had already passed. While he was busy removing all of those sheets at once from the calendar, his waking lover surprised him, and the humor of the incident was excuse enough for them to spend almost the entire morning celebrating between laughter and frolicking. They found in that joyful state of euphoria that even the smallest incident was reason enough for merriment. Naturally, given the interwovenness in which that loving pair found themselves, everything ended in kisses and hugs.

Their daily schedule consisted of similar scenes. But that morning's, in contrast, took on a transcendental and serious note. It seemed that Eugenia needed to tell her partner something very important, and apparently it was difficult for her to do so. Eventually Ernesto guessed, rather than deducing what it was from Eugenia's half-spoken sentences, nervous bouts of laughter, unusual blushing, and almost inaudible whispers in his ear.

There is in the history of every honeymoon an almost scripted episode that has, since early days, been exploited by novelists with more or less bad taste. It is that poetic and interesting moment in which the wife shares with her spouse the happy news of the success that their sleepless nights have begun to propagate in favor of the species—that in her belly the blessed fruit of their love beats.

There was no other motive for Eugenia's awkwardness, nor was there any other important news that, amid their frolicking, she told her beloved.

What is curious and worthy of pointing out is the effect that the news had on Ernesto. He who in the first years of his youth believed that he was completely happy and satisfied with a love that was sterile and later carried out his job as official reproducer with notable fervor and efficiency, but without dedicating a single thought to his offspring, upon learning that Eugenia's flesh was mixing with his to create the flesh and soul of another life that would be the soul and flesh of both of them, felt what he had never felt nor believed he could feel. Knowing that he would have an adorable child, who would also be the child of the woman he adored, he understood with exactitude the very purpose of his existence; he saw clearly the motive of his life, in the survival of his very being through the cycle of life and death.

For love to deserve being called complete, it is not enough for it to fulfill the physiological, aesthetic, and sentimental aspirations of a human couple. It also has to fulfill its first and natural purpose, which is the propagation of the species. When it does not fulfill each and every one of these purposes, it degenerates into an unconscious and brute act of breeding or turns into a sterile sentimentalism that almost borders on the pathological.

The future began to exist once again for the young lovers. From that moment on, time became divided by months and days. The time that remained—and together they would count—up to the moment in which, leaning over the edge of an immaculate crib, time would be spent contemplating the rosy cheeks of a newborn, a baby like any other, but for them, different than the rest and the most beautiful of them all.

It was then that Ernesto was able to understand just how useful Dr. Pérez Serrato's informative talk had been for him, despite how bored he'd been during his initial visit to the Institute of Eugenics. Thanks to that talk, he was perfectly informed about the gestation of a child through the scientific method in use during that period, and he could explain it to Eugenia, who was completely ignorant of the process. Proud of his knowledge and satisfied with the attention with which an interested and grateful Eugenia listened to him, Ernesto started to feel like an expert and detailed the stages of the process, from the extraction of the ovum from the uterus to its placement it in the peritoneum of the gestator, up to the solemn final surgical delivery. He described how they would have to anxiously await each of these steps and intimated how intense their emotions would be while observing, eager and locked in an embrace.

They spent the rest of the day immersed in these projects and hopes, discreetly mixing in, as was expected, indispensable kisses and hugs. But Ernesto didn't feel happy about everything. It seems that with the reemergence of his future, time was challenging the unity of his three natural stages in life and the past was not going away without a fight. And the past resurrected itself in the unwelcomed form of regret, regarding something deep in the corner of his conscience that spoke faintly about Celiana, of how cruel he had been with her. In the high esteem that he now held himself, Ernesto urgently felt the need to pay his dues to the past. He decided to do it as soon as possible, and he thought about how best he could do it. Ernesto first thought about bravely facing his former lover in person and talking frankly. He later thought that it would be easier to write Celiana a letter. He finally decided that the most practical and feasible way was to find Miguel and beg him to deliver his crushing last good-bye to Celiana.

And as if this thought—stuck in Ernesto's mind all afternoon—had the telepathic strength of an evocation, Miguel knocked on the door of the chalet that very evening, as the young lovers were discovering that the time reserved for after-dinner conversation also provided a new outlet for their cooing and caresses.

Embarrassed and babbling, Ernesto didn't know how to act in front of his old friend. With his usual frankness, Miguel took the embarrassment out of the situation by saying,

"You are an absolute pig, Ernesto, or better yet, completely irresponsible. I'm not asking you for an explanation for your behavior, because I know perfectly well the cause of it, and I was the first to foresee it, as you might recall, but even if you have lost your sense of shame, you haven't lost your memory too."

"Don't be hard on me, Miguel. I would have wanted . . . ."

"No, Ernesto. The preterit pluperfect of the subjunctive is an absurd verb tense that should be erased from the conjugation. Things don't happen twice, and what 'would have been' is not, has not been, and never will be. By the laws of nature, in the play of love one of the actors always finishes his part before the other. You have finished your lines before Celiana and if you had been only one of multiple lovers you would be perfectly in your right to leave her without taking notice of her fate. But you have been her favorite pupil, her creation, her child. You owe her everything that you are and the little that you cherish in life. This gratitude, then, requires that you act like a gentleman. I have come ready to demand—if begging isn't enough—that you do whatever it takes to comply with the sacred responsibility."

"What do you want me to do?" asked Ernesto. "You tell me."

"Celiana is dying on us, Ernesto. But what is killing her isn't exactly your abandonment of her but the senseless struggle that her soul is waging between certainty and hope. Rip the hope out of her with a direct, sincere, and fair good-bye letter. I am still confident that her exceptional mind, full of goodness and justice, will respond accordingly and regain a sense of balance. Because I want to help resolve this situation and I understand that your life now probably doesn't leave you either time or the will to write, I bring you the letter already written. Here you have it. If you agree with what it says, you don't have to do anything but sign it."

"No, Miguel, that is too much," said Ernesto without taking the letter that his friend offered him. "I tell you that this very night I will write a letter and send it by mail."

"No. Write it now. I will wait. Everything is planned," Miguel added, taking a sheet of paper and a fountain pen from his large shirt pocket and handing them to the young man.

Ernesto obliged without saying a word and there in the living room, on a coffee table, he quickly wrote out a new, short, concise, and sincere letter. In it he spoke to Celiana with the raw frankness of the truth, without attenuation or false sorrow and without resorting to sophisms to justify the unjustifiable. Ernesto signed it, sealed the envelope, and handed it to the painter.

Miguel took the letter and afterward, calm, unmoved, standing tall, he shook his friend's hand and left without saying a word.

Eugenia, who from a doorway had watched with surprise as the whole scene unfolded, went up to her lover, looking serious and worried for the first time since they had begun living together, and gently asked him,

"Who was that extremely bald and stern man? Are you already starting to keep secrets from your little lady?"[33]

Ernesto stared at her for a moment and replied,

"This, my dear, is the past that has died once and for all and that I have just buried. Now, for me, the only things that exist are the present and the future. . . . And since both are embodied in you, the only love of my life, come to my arms."

33. The original word in Spanish is *mujercita*, which literally means "little woman" but is also an endearing term for "wife." However, since *Eugenia* proposes a model of families based on free love and nonblood groups, we have opted for "little lady" to suggest a special relationship of lovers/partners but not necessarily a lawfully wedded "wife."

↝ *14* ↜

*L*ying down on an easy chair with the listlessness of a sick woman, facing the large window in her study, Celiana gazed out as the warm day became evening. The sky was a solid dark gray, without the usual abundance of purples and golds, such that to the west the sun's rays were barely able to fall to the ground in three slanting lines. The unusual sadness of that painful afternoon seemed to add to the intense bitterness displayed by the expressionless look of those eyes, the main attraction of a feminine face that once had been so alive and intelligent.

Carrying the letter, not knowing if it was fatal or lifesaving, Miguel entered and stopped for a moment to contemplate his friend with boundless pity. Just then Celiana slowly and clumsily lit one of those toxic and treasonous cigarettes. Void of free will, the vice entangled her more and more in its tentacles. "Everything is now useless," thought Miguel, and he almost decided against giving Celiana the letter.

"What are you doing and what is on your mind, sister?" he finally said as he approached her and caressed her matted and uncombed hair.

"Are you so dim-witted that you have to ask me, Miguel? What do you want me to think about when my will is no longer able to choose the object of its thoughts? What do I do? You already see, I try to not think about anything. Oh, if only I could once and for all. . . . Why don't you help me, my brother, the only one who never deceived me?"

"Life, Celiana, is an invaluable gift, since we only have one chance at it, and our every test of wisdom is in living it to the fullest. How much fulfillment life still has in store for you! You, who still have a store of youth and exceptional talent that can see you through to the triumphs and highest peaks of glory! In this life that you despise there are plenty of beautiful ideals left to which you can devote the abundant energy of your spirit. What is it, in short, that you have lost? The love of a rude and dumb child who didn't deserve what you gave him.

Love is but one of many means that we can count on to enjoy life. From semi-barbaric times its lances have fostered drama."

"You are lucky to have always been able to balance theory with practice when it comes to this subject. I can't, Miguel. That past that you correctly refer to as semibarbaric has deep roots in my heart—a heart that, by not knowing how to love without becoming impassioned, has made a disgrace out of my entire life."

"I think that what has made you suffer, more than delusion itself, is the foolish struggle that you maintain between the proof of your abandonment and the hope of winning back Ernesto. You would have given up by now if he had opened up to you at the moment he fell so madly in love with Eugenia, which made it impossible for him to continue living by your side."

"It's possible, Miguel. But it is too late for me to give up. I have lost the will to choose a new ideal for my life, and I even have lost the will to live."

"And would it not calm your spirit if he now wrote you a letter saying good-bye once and for all?"

"You, you have the letter! Stop beating around the bush and give it to me!" Celiana said sharply.

"Take it," replied Miguel as he handed it to her, and as she ripped the letter from his hand, she eagerly kissed it, trembling as she opened it and seeming to forget that Miguel was even there.

Miguel stepped back a little so that he could better observe the psychological phenomenon.

The letter read,

Unforgettable Celiana:

You once told me that pretending to love was more cruel than forsaking love. I cannot nor should not continue deceiving you. A new love has killed that which I once had for you and that made us so happy. I only ask your forgiveness for having allowed so much time to pass between the day when I stopped loving you and today, when I tell you.

As for the other good graces that you showed me, I will never forget those. Good-bye.

ERNESTO

As harsh and heartless as that letter was in its laconic frankness, it didn't really say anything that Celiana didn't already know. However, after reading it

she felt a complete void in her mind. Where were her ideas and memories?. . . .
Without shedding a tear, Celiana walked mechanically toward the desk and sat
down as if she were going to write something. Her hands shuffled through papers
as if looking for notes. But they soon stopped their nervous hustle and bustle
and rose up to roll and light a fatally toxic cigarette. She inhaled the smoke
with anxiety and, exhaling slowly, smiled with the silliness of delusion.

After finishing the marijuana cigarette, Celiana stood as if sleepwalking
and, with Miguel following her from a distance, went downstairs. She went to
the living room, invaded by the approaching shadows of the evening, and sat at
the piano. Her hands stayed limp, clumsy, and sluggish for a long time on the
keys, and when they finally lifted up it was to roll and light another joint. Slowly
inhaling and exhaling, Celiana smiled, smiled. . . .

The complete and total ruin of that powerful mind was final. Everything
was gone: ideas, memories, emotions, and willpower. All that was left was the
insatiable desire to smoke.

Back at her side and caressing her disheveled hair without her seeming to
notice, Miguel waxed philosophical,

"Love is arbitrary and master of the universe. It is the reason why the stars
sparkle, the flowers smell, and the birds sing. Why, if in all other beings there is
an abundance of life and happiness, is there for humans a strange mix of pleasure
and torture? Is social progress, gained at the expense of so many tears, not
worth anything in the end? Love is now free from all of those obstacles and
prejudices that before tried to get in the way of fulfilling its divine laws. But it
still has not freed itself from the burden of pain. Othello no longer strangles nor
does Werther commit suicide, but man still suffers and cries because of love.
Why don't men learn to love as the birds and the butterflies love? . . . .[34]

"But no. It can't be and it shouldn't be. Human suffering—moral pain, the
distinguished loftiness of our species—is our divine birthright. For the bird, the
insect, or the wild beast, love is nothing more than the fleeting moment of
pleasure itself. For man, the present is only a moment between the past and the
future. This is why he keeps coming back a thousand and one times to this
delightful pleasure. He relives it in his imagination and enjoys it all over again,
and, even more so in the moments of pain or pleasure, he suffers or enjoys it as

34. *The Sorrows of Young Werther* is a loosely autobiographical epistolary novel by
Johann Wolfgang von Goethe, first published in 1774. The character of Werther,
embroiled in a love triangle but unable to inflict harm on the other, shoots himself in the
head after leaving a suicide note. He died a short time later from the injury.

he waits or craves it and when he remembers or longs for it. And for this reason, in the preparation of Citeres's divine nectar, the sorrow of tears is an indispensable ingredient."[35]

Celiana lit another joint. Miguel watched her with sadness. It was one of those losses that, in its triumphant march, love and life toss to the side of the road.

Mérida, July 14, 1919

The End

35. Citeres (also called Cythera) was the birthplace of Aphrodite (Venus). See Hesiod, *Theogony*, in *Hesiod*, trans. Richard Lattimore (Ann Arbor: University of Michigan Press, 1991), lines 199–200.

Social and Biological Reproduction
in Eugenia

In many ways, the social system of free love and the reproductive apparatus Eduardo Urzaiz describes in *Eugenia* allow for significant changes in gender and sexual roles, promoting gender equality and departing radically from gender conventions of the late nineteenth and early twentieth centuries to construct a futuristic utopia.[1] However, in other ways, *Eugenia* relies on traditional stereotypes of males and females and suggests that gendered characteristics of each sex have biological roots, perhaps offering a dystopian warning against taking revolutionary social change too far. One way to make sense of Urzaiz's contradictory postures toward gender roles, sexual behavior, and family structure as they are related to gendered expectations of males and females is to use them as lenses to explore complex Mexican postrevolutionary social, political, and economic reform programs in which Urzaiz was very involved. The Yucatán constituted a vibrant "laboratory of the Revolution," in which revolutionaries tested and adapted national initiatives in hopes of achieving change at the provincial and local level.[2] One important component of such laboratories and their revolutionary work was initiatives intended to modernize gender roles and give women new political and economic opportunities.

This essay examines *Eugenia*'s contradictory claims regarding gender roles against the complex postrevolutionary context in which the novel was written. It begins by reviewing changes in women's legal rights, responsibilities, and status at the federal and Yucatecan level in the years immediately following the Mexican Revolution. It also traces welfare initiatives carried out nationally and in the state of Yucatán, discussing how these, as well as legal changes, strengthened an association between women as mothers and the provision and receipt of welfare services. From here, it turns to a focus on a particularly controversial public health project: a campaign promoting Margaret Sanger's ideas about and specific methods to use birth control. The reaction to birth control, both within Yucatán and beyond, resulted in the celebration of Mother's Day in Mexico, as a way to encourage women to have more, not fewer, children. By examining each of these themes, this essay shows how *Eugenia* engages with local (Yucatecan), national (Mexican), and international ideas about women's legal status; women's social, political, and economic roles, particularly as providers and receivers of welfare services and as mothers; and population loss and growth as connected to political-economic development.

A Gendered Examination
of Mexican Revolutionary Citizenship

Postrevolutionary Mexican reformers were concerned with revising old laws and creating new ones to facilitate progressive social change. Some of these laws had significant repercussions for gender—especially women's—roles in connection with the regulation of family organization and sexual behavior. A major theme driving much of the legal reform that impacted women was the question of how to define and assign the rights and responsibilities of citizenship. The idea of citizenship, especially in postrevolutionary Mexico, is therefore a useful place to begin this discussion of Mexican revolutionary-era changes in gender roles, the construction of families, and sexual relationships as seen in *Eugenia*.

T. H. Marshall provides a useful model for examining differentiations in citizenship rights developed in the context of western, democratic nation-states. He argues that three major types of citizenship rights were granted in different historical epochs. First, civil citizenship rights (such as the right to freely express oneself; to enter contracts, including marriage and work; to acquire and to defend one's property; to pursue an education; and to practice the religion of one's choice) were defined in the eighteenth century, with the appearance of the enlightenment discourses of freedom and the rights of man, and were first enjoyed by men. Second, political rights, most notably the right to vote and to be elected, were granted first to a restricted group of male property owners and/or literate men and later extended to other members of national communities during the nineteenth and twentieth centuries. Third, social (and often economic welfare) rights such as housing and health care, security, and the right to share in one's community's social heritage emerged mostly in the twentieth century.[3] Marshall's scheme corrects the tendency to focus discussions of citizenship on political rights, which, historically, were usually afforded exclusively to men, and in doing so, reveals other kinds of citizenship rights that women have historically possessed, including "the ability to marry, work, own property, and make a will."[4]

Throughout Mexico's nineteenth-century process of state-building (following independence from Spain in 1821), individual and collective understandings of race, class, and gender roles and identities all impacted who was considered a citizen and what roles individuals and groups would play in Mexico's society, economy, and government. For example, one's age, gender, level of education, and status as a landowner or nonlandowner could determine citizenship and civic rights.[5] Consequently, women were often historically denied access to the same rights and benefits of citizenship granted to certain groups of men in constitutional and other kinds of law.

Mexico's historical and contemporary constitutions have used the Spanish word *ciudadanía* to define Mexicans and Mexican citizens and to delineate citizens' rights and responsibilities.[6] The differential treatment of women vs. men as citizens in Mexico was historically encouraged by the fact that definitions of ciudadanía in Mexican constitutions, including that issued in 1917 at the close of the Mexican Revolution, created an ambiguity in reference to the legal status of women. Article 34 of the Constitution of 1917, following the language utilized in the Constitution of 1857, defined citizens of the republic as eighteen-year-old married or twenty-one-year-old unmarried mexican*os* (a term that could refer only to Mexican males or to all Mexicans—Mexican males and females), leaving it unclear whether or not Mexican women (mexican*as*) fell into this category. Because of this ambiguity, individual laws were frequently applied differently to women than to men.

Thus, Mexican constitutional law did not explicitly deny women the right to exercise the obligations, or receive the benefits, of citizenship, including even such political prerogatives as voting and being elected to office. This freedom of interpretation was, however, collapsed by the June 1918 national election law, which stated that all Mexican *men* eighteen years of age if married or twenty-one if single had the right to vote.[7] Consequently, women were not allowed to vote in municipal elections until December 1946, when congress amended article 115 of the Constitution of 1917, or in federal elections until October 1953, when congress approved the modification of article 34.[8]

Such legal changes resulted from a feminist campaign to increase women's political, economic, and social participation in the *cosa pública*, Mexico's public sphere or civil society, which women activists initiated at the 1916–17 constitutional assembly.[9] And yet, even as they campaigned for women's rights between 1916 and 1953, feminists, as well as their opponents, utilized the terms *ciudadanía* and *ciudadana* to refer almost exclusively to women's *political* rights. When discussing women's roles and rights as workers, they did not use the term *ciuda-danía*.[10] And when glorifying women's roles as housewives and mothers, they used the term *ciudadanía* only to refer to a woman's male children.[11] Nonetheless, thanks in part to their organizing, between the end of the revolution in 1917 and 1953, the year that they acquired the right to vote in national elections, Mexican women acquired a new legal status and related public role as ciudadanas, a transformation related to an increase in both the numbers and recognition of women working as wage earners and civic actors.[12] In this process, the term and concept of ciudadanía came to constitute a new aspect of womanhood that coexisted and interacted with an older, private, tacitly recognized role of women citizens as domestic caretakers and creators of male citizens as wives and mothers.[13]

Mexican Women's Civil Rights up to 1917

All Mexican constitutions have defended the quintessential liberal civil rights to freedom of opinion, speech, and print. Many of them have also defended the right to property, security, and education.[14] The Constitution of 1857 was the first to allow some freedom of religion; those preceding it declared Roman Catholicism to be the only legitimate religion in Mexico.[15]

Given constitutional ambiguities in defining a citizen, it is unclear to what degree such rights applied to women. Most likely Mexican civil rights were articulated primarily for men's protection, given that other legislation, particularly that regulating family life, limited women's economic and political participation in the public sphere (where freedom to express one's opinion, defend one's property, and acquire an education were most relevant) according to their marital status. For example, Mexico's first civil codes, written in 1870 and 1884, differentiated women's civil rights based on their marital status, granting single, widowed, and separated women *patria potestad* ("the right to control [their] child[ren] and [their] property, and to use any income from that property for [their] own benefit"[16]), as well as juridical capacity in all but special cases, while restricting *married* women's movement by requiring that they live with their husbands and giving their husbands only patria potestad.[17] Such laws also retained a double standard; married and widowed fathers were entitled to such rights regardless of their behavior, whereas women retained them only if they remained single and avoided scandal.[18] Husbands were also the legitimate administrators of any common property within marriages while wives needed their husbands' permission to appear in court and were required to obey their husbands in the domestic sphere and in the education of their children, in exchange for protection.[19]

Mexico's 1870 and 1884 civil codes not only granted married men more rights than married women but they also instituted vulnerabilities for unmarried women vis-à-vis unmarried men. For example, although the 1870 and 1884 civil codes lowered the age of majority for men and women from twenty-five to twenty-one years, thereby releasing children from their father's patria potestad upon reaching that age, the codes required single women to obtain parental permission to move out of the family home until age thirty in order to guard their reputations.[20] Thus, although daughters could manage property, hold jobs, enter contracts, and marry without paternal permission at age twenty-one, they had to wait until they were thirty to choose their own residences.[21]

Single and married women were also affected by two broader legal processes characterizing nineteenth-century Latin America: the dispossession of land from "corporate" entities such as the Catholic Church and indigenous communities and the secularization of society (as the state took over schools, hospitals, the function of a civil registry, and other institutions traditionally managed by the church). Both initiatives encouraged the rise of private and individualist (as opposed to community or corporate) ownership and legal control and aimed to weaken the church. Yet although both began a process of the state usurping patriarchal authority from families (embodied in husbands and fathers), they did not, generally, empower women.

In Mexico, nineteenth-century laws promoting the rise of privately owned land eliminated an important legal protection that women had enjoyed since colonial times, the right to their share of family property, by "dropp[ing] the requirement that parents with the means to do so endow their daughters" from the 1870 civil code, and "abolish[ing] the *legítima*, . . . the equal share of parental property guaranteed to each child, female and male," from the 1884 code.[22] In addition to weakening women's historic rights to property, secularizing reforms also "tended to reinforce wives' subordination to patriarchal authority" by weakening the church's ability to provide its traditional "protection of sexual equality within marriage."[23] At the same time, secularization encouraged the passage of new laws helping women challenge male violence.[24]

In *Eugenia*, Urzaiz presents a world in which women especially are freed from such sexually differentiated laws because the institution of marriage itself has disintegrated and nuclear families have been replaced by family groups composed of individuals who are drawn to one another through "affinity of character, . . . pleasures, and aspirations."[25] Urzaiz also recognizes the role of a secular state privileging science over religion in transitioning from nuclear families to family groups. He articulates this understanding through Celiana, who, as she writes a lecture on the history of the family, explains that the group arose as "religious prejudices gradually faded and the legal system became simplified."[26]

Urzaiz's model of family groups is related to an interest in "free love," a concept intriguing to thinkers and activists around the world in the 1910s and early 1920s that also helped to stimulate significant changes to civil law and had important effects on women's legal status in Mexico at the end of the revolution. The first revolutionary transformation of Mexican civil legislation that was in accordance with a free-love orientation was President Venustiano Carranza's December 29, 1915, federal decree redefining the term "divorce" from meaning "separation from the home but not the dissolution of marriage" to the "rupture of the marital vow and the abandonment of one's partner, conferring the possibility to form a new union if desired" and laying out legitimate reasons that husbands or wives could initiate dissolution of an unhappy marriage. This legislative act set off a decade-long process of revising national and state divorce and marriage laws revealing concern with the presence of love, happiness, and the fulfillment of appropriate rights and responsibilities on the parts of both partners in a marriage and establishing legal procedures to take action if such components were absent.[27]

State-by-state implementation of divorce and marriage law reform in Mexico began after Carranza issued a second article on January 29, 1915 (exactly one month after the first) that was designed to ensure enactment and enforcement of the new divorce laws. This second article was a "constitutional order mandating that all Mexican Governors modify their respective civil codes to include divorce as part of their state laws" and it resulted in the adoption of these laws by most Mexican states between 1915 and 1917.[28]

Women gained new rights as Carranza incorporated and built further on the new divorce law in the 1917 Ley de Relaciones Familiares (Law of Family Relations), which afforded a woman the possibility of not living with her husband if his living conditions were unhealthy; conferred patria potestad to both parents; made spousal obligations more reciprocal and more empowering to the wife in the domestic sphere by requiring the husband to provide food and meet household costs, and the wife to "take charge of caring for children, the government and direction of the home"; and modified articles relating to marital property, stating that the "woman needs permission from her husband to work, but she is capable of administering her own properties without permission of her husband."[29]

However, although the divorce decrees and Law of Family Relations allowed some advances for women, they did not treat divorced men and women equally. When couples separated, the law called for the wife to be deposited in the house of a decent person if she was the cause of divorce and for measures to be taken to ensure that the man did not harm the woman.[30] Children would be placed in the care of the innocent parent, with the guilty partner recovering rights over children in the event of the innocent partner's death. The mother that conserved patria potestad over her children would lose it if she engaged in prostitution or had an illegitimate child.[31] The father was to continue supporting his ex-wife and children as long as the woman did not cause the divorce, re-marry, or live dishonestly. By contrast, the innocent husband only had a right to financial support when he could not find work and lacked property with which to subsist.[32] Adultery committed by the wife was always grounds for divorce, while it only warranted divorce for a husband if he had committed adultery in the home, kept a mistress, or created public scandal by mistreating and/or permitting his mistress to mistreat his wife.[33] The 1917 law also denied the woman the right to remarry within three hundred days after the separation from her first husband and defined measures to be taken in case the woman was found pregnant.[34]

Such gendered distinctions in the law show that men were assumed to be workers who provided for their families while women were assumed to be stay-at-home wives and mothers supporting their husbands' economic and civic action and their children's development while also depending on their husband for economic resources. The fact that women needed to wait approximately ten months (well beyond the point at which they would typically "show" that they were pregnant) before remarrying after divorce reveals efforts to regulate women's sexuality as well as differential treatment of women as independent juridical and economic actors as compared to men. Presumably, a man was free to remarry even if his recently divorced (ex-)wife carried his unborn child. A woman, on the other hand, had to prove the paternity of her unborn child in order to claim benefits for her child as a dependent of her ex-husband. In order to prove this paternity, a woman would have to be celibate for the three-hundred-day period, effectively remaining faithful to her ex-husband and re-inscribing the legal and financial dependency she had on him as his wife (for now he would provide child support and eventually inheritance for the child as well). This dynamic invokes moral standards and codes from the colonial era, when women's honor was tied to their chastity, in direct contrast to men's honor, which was proven by their ability to keep their word and demonstrate military prowess and virility.[35]

In the state of Yucatán, revolutionary governors embraced and adopted Carranza's reforms in family and divorce law, demonstrating the way that Yuca-tán and other states functioned as laboratories of the national revolution. The

Yucatecan governor Salvador Alvarado (1915–18) legalized divorce by reforming the state civil code on May 26, 1915.[36] In 1918, Alvarado introduced further changes in a new Yucatecan civil code based on Carranza's 1917 Law on Family Relations.[37] Alvarado and other proponents of divorce argued that such laws would help liberate women from economic and moral dependency on men by decreasing the practice of common-law marriage and by giving women a legal outlet to escape unsatisfying marriages or "the condition of slavery" in which many found themselves.[38] They also claimed that divorce would help to ensure that conjugal unions were founded "on mutual esteem and love" rather than status or economic-based interests.[39] As a corollary, "the option to divorce and remarry would improve lower-class morality by encouraging the poor to marry, thus reducing 'to the minimum the illegitimate unions among the popular classes, who form the immense majority of the Mexican nation.'"[40]

Opponents, on the other hand, warned that divorce would encourage free love and polygamy, destroying the traditional home and the family, threatening female honor and challenging parental authority, by leading illegitimate children to choose the parent that suited them best.[41] Feminists generally opposed divorce on the grounds that it would hurt rather than help married women," by encouraging men to abandon their wives for other women.[42] Feminist fears that the law would not protect women were, in fact, confirmed by the law's many double standards, such as the fact that it allowed a man the right to legally separate from his wife if she committed adultery under any circumstances, while making male adultery grounds for divorce only in certain situations, and that it required female divorcées to live honest and honorable lives (free from prostitution or birthing illegitimate children), to maintain patria potestad and custody, and to wait three hundred days until remarrying.

In spite of such critiques, the Yucatecan governor Felipe Carrillo Puerto (1922–24) further liberalized divorce laws, particularly with a March 1923 law granting divorce at the request of only one conjugal partner, with or without the spouse's knowledge or consent.[43] According to Stephanie Smith, this new law reflected Felipe Carrillo Puerto's ideas on free love. Carrillo Puerto, along with some of his collaborators, viewed love as the key to a successful and happy marriage, and divorce as a way out of a loveless marriage. Since marriage was based on mutual love, only one partner needed to fall out of love to justify divorce.[44]

The promulgation of the March 1923 divorce law was one of Carrillo Puerto's most visible "feminist" acts. The governor had an important ally in this and other initiatives aiming to "liberate" women in his sister, Elvia Carrillo Puerto, who helped him establish feminist leagues of resistance throughout the

Yucatán, mobilizing women to bolster state reform projects while being exposed to new political and social mores.[45]

According to Monique Lemaître, Elvia Carrillo Puerto was also a proponent of free love. In 1891, at the age of thirteen, she married. She was widowed at twenty-one.[46] Her first husband and her brother significantly influenced her intellectual and political development, encouraging her to read and discuss feminist and socialist texts, rationalist pedagogy, and history. Her husband also introduced her to birth control through the gift of a pessary.[47] Elvia Carrillo Puerto's marriage was therefore more of a companionate partnership than many other marriages of her era.

After her first husband's death, Carrillo Puerto's feminist career took off. In the 1920s she played a central role in the organizing of Yucatecan feminist leagues and participated in national feminist conferences and the national women's suffrage movement through her membership in major coalition women's organizations.[48]

During these years Elvia also became a passionate advocate for free love. As she explained in 1922, she wanted "women to enjoy the same liberties as men[,] . . . to detach themselves from . . . material, sensual, and animal instincts, to uplift themselves spirituality and intellectually[,] . . . [and to acquire] . . . a more dignified and happier life in an environment of sexual liberty and fraternity."[49] At the 1923 Pan American Women's Conference, she presented controversial arguments favoring the use of contraception and practice of free love. At the same time, at this and the 1925 Congress of Women of the Race, she also argued for the sanctity of the marital contract and claimed that people should marry for love only, not for religious, civil, or economic reasons.[50]

According to Dra. Valdillo, an informant for the anthropologist Robert Redfield, Elvia "lived with men without marrying them or, if she did, it was only by a socialist ceremony . . . in the Casa del Pueblo. . . . She scandalized everybody."[51] This claim is not corroborated by other archival documentation or newspaper commentary, but it suggests that Carrillo Puerto personally demonstrated her beliefs in free love through her second marriage and divorce. She felt no reason to stay in a marriage without love.[52]

Elvia and Felipe Carrillo Puerto's commitment to free love connected them to contemporary free-love advocates in other countries. For example, George Robb argues that turn-of-the-century Great Britain's focus on battling degeneration "as a means of social control and an instrument for enforcing sexual conformity" involved an often overlooked discourse "attribut[ing degeneration] to traditional morality."[53] According to British proponents of free love, the "concern for gentility and delicacy had thwarted the life force among the English middle classes" and if "new" or "super" men and women were to "rescue the British people from degeneration, they had to discard much of their cultural baggage that had retarded racial progress—to this end, a number of people advocated free love over traditional marriage."[54]

The idea that free love would improve the race centered on an old and a new idea about the relationship between sex and reproduction. The old idea was that procreation was the intended and natural result of sex. The sexologist and eugenicist Marie Stopes and the science fiction writer H. G. Wells both drew on this age-old claim, arguing that "every lover desires a child. Those who imagine the contrary . . . know only the lesser types of love" and "physical love without a child is a little weak."[55] The new idea, articulated by doctors, writers, and activists who advocated free love as a means to promote eugenics, was that sexual attraction was nature's way of choosing an ideal mate. Thus, the language of free love connected eugenics to procreation, arguing that free love would result in eugenically superior offspring.

Doctors who drew on such arguments explained that traditional ideas about sexuality and traditional sexual behaviors not only diminished women's sexual pleasure and stifled passion and creativity but could actually result in degenerate offspring. The sexologist Havelock Ellis believed that the cult of female purity "rendered difficult for [woman's] satisfaction of the instinct of courtship, which is the natural preliminary of reproductive activity," and his colleague Marie Stopes claimed there was a direct correlation between sexual pleasure and the quality of one's offspring.[56] The psychologist Stella Browne relatedly argued that "absolute freedom on the choice of woman's part, and intense desire both for her mate and her child, are the magic forces that will vitalize and transfigure the race."[57]

Eugenia follows such logic to an extent, by allowing selected breeders to choose among one another (rather than assigning mates) and by promoting "free love" through the rise of the "group" in place of the nuclear family. Twenty-six years after the publication of *Eugenia*, Urzaiz was still promoting the companionate marriage ideal, which he claimed to be gaining popularity. Writing in the University of Yucatán's journal *Orbe*, Urzaiz argued that the modern marriage must incorporate mutual sexual satisfaction, support in the work of living, and self-growth for both partners. Women, he argued, could expect "economic sustenance, material protection, intellectual direction, and moral support" in return for their understanding maternal instinct, carnal satisfaction of the male libido, and intellectual friendship.[58]

Together, George Robb and Eduardo Urzaiz reveal that the definition of free love in the early twentieth century was open to interpretation. Robb writes that for some, it simply meant the ability to choose one's marital partner, free from family or other constraints, while for others "free love referred to monogamous unions between men and women outside of marriage, based on mutual affection, interests, and sexual compatibility."[59]

Free love appeared "as a social panacea in a number of popular novels that celebrated eugenics and procreation outside of marriage," as well as a subject to explore in journalism and cinema.[60] However, Robb qualifies, such discussions often gave voice to "libidinous, male fantasies of the new woman" and displayed "naïvete about the economic implications of free love and practical responsibilities of child rearing," leading suffragists to claim that some portraits of free love "malign[ed] feminism by associating it with sexual promiscuity."[61]

In 1928, Mexican lawmakers issued a revised federal civil code that reflected some of the demands made by feminists.[62] In reaction to petitions by delegates to the 1923 Pan American Women's Congress, the 1928 civil code removed the articles stipulating that mothers would lose their right to the patria potestad if they behaved immorally and prohibiting women from remarrying for three hundred days after separation from their first spouses.[63] The code also modified articles prescribing support from one divorced party to another and referring to adultery and granted women the right to participate in civil suits, draw up legal contracts, act as guardians, practice law without restriction, leave home at the same age as men, work in jobs or professions of their choice, and administer marital property as long as these acts did not harm the home.[64]

However, not all aspects of the code were changed in response to feminist demands. The code retained the stipulation that a woman be placed in the home of a decent person if she was the cause of divorce and did not implement feminist demands to make the investigation of paternity as rigorously enforced as the investigation of maternity.[65] The retention of such rules reveals the survival of efforts to regulate women's sexuality.

Thus, in 1928, family law as expressed in civil codes continued to differentiate between men and women by explicitly defining male and female roles and rights in the home unequally. This legislation prescribed the home as women's ideal sphere of action and favored a normative social vision of the married family, with a working husband and father providing for his wife and children.

In addition to setting the backdrop for *Eugenia* and characterizing Mexican family (including marriage and divorce) law, conflicting understandings of the meaning of marriage and free love and related double standards in civil codes affected other kinds of civil law. For example, Mexican agrarian law, which defined the civil right to own, develop, and cultivate land, followed the paternalistic tendencies of the civil code and the Law of Family Relations to define women's juridical rights in relation to her civil status. The effects of paternalistic law on women were compounded by an additional legal shift brought by the revolution and marked by the 1917 constitution: the transformation from a core concept of individual rights for citizens to one of rights for the local, state, or national collective (or community of citizens).

Before 1917, Mexican constitutional law utilized the ambiguous category of mexicanos to define who had the right to own Mexican land and treated property primarily as an individual right.[66] In contrast, article 27 of the 1917 constitution defined property as a social resource, thereby demonstrating the revolutionary regime's concern with mediating individual and social or state needs to have access to important resources.[67] Thus, in article 3 of the Ley de Ejidos (Law of Ejidos), President Obregón granted juridical control over land to communities with particular political categories (*pueblos, rancherías,* or *congregaciones*), as well as to individual heads of families. This individual clause was paternalistic, for women only had rights as heads of households in the absence of a husband (that is, if they were "single women or widows that [had] . . . family to tend to").[68]

Thus, in many ways, revolutionary and postrevolutionary civil law continued to differentiate between men and women, either by not mentioning women in legislation defining basic civil rights and liberties, making it unclear whether or not such laws pertained to women, or by explicitly defining male and female roles and rights in and related to administration of the home unequally. In general, postrevolutionary civil law continued the nineteenth-century trend of prescribing the home as women's ideal sphere of action. At the same time, however, twentieth-century legislation began to build a base for a more egalitarian, reciprocal model for domestic relations and for feminist petitions to be received, and when acceptable to legislators, to be met. The 1928 civil code was not significantly modified again until the 1970s.

Mexican Women's Political Rights

The central political prerogative of Mexican citizenship has been the right to vote and to be elected to office, as articulated in Mexican constitutions since 1814.[69] Constitutional law granted suffrage universally to gender-neutral ciudadanos mexicanos who met particular requirements that changed from constitution to constitution (such as earning a minimum income, owning land, and/or being literate).[70] Despite feminist petitions to change constitutional language to explicitly give women citizenship rights, the 1917 constitution continued using the term "mexicanos," thus leaving the article concerning citizenship and suffrage rights open to interpretation until the June 1918 national election law explicitly denied women the right to vote.[71]

Nonetheless, at the time Urzaiz wrote *Eugenia*, Yucatecan governors supported the idea of women voting and women being elected, as is evident in Alvarado's allowing consideration of a resolution for female suffrage to be presented at the 1916 feminist conference he organized, and Carrillo Puerto's nominating women recommended to him by feminist leagues as candidates for his party, resulting in the popular election (by male voters) of four female members of the Feminist League Rita Cetina Gutiérrez to public office in 1922. Urzaiz does not, however, mention any electoral activity in *Eugenia* or indicate whether women hold positions of political authority in Villautopia. This is a notable omission. With the exception of the male head of the Institute of Eugenics, the novel does not introduce readers to any government authorities in Villautopia (the capital of a twenty-third-century Central American subconfederation), and Urzaiz does not explain how authorities are chosen or selected. This is strange, particularly considering the details he provides on Villautopia's socioeconomic and public welfare system.[72] It is also peculiar since a major factor in the outbreak of the Mexican Revolution itself was popular opposition to President Porfirio Díaz's continued occupation of the presidency, which resulted in a commitment on the part of revolutionary activists and leaders to achieve an appropriate balance of socialist and electoral democratic features in Mexico's postrevolutionary political system.

Mexican Women's Social Citizenship Rights

The most significant initiatives to provide Mexican citizens, in general, and women more specifically, with social welfare rights have been inserted into labor legislation. During the first half of the nineteenth century no laws protecting or guaranteeing workers' rights existed. However, in response to the pressures of newly formed workers' unions, the Civil Code of 1870 regulated workers' contracts, and the 1884 code added the regulation of domestic service.[73]

In the twentieth century, beginning with the 1917 constitution, workers' guarantees in Mexican law increased significantly. Article 123 stipulated a maximum workday of eight hours (seven hours for night work) with one day of rest for every six days of work and defended the Mexican worker's right to safe, hygienic work facilities, compensation in the event of on-the-job accidents, and the ability to organize, strike, and bargain.[74] Employers in agricultural, industrial, mining, or other kinds of work located away from towns or cities had to provide "comfortable and healthy housing," schools, and medical services to serve the working community.[75] When this population exceeded two hundred habitants, a space had to be reserved for the establishment of a market, municipal buildings, and centers of recreation. Factory owners employing more than two hundred employees had to provide similar services.[76]

Treatment of women's work in article 123 indicates that labor laws reinforced previously discussed gender ideals shaping civil legislation prescribing men as wage earners and civic actors and women as stay-at-home wives and mothers. Article 123 articulated women's entitlement to wages equal to men's for equal work, but only after referring clearly to the idea of a paternalistic family wage, arguing that "the minimum salary that the worker must enjoy, is that considered sufficient, attending to the conditions of each region, to satisfy the normal needs of life of the worker, his education and honest pleasures, considering him as head of a family.[77] This suggests that men were preferred for employment, but if women were hired, they were entitled to the same wages and conditions as men.

This preference for male employees was reinforced by protective legislation that prevented women and minors from working in unhealthy or dangerous environments and that required employers to provide pregnant women with exemption from demanding physical work for the three months before childbirth; one month of paid leave after childbirth, with conservation of employment; and two extra rest periods during the period of lactation for breastfeeding.[78] In the Yucatán, Governors Alvarado and Carrillo Puerto enforced federal law and added legal reforms aiming to improve the working conditions of female domestic servants.[79]

In addition to freeing women from the double standards of civil law, Villautopia's abolishment of marriage and the nuclear family rejects the prominent social ideal of Urzaiz's time of men as family wage earners and women as angels of the house and grants men and women equal opportunity in various social and economic roles. The reader is introduced to male and female office staff, researchers, and doctors at the Institute of Eugenics; intellectuals, academics, and artists among Celiana, Miguel, and their colleagues and friends; food service and waitstaff; college students; and representatives of a leisure class to which Ernesto belongs. Furthermore, because embryos are removed from their biological mothers soon after conception, transferred to male gestators, and raised in state-run facilities by nannies, there is no need for protective legislation for women.

Despite this radical departure from the actual historical sexual division of labor present when Urzaiz wrote *Eugenia*, Urzaiz retains some early twentieth-century gender stereotypes in Villautopia. He continues to associate femininity and women with parenting and welfare service provision, as is seen in his descriptions of Celiana as highly maternal in nature, which he indicates is a feminine virtue. As he writes, "like almost every other woman of her time who preserved the ancestral instinct of motherhood, Celiana became a teacher . . . satisf[ying] her desire to love children, the weak, and those in need of protection. . . . In centuries past, such a woman would have made an excellent mother."[80]

The director of the Institute of Eugenics, Dr. Remigio Pérez Serrato, also glorifies women's maternal roles, explaining to his African colleagues and Ernesto that maternalism remains a feminine virtue, but that it has been improved through Villautopia's system of selective sterilization. According to him, "since woman was freed from the physiological yoke of gestation . . . her love for children has become more general and less selfish. Those women in whom the instinct of motherhood still thrives find ample room to act on it by caring for and raising small children."[81] Relatedly, in order to effectively carry fetuses transplanted into their intestinal cavities to term, male gestators are injected with hormones that feminize them.[82] Consequently, "during the gestational period all erotic impulses in them disappear and, in time, their effectiveness and their inclinations are definitively altered. They become aficionados of feminine pastimes and occupations," such as playing the piano, chess, or billiards; knitting, crocheting, and sewing; and reading novels and newspapers.[83] Serious reading is, however, prohibited, as extreme intellectualism is undesirable for male and female reproducers and also perhaps viewed as unfeminine, suggested in the fact that Celiana is the only character that Urzaiz points to as sterilized for "excessive intellectual curiosity."[84] *Eugenia* offers no examples of highly intelligent men disqualified from reproducing. On the contrary, the director of the Institute of Eugenics, who is described as highly intelligent, was allowed to reproduce, and one of his daughters ultimately ended up as part of his family group.

In contrast to women's tendency toward maternalism, Pérez Serrato claims that man "has always been, and continues to be, more selfish. Many—if not all—are like a tree that does not know where the wind carries the pollen of its flowers," and, he adds, "men were like this in the past, in those patriarchal times that our sappy moralists and sentimental poets so long for."[85]

Early in his novel, Urzaiz suggests that Celiana and Ernesto conform to such stereotypes. After Ernesto accepts his position as an official reproducer, Celiana resolves to "be the self-sacrificing friend, the loving mother, able to dry away the tears he shed over other women and stop his heart from being hurt."[86]

Ernesto, for his part, "had managed to clearly distinguish between mere carnal possession, instinctive and mechanical," which he would use in taking lovers for the purposes of reproduction, "and the pure and idealistic affection of a heart in love," which he would continue to hold for Celiana.[87] "This is a dualism of subtlety . . . that men have been instituting with ease for years, but that only a few highly superior women have been able to comprehend."[88] However, in the last chapters of *Eugenia* such differences dissolve, as Ernesto abandons Celiana for Eugenia and Celiana increasingly withdraws from her work and society and spends her days escaping into a marijuana-induced haze.

Mexican Postrevolutionary Welfare Institutions

The creation of welfare institutions accompanied the rise of labor legislation. During the nineteenth century, the Catholic Church provided most welfare services, as it had during the colonial era. This changed in the early twentieth century, in response to the revolution's demand for government-supported aid programs. In 1914, Mexico City's Department of Public Welfare created sanitary brigades to treat wounded soldiers and civilians. In 1915, a new Department of Aid built homeless shelters and schools for war orphans. In 1917, the constitution placed all charity and welfare organizations under government control.[89] A wide range of revolutionary reformers, including soldiers, lawyers, doctors, teachers, nurses, social workers, and activists, also joined and/or founded religious and civil organizations fighting prostitution and promoting temperance, public health, and education.

A central postrevolutionary state welfare institution was the Secretaría de Educación Pública (Secretariat of Public Education, SEP), which was created in 1921 and greatly expanded public education from that offered by the Porfirian Secretaría de Instrucción Pública (Secretariat of Public Instruction).[90] The SEP aimed to shape new, revolutionary male and female citizens by teaching them not only traditional subjects such as reading, writing, math, and social studies but also important life skills, appropriate to their sex, such as agriculture and construction, cooking, home economics, and childcare.[91] Public schools were supported by article 3 of the 1917 constitution, which "established that every individual had the right to receive an education" and that "primary and secondary education was to be free, secular, and compulsory."[92] Thus, schools sought to create a "modern Mexican civil society: as the provider of skills, attitudes, linkages, and behaviors that would create citizens who would seek a new pact, a new language, and a new set of political relations," and education constituted a pillar of and metaphor for postrevolutionary reform and state-building projects.[93]

Three years later, the Porfirian Consejo Superior de Salubridad (Health Council) was replaced with the Departamento de Salubridad Pública (Department of Public Health). This new Department oversaw the Hospital General (General Hospital), Hospital Morelos (Morelos Hospital, dedicated to syphilitics), and La Castañeda (mental health hospital).[94] La Castañeda emerged the same year the revolution erupted (1910), replacing the Catholic San Hipólito (Saint Hipolito) and the Divino Salvador (Divine Savior) hospitals, which treated mentally ill men and women, respectively, and its creation represented not only the transition from the church to the state as providers of mental health care but also from "custody and charity to therapy and correction in the history of mental health policy."[95]

Women played important roles in the construction of Mexican welfare institutions, both as welfare providers and recipients. In both capacities, women demonstrated "symbolic and real links between femininity, maternity, welfare provision, and the Mexican state"—connections that were strengthened by politicians' and activists' tendency to use maternalism, a strategic glorification of women's roles as mothers and of maternal characteristics, such as nurture and moral virtue, for political ends, arguing, for example, for increased women's political opportunities and rights, or for women's "qualifications as welfare providers and recipients."[96]

In the late nineteenth century, women emerged as the majority of practitioners in care-giving professions such as schoolteaching and nursing, making them key players in the emergence of the welfare state, and by 1910, they "had created, funded, and administered . . . welfare institutions," dedicated to taking care of orphans and working mothers' children, reforming prostitutes, and teaching women improved hygiene, childcare, and homemaking skills. This work served as a precursor to women's roles during the revolution as "nurses, teachers, and *soldaderas* (female combatants and camp followers)," which positioned them as central players in postrevolutionary campaigns to create new rural schools, spread literacy, improve public health, and provide job training.[97]

One can see the close relationship between women and welfare provision during the revolutionary period in the state of Yucatán. Against the backdrop of the women's conferences, educational and employment opportunities, and legal initiatives patronized by Alvarado and Carrillo Puerto, women's organizations dedicated largely to providing welfare services, particularly to women and children, proliferated during the late teens and early twenties. Thus, while Alvarado was governor, women's organizations fought alcoholism, drug use, and prostitution; set up cooperative kitchens to feed working women and their children; administered milk programs for poor children; promoted literacy; and educated women about home economics and hygiene.[98] It was in this context that Governor Carrillo Puerto, with significant help from his sister, Elvia Carrillo Puerto, established feminist leagues of resistance throughout the Yucatán, which sought to mobilize women to bolster state reform projects and expose them to new political and social mores.[99] By 1923 at least forty-nine feminist leagues existed in the state of Yucatán.[100]

Through such mobilization Alvarado and Carrillo Puerto significantly bolstered the feminist movement in the Yucatán by incorporating it into broader state initiatives. However, they did not create Yucatecan feminism. The Yucatán peninsula produced a vibrant and radical feminist movement that preceded women's organizing in most other parts of Mexico. And it was the women who belonged to organizations such as La Siempreviva who served as *precursoras* and founded a viable base for the feminist state-building initiatives carried out by Alvarado and Carrillo Puerto.[101] These women and others, such as Elvia Carrillo Puerto, familiarized themselves with feminist and other revolutionary ideologies and went on to create new feminist organizations, such as the Liga Feminista Rita Cetina Gutiérrez and the Liga de Resistencia Feminista Obrera (the Feminist Worker League of Resistance).[102] Such feminist organizations advocated for civil, political, and economic legal reforms, and often did so with maternalist strategies, highlighting women's maternal welfare services as evidence of their ability to benefit their communities through wage labor and civic and political action. Although this strategy was often successful—most notably when women used it to secure the right to vote in municipal elections in 1946 and national ones in 1953—it also reinforced conventional stereotypes of women as mothers and wives, and as suitable for "feminine" professions such as teaching, nursing, and welfare services.[103]

All forms of Mexican citizenship rights—civil, political, and social—suggest that Mexican postrevolutionary law generally conferred the rights and privileges of citizenship (including the civil rights to marry and divorce, decide whether and when to have children, provide legal guardianship to one's children, and inherit and bequeath property from one's ancestors and to one's descendants and heirs; political rights such as voting and being elected; and economic rights to work, earn a wage, and own property) to men universally, while prescribing and limiting access for women to such legal prerogatives according to their civil (marital) status.

Along these lines, Gabriela Cano and Elizabeth Dore point to ways that Mexico's 1917 constitution demonstrates Carole Pateman's argument that the

Enlightenment's social contract, which formed the basis of modern democratic civil societies and assumed the existence of a universal fraternal citizenship that granted universal rights and freedoms, was predicated on a sexual contract, in which women became subordinate to men when they entered into the civil contract of marriage.[104] One indication of the existence of a sexual contract in revolutionary Mexican legislation is that the Constitution of 1917, following the language utilized in the Constitution of 1857, allowed a man to become a citizen at a younger age if he was married than if he was single.[105] In this way, the Mexican 1917 constitution accelerated a man's acquisition of a superior civil status when he claimed a wife as a dependent.[106]

One way to reconcile some postrevolutionary leaders' support of feminist proposals and legal initiatives to grant women more rights and challenge legacies such as the sexual contract is found in Gabriela Cano's suggestion that some postrevolutionary leaders were receptive to feminism in part because they viewed it as a way to combat the church's influence, a goal that the postrevolutionary state embraced with more force than the Porfirian one.[107] The 1917 constitution prohibited the existence of religious primary schools and welfare institutions, claimed the right to seize and nationalize church property, called for the state regulation of the amount of practicing clergy and churches in the Mexican republic, and denied the church juridical status.[108] The 1917 constitution was also the first to defend freedom of religion in Mexico, ending the practice of declaring Roman Catholicism the only true or official Mexican religion.[109]

Urzaiz, the Yucatecan Birth Control Campaign, and the Introduction of Mother's Day to Mexico

Urzaiz played an important role in several initiatives addressing inequalities related to gender, class, and racial difference, all of which were integral components of the Yucatán's revolutionary program. As a teacher, practicing doctor, educational and medical administrator, artist, and scholar, Urzaiz worked with Alvarado, Carrillo Puerto, feminist activists, and other postrevolutionary reformers and had a direct impact on educational and medical campaigns—whether to increase Mexican literacy rates, improve hygiene, or teach women skills to help them earn money to support their families.

Significantly, evidence suggests that Urzaiz participated in what was probably the most controversial initiative of the feminist leagues sanctioned by Governor Carrillo Puerto: the promotion of birth control through articles in socialist party periodicals, speeches on the subject at socialist assemblies, and the printing and distribution of at least five thousand copies of Margaret Sanger's pamphlet "The Regulation of Natality or the Compass of the Home: Sure and Scientific Means to Avoid Conception" to adult members of leagues of resistance and newly married couples via the civil registry.[110] According to Anne Kennedy, executive secretary of the American Birth Control League, who visited the Yucatán in 1923 as a representative of Margaret Sanger, the Yucatecan government planned for further dissemination of contraceptive information and materials.[111] Kennedy announced plans to establish two clinics in Mérida to aid women in the use of contraception: one in the Hospital for Women and Children and another in the red-light district to service prostitutes.[112] Kennedy also reported that Dr. Urzaiz gave lectures on birth control in his medical classes, encouraging new doctors to inform women about contraception.[113] *Eugenia* further demonstrates Urzaiz's interest in such issues.

Urzaiz's and other Yucatecans' interest in and efforts to promote birth control drew attention far beyond the Yucatán, generating a national debate in Mexico involving highly sensitive issues of race and class and linking to international eugenic discourses. Sanger's pamphlet (which constituted the main piece of propaganda used in the Yucatecan birth control campaign) explicitly called for the state regulation of births "to preven[t] having children born to degenerate or sick parents" and explained that this system would also lift economic pressure from poor families burdened with too many offspring.[114] Such poor families in the Yucatán tended to be indigenous and darker skinned than the whiter, wealthier, and more educated activists who encouraged them to use birth control and limit their reproduction. Thus, the Yucatecan birth control campaign constituted an effort by one particular racial/ethnic class or sector of society to limit reproduction by another.

Yucatán's conservative Catholic newspaper, *La Revista de Yucatán*, voiced the opposition of various individuals and groups to Sanger's pamphlet and the birth control campaign itself, although they did not question the classist and racist tendencies of the Yucatecan birth control campaign.[115] Such critics included conservative organizations, which not surprisingly found Sanger's pamphlet offensive;[116] known members or collaborators of the socialist regime;[117] "members of the Liga Feminista 'Rita Cetina Gutiérrez,'" who appeared in the offices of the *Revista* to complain about a league meeting in which some members advocated the publication and distribution of Sanger's pamphlet;[118] and two large groups of Yucatecans: more than six hundred Yucatecans presenting a petition to the state's Procuraduría de Justicia (Office of the Attorney General), arguing that the ideas expressed in Sanger's pamphlet violated the laws of nature and the state penal code; and a group of hundreds of women forwarding a petition urging public schoolteachers and mothers to fulfill their duties of defending the honor and glory of the Yucatecan and Mexican home by ignoring the pamphlet.[119]

In these articles, the *Revista* used two main tactics to attack the birth control campaign. First, in articles by civic groups opposing the state government, and even more significantly in complaints from collaborators of the socialist regime, it suggested that the socialist administration's hold on political power in the state was tenuous and limited by internal fissures. Second, the *Revista* played on the fears of Yucatecan society that the birth control campaign, like revolutionary programs in general, would result in the loss of tradition, stability, and morality. In several of its articles alluding to birth control, the *Revista* criticized socialist education and alluded to a link between socialist schools and the dissemination of Sanger's pamphlet, thereby propagating a rumor that the government was directing propaganda about birth control at schoolchildren, which, although false, fueled the reactionary fever.[120]

The *Revista*'s attack on birth control formed part of its consistent critique of Yucatán's socialist state administration. The *Revista* constituted the primary opposition voice in the state during this period, often upholding the points of view of interest groups who found their power challenged by revolutionary administrations—especially the church and landowners. It was sophisticated in this criticism; the *Revista* was an exemplary newspaper for its time, using state-of-the-art equipment and a quantity and quality of reporting uncommon in Mexico at large.[121] It preceded the two great daily national newspapers of its era, *El Universal* and *Excelsior*, and was the second in a string of newspapers run by the prominent political critic and newspaperman Carlos Menéndez.[122]

In addition to its treatment of the birth control campaign within the context of regional politics, the *Revista* linked questions of family planning to national and global trends. These links are most apparent in the *Revista*'s use of pronatal-ist (pro-reproductive) ideology and its cooperation with the national newspaper *Excelsior* in a campaign promoting Mother's Day in Mexico.

Pronatalist rhetoric had been popular in Mexico and beyond during the nineteenth century, and its resurgence in the interwar era has been documented throughout the western world. In Europe and the United States, pronatalist arguments responded to death caused by World War I.[123] In Mexico, pronatalism was inspired by this global discourse, as well as by the Mexican Revolution. At the end of the war, Mexicans shared a general perception of a legacy of destruction and the need for reconstruction. Integral to this worldview was a sense of population decline, which was not imaginary. During the nineteenth century, Mexico's population grew steadily, booming during the prosperity of the Porfiriato. The revolution, however, brought about a significant rupture in this growth. Conservative estimates suggest that between 1910 and 1921 Mexico's population dropped from fifteen to fourteen million people.[124] This loss had a profound effect on the Mexican people, leading some to respond with calls for increased natality to replenish the dwindling population.[125]

Several articles printed by the *Revista* during this period warned against falling birth rates and favored pronatalist policies, making direct allusions to the Yucatecan birth control campaign. On March 19, 1922, the *Revista* discussed France's awarding of prizes of 25,000 francs to the parents of two large families, with twenty-two and nineteen children, respectively. The Yucatecan newspaper explained that "this information which we take from the *New York Times* could not be more suggestive, and contrasts with the propaganda being realized actually in Yucatán."[126] With the same goals, on April 4 the newspaper reported that in the month of March, Mexico City witnessed 609 births and 1,615 deaths. It lamented that "despite this . . . [the Italian labor activist] León Marvini just left for Mexico, bringing a large quantity of [Sanger's] obscene pamphlets, which provide the means to restrict natality."[127]

The national newspaper *Excelsior* echoed the *Revista*'s protests against birth control, as well as its pronatalist orientation. It reported that many Yucatecan mothers organized protests in the streets and "invaded schools begging professors not to distribute the immoral pamphlets."[128] Soon, *Excelsior* went beyond mere criticism and launched a campaign to establish Mother's Day in Mexico, to counter the socialist and feminist tendencies of Yucatán.[129] *Excelsior* publicized its idea, announcing that the tenth of May "be consecrated, in a special manner, to render an homage of affection and respect to the mother. . . . Today, in the southeastern extreme of the country, a suicidal and criminal campaign against maternity has been developed. While in Yucatán official elements have not hesitated in launching a grotesque propaganda, denigrating the highest function of woman, it is essential that the entire society manifest . . . that in no way have we arrived at such an aberration as that which extreme rationalists preach."[130]

Excelsior suggested that Mother's Day was part of an international pronatalist discourse, reporting that "since the end of the Great War, Mother's Day has been given more consideration and attention than prior to the struggle." Mexico should follow the examples of Europeans, Asians, and other Americans in devoting one day of the year to mothers.[131] *Excelsior* propagandized Mother's Day in articles speaking positively of the initiative, in challenges to its readership to participate in the homage, and in the publication of letters of support from individuals and groups.[132]

The *Revista* supported *Excelsior*'s Mother's Day project, reporting that *Excelsior* was "disseminating a noble idea: to celebrate Mother's Day; . . . to glorify the Mexican mother. . . . The thinking suggested by this . . . could seem small. . . . However, it is grand. . . . It must be considered transcendental. Because it is a moral example. Because it indicates a tendency of human elevation."[133]

Urzaiz's awareness of depopulation concerns and his willingness to advocate birth control in such a climate are clear in his advocacy in *Eugenia* of male pregnancy as the solution to "the necessity to rapidly repopulate the land" "in light of growing Malthusianism on the part of men and *tocofobia* [the fear of childbirth] on the part of women."[134] It is very interesting that Urzaiz refers to Malthusianism as a historical phenomenon (an event that occurred at a particular time, rather than a theory to explain population trends), since, at the time Urzaiz wrote *Eugenia*, Mexicans—including Yucatecans—were arguing over Malthusian theories in the context of significant depopulation resulting from the Mexican Revolution. Thus Urzaiz, like Sanger, favors encouraging certain less desirable parents (at least less desirable parents of multiple offspring) to limit reproduction with birth control, while encouraging more suitable potential parents to reproduce.

Conclusion

One of Urzaiz's interests and concerns in every aspect of his work—as a teacher, doctor, and writer—was to examine, question, and, if he deemed it appropriate, work to change women's roles, presumably in order to improve women's lives and increase their status. Urzaiz was an advocate for girls' and women's education and for women's health and birth control options. Through such work he participated in many revolutionary projects that questioned the status quo, something *Eugenia* also does. However, it is more debatable whether Urzaiz (or his revolutionary allies) ultimately succeeded in significantly changing current gender and family structures and ideologies, and if so, if these changes gave women new opportunities and improved women's—and men's—lives for the better. As this chapter has shown, revolutionary and postrevolutionary Mexican legislation, at the national and state levels, tended to be cast in a paternalistic framework, treating women of certain stature (married and/or mothers) as dependents in need of protection. This tendency to associate women with motherhood and caring professions (teaching, nursing, social work, etc.) was also evident in women's roles in new welfare institutions created at the national and state level.

Similarly, although Urzaiz and others introduced birth control, a technology that offered women the possibility of choosing not to be mothers, to Mexico, they marketed it through government propaganda that targeted certain groups, rather than promoting contraception as a tool for any woman to choose to use (or not). Some Mexicans went even further in disempowering women regarding birth control: opponents to birth control decided that it should not be left up to women to make this choice at all; Mexico was not in a position to be encouraging anyone to limit reproduction and they instead favored an initiative to glorify motherhood, the celebration of Mother's Day.

Thus, the entire social apparatus that surrounded Urzaiz (laws, welfare institutions, medical and family planning information and services, social mores, and popular culture) cast women primarily as mothers and/or caregivers. In addition, Urzaiz had a loving, stay-at-home wife who kept a busy household comprised of fourteen children, extended family, and, at times, even friends, running smoothly. Authors of biographical sketches of Urzaiz consistently describe him as a lover of humanity who was dedicated to bettering the lives of his students, his patients, women, and anyone he encountered. Doña Candelaria Souza de Fernández, who considered Urzaiz a mentor and dear friend, went so far as to describe Urzaiz as "un grán feminista" (a great feminist).[135] Yet it is important to acknowledge the fact that Urzaiz's great generosity and his ability to work on behalf of women and others would have been challenging if not impossible without the support of his wife, who was able to make his house more than a "bourgeois residence to which any professional of his stature would have felt entitled, but an open home that embraced in its warmth more than a few refugees" alongside their fourteen children," precisely because she did not develop a career.[136] Urzaiz's wife's dedication to supporting her husband and family is illustrated in two episodes in which she dedicated herself to taking care of Urzaiz. These two events in Urzaiz's life are both described in Carlos Urzaiz Jiménez's biography, and are the passages in the book in which his mother receives the most attention. First, in 1920, when Urzaiz had to have his eye removed after he acquired an ocular infection, his wife arranged to have Urzaiz's brother (Carlos's uncle) live with them to help keep the extremely busy and full household routine running smoothly while he recovered.[137] According to Carlos, at this time (one year after the publication of *Eugenia*), at least twelve of Urzaiz's fourteen children had been born. Urzaiz would have been forty-three or forty-four. Similarly, when a much older Urzaiz (seventy-six) suffered a heart attack in February 1953 while he was in Mexico City on business, Doña Rosita "flew to his side" and spent three months with him in the National Institute of Cardiology trying to lift his spirits (which were uncharacteristically low) until she could bring him home to Mérida.[138]

Thus, Carlos Urzaiz Jiménez describes Doña Rosita Jiménez as a strong and capable wife and mother, but he only mentions her a few times in the biography he dedicates to her husband, and every time she is only brought up in the context of her caregiving roles as a wife and mother. In fact, Urzaiz Jiménez never explains how Urzaiz met his wife or how long they courted before marrying. Given *Eugenia*'s exploration of free love and Urzaiz's reputation as a feminist, more information would be helpful.

Eugenia itself illustrates the limitations of Urzaiz's imagination regarding gender roles. Although *Eugenia* offers equal opportunity to men and women in a range of professions, eliminates the need for protective labor legislation related to women's reproductive roles as mothers, and rejects early twentieth-century social ideals of men as family wage earners and women as angels of the house characterizing the era in which the novel was written, the novel preserves some core, conventional gender stereotypes. For example, Urzaiz suggests that Villautopian women are particularly suited toward parental and maternal work such as teaching, childcare, and welfare services, while men have a stronger sex drive than women and find it easier to separate the act of sex from the emotional attachment of love. In explaining that Celiana was sterilized partly because of her excessive intelligence, he suggests that men are naturally more intellectual and removed (and less parental), whereas intelligence in a woman could have a negative effect on her reproductive capabilities. One likely explanation for Urzaiz's inability to escape gender stereotypes and the contradictions this poses in gender representations in *Eugenia* is that Urzaiz's vision was limited by the boundaries of scientific (including biological and eugenic) and social scientific (including sociological and psychological) knowledge achieved and theories formulated in 1919. Perhaps it was not possible for Urzaiz to imagine a more progressive world than the one he described in *Eugenia*. Another possibility is that Urzaiz is cautioning against overly zealous, revolutionary change—pointing to the dystopian aspects of his novel.

NOTES

1. Nineteenth-century middle-class gender roles throughout the western world centered on the doctrine of separate spheres, which prescribed woman's proper role as an "angel of the house" who would make the home a peaceful haven from the fast-paced, competitive atmosphere of the shop, office, and street, where men dominated in activities of economic and political exchange as well as sexual pursuit. For an introduction to the Victorian doctrine of separate spheres and cult of true womanhood as historical and historiographical constructs, see Barbara Welter, "The Cult of True

Womanhood: 1820–1860," *American Quarterly* 18 (1966): 151–74, and Linda K. Kerber, "Separate Spheres, Female Worlds, Woman's Place: The Rhetoric of Women's History," *The Journal of American History* 75, no. 1 (1988): 9–40. For an excellent article on the manifestation of this model in late nineteenth-century Mexico, see William French, "Prostitutes and Guardian Angels: Women, Work, and the Family in Porfirian Mexico," *Hispanic American Historical Review* 72, no. 4 (1992): 529–53.

2. See Benjamin and Wasserman, *Provinces of the Revolution*, for a broad discussion and several examples of provincial Mexican revolutionary laboratories. See Joseph, *Revolution from Without*, for the application of this framework to Yucatán.

3. T. H. Marshall, *Citizenship and Social Class and Other Essays* (Cambridge: Cambridge University Press, 1950), 11. Marshall's scheme is helpful because of its delineation of different kinds of citizenship rights, especially the social category of citizenship. It has, however, been justly criticized for its anglo- and male-centrism. For critiques, see Will Kymlicka and Wayne Norman, "Return of the Citizen: A Survey of Recent Work on Citizenship Theory," *Ethics* 104 (1994): 352–81; Louise A. Tilly, "Women, Work, and Citizenship," *International Labor and Working Class History* 52 (1997): 2; and Ana Shola Orloff, "Gender and the Social Rights of Citizenship: The Comparative Analysis of Gender Relations and the Welfare States," *American Sociological Review* 58 (1993): 309. For further theorizing on the problems of women's citizenship, see also Flora Anthias and Nira Yuval-Davis, *Women, Nation and State* (New York: St. Martin's Press, 1989); Sarah Radcliffe and Sallie Westwood, eds., *Remaking the Nation: Place, Identity and Politics in Latin America* (New York: Routledge, 1996); and Chandra Talpade Mohanty, Ann Russo, and Lourdes Torres, eds., *Third World Women and the Politics of Feminism* (Bloomington: Indiana University Press, 1992).

4. Donna Guy, "White Slavery, Citizenship and Nationality in Argentina," in *Nationalisms and Sexualities*, ed. Andrew Parker, Mary Russo, Doris Sommer, and Patricia Yaeger (New York: Routledge Press, 1992), 205.

5. For example, the Siete Leyes of 1836 and Bases Orgánicas of 1843 required a Mexican to earn a minimum income in order to be considered a citizen, participate in elections, and have the right to be elected to office (see arts. 7–8 [p. 96] and 18–20 [p. 129], respectively, in H. Congreso de la Unión, *Las constituciones de México, 1814–1989* [Mexico City: Comité de Asuntos Editoriales, 1989]). The Bases de Organización Política de la República Mexicana of 1834 also stipulated that after 1850 citizens would have to be able to read and write to exercise their political rights (art. 18, p. 129).

6. *Ciudadanía*, which translates to English as "citizenship," originates in the Latin *civitis*, a generic quality of Roman citizens, understood as those pertaining to a social, politically structured group defined by what is today called sovereign. See "Ciudadanía," in Instituto de Investigaciónes Jurídicas, *Diccionario Jurídico Mexicano*, 4th ed. (Mexico City: Editorial Porrúa, 1991), 469. The first liberal constitution applied to Mexico was the Spanish Constitución of Cádiz, drawn up in 1812, as part of a movement to unite the various kingships of Spain against the Bonapartes. This constitution included three articles articulating equal rights among Indian, African, peninsular, and

creole Spaniards in Spain and in Spanish colonial territories, thus identifying and promoting a notion of common citizenship for all kingdoms of the Spanish empire. See "Ciudadanía," in *Diccionario Electoral* (Costa Rica: CAPEL, Instituto Interamericano de Derechos Humanos, 1989), 111.

The Mexican Constitución de Apatzingán (1814), inspired by the independence hero José María Morelos, utilized the term *ciudadano* frequently to refer to civil and political rights and to the purpose of the state. This constitution defined citizens of America as those born in America (chap. III, art. 13, p. 46, in H. Congreso de la Unión, *Las constituciones de México*), and in various articles it explained that the purpose of the state and its laws were to be applied equally to and in benefit of all citizens (chap. IV, arts. 19, 21; chap. V, arts. 24, 25, 27, 28, 30, 32, and 37, pp. 46–47).

The federal Constitución de 1824 did not address themes of membership of a state or citizenship, but the Constitución [de Siete Leyes] de 1836 defined citizens as Mexicans by virtue of being born in Mexico, born to a Mexican parent (*padre*, which could also mean father only), or by naturalization, who earned an annual income of at least one hundred pesos from honorable and honest work, industry, or capital acquisition or acquired a special certificate (*carta*) of citizenship (art. 7, p. 96). Likewise, the Bases Orgánicas de la Republica Mexicana (1843) defined citizens as Mexicans who had completed eighteen years of age and were married, or twenty-one without being married, and had an annual income of at least two hundred pesos earned from honest physical capital, industry, or personal work. Furthermore, from the year 1850 on, in addition to having the required minimum income, those arriving at the age of citizenship would also need to know how to read and write in order to exercise their political rights (art. 18, p. 129).

The Constitución de 1857 provided close to the original text of the law found in the Constitución de 1917 (whose reforms provide current legislation), defining Mexicans as those who were born within or outside the Mexican republic to Mexican parents, were foreigners who had become naturalized, or were foreigners who had acquired real estate in the Mexican republic or had Mexican children (title I, sec. II, art. 30, p. 162), and defining citizens as Mexicans who had completed eighteen years of age if married or twenty-one if not, and had an honest way of life (title I, sec. IV, art. 34, p. 162). The Constitución de 1857 also stated that Mexicans had the obligation of defending the independence, territory, honor, rights, and interests of the nation and contributing to public expenses (title I, sec. II, art. 31, p. 162). In exchange, they received preference over foreigners for all jobs and positions of authority (title I, sec. II, art. 32, p. 162). Citizens, likewise, were responsible for voting in popular elections, being elected to political positions, jobs, or commissions for which they had the qualities that the law established, participating in political affairs, taking up arms in the army or national guard for the defense of the republic and its institutions, and exercising all classes of business and rights of petition (title I, sec. IV, arts. 35–37, pp. 162–63).

The Constitución de 1917 defined as Mexicans those persons born inside or outside Mexico to Mexican parents, naturalized foreigners, and foreigners with Mexican children who had not expressed a desire to maintain their former nationality (title I, chap. II, art. 30, p. 186). Obligations of Mexicans were to make sure any children or minors under fifteen years of age for whom they were responsible attended public or private school; to acquire civic and military instruction so that they could aptly exercise the rights of citizenship; to enlist and serve in the national guard in order to defend the independence, territory, honor, rights, and interests of the country; and to contribute to public expenses. In exchange, Mexicans received the right to preference for jobs and positions of public authority (title I, chap. II, arts. 31 and 32, pp. 186–87). The prerogatives and responsibilities of citizenship included voting in popular elections, being elected to positions of popular election or named to any other position or commission when having the qualities established by the law, being involved in political affairs, taking up arms in the army or national guard for the defense of the republic and its institutions, exercising all classes of business and the rights of petition, and inscribing oneself in the civil registry (title I, chap. IV, arts. 35 and 36, p. 187).

7. Ward Morton, *Woman Suffrage in Mexico* (Gainesville: University of Florida Press, 1962), 9.

8. "Para la mujer votar y ser votada a cargos municipales," *El Nacional*, December 6, 1946; "Deben votar las mujeres," *El Nacional*, December 7, 1946; "Voto municipal para las mujeres mexicanas," *El Nacional*, December 9, 1946; "El voto femenino se aprobó en el Senado," *El Nacional*, December 11, 1946; "Se aprobó el voto de la mujer," *El Nacional*, December 24, 1946; "Triunfo de la mujer mexicana," *El Nacional*, December 26, 1946; *Diario Oficial, Organo del Gobierno Constitucional de los Estados Unidos Mexicanos*, July 17, 1947; *El Nacional*, October 7, 1953, 8; *Excelsior*, October 7, 1953, 1; *Novedades*, October 7, 1953, 1; and *Diario Oficial, Organo del Gobierno Constitucional de los Estados Unidos Mexicanos*, October 17, 1953.

9. Chris Boyer originally suggested translating *cosa pública* as "civil society" at a LASA meeting in 2000. I am grateful for his insights. I follow John Ehrenberg in defining civil society as a sphere or set of "social relations and structures" that is separate from, yet connected to, the "political and administrative mechanisms of the state and the state-regulated part of the economy" (John Ehrenberg, *Civil Society: The Critical History of an Idea* [New York: New York University Press, 1999], 235). Civil society, for Ehrenberg and others, is comprised of social institutions and organizations that allow citizens to lobby for their interests to be met and that compensate for deficiencies in political and economic policy. Such institutions and organizations include churches, families, labor unions, ethnic associations, economic and political cooperatives, environmental groups, neighborhood associations, women's organizations, and charities (Kymlicka and Norman, "Return of the Citizen," 363). Mexico's 1916–17 constitutional assembly marked the official closure of the military phase of the revolution and the initiation of the post-revolutionary period and consolidation of the revolutionary regime.

10. For example, article 123 of the 1917 constitution, the 1931 Ley Federal de Trabajo, and the 1943 Ley Del Seguro Social do not use the term *ciudadanía*.

11. Gabriela Cano explains that a key argument made against women's suffrage at the 1916–17 constitutional convention was that women's differences from men relegated them to an enclosed private sphere, separate from the public sphere in which political activity occurred. The only appropriate way for women to participate in politics was by influencing their fathers, husbands, and brothers. See Gabriela Cano, "Las feministas en campaña: La primera mitad del Siglo XX," *Debate Feminista* 2, no. 4 (1991): 277.

12. See chapter 5, "Producers or Consumers: Female Wage Labor, Household Management, and the Mexican Miracle," in Buck, "Activists and Mothers," for examination and documentation of such trends.

13. See Buck, "Activists and Mothers," for a much broader discussion of this process.

14. The Cádiz Constitution of 1812 defended the right to freedom of speech and print in article 371 (title IX, chap. I, p. 433, in H. Congreso de la Unión, *Las constituciones de México*).

The Constitution of Apatzingán in 1814 defended the freedom of speech and press in article 40 (title I, chap. V, p. 47); equality, security, property, and freedom in article 24 (title I, chap. V, p. 46); the right to work in article 38 (title I, chap. VI, p. 46); and the right to education in article 39 (title I, chap. VI, p. 47). The Constitution of 1857 articulated freedom of expression, writing, publishing, and petition (title I, sec. I, arts. 6–8, pp. 159–60).

15. Title II, chap. II in the 1812 Constitution of Cádiz, p. 404, in H. Congreso de la Unión, *Las constituciones de México*; art. 1 of the 1814 constitution, chap. I, p. 45; and art. 3 of the 1824 constitution, title I, p. 75.

16. Silvia M. Arrom, "Changes in Mexican Family Law in the Nineteenth Century: The Civil Codes of 1870 and 1884," *Journal of Family History* 10, no. 3 (September 1985): 308.

17. Kathryn Sloan explains that Mexico's first national civil code was actually the civil code for the federal district (Mexico City) and the state of Baja California. This was first issued in 1870 and was revised in 1884. See Kathryn Sloan, "Defiant Daughters and the Emancipation of Minors in Nineteenth-Century Mexico," in *Girlhood: A Global History*, ed. Jennifer Hengren and Colleen A. Vasconcellos (New Brunswick, NJ: Rutgers University Press, 2010), 366. On the differentiation of women's civil rights in relation to their marital status, see Dr. Rafael Rojina Villegas, "Capacidad de la mujer en el derecho civil y condición juridical de la mujer Mexicana," in *La situación jurídica de la mujer mexicana*, ed. Alianza de Mujeres de México (Mexico City: Alianza de Mujeres de México, 1953), 14. On patria potestad, see Arrom, "Changes in Mexican Family Law," which cites arts. 268–71 and 391–92 of the 1870 code and arts. 245–49 and 365–66 of the 1884 code to illustrate these distinctions between male and female rights to the patria potestad (308). On the restriction of women's movement, see arts. 32, 199, and 204 of the 1870 civil code (*Código Civil del Distrito Federal y Territorio de Baja California, con su parte expositiva e indices respetivos*, new ed. [Mexico City: Imprenta Comercio de Dublan y Chavez, 1878], 6 and 24, respectively), and arts. 32 and 195 of the 1884 civil code (*Código*

Civil del Distrito Federal y Territorios de Tepic y Baja California Promulgado en 31 de marzo de 1884,
ed. Antonio de J. Lozano, annotated ed. [Mexico City: Librería de la Vda. de C. Bouret,
1902], 24 and 59, respectively).

18. Arrom, "Changes in Mexican Family Law," 308–9.

19. Regarding marital property, see art. 205 of the 1870 civil code (*Código Civil* 1902,
p. 59) and art. 196 of the 1884 code (*Código Civil* 1878, p. 59). On women's court appearances, see arts. 206 and 207 of the 1870 civil code (*Código Civil* 1878, p. 24) and arts. 197
and 198 of the 1884 civil code (*Código Civil* 1878, p. 59–60). Both codes did, however, add
articles granting a judicial authority the right to authorize the wife's participation if,
according to both codes, the husband was present but unjustly refused to grant his wife
permission to be involved in litigation. The 1884 civil code also allowed for this if the
husband was absent from the home (art. 209, *Código Civil* 1878, p. 25, and arts. 200–201,
Código Civil 1902, p. 60). Regarding the requirement of wives' obedience to their husbands,
see art. 201 of the 1870 civil code (*Código Civil* 1878, p. 24) and art. 192 of the 1884 civil
code (*Código Civil* 1902, p. 59).

20. Arrom, "Changes in Mexican Family Law," 307. Arrom cites arts. 415 and 464
of the 1870 code and arts. 388 and 596 of the 1884 code.

21. Arrom, "Changes in Mexican Family Law," 308. Arrom cites art. 695 of the
1870 code and art. 597 of the 1884 code for stipulations regarding daughters' residences.

22. Arrom, "Changes in Mexican Family Law," 313.

23. Elizabeth Dore "One Step Forward, Two Steps Back: Gender and the State in
the Long Nineteenth Century," in *Hidden Histories of Gender and the State in Latin America*,
ed. Elizabeth Dore and Maxine Molyneux (Durham, NC: Duke University Press, 2000),
17. Such changes are evident in Mexico's 1870 and 1884 civil codes; see Arrom,
"Changes in Mexican Family Law," and Ana María Alonso, "Rationalizing Patriarchy:
Gender, Domestic Violence, and Law in Mexico," *Identities: Global Studies in Culture and
Power* 2, nos. 1–2 (September 1995): 29–47.

24. Dore, "One Step Forward, Two Steps Back," 17. See also Arrom, "Changes in
Mexican Family Law," and Alonso, "Rationalizing Patriarchy."

25. Urzaiz, *Eugenia*, 13.

26. Ibid.

27. Carranza's "Ley Sobre el Divorcio," issued on December 29, 1914, was published
on January 2, 1915, in the newspaper *El Constitucionalista* (Veracruz, Veracruz). The full
text of the law can also be found in Eduardo Pallares, ed., *Leyes complementarias del* Código
Civil (Mexico City: Herrero Hermanos Sucessores, 1920), 412–16. See arts. 239 and 240
of the 1870 and 1884 civil codes for the original legal definitions of divorce that Carranza's
law changed. For further discussion, see Ann S. Blum, *Domestic Economies: Family, Work,
and Welfare in Mexico City, 1884–1943* (Lincoln: University of Nebraska Press, 2009), 105;
Manuel F. Chávez Asencio, *La familia en el derecho*, vol. 2, *Relaciones jurídicas conyugales*,
4th ed. (Mexico City: Editorial Porrúa, 1997), 444; Anna Macías, "Felipe Carrillo Puerto
and Women's Liberation in Mexico," in *Latin American Women: Historical Perspectives*,
ed. Asunción Lavrin (Westport, CT: Greenwood Press, 1978), 293; Stephanie J. Smith,

Gender and the Mexican Revolution: Yucatán Women and the Realities of Patriarchy (Chapel Hill: University of North Carolina Press, 2009), 123–24; Lionel M. Summers, "The Divorce Laws of Mexico," *Law and Contemporary Problems* (1935): 311; and Rafael Rojina Villegas, *Compendio de derecho civil*, 7th ed., vol. 1, *Introducción, personas y familia* (Mexico City: Editorial Porrúa, 1997), 376, cited in Smith, *Gender and the Mexican Revolution*, 207n26.

28. Summers, "The Divorce Laws of Mexico," 311; Manuel F. Chávez Asencio, *La familia en el derecho*, 4th ed., vol. 2, *Relaciones jurídicas conyugales* (Mexico City: Editorial Porrúa, 1997), 444, cited in Smith, *Gender and the Mexican Revolution*, 124 and 207n27.

29. On living conditions, see Secretario del Estado, *Ley sobre relaciones familiares expedida por el C. Venustiano Carranza* (Mexico City: Imprenta del Gobierno, 1917), chap. IV, art. 41, p. 22. Regarding patria potestad, see *Ley sobre relaciones familiares*, chap. XV, art. 241, p. 52. Regarding spousal obligations, see *Ley sobre relaciones familiares*, chap. IV, art. 44, pp. 22–23. On marital property, see *Ley sobre relaciones familiares*, chap. IV, art. 45, p. 23.

30. *Ley sobre relaciones familiares*, chap. VI, art. 93, p. 30.

31. Ibid., art. 97, p. 31.

32. Ibid., art. 101, p. 32.

33. Ibid., art. 77, p. 28.

34. Ibid., chap. VII, art.140, p. 38.

35. For excellent introductions to the literature on honor in colonial Latin America, see Asunción Lavrin, ed., *Sexuality and Marriage in Colonial Latin America* (Lincoln: University of Nebraska Press, 1989), and Lyman L. Johnson and Sonya Lipsett-Rivera, eds., *The Faces of Honor: Sex, Shame, and Violence in Colonial Latin America* (Albuquerque: University of New Mexico Press, 1998).

36. *Ley Sobre el Divorcio; Reformas de varios artículos del Código del Estado de acuerdo con la ley de 29 de diciembre de 1914*, cited in Smith, *Gender and the Mexican Revolution*, 125 and 207n36. See *Diario Oficial de Yucatán*, May 27, 1915, for the original reform of the civil code adopting Carranza's divorce law in the state of Yucatán.

37. *Código Civil del Estado de Yucatán (1919)*, p. 40, cited in Smith, *Gender and the Mexican Revolution*, 125 and 207n37. For a well-documented demonstration of how such laws affected Yucatecan women in practice, see Stephanie J. Smith, "'If Love Enslaves . . . Love Be Damned!': Divorce and Revolutionary State Formation in Yucatán," in *Sex in Revolution: Gender, Politics, and Power in Modern Mexico*, ed. Jocelyn Olcott, Mary Kay Vaughan, and Gabriela Cano (Durham, NC: Duke University Press, 2006), 99–111, and chap. 4 of Smith, *Gender and the Mexican Revolution*.

38. Carmen Ramos and Ana Lau, *Mujeres y revolución, 1900–1917* (Mexico City: Instituto Nacional de Estudios Históricos, 1998), 311–14.

39. Ibid., 273.

40. Blum, *Domestic Economies*, 110, citing Ramos and Lau, *Mujeres y revolución*, 311–14.

41. Ramos and Lau, *Mujeres y revolución*, 274 and 281.

42. Anna Macías, "The Mexican Revolution Was No Revolution for Women," in *Latin America: A Historical Reader*, ed. Lewis Hanke (Boston: Little, Brown, 1974), 593.

43. "Ley de Divorcio, Reformas al Código del Registro Civil y al Código Civil del Estado," supplement to no. 7803 of the *Diario Oficial del Gobierno Socialista del Estado de Yucatán*, April 3, 1923, Mérida, Yucatán.

44. Smith, *Gender and the Mexican Revolution*, 134.

45. Macías, "Felipe Carrillo Puerto and Women's Liberation in Mexico," 289–91; Joseph, *Revolution from Without*, 216–20; and Piedad Peniche, "Las ligas feministas en la revolución," *Unicornio* (1996): 9–10. By 1923 at least forty-nine feminist leagues existed in the state of Yucatán ("Relación de Ligas de Resistencia," September 1, 1922, Archivo General del Estado de Yucatán [AGEY], Ramo Poder Ejecutivo [RPE] Caja [C] 773, Legajo [L] 769, and Report from the Secretario General of the Yucatán relating the contents of a report from the Liga Central de Resistencia to the Secretario General, May 30, 1923, AGEY RPE C 770).

46. Monique J. Lemaître, *Elvia Carrillo Puerto: La monja roja del Mayab* (Monterrey, Nuevo León: Ediciónes Castillo, S.A. de C.V., 1998), 33, 34, and 39, and Acrelio Carrillo Puerto, *La familia carrillo Puerto de Motul con la Revolución Mexicana* (Mérida, 1959), 87.

47. Lemaître, *Elvia Carrillo Puerto*, 32–33.

48. She attended the 1923 Pan American Women's Conference; the 1925 Congreso de Mujeres de la Raza; all three Congresos Nacionales de Mujeres Obreras y Campesinas in 1931, 1933, and 1934; and the Liga de Mujeres Ibero y Hispanoamericanas' conference on prostitution in 1934. She was a member of the Frente Único Pro Derechos de la Mujer (FUPDM) and the Liga Nacional de Mujeres (LNM). She also founded and served as president of the Liga Orientadora Socialista Feminista. This organization drew its membership from among Elvia Carrillo Puerto's coworkers at the Secretaría de Economía Nacional and from groups of campesinas in central Mexico and the Yucatán. It aimed to help homeless children, single mothers, and devalued women, including prostitutes (Lemaître, *Elvia Carrillo Puerto*, 131–38). After the *delahuertista* rebellion forced her into hiding in 1924, Carrillo Puerto went to Mexico City, which made it easier for her to connect with women active on a national scale.

49. "Quiero que mis hermanas, las mujeres, gocen de las mismas libertades que el hombre," *El Popular*, August 1, 1922.

50. "El amor libre y el sufragio femenino fueron discutidos ayer por la convención feminista," *El Demócrata*, May 26, 1923, 3, and "Como piensan y que desean las principales delegadas," *Excelsior*, July 8, 1925, 1.

51. "Field Notes from Merida by A. T. Hansen," from box 47, folders 19–24, Robert Redfield Papers, Special Collections, Joseph Regenstein Library, University of Chicago. I am grateful to Anne Rubenstein for sharing this documentation with me. The Casa del Pueblo, or the house of the people, a government-sanctioned community center in Mérida, was inaugurated in 1928 and offered educational workshops and meeting spaces to various activist groups.

52. Lemaître, *Elvia Carrillo Puerto*, 42.

53. George Robb, "The Way of All Flesh: Degeneration, Eugenics, and the Gospel of Free Love," *Journal of the History of Sexuality* 6, no. 4 (April 1996): 590.

54. Ibid., 593. Robb uses the terms "supermen" and "superwomen" in reference to George Bernard Shaw's arguments in *Man and Superman* (New York: Brentano's, 1905). I am associating this term here with "new men" and "new women," which Robb uses elsewhere in the article, and which connects to other literature.

55. Robb, "The Way of All Flesh," 595.

56. Ibid., 591.

57. Ibid., 593.

58. Eduardo Urzaiz, "El hogar del porvenir: Amor, monogamia, y matrimonio," *Orbe*, no. 6 (April–May 1945): 5–8.

59. Robb, "The Way of All Flesh," 593.

60. Ibid., 596. Robb cites a 1913 article from the feminist paper the *New Free Woman*; literary work by George Sand, Bernard Shaw, and H. G. Wells; and the historical example of utopian communities inspired by the socialist thinking of Charles Fourier (593).

61. Ibid., 597.

62. "Código Civil para el Distrito y Territorios Federales en Material Comun y Para Toda la Republica en material Federal," *Diario Oficial*, May 26, 1928, 71.

63. Ibid., art. 286.

64. Ibid.; see arts. 288 (support); 269 (adultery); 169, 170, 171 (legal and other rights). See also Macías, *Against All Odds*, 119.

65. See feminist demands in "Resoluciones tomadas por el Primer Congreso Feminista, convocado por la Sección Mexicana de la Liga Panamericana, para la elevación de la mujer de 20 a 30 de mayo de 1923," reproduced in Gabriela Cano, ed., "México 1923: Primer Congreso Feminista Panamericano," *Debate Feminista* 1 (March 1990): 303–18. In 1953 the Alianza de Mujeres was still making similar claims, explaining that arts. 60, 385, and 386 of the civil code required investigation of maternity and the same obligation should exist for the father. See Licenciada Margarita Lomeli, "La mujer en el derecho civil mexicano, primera parte," in Alianza de Mujeres de México, *La situación jurídica de la mujer mexicana*, 45–46.

Relatedly, the Alianza de Mujeres also pointed to an important discrepancy between legislation in the civil code and that in the Código de Comercio. Articles 8 to 11 in the Código de Comercio required a woman to have permission from her husband to work. The Alianza demanded that the commercial code be reformed to match the civil code's defense of a woman's right to work (see Lomeli, "La mujer en el derecho civil mexicano," 41).

66. According to Martha Chávez Padrón, Mexican agrarian law was historically characterized by a tension between legal definitions of land as an individual right and as a collective resource of the national community. She argues that the Constitution of 1917 reclaimed a definition of property as a social resource, using art. 27 to define land and water as originally corresponding to the nation. Chávez claims that in this act, drafters of the constitution restored a juridical status of property that existed in pre-colonial Aztec law (Martha Chávez Padrón, *El derecho agrario en México* [Mexico City:

Editorial Porrua, 1974], 308–9). See also art. 24 of the Constitution of 1824 and art. 27 of the Constitution of 1857.

67. Article 27 of the Constitution of 1917 "gave the nation direct ownership of the country's natural resources and subsoil rights" and the corresponding "right to expropriate property and redistribute land when it was deemed of public utility. This . . . helped pave the way for significant land distribution programs . . . benefiting hundreds of thousands of Mexicans" but it could also be used to take communal land away from communities. Quotes are taken from Enrique C. Ochoa, "Constitution of 1917 (Mexico)," in *Encyclopedia of Social Welfare History in North America*, ed. John M. Herrick and Paul H. Stuart (Thousand Oaks, CA: Sage Publications, 2005), 69. See also Chávez Padrón, *El derecho agrario en México*, 308.

68. See arts. 1 and 78 of the Ley de Ejidos.

69. The 1814 Constitution of Apatzingán expressed that all citizens had the right to vote for *diputados* (deputies) and representatives to *juntas electorales de parroquia* (electoral parish committees) (arts. 6, p. 45, and 64–66, p. 49, in H. Congreso de la Unión, *Las constituciones de México*).

The 1857 constitution stated that the obligations of citizens included voting in popular elections, holding offices of popular election when elected to do so, serving in the army or national guard, and exercising all classes of business and rights of petition (title I, sec. IV, arts. 35–37, pp. 162–63).

The Constitution of 1917 also called on citizens to vote in popular elections, serve in offices of popular election when selected to do so, serve in the army or national guard, and exercise the right to petition in all classes of business (title I, sec. IV, arts. 35 and 36, p. 187).

70. The 1857 exclusion of illiterate mexicanos from enjoying the rights of citizenship was based on the Bases Organicás stipulation that after 1850, citizens would have to be able to read and write to exercise their political rights (art.18, p. 129, in H. Congreso de la Unión, *Las constituciones de Mexico*).

71. For the reference to the June 1918 National Election Law, see Morton, *Woman Suffrage in Mexico*, 9. A sustained campaign for women's suffrage was initiated at the Querétaro Constitutional Convention of 1916–17, when the revolutionary activist and feminist Hermila Galindo and the revolutionary general Silvestre González pressured delegates to consider giving women suffrage rights (Cano, "Las feministas en campaña," 272–76, and the *Diario de Debates*, 1:586 and 2:829–30, 2:982–83, cited in Cano). Women acquired the right to vote in municipal elections through previously mentioned reforms to constitutional art. 115 enacted in 1946, and in federal elections through reforms to constitutional art. 34 enacted in 1953.

72. *Eugenia*, 63–66.

73. Alianza de Mujeres de México, *La situación juridical de la mujer mexicana*, 142.

74. Title 6, art. 123, secs. I, II, IV (regulation of workday and week); XV (safety conditions); XIV (worker's compensation); and XVIII–XXII (organizing rights), pp. 199–200, in H. Congreso de la Unión, *Las constituciones de México*.

75. Title 6, art. 123, sec. XII, p. 199, in ibid.

76. Title 6, art. 123, sec. XIII, p. 199, in ibid.

77. "Para trabajo igual debe corresponder el salario igual, sin tener en cuenta sexo ni nacionalidad" ("Equal work must be matched by equal pay, regardless of sex or nationality"). Title 6, art. 123, sec. VI, p. 199, in ibid.

78. Title 6, art. 123, secs. III and V, p. 199, in ibid.

79. Macías, "Felipe Carrillo Puerto and Women's Liberation in Mexico," 288, and Macías, "The Mexican Revolution Was No Revolution for Women," 463–65.

80. Urzaiz, *Eugenia*, 14.

81. Ibid., 41.

82. Ibid., 29.

83. Ibid., 35. The description of gestators engaged in "feminine" pastimes can be found on p. 35.

84. Ibid., 14.

85. Ibid., 41.

86. Ibid., 47–48.

87. Ibid., 49–50.

88. Ibid., 50.

89. Nichole Sanders, "Mother and Family Programs (Mexico)," in Herrick and Stuart, *Encyclopedia of Social Welfare History in North America*, 239–40.

90. Katherine Elaine Bliss, "Social Reform and State-Building (Mexico)," in Herrick and Stuart, *Encyclopedia of Social Welfare History in North America*, 344.

91. Laurence Armand French and Magdaleon Manzanárez, "Mexico," in *World Education Encyclopedia*, 2nd. ed., ed. Rebecca Marlow-Ferguson (Detroit: Gale, 2001), 2:881.

92. Ochoa, "Constitution of 1917 (Mexico)," 69.

93. Mary Kay Vaughan, *Cultural Politics in Revolution: Teachers, Peasants, and Schools in Mexico, 1930–1940* (Tucson: University of Arizona Press, 1997), 24.

94. Bliss, "Social Reform and State-Building (Mexico)," 343.

95. Cristina Rivera-Garza, "General Insane Asylum: La Castañeda (Mexico)," in Herrick and Stuart, *Encyclopedia of Social Welfare History in North America*, 148.

96. Sarah A. Buck, "Women and Social Welfare (Mexico)," in Herrick and Stuart, *Encyclopedia of Social Welfare History in North America*, 444.

97. All quotations in this paragraph are from ibid., 444–45.

98. Soto, *Emergence of the Modern Mexican Woman*, 67–81; Soto, *The Mexican Woman*, 49–53; Macías, *Against All Odds*, 64–80; Macías, "Felipe Carrillo Puerto and Women's Liberation in Mexico," 287–88; Joseph, *Revolution From Without*, 105; Peniche, "Las ligas feministas en la revolución," 8–9; Cano, "Congresos feministas en la historia de México," 24–26; and Lau, "Una experiencia feminista en Yucatán, 1922–1924," 12–14.

99. Macías, "Felipe Carrillo Puerto and Women's Liberation in Mexico," 189–91; Joseph, *Revolution from Without*, 216–20; Peniche, "Las ligas feministas en la revolución," 9–10.

100. See "Relación de Ligas de Resistencia," September 1, 1922, AGEY R PE C 773 L 769, and Report from the Secretario General of the Yucatán relating the contents of a report from the Liga Central de Resistencia to the Secretario General, May 30, 1923, AGEY R PE C 770.

101. La Siempreviva was one of Mexico's earliest feminist societies formed in late nineteenth-century Yucatán by the teacher and poet Rita Cetina Gutiérrez (Macías, *Against All Odds*, 61; Soto, *Emergence of the Modern Mexican Woman*, 67).

102. Macías, *Against All Odds*, 92; Soto, *Emergence of the Modern Mexican Woman*, 86–87; Soto, *The Mexican Woman*, 58–59; and Lau, "Una experiencia feminista en Yucatán," 12. According to Monique Lemaître, Elvia Carrillo Puerto created Yucatán's first Liga Feminista in 1912, and she created the Liga Rita Cetina Gutiérrez in 1919 while in exile in Mexico City (Lemaître, *Elvia Carrillo Puerto*, 71–72).

103. See Buck, "Activists and Mothers," for a study of how Mexican women activists shifted from equal-rights to difference-based maternalist strategies in suffrage organizing over the course of the 1920s, 1930s, and 1940s.

104. See Carole Pateman, *The Sexual Contract* (Palo Alto, CA: Stanford University Press, 1988), cited in Dore, "One Step Forward, Two Steps Back," 16; and Pateman, "Feminismo y democracia," *Debate Feminista* 1 (March 1990): 7–28, cited in Cano, "Revolución, feminismo y ciudadanía en México," 303.

105. Title I, chap. IV, art. 34, p. 187, in H. Congreso de la Unión, *Las constituciones de México*.

106. Dore, "One Step Forward, Two Steps Back," 16.

107. Gabriela Cano, "The Porfiriato and the Mexican Revolution," in *Nation, Empire, Colony: Historicizing Gender and Race*, ed. Ruth Roach Pierson and Nupur Chaudhuri with the assistance of Beth McAuley (Bloomington: Indiana University Press, 1998), 113 and 115. The Porfirian state relaxed the hostile posture toward the church promoted by mid-nineteenth-century liberals, evident in the fact that Catholic influence and activities such as the construction of new dioceses, parishes, seminaries, religious orders, and beneficent institutions increased during the Porfiriato. See Patience A. Schell, *Church and State Education in Revolutionary Mexico City* (Tucson: University of Arizona Press, 2003), 4, and Kristina Boylan, "Mexican Catholic Women's Activism, 1929–1940" (PhD diss., Oxford University, 2000), 58–59.

108. See title 1, chap. I, arts. 3, p. 179, 27, p. 184, and 130, p. 186, of the 1917 constitution in H. Congreso de la Nación, *Las constituciones de México*.

109. See title 1, chap. I, art. 24, p. 182, in H. Congreso de la Nación, *Las constituciones de México*.

110. Margaret Sanger, "La regulación de la natalidad o la brujula del hogar: Medios seguros y científicos para evitar la concepción" (Mérida, Yucatán: Centro de Apoyo CII, 1922). Margaret Sanger was an American nurse. She was significantly influenced by sexology and committed to social justice causes and socialism. According to James Reed, she "combined a feminist vision with a prophetic style," arguing that "women in

control of themselves would remake the world by restricting the production of children and revaluing human life cheapened by plenitude" (James Reed, *The Birth Control Movement and American Society: From Private Vice to Public Virtue* [Princeton, NJ: Princeton University Press, 1983], 129 and 131).

Sanger begins by explaining the motivations for limiting natality and continues by providing a simply written, no-nonsense guide to various forms of birth control, including the rhythm method and withdrawal, condoms, douches, pessaries, sponges, and suppositories. Juan Rico claims that the first copies of Sanger's pamphlet were made available in March 1922 (Juan Rico, *La huelga de junio* [Mérida, Yucatán, 1922], 164).

111. A July 3, 1923, letter from Anne Kennedy to Felipe Carrillo Puerto, written in advance of her trip, indicates that she planned to arrive in Progreso on August 12 or 13 to report on clinical work in America and, if desired, "give a demonstration of methods" and leave "some definite outline for organized clinical work" in Yucatán. She planned to go on to Mexico City to arrange a meeting for Sanger in September. Kennedy also states that Dr. Ernest Gruening had communicated Carrillo Puerto's desire to have Sanger visit, "if [Sanger] could speak Spanish. Unfortunately, Mrs. Sanger [did] not speak the language," which explains why Kennedy was coming instead. The letter is reproduced in Adolfo Ferrer, *El archivo de Felipe Carrillo: El callismo, la corrupción del regimen obregonista* (New York: Carlos Lopez Press, 1924), 57.

112. The degree to which the government was involved in the publication and distribution of Sanger's pamphlet is somewhat unclear. Rico attempted to clarify the role of Carrillo Puerto's ruling Partido Socialista del Sureste (PSS) in the birth control campaign. He wrote that the Liga Central de Resistencia printed Sanger's pamphlet for distribution within other *ligas*. He went on to quote *Diario Oficial*, which declared that "the state government . . . [never] ordered the printing much less the distribution of the pamphlet . . . [although] . . . it declares itself in solidarity with all of the propaganda of social reform carried out by the Central Liga" (Rico, *La huelga de junio*, 164).

Kennedy suggested that the government played a more direct role in Yucatán's birth control campaign. She claimed to have "had many conversations on the establishment of clinics," which would be established "under the direction of the government" and would be "supervised by the Junta de Sanidad." She also reported that Governor Carrillo Puerto personally accompanied her on a tour of Mérida and arranged meetings for her with the Junta de Sanidad and doctors to discuss practical applications of birth control during her visit ("Interesantes entrevistas entre la Señora Kennedy y nuestro 'leader' el ciudadano Felipe Carrillo Puerto, acerca del control de los nacimientos," *Tierra* 28 [November 4, 1923]: 9 and 23).

In 1924, Ernest Gruening, who helped to arrange Kennedy's visit, stated that "birth-control information was . . . freely available in Yucatán, and with the assistance of . . . Kennedy . . . two clinics—the first to be legally established in this hemisphere— were recently opened in Mérida" (Ernest Gruening, "Felipe Carrillo," *The Nation*, January 16, 1924, 62).

113. "Interesantes entrevistas entre la Señora Kennedy y nuestro 'leader' el ciudadano Felipe Carrillo Puerto," 9 and 23. This article was a reprint of a report on Kennedy's
trip published in Margaret Sanger's magazine *Birth Control* in October 1923.

114. Sanger, "La regulación de la natalidad," 4.

115. "Justa protesta de numerosos profesores," *La Revista de Yucatán*, March 9, 1922,
1; "El asunto de los folletos inmorales denuncia presentada por numerosísimos ciudadanos al C. Procurador Gral. de Justicia," *La Revista de Yucatán*, March 10, 1922, 3; "Protesta de la Liga de Acción Social contra el folleto aquel," *La Revista de Yucatán*, March 11,
1922, 3; "A las señoras, y señoritas, profesoras de las escuelas oficiales del estado y a las
señoras madres de familia de Yucatán," *La Revista de Yucatán*, March 12, 1922, 5.

116. A good example of such conservative organizations was the Liga de Acción
Social, a nonpolitically and nonreligiously partisan organization that was founded on
February 1, 1909, to "procure social betterment" and to foster private initiatives and
sentiments of individual responsibility ("Estatutos de la Liga de Acción Social: Reformados el 6 de noviembre de 1944," Liga de Acción Social, Mérida, 1944, archived at the
Centro de Apoyo a la Investigación Histórica del Estado de Yucatán, Biblioteca Yucatanense [CDA] CXLVI 1944 1/2 14). Despite its purported nonpartisanship, however, Faulo M. Sánchez Novelo claims that the organization was created by a group of
hacendados (wealthy plantation owners) who were inspired by "the social doctrine of
the Catholic Church, renewed by León XIII" (Faulo M. Sánchez Novelo, *José María
Iturralde Traconis, "El Kanxoc": Ideología y política en un regimen socialista yucateco* [Mérida:
Maldonado Editores, 1986], 15). Between 1909 and 1925, the league's activities included
the creation and celebration of several civic holidays, projects to further public rural
education, the organization of baseball and tennis competitions, campaigns against
alcoholism and immoral cinematography, and initiatives to industrialize henequen
production ("Principales Sucesos de la Liga de Acción Social desde su fundación," Liga
de Acción Social, Mérida, 1954, CDA CLXXII 1954 2/2 11). See the league's complaints
about Sanger's pamphlet in the *Revista de Yucatán*, March 11, 1922, 3.

117. For example, Professor Augusto Molina Ramos, a participant in feminist
league activities, wrote an article criticizing rationalist education (*La Revista de Yucatán*,
March 12, 1922, 5). To see reports on Molina Ramos's involvement in feminist league
activities, see "La fiesta de la Liga Feminista 'RCG,'" *El Popular*, February 7, 1922, 4,
and "Asamblea de la Liga Feminista 'RCG,'" *El Popular*, November 15, 1922, 3. Similarly,
a socialist teacher, journalist, legislator, and close collaborator of Felipe Carrillo Puerto,
Professor Edmundo Bolio, resigned from his position in the state education council in
protest of the birth control campaign ("Protesta de la Liga de Acción Social contra el
folleto aquel," *La Revista de Yucatán*, March 11, 1922, 3). For biographical information on
Bolio, see "Bolio Ontiveros, Edmundo," in *Diccionario histórico y biográfico de la Revolución
Mexicana*, ed. and published by Instituto Nacional de Estudios Históricos de la Revolución
Mexicana (INEHRM), CD ROM, 1994. Bolio Ontiveros also attended at least one
session of the LRCG on February 22, 1922 ("Por la liga feminista 'RCG,'" *El Popular*,
February 24, 1922, 4).

118. "Justa protesta de numerosos profesores," *La Revista de Yucatán*, March 9, 1922, 1.

119. "El asunto de los folletos inmorales denuncia presentada por numerosísimos ciudadanos al C. Procurador Gral. de Justicia," *La Revista de Yucatán*, March 10, 1922, 3; "A las señoras, y señoritas . . . ," *La Revista de Yucatán*, March 12, 1922, 5.

120. Sources that accused schoolteachers of disseminating the pamphlet to schoolchildren include "Justa protesta de numerosos profesores," *La Revista de Yucatán*, March 9, 1922, 1; "El reparto de folletos inmorales relacionados con la maternidad, ha causado una enorme indignación en todos los círculos sociales," *Excelsior*, March 10, 1922, 7; "A las señoras, y señoritas . . . ," *La Revista de Yucatán*, March 12, 1922, 5; "Se comenta en Veracruz la circulacion en Yucatán de los folletos aquellos," *La Revista de Yucatán*, March 17, 1922; and Adolfo Ferrer, *El archivo de Felipe Carrillo: El callismo, la corrupción del regimen obregonista* (New York: Carlos López Press), 55. Juan Rico, from the Confederación Regional de Obrera Mexicana in the Yucatán, wrote that "the pamphlet has not been distributed in state schools, as it was written . . . for adults and not children" (Rico, *La huelga de junio*, 164), and Esperanza Velázquez Bringas wrote that "the conference and the pamphlets . . . have been distributed, yes, but among women and adults" ("Alerta, mujeres del proletariado," *El Popular*, March 10, 1922, 2).

121. *Enciclopedia Yucatanense* (Mexico City: Edición Oficial del Gobierno de Yucatán, 1977), 5:87; *Diario de Yucatán*, May 31, 2000, 9–11; "Menéndez, Carlos R.," in INEHRM, *Diccionario histórico y biográfico de la Revolución Mexicana*.

122. Menéndez frequently found himself at odds with Yucatán's powers of the moment. Although he was involved in the early stages of the Mexican Revolution and viewed himself as a zealous propagator of democracy, he later protested against the abuses of power of revolutionary and postrevolutionary socialist regimes in the state of Yucatán. Consequently, he lost close friends to political feuds and found himself in Mérida's prison and in foreign exile several times between 1912 and 1933, when Mexico's supreme court freed him from his last jail sentence. During the 1920s and 1930s he opposed the socialist administrations of Governors Felipe Carrillo Puerto, José María Iturralde, and Bartolomé García Correa (*Diario de Yucatán*, May 31, 2000, 9–12). Through this orientation he became one of the major conservative forces of Yucatán. He consistently criticized the policies of his former friend and colleague Felipe Carrillo Puerto, and publicized and supported the *delahuertista* rebellion in Yucatán, which resulted in Carrillo Puerto's death and the end of his administration (*Diario de Yucatán*, May 31, 2000, 10–11; Sánchez Novelo, *José María Iturralde Traconis*, 16). Menéndez was also a founding member of the Liga de Acción Social ("Liga de Acción Social," in INEHRM, *Diccionario histórico y biográfico de la Revolución Mexicana*).

123. For citations on global population trends and debates during this period, see the essay "*Eugenia* and Eugenics" in this volume, 158–60.

124. Francisco Alba, *La población de México: Evolución y dilema* (Mexico City: El Colegio de México, 1977), 18. Michael C. Meyer and William L. Sherman suggest an even higher decrease of 1.5 to 2 million people, amounting to a decline of as much as one-eighth of

the population (*The Course of Mexican History*, 5th ed. [New York: Oxford University Press, 1995], 552). The Instituto Nacional de Estadística, Geografía e Informática (INEGI) claims that the population was 14,334,780 in 1921 (INEGI, *Estadísticas históricas de México* [Mexico City: Instituto Nacional de Estadística, Geografía e Informática; Instituto Nacional de Antropología e Historia; SEP, 1985], 1:21).

125. In reality, the population decline evident at the end of the revolution was more a result of Spanish influenza and temporary or permanent immigrations to the United States than to deaths resulting from the revolution or decreasing birthrates (Alba, *La población de México*, 18). However, natality was a more obvious target with higher symbolic power.

126. "La regulación de la maternidad en Francia," *La Revista de Yucatán*, March 19, 1922, 12.

127. "Rapidamente disminuye la natalidad en la Republica, al mismo tiempo aumentan L'defunciones; . . . se teme que ocurra en nuestro país lo que ha pasado en Francia," *La Revista de Yucatán*, April 4, 1922, 1.

128. "El reparto de folletos inmorales relacionados con la maternidad, ha causado una enorme indignación en todos los circulos sociales," *Excelsior*, March 10, 1922.

129. Marta Acevedo, *El 10 de Mayo* (Mexico City: Cultura/SEP, Martín Casillas Editores, 1982).

130. *Excelsior*, April 13, 1922, 10.

131. "Para glorificar el amor a la madre habrán de unirse los mexicanos en Toda la Nación," *Excelsior*, April 15, 1922, second section, 7.

Excelsior's allusion to Mother's Day celebrations in other parts of the world points to a historical reality. The celebration of motherhood has old roots in the western world. Both the ancient Greeks and the Romans held festivals for mothers, and medieval Christians in Eastern and Western Europe adapted such celebrations into their religious cosmology. See Stephen G. Christianson, ed., *The American Book of Days*, 4th ed. (New York: H. W. Wilson Company, 2000), 353.

Modern celebrations of Mother's Day followed. In the mid-nineteenth century, Julia Ward Howe campaigned in the United States for July 4 (Independence Day) to be changed to Mother's Day in an effort to promote peace, and Anna Reeves Jarvis promoted the idea of Mother's Friendship Day as a time to reunite divided families during the Civil War (Christianson, *The American Book of Days*, 353).

In the early twentieth century, the US Congress responded to petitions by Anna Reeve Jarvis's daughter (named Anna M. Jarvis) for the officialization of Mother's Day with a joint resolution to reserve the second Sunday in May "for displaying the American Flag, and as a public expression of our love and reverence for the mothers of our country" (Christianson, *The American Book of Days*, 354).

International social, political, and economic trends favored the celebration of Mother's Day. Mother's Day was appealing in part because it "honored the traditional role of women in the family home . . . [and] reassured those who were uneasy about the 'new womanhood' that emerged as a result of World War I," and it also constituted a "viable commercial holiday for various business concerns, who therefore widely publicized it as an important event" (Wendy Woloson, "Mother's Day," in *St. James Encyclopedia of Popular Culture*, ed. Sarah Pendergast and Tom Pendergast [Woodbridge, CT: St. James Press, 2000], 3:417–18).

In Germany, Mother's Day appeared in 1922 through the promotion of an odd coalition of florists, nonprofit organizations, conservatives, and church groups who introduced the holiday right after Germany's defeat in World War I "to cover up [economic and political] disorder" and "reinforce tradition" (Karen Hausen, "Mother's Day in the Weimar Republic," in *When Biology Became Destiny: Women in Weimar and Nazi Germany*, ed. Atina Grossman, Renate Bridenthal, and Marion Kaplan [New York: Monthly Review Press, 1984], 132). In France, the Vichy regime of the early 1940s used Mother's Day as part of their overall campaign of French renewal through "work, family, and the fatherland" promoting sacrificial, loyal mothers' work for national development; see Miranda R. Pollard, *Reign of Virtue: Mobilizing Gender in Vichy France* (Chicago: University of Chicago Press, 1998), xiii, 45–50. And in Italy, Mussolini's fascist government found Mother's Day was a viable tool to mobilize women and families behind the regime; see Victoria De Grazia, *How Fascism Ruled Women: Italy, 1922–1945* (Berkeley: University of California Press, 1992), 71.

132. "Es bien acogida la idea para celebrar el dia de las madres," *Excelsior*, April 14, 1922, 3; "La Secretaria de Educación hace suya la iniciativa del 'día de las madres,'" *Excelsior*, April 24, 1922, 3; "EL DIA DE LAS MADRES; EXCELSIOR prentende que el diez de mayo de todos los años sea consagrado por los hijos a enaltecer en vida o en memoria a quienes les dieron el ser," *Excelsior*, April 13, 1922, 1. Advocates included Carmen Ramos, who supported the idea of Excelsior, particularly since she had been a member of a group who tried to institutionalize Mother's Day in Mexico in 1916 ("Para glorificar el amor a la madre habrán de unirse los mexicanos en toda la nación," *Excelsior*, April 15, 1922, second section, 7); the Knights of Columbus ("Los caballeros de colon secundarán la iniciativa de Excelsior para honrar a las nobles madres," *Excelsior*, April 29, 1922, 10); and the factory worker Señorita Camacho, who suggested that the factory where she worked organize a collection from the children of the women working there and return the amount deposited by each child to them on the eve of Mother's Day to buy flowers ("Noble y brillante proposición de una dama para celebrar el 'Día de las Madres,'" *Excelsior*, May 19, 1922, second section, 3).

133. Luis G. Urbina, "El mundo de las almas y el dia de las madres," *La Revista de Yucatán*, May 7, 1922, 9.

134. Urzaiz, *Eugenia*, 66. Malthusianism refers to the practice of supporting family planning techniques, in adherence to Thomas Malthus's argument that without regulation, population would grow exponentially and unsustainably, outstripping available resources and resulting in social problems and unrest.

135. Sarah Buck Kachaluba, interview with Doña Candelaria Souza de Fernández, July 1, 2014, Mérida, Yucatán.

136. Souza, "Prólogo," 11.

137. Urzaiz Jiménez, *Oficio de mentor*, 42.

138. Ibid., 71.

Eugenia and Eugenics

The letter summoning Ernesto, the main character of *Eugenia*, to become an Official Reproducer of the Species introduces the reader to the eugenic principles that govern the reproductive apparatus of Villautopia, the utopian community depicted in the novel, by explaining that he has been selected as a breeder "in recognition of [his] robustness, health, beauty, and other favorable conditions."[1] The fact that it is positive physiological qualities that make Ernesto desirable as a breeder shows that early twentieth-century Mexican intellectuals were aware of eugenic ideas and practices. In fact, at the time Urzaiz was writing, Mexico had begun to develop one of the most rigorous eugenic programs in the Americas—a program that rivaled better-known initiatives in interwar Europe and the United States.[2] *Eugenia* provides an excellent lens through which to examine Mexican experimentation with eugenics.

In Villautopia, official breeders, such as Ernesto, are selected via medical and psychiatric evaluations, while the rest of the population is sterilized. Selective reproduction is designed to improve the species, which the director of Villautopia's Institute of Eugenics, Dr. Remigio Pérez Serrato, explains as he provides a tour of the institute's facilities: "In the societies of yesteryear, the most intelligent, most astute, or the richest triumphed, and since they were generally also the worst off physically, that meant that the species degenerated at an alarming rate."[3] Pérez Serrato also indicates that Villautopia's population is improving so much that "each year the number of children sterilized diminishes; the day will come when the procedure is performed only when the excess of inhabitants requires the restriction in the number of births."[4]

Although these passages in *Eugenia* suggest that Urzaiz embraced eugenic initiatives, other excerpts indicate that Urzaiz may have had more ambivalent feelings about eugenics. For example, before his glowing summary of eugenic programs in Villautopia, Pérez Serrato explains that "the most advanced nations of [the past] tried to the best of their abilities to undertake artificial selection. Out of these trials eugenics was born, but this science, which today is perfectly regulated, [and] has reached maximum development[,] . . . had to be limited by purely mitigating measures, and its results were all but absurd."[5]

Comparing the ideas and practices described in *Eugenia* with Mexican and global trends from the time that Urzaiz was writing can provide the necessary contextualization to examine Urzaiz's opinions and is particularly helpful in exploring the following historical phenomena in local (Yucatecan), national (Mexican), and global contexts: eugenics thought and initiatives; theories of racial uplift, such as *indigenismo* (an idealization of pre-Columbian "Indians" and precolonial indigenous cultural practices) and *mestizophilia* (a glorification of mixed indigenous-hispanic people and their culture); debates between those using eugenics to argue for population decline and those advocating population increase; and the way that medical professionals, particularly obstetricians, psychiatrists, and sexologists, understood the relationship between eugenic principles and procreation.[6]

Reconstructing a Narrative of Eugenic Thought and Initiatives in Mexico, Latin America, and the World

Latin American historians have described eugenics as a "scientific" approach to managing the "hereditary makeup of the human species" and as "a set of theories and policies aimed at controlling and monitoring the reproduction of individuals and social groups."[7] As all of these things, "eugenics" has varied widely in its historical manifestation and constituted an appealing tool for social and political reformers across the globe, ever since Francis Galton coined the term "eugenics" in 1883.[8]

Examples of eugenic thought and policies have continued to manifest themselves in many times and places up to the present day, but eugenic projects were especially prominent between the 1880s and the 1920s.[9] Important groundwork for later theories regarding inheritance (which were, in turn, applied to eugenics) was laid by Jean-Baptiste Pierre Antoine de Monet, the Chevalier de Lamarck, whose *Philosophie zoologique* (1809) suggested that changes in animal species inspired by external, environmental conditions could be handed on to future generations.[10] Lamarck also believed that "living forms gradually but inevitably progress[ed] toward higher levels of organization," a general evolutionary orientation (labeled progressionist evolutionary theory) that many would cling to for the remainder of the century and beyond.[11]

The degree to which the British naturalist Charles Darwin's discoveries regarding nonhuman species' adaptations to the environment (published in *On the Origin of Species* [1859]) could be used as a base for later eugenic theories is a source of controversy.[12] Yet while "one premise of everything Darwin believed about inheritance was that characters acquired during an organism's lifetime could be transmitted to their offspring," Darwin viewed *natural*—not artificial (or human-driven)—selection as the main mechanism driving evolution.[13] Darwin was also reluctant to use his findings to argue for human evolution from animals and did not discuss this possibility in *On the Origin of Species*. Nonetheless, many speculated about this correlation following its publication.[14]

Darwin was nonetheless interested in the work of the sociologist Herbert Spencer and Darwin's cousin Francis Galton, engaging in exchanges with them and influencing their theories of "survival of the fittest" and eugenics, respectively.[15] As Spencer argued in *Principles of Sociology* (1896), human communities evolve from "socially static, undifferentiated societ[ies] to . . . utilitarian, socially dynamic, differentiated societ[ies] where social structures and functions transform to meet needs" through an evolutionary process in which change for individuals, groups, or social systems occurred as "survival of the fittest."[16] Spencer's adaptation of Darwinian evolution to the idea of "survival of the fittest" as it pertains to humans has been associated with a school of thought and social movement labeled as social Darwinism.[17]

Significantly, Darwin adopted the term "survival of the fittest" to discuss natural selection in later editions of *On the Origin of Species*.[18] Darwin and Spencer agreed that organisms struggled to survive by developing skills to effectively compete against other organisms and adapt to environmental change within a world defined by limited resources, but they disagreed about how organisms acquired such skills. For Spencer, they were cultivated through competition, whereas for Darwin, they were acquired by chance, through accidental mutations.[19] Darwin's observations on the HMS *Beagle*'s second voyage (1831–36) and work that he did after returning to Britain, including research on breeders' attempts to shape the characters of animals and the reading of Thomas Malthus's *Essay on the Principle of Population* (1798)—a study warning of the perilous results of human overpopulation—led him to different conclusions on species' adaptation to the environment than the progressionist evolutionary theory favored by Spencer.[20] Nonetheless, Darwin and Spencer shared a commitment to the idea of natural selection, and this was the principle both applied to humans and society through the concept of "survival of the fittest"—not an interest in initiatives characterized by human-driven (artificial) selection, which were at the heart of eugenic movements.

In contrast to Darwin and Spencer's affirmation of the principle of natural selection, Galton's explorations of how mechanisms of inheritance could be used to better the human race eventually led him to coin the term and found the field of "eugenics"—a movement exploring and promoting "the science of improving the stock" through human and artificial (unnatural) intervention.[21] Despite such disparate views on whether humanity was best served by "natural selection" or artificial (eugenic) selection, Galton credited Darwin with inspiring him to begin his investigations. Galton articulated his initial discoveries in the publication of "Hereditary Talent and Character" (1865).[22] Galton's research informed a decades-long debate as to whether human physical, intellectual, and moral characteristics were "innate" or a product of the physical, historical, and sociocultural context or environment. Galton's contribution was asserting that "the laws of inheritance applied to humans just as much as they did to other animals," thereby connecting questions of human reproduction to "anxieties about biological decline that Darwin had provoked" and promoting "a 'hard' concept of heredity" over the "conventional 'soft' or Lamarckian belief in the inheritance of acquired characters."[23] Galton also introduced the phrase "nature and nurture . . . to describe the conflict between biological . . . and environmental determinism." He favored hard, biological theories of inheritance (nature).[24]

Although Darwin did not share Galton's eugenic orientation, Darwin was interested in the mechanisms of inheritance that Galton's work addressed, and Darwin acknowledged Galton's influence in the development of theories articulated in his highly influential *The Descent of Man and Selection in Relation to Sex* (1871), which explored how human evolution related to the broader processes Darwin had discussed in *On the Origin of Species* and took on such issues as the dominant role of females in choosing mating partners and sexual selection, evolutionary psychology, evolutionary ethics, and differences between human "races" and "sexes."[25]

While Darwin, Spencer, and Galton were developing biological and social ideas about human evolution, Gregor Mendel (1822–84) was experimenting on peas to discover what determined such characteristics as color and flower, pod, or seed structure, and how such characteristics related to inheritance. After crossbreeding different varieties of peas between 1856 and 1863, Mendel concluded that inheritance demonstrated "law-like" principles, with physical characteristics "determined by factors transmitted unchanged through generations."[26] Few scientists, however, learned of Mendel's work at that time; it wasn't until the turn of the century that Mendel's findings were rediscovered, playing a major role in the development of "classical genetics." Thus, although

Mendel's research had nothing to do with human evolution, it contributed to the development of genetic theories that some eugenicists adopted a few decades later. By the time of Galton's death in 1911, "eugenics had become popular, thanks in large measure to the rediscovery of Gregor Mendel's law of heredity in 1900."[27]

Mexico's engagement with evolutionary and eugenic theories occurred in a period of dramatic political-economic contests, which arose out of Mexico's long civil war for independence from Spain, between 1810 and 1821. In the aftermath of this struggle, two ideological and political factions vied for power for decades: those generally called centralists (since they felt power and authority was best concentrated in a hierarchical system grounded in a strong central power) and those called federalists (since they preferred a more democratic diffusion of power and representation throughout smaller organizations, at the state/provincial and even local level).[28] The centralists tended to favor the influence of the Catholic Church in such sociopolitical affairs as marriage and education, as well as traditional political and social conventions, such as monarchy and aristocracy, making them "conservatives," while the federalists were generally anticlerical and more amenable to newer constitutional democratic political systems and to creating opportunities for upward mobility, making them "liberals."

The centralist/federalist, conservative/liberal struggle between independence (1821) and the outbreak of the Mexican Revolution (1911) is often divided into three periods. The first (1821–55) was a period of war in which foreign powers and internal leaders vied for power in Mexico. During this era, the army commander Antonio López de Santa Anna led Mexican troops and also moved in and out of the presidency until the Revolution of Ayutla (1854–55) forced him into his last exile. Santa Anna's volatile political career and periods of exile were related to his military responsibilities in battles that resulted in Mexico losing much of its territory to the United States.

The Revolution of Ayutla and downfall of Santa Anna initiated the liberal era (1855–76), which is closely associated with the lawyer Benito Juárez, who served as president from 1858 until his death in 1872, promoted a liberal ideology emphasizing economic growth, and sought to disempower the church vis-à-vis the state.[29]

The third and final period (1876–1911) began when the army general Porfirio Díaz, a liberal war hero, engineered a revolutionary coup in the fall of 1876, followed by his election to the presidency and assumption of office on May 5, 1877.[30] Díaz served as president from 1877 to 1880 and again from 1884 to 1911, when he was overthrown with the outbreak of the Mexican Revolution. During the period of 1880–84, Manuel González, with Díaz's full support, occupied the post.[31]

Díaz and his allies accelerated mid-nineteenth-century Mexican liberals' emphasis on economic and industrial growth with the goals of establishing "modern" urban infrastructures (for water, transportation, sanitation, public lighting, and telephones). Because Porfirian leaders looked to European models for development, Porfirian infrastructures, buildings, and institutions (such as roads, tram and train tracks, schools, museums, theaters, and hospitals) often mimicked European architectural design, fashion, and art styles.

The liberalism shaping the Juarista and Porfirian eras was based heavily on positivism, an intellectual movement attributed particularly to Auguste Comte, which brought together initiatives in nineteenth-century social science and philosophy to describe and address issues arising from scientific and industrial development.[32] For Comte, "all knowledge was . . . derivable from sensory experience[,] le[aving] no room for religious superstitions"; "society followed the same hard, inexorable laws that scientists found in chemistry, biology, and physics"; and all areas of study, including humanistic disciplines, should privilege scientific knowledge and analysis.[33] In Latin America, liberal leaders embraced positivism as a way to address current socioeconomic and political problems, applying positivism to education in particular, prioritizing math and science over rhetoric, literature, and theology, with the goal of creating a progressive, anticlerical citizenry motivated to aid Mexico in its political, social, and economic development. Thus, in Mexico, positivism grew out of local events and needs and was driven by local "'positivist' politicians" as much as the ideas of European positivist intellectuals.[34]

Comte, like other nineteenth-century philosophers, including Friedrich Hegel and Karl Marx, embraced a teleological, progress-oriented notion of history based on society's evolution through a series of stages, which, in Comte's imagination, were mythical, metaphysical, and positive. Individuals passed through parallel stages of mental development as their understanding of the governing forces and order of the world changed from animistic, supernatural beings to abstract powers of the universe, to facts that could be expressed through statistics and verified by experience.[35]

In Mexico, Gabino Barreda, appointed by President Benito Juárez to help formulate educational reforms resulting in the Ley Orgánica de 1867, introduced Comtian positivism as an educational program.[36] During the Porfiriato, the lawyer, historian, poet, and educator Justo Sierra built upon this positivist base as subsecretary and secretary of education, broadening Mexico's network of public primary and secondary schools and creating a national university. Such schools privileged positivist and scientific principles but also retained the study of language, literature, and arts. Thus in Mexico, Comtian positivism, with its evolutionary, progressionist tendencies, helped to create an intellectual climate open to exploring Darwin's and others' theories of inheritance and evolution and Spencer's applications of these theories to humans with the concept of the "survival of the fittest."[37] Although the term "social Darwinism" was not used heavily (if at all) in Porfirian Mexico, the intellectual historian Charles Hale argues that Mexico and Latin America were both characterized by a "vogue of Social Darwinism" after 1870 and this "was a demonstration of the influence of Spencer . . . not of Comte."[38]

Darwinism entered Mexico primarily through the distribution of French texts, including the French translation of Darwin's *Descent of Man*, not *On the Origin of Species*. The earliest Mexican citations of Darwin appeared in two 1875 articles by Justo Sierra, which examined the relationship between spiritualism, religion, and science; defended scientific analysis and debate; compared the evolutionary theories of Darwin and Alfred Russell Wallace; and advocated incorporating the ideas of evolution into the teaching of history. Mexican scientific publications engaging with Darwinist theory followed. A final indication of Mexicans' interest in Darwinism in the 1870s is the claim of Justo Sierra's brother, Santiago Sierra, to be translating Darwin's *Descent of Man* into Spanish as *La filiación del hombre*, a work that never materialized, probably because Santiago was killed in a duel before he could publish.[39]

It is significant that Mexican educators, scientists, and intellectuals did not mention Darwin in publications until the 1870s; that it is *The Descent of Man*, not *On the Origin of Species* that is cited; and that it was through French editions that these works became known. Unlike *On the Origin of Species*, *The Descent of Man* directly addressed questions of human evolution and applied the concept of "survival of the fittest," and French editions of Darwin emphasized Lamarckian theories of the inheritance of acquired characteristics and progressionism more than those in English.

The general value of positivism and "scientific" ideas—including social Darwinist ones—driving late nineteenth-century reform helps to explain the label of *científicos* ("scientifics"), applied derisively to reformist Porfirian leaders.[40] The científicos coalesced in 1892 as a group of young intellectual professionals who met in the law office of Porfirio Díaz's father-in-law, Romero Rubio, to engineer the reelection of Díaz. The group soon constituted a political cadre leading a broader political, intellectual, and social reform movement. They were important predecessors for postrevolutionary leaders such as Urzaiz, laying foundations for postrevolutionary initiatives that reflected and effected changes in race, class, and gender roles and were informed by and manifested in eugenic initiatives.

Bolstering the Díaz regime's dedication to "order and progress," the científicos were convinced of the need to industrialize and modernize Mexico and agreed that Indian and "hybrid" races such as mestizos were degenerate and were impeding this agenda. However, they did not share a common understanding of Darwin's ideas or positivism and they disagreed on the best way to combat the problem of degeneracy. Some científicos aimed to whiten the Mexican population by encouraging European immigration, whereas others privileged assimilation of Indians, especially through educational initiatives. Justo Sierra, a científico from the first meetings in Romero Rubio's office, was very engaged in such debates. Sierra sought to increase the number of mestizos and believed that European immigration was one approach to overcoming national deficiencies resulting from the prevalence of Mexico's indigenous population, but when the Díaz regime had limited success attracting European immigrants, Sierra pushed for assimilating education as an alternative.[41]

The "inherent logic" of Porfirian economic development attacked indigenous communities and indigenous culture and thereby supported a focus on racial improvement as central to national modernization—whether such improvement was achieved through increased miscegenation or immigration as strategies to increase the number of mestizos, or educational uplift for ignorant and backward "Indians." Drawing on liberal trends from the age of Juárez, the Díaz regime seized "corporate" landholdings that belonged to the church or indigenous communities in order to promote private landownership, industrial and agricultural development, and such projects as railroad and road construction and oil extraction. Against this developmentalist backdrop, many characteristics, including skin tone and phenotype, language, dress, religion, social organization, and cultural practices informed racial and ethnic identity. All of these factors were based on social interpretation and could be changed; through "education, migration, and occupational shifts . . . Indians could become Mestizos . . . [and] . . . [u]pwardly mobile individuals were 'whitened.'"[42] Porfirio Díaz himself demonstrates the fluidity of Mexican racial identity in this period. One historian states that he was "'an almost pure mixtec' Indian," whereas a contemporary counters that "of supposed [*sic*] only one-eighth Indian blood," he was, "in fact, 'probably all white.'"[43] Díaz is also rumored to have used facial powder to whiten himself.[44]

Thus, in the late nineteenth and early twentieth centuries, some Mexican intellectuals and leaders began to champion the mestizo as an ideal blend of indigenous and Hispanic heritages and traits and the basis for model modern

Mexican citizens. For example, Andrés Molina Enríquez drew upon the ideas of Comte, Spencer, Darwin, and others to "hai[l] the mestizo as the beacon of national progress" in his widely read *Los grandes problemas nacionales* (*The Great National Problems*, 1909).[45]

The dynamic climate of growth and reform characterizing turn-of-the-century Mexico makes it an excellent case study to explore why societies around the world who were grappling with historical characteristics of "modernization" were so receptive to eugenics during this era. Over the course of the nineteenth century, industrialization, urbanization, migration, and population growth and decline gave rise to new social problems that citizens and governments responded to with new ideas about the state, including making "populations—people and their bodies—increasingly . . . the business of government, to be improved physically and morally."[46] In Mexico and elsewhere such historical processes (industrialization, urbanization, migration, demographic changes, and a corresponding increasing government regulation of the human body) related to the fact that during the late nineteenth and early twentieth centuries "authoritative claims for governance and rule—whether national, regional, or colonial—shifted from the religious to the scientific realm. Under the canopy of secularization and rationalization, this protracted, uneven, and perennially incomplete transition was deeply interpenetrated with the emergence of original forms of medical and biological knowledge."[47] The concept of *race* informed such concerns and debates as well. Race, "perhaps more than any other social concept, . . . is preeminently modern," and "notions surrounding race emerge only in times we consider modern, that is, at the beginning of the 1500s, immediately after the Conquest of the Americas by Spain."[48] Concerns with racial difference infused individual, group, and governmental responses to migration, urbanization, poverty, and related social issues. For all of these reasons, "eugenics arose out of a constellation of recognizably modern issues and soon became a signal for, and almost a symbol of, modernization," and, more than a "clear set of scientific principles," eugenics offered reformers and governors "a 'modern' way of talking about social problems in biologizing terms."[49]

The modern nature of eugenics is also evident in the fact that eugenicist writers used modernist scholarly and literary strategies to authorize eugenic thought. For example, they "creat[ed] a classical lineage" for the discipline, writing about ancient traditions of withdrawal of aid to undesirable children and adults.[50] In *Eugenia*, Urzaiz compares his characters and the world of Villautopia to classical Greece as well as to Enlightenment-era Europe. Urzaiz also draws scenes in which characters discuss key ideas or social institutions in scholarly societies or salons, evoking Socratic dialogues.

In 1883, the same year that Galton coined the term "eugenics"—thereby helping to make eugenic thought a signature feature of modern, fin-de-siècle thinking and reform—the zoologist August Weismann shared his observations on cell division, distinguishing between "germ cells" (today called "genes), which carried inheritable information, and "somatic cells" responsible for all other bodily functions. This distinction constituted an important addition to knowledge about mechanisms of inheritance that geneticists would build on in the future, in combination with the rediscovery of Mendel's theories.[51]

Postrevolutionary Reform and Eugenics in Mexico

It was on the heels of this intellectual genealogy that Urzaiz published *Eugenia* in 1919. By this time, eugenicists in Mexico and beyond had various biological (including genetic) and sociological studies and arguments to inform their work. Some of these privileged the role of environmental reforms in nurturing positive physical and social characteristics that future generations could inherit. Others emphasized the importance of hard, immutable traits passed on within living organisms through biological heredity. Such scientific and social scientific literature could be used to justify *positive* eugenic policies and initiatives encouraging the development of desirable (positive) biological and social traits through environmental reforms, maternal and child welfare programs, public health campaigns, and pronatalist propaganda encouraging individuals and groups displaying positive traits to reproduce, or *negative* eugenic practices aiming to limit or prevent the reproduction of individuals or groups displaying undesirable (negative) traits, including sterilization, contraception, segregation, abortion, and in some cases, decisions to end the lives of the weaker or less fit through euthanasia or nonintervention in the case of illness, injury, or maldevelopment.

Turn-of-the-century eugenics movements around the world focused on marriage and sexuality—as both related to reproduction—in their efforts to promote the improvement of human offspring. In postrevolutionary Mexico, puericulture, the science of cultivating (including parenting—particularly mothering) the child and hygienic reform were considered key tools in this quest. Puericulture involved defining childhood as a separate stage of life and observing, regulating, controlling, and protecting children through welfare institutions (such as poorhouses and orphanages), schools, laws, and the oversight of social workers, nurses, and doctors. In Mexico, such initiatives were accompanied by the rise of a new literature on mothering and hygiene that began during the Porfiriato and intensified after the Mexican Revolution.

Increased attention to children, the recognition of childhood as a particular stage of life, and the rise of new maternal and child welfare programs are also evident in increasing efforts to use schools as a way to promote and enforce hygienic practice. In 1882, medical professionals and educators came together in Mexico City at a pedagogic hygiene congress to discuss ways that schools could promote health and hygiene. Following the introduction of compulsory primary education up to age ten in 1888, Mexico City's municipal primary schools were federalized in 1896, giving rise to the first permanent body to address school hygiene: the Secretaría de Justicia e Instrucción Pública's (The Secretariat of Justice and Public Instruction) Inspección Médica e Higiénica (Medical and Hygienic Inspection Service), which hired inspectors to check students' health and school facilities, ensure that students were being vaccinated, and collect anthropometric data through monthly visits.[52]

The collection of anthropometric data contributed to the evolving definition of childhood and furthered eugenic reform, since Mexican school inspectors began gathering data that doctors used to calculate the "anatomical and physiological averages of Mexican children, from birth until . . . 24 years."[53] In 1908 this practice widened significantly when the Secretaría de Instrucción Pública y Bellas Artes (Secretariat of Public Instruction and Fine Arts) mandated general medical inspections and created the Departamento de Antropométrica Escolar (Department of School Anthropometrics) to trace students' development, thereby adopting techniques introduced by Francis Galton, the inventor of eugenics, who had established the world's first anthropometric lab in 1884 to generate statistics on individuals in order to chart national developmental trends. Consequently, by the "early 1910s, a little over five years after Alfred Binet had invented his test to ascertain the mental age of French schoolchildren, Mexican educators and pediatricians began to urge that scales and instruments capable of discerning signs of mental retardation and abnormality be incorporated into the pedagogical repertoire of the classroom."[54]

Some Mexican professionals specializing in child welfare continued to use anthropometric testing as a eugenics strategy after an interval of disruption posed by the Mexican Revolution. Several examples of Mexicans who were engaged with both anthropometric testing and eugenics in the postrevolutionary era were involved in two child welfare conferences, held in 1921 and 1923, which brought together teachers and school administrators, doctors, eugenicists, hygienists, social workers, lawyers, politicians, and others.[55] Eugenics was one of six official thematic tracks organizing the conferences, and at the first conference, delegates approved a proposal for the eugenic sterilization of criminals.[56] Conference delegates who were visible advocates of eugenics included the physiologist J. Joaquín Izquierdo, chair of the eugenics section at the second conference, who had also "presented a paper on his [own purportedly] illustrious Spanish genealogy at the Second International Congress of Eugenics in New York two years earlier"; Alfredo Saavedra, "then a young medical school graduate," who went on to found the Sociedad Eugénica Mexicana para el Mejoramiento de la Raza (Mexican Eugenics Society for the Betterment of the Race) in 1931; the obstetrician Antonia Ursúa, who was an active member of the Mexican Eugenics Society from its foundation in 1931 until the 1950s and presented at both congresses on child hygiene; and the journalist and lawyer Esperanza Velázquez Bringas, who played a central role in the eugenic advocacy of birth control in the state of Yucatán, as will be examined shortly, and gave a presentation at the first congress in the eugenic track titled "The Psychological Influence of the Woman on Her Child during Gestation."[57]

Rafael Santamarina was also a key participant at the two child welfare congresses and a central figure in the use of anthropometric testing in Mexico. Although his links to Mexico's eugenics movement are a little less direct than the individuals cited above, there are two connections worth highlighting. First, following his participation in both child welfare conferences, Santamarina was named the head of the Servicio Higiénico Escolar (School Hygiene Service) in 1924, when it was reorganized as the Departamento de Psicopedagogía e Higiene (Department of Psychopedagogy and Hygiene) and moved from the oversight of the Departamento de Salubridad Pública (Department of Public Health) to the Secretaría de Educación Pública (Secretariat of Public Education).[58] According to Alexandra Stern, the School Hygiene Service, founded in 1920, was the "cornerstone" of government-sponsored eugenics in early twentieth-century Mexico, aiming to "establish standards of 'normal' development for children of all ages, participate in international conferences on child welfare, enforce sanitary laws and building codes in the schools, and compile anthropometric data of pupils."[59] And it was this state agency (the School Hygiene Seervice, succeeded by the Department of Psychopedagogy and Hygiene) that turned the concluding recommendations of the Mexican congresses on child welfare into action items. Such recommendations included offering puericulture courses to women and girls, constructing playgrounds and child hygiene centers, forming sanitary brigades to visit potential and pregnant mothers, and continuing anthropometric and psychometric testing of Mexican children.[60]

In 1927, Santamarina attended a conference hosted by the Pan American Central Office of Eugenics and Homiculture in Havana, Cuba, and drew on his knowledge of anthropometric testing to challenge the conference organizers, the Cuban physician Domingo F. Ramos Delgado and the American eugenicist Charles B. Davenport, whose "goal for the conference was to approve a 'Code of Eugenics and Homiculture' . . . mandat[ing] the classification of all inhabitants of the Americas as 'good,' 'bad,' or 'doubtful,'" limiting immigration to those in the "good" category, and working to reduce reproduction by those in the "bad" or "doubtful" categories through sterilization and isolation.[61] Santamarina articulated his objection by questioning "the reliability of physical and mental tests . . . used to claim the inferiority of Mexican child immigrants in the United States" and argued that the Mexican population was improving through measures such as investment in rural schools and labor laws.[62] Thus, Santamarina had an interest in eugenics and, like Galton, he saw anthropometric testing as a useful strategy to promote population improvement. However, he cautioned that such testing needed to be designed and implemented appropriately to work.

A few years after the School Hygiene Service changed into the Department of Psychopedagogy and Hygiene, President Emilio Portes Gil created another complementary welfare service—the Servicio de Higiene Infantil (Child Hygiene Service) under the umbrella of the Department of Public Health, which gave rise to an organization that was important to the institutionalization of eugenic initiatives in Mexico: the Sociedad Mexicana de Puericultura (Mexican Society of Puericulture). The director of the Child Hygiene Service, Dr. Isidro Espinosa de los Reyes, who had given a lecture, "Notes on Intrauterine Puericulture," in the eugenics track at the First Mexican Congress of the Child, recruited respected physicians to join the new organization through handwritten letters. The puericultural society had a eugenics wing and provided a forum for the physicians who would found the Mexican Eugenics Society two years later (in 1931), and over the next twenty-five years, the two societies' members, topics of discussion, and activities constantly overlapped. Espinosa de los Reyes also wrote a narrative history of the Child Hygiene Service, which directly linked its creation to the First Mexican Congress of the Child's eugenics section.[63]

Postrevolutionary Mexico's engagement with reform projects informed by eugenics, puericulture, and hygienic standards aiming to create a new revolutionary citizenry shares tendencies seen in a series of national authoritarian case studies that emphasized the creation of a "new man" (and relatedly, a new woman and new child). Similar to the governments of fascist Italy, Nazi Germany, Francoist Spain, Salazar's Portugal, Vichy France, and Bolshevik Russia, postrevolutionary Mexican leaders and reformers articulated their proposal to "transform Mexican society through a process of racial purification," which drew upon Enlightenment-era revolutionary utopian thought;

nineteenth-century arguments regarding the role of nature (biological inheritance) versus nurture (environmental influence) in human individual and social development; and early twentieth-century corporatist, mass political strategies.[64]

Mexico's postrevolutionary project, centered as it was on racial improvement, had at least two major thrusts: first, a cultural revolution that aimed to change the mentality, psychology, and conscience of the Mexican citizenry through anticlerical and educational campaigns focusing on literacy, hygiene, and home economics skills; and second, an anthropological revolution based on *mestizaje* (miscegenation and related cultural mixing between the Spanish and indigenous elements of the population).[65] Educational campaigns—carried out by teachers, as well as feminists, nurses, doctors, social workers, and other professional reformers—sought to replace religious ideas and structures with secular ones overseen by the state; encourage the speaking, reading, and writing of Spanish instead of indigenous languages; discourage alcohol and drug use; encourage middle-class behavior and mentalities in such areas as hygiene, nutrition, fashion, and courtship and sexual expression; and promote an age-specific, gender-appropriate role to each member of a family. As seen in the relationship between child welfare congresses, state institutions patronized by the secretariats of public health and education, and the Mexican societies of puericulture and eugenics, postrevolutionary Mexican educational institutions and campaigns were organized in tandem with eugenic organizations and initiatives, and postrevolutionary Mexican educational campaigns reflected eugenic values and goals: to improve the physical and mental health of Mexico's population. This national context explains Paul Eiss's assertion that "from the porfiriato [*sic*] through the revolution of Salvador Alvarado (1915–1918), indigenous education in Yucatán was imagined, organized, and instituted under the sign of redemption" with the school replacing the church as the social institution charged with the well-being of Mexicans—including "Indians."[66]

Many reformers also believed that racial mixing, brought about through the anthropological revolution, would result in the gradual inheritance and dominance of positive traits and the eradication of degenerative traits. Taking over such functions allowed the state to usurp the paternal authority of the church and family, giving rise to Mexico's "*papá estado*" (papa state).

The years immediately following the Mexican Revolution were violent and politically volatile, as the multiple factions that participated in the revolution competed for power, giving rise to constant rebellions and assassinations. Beatriz Urías Horcasitas suggests that in this context, "new concepts of mestizaje and purification of degenerate inheritance functioned as an ideological mechanism allowing the simultaneous expression and containment of violence that war had unleashed," as the language of race provided a "socially acceptable and scientifically validated" way for power contenders to identify social characteristics, individuals, and groups that they hoped to make prevalent in the social order.[67]

Thus, during the 1920s, the language of race served as a powerful tool for postrevolutionary Mexican leaders to build a strong revolutionary party that combined elements of corporatist-populism, authoritarian bureaucracy, and democratic socialism.[68] Over the course of the following decades, the Partido Nacional Revolucionario (Revolutionary National Party, PNR), which became the Partido de la Revolución Mexicana (Mexican Revolutionary Party, PRM) and then the Partido Revolucionario Institucional (Revolutionary Institutional Party, PRI), was increasingly centralized, consolidated, and strengthened, largely through a corporatist structure that used mass organizations to incorporate farmers, industrial workers, military personnel, white collar workers, and women, among others.

In many ways Mexican race ideology, eugenics, and the corporatism to which they were linked evolved much as they did in other parts of Latin America.[69] Mexico's tendency to develop eugenic organizations and initiatives in connection with public puericultural and hygiene programs reflected a general trend in Latin America of relying on social reform to improve the health and abilities of reproducers and their children (operating effectively within a corporatist political-economic structure and also conforming to neo-Lamarckian theories favoring environmentally driven change and the inheritance of acquired characteristics). Mexico and other countries also developed propaganda encouraging individuals to select reproductive partners carefully so that their children would have desirable characteristics. Nancy Leys Stepan describes prenuptial tests and marriage licenses as "non-coercive" eugenic strategies to limit undesirable marital unions and reproduction on the one hand and encourage desirable ones on the other. Stepan argues that this approach to regulating reproduction demonstrated the political and social influence of the Roman Catholic Church, which opposed negative eugenic practices such as contraception and sterilization because it viewed human reproduction as falling under the authority of God only. The state and civil society, according to the church, had no right to tamper with the practices or results of human reproduction, even when those results might be considered physically and mentally unfit.[70]

However, in other ways, Mexico favored negative eugenic techniques not commonly advocated in other Latin American countries. One example of a negative eugenic orientation is the previously mentioned resolution at the 1921 child welfare conference to sterilize criminals.[71] Another is Dr. Rafael

Carrillo's suggestion at the same conference to encourage unfit mothers to "avoid impregnation" or undergo sterilization.[72] A third example is found in the eugenic implications of birth control proposals considered in Yucatán.

Eugenic aspects of postrevolutionary Mexican arguments in favor of birth control are clear in a speech given by the journalist, pedagogue, lawyer, and feminist Esperanza Velázquez Bringas to members and guests of the feminist league "Rita Cetina Gutiérrez" in Mérida, Yucatán, in February 1922.[73] Velázquez Bringas enthusiastically made the following claims:

> Socialism advises us to free the proletariat of all the disgraces that it has experienced for some time.
>
> Eugenics has the obligation of making a selection of individuals for the good of the race. I've seen . . . proletarian families . . . in which the number of children arrives at ten or twelve . . . [and in which] . . . the resources of the father are not enough . . . [and] . . . the mother is forced to help those children grow up without proper nutrition, without the ability to study . . . [and] without the power to play.[74]

Because of this, she argued, "WE HAVE TO RESTRICT THE NUMBER SO THE PRODUCT WILL BE GOOD." She then proposed a series of eugenic congresses to "make women understand . . . [that this] . . . is a necessity in favor of the proletariat and the race."[75]

Velázquez Bringas's statements closely echoed those of the American nurse Margaret Sanger in her pamphlet "The Regulation of Natality or the Standard of the Home: Safe and Scientific Methods to Avoid Conception," which advocated family planning and described different forms of birth control; it was translated into Spanish and printed and distributed in Mérida, Yucatán, in 1922.[76] As Sanger wrote, the regulation of natality was "a necessity of modern societies. . . . No animal has more offspring than it can take care of, but a poor worker in the city has to support ten or twelve children. . . . The ideal for future society is that the state regulate births, through organized scientific corporation, but until we arrive at this ideal we need to put all our effort and knowledge into preventing having children born to degenerate or sick parents."[77] Drawing on ideas of various social theorists, Sanger and Velázquez Bringas suggested that birth control technology should be used by certain social groups (namely working-class urban and rural women, who—in the case of Yucatán—were likely Mayan or mestizo) in order to limit reproduction, thereby discouraging individuals with certain characteristics from reproducing in favor of others.[78]

At the same time, the politicians and reformers—including feminists—who organized and propagandized the Yucatecan campaign tended to be educated, middle-class, white or light mestizo, male and female professionals. Such characteristics are evident in reports on the campaign. For example, Ann Kennedy, executive secretary of the American Birth Control League, who visited the Yucatán in 1923 as a representative of Margaret Sanger, indicates that initiatives were limited to Mérida (where such professionals lived and worked).[79] Furthermore, we have not found a single reference to a birth control clinic or to classes on birth control in or outside Mérida in Yucatecan archives or newspapers. There is no evidence of urban or rural proletarian women engaging in discussions about or practicing the birth control measures advocated by Sanger and Velázquez Bringas. Rather, the campaign appears to be led by more educated, middle-class male and female reformers, directing propaganda at working-class, urban, and rural women.

These tendencies characterizing the birth control campaign are critiqued in a cartoon published in the Yucatecan satirical magazine *Chispas*. In this cartoon, one sees a busy urban white man bustling through a Mayan village holding Sanger's pamphlet in his left hand and a vinegar douche in his right. He passes a bedraggled pregnant woman with three dirty, loud children, who exemplify the subjects in need of such literature. The caption reads "The Patria [Fatherland] Is Saved!" With this sarcastic commentary, *Chispas* suggested that Sanger's pamphlet was directed at Yucatán's rural poor, who were conceived of as dirty, ignorant, and in need of salvation. As such, it both questions and emphasizes Yucatecan revolutionaries'—including feminists'—associations between birth control, progress, and development.

The birth control campaign in Yucatán was effectively stymied through critiques such as that articulated in the *Chispas* cartoon, and, even more significantly, through articles in the *Revista de Yucatán* and *Excelsior* that resulted in the celebration of Mother's Day in Mexico.[80] However, although they quickly declined in popularity in Yucatán, proposals for the use of contraception had spin offs in the states of Querétaro and Veracruz. In March 1922, the Querétaro secretary of government asked the Yucatecan governor Carrillo Puerto to send him some of Sanger's pamphlets to distribute.[81] In April, the Veracruz newspaper *El Dictamen* reported that the Italian activist León Marvini (a likely candidate for the man in the *Chispas* cartoon), who worked for Yucatán's State Committee on Education and participated in the Yucatecan birth control campaign, brought ten thousand pamphlets to the state of Veracruz and was seen distributing them in the port city.[82]

"The Patria [Fatherland] Is Saved!," *Chispas*, no. 272 (March 1, 1922).

Postrevolutionary Mexican Movements for Racial Uplift: Indigenismo and Mestizaje

In addition to the birth control campaign, another way to examine ideas about race—including those infused with eugenic initiatives—in postrevolutionary Mexico is to look at reform intended to achieve racial uplift, often wrapped into the broader revolutionary goal of modernizing Mexicans. Indigenous Mexicans, understood both as "traditional" and "backward," constituted a key target of such reform, and a general commitment to indigenismo—an intellectual orientation that manifested itself in concrete political, economic, and social initiatives—aimed to simultaneously hold up traditional indigenous achievement and to modernize and thereby change real, contemporary "Indians" and indigenous culture. *Indigenistas* built upon Porfirian thinkers who had expressed earlier versions of mestizophilia, such as Justo Sierra and Andrés Molina Enríquez.

The archaeologist and anthropologist Manuel Gamio and the intellectual and politician José Vasconcelos, who served as the federal minister of education from 1921 to 1924, are the most well-known architects of postrevolutionary Mexican indigenismo. Gamio is known for his work excavating Mesoamerican indigenous ruins and for *Forjando Patria: Pro Nacionalismo* (*Forging the Nation: Pro-Nationalism*), his 1916 treatise on the cultural assimilation of indigenous Mexicans into Mexico's mainstream, racially mixed (mestizo) society. Vasconcelos's similar belief in the rise of mestizaje as key to Mexico's future was most famously articulated in *La raza cósmica* (*The Cosmic Race*, 1925), which prophesized that it was America's "divine mission" to become "the cradle of a fifth race into which all nations [Amerindian, Asian, White, and Black would] fuse with each other to replace the four races that have been forging History apart."[83] In the process, Vasconcelos claimed, "unity will be consummated . . . by the triumph of fecund love and . . . improvement of all . . . races."[84] One indication of the popularity of Vasconcelos's vision is that in 1930, Mexican "statisticians dropped [nineteenth-century] 'racial' categories . . . from the census, thus implicitly endorsing a belief in a homogeneous mestizo population."[85]

Vasconcelos was probably a stronger influence on Urzaiz than Gamio, given Urzaiz's work as a teacher and administrator from the elementary through the postdoctoral level. In fact, Urzaiz directly communicated with Vasconcelos when he secured funds for the establishment of the Universidad Nacional del Sureste in 1922 and he likely had other contact with Vasconcelos as well.[86]

According to Vasconcelos, America had not only the opportunity but the purpose and destiny of becoming the site of the rise of a new kind of human race: a cosmic race. As he writes, "America was not kept in reserve for five thousand years" merely to be conquered by white men" but instead to be the cradle for the "mixed race that inhabits the Ibero-American continent," which is destined to "become the first synthetic race of the earth."[87]

This synthetic race, according to Vasconcelos, would be characterized by physical, intellectual, and spiritual perfection, having moved through three stages of social development: a material/warlike phase; an intellectual/political phase (in which the world was currently operating); and a futuristic, spiritual/ aesthetic stage in which humanity would be liberated from rules and norms, operating instead "in a state in which everything that is born from feeling will be right" with "constant inspiration."[88] The cosmic race would bring together the best characteristics of humanity that emerged through this evolutionary process.

Although he shared a three-stage, evolutionary vision of history with his positivist antecedents, Vasconcelos "distanc[ed] himself from Porfirian *científicos*, whom he saw as too wedded to Darwin and Comte," privileging spiritual and artistic explorations of indigenismo over Gamio's and others' more "scientific" approaches.[89] Making sense of Vasconcelos's engagement with aestheticism— which is central to his approach to race—requires recognition of the inherent modernity of an intellectual focus on the aesthetic. Before the Enlightenment, particularly during the classical era, artistic contemplation was not independent of other kinds of thinking. Art was not an object of analysis; rather, it was an integral part of social, cultural, and political life. Vasconcelos and other modern-ist thinkers privileged an aesthetic sensibility with the goal of "mak[ing beauty] a social norm," and for Vasconcelos the "entire history of mankind ha[d] moved teleologically toward an epoch when humans [would] finally be able to be aesthetic beings, freed from practical demands and utilitarian concerns."[90]

Vasconcelos's articulation of an aesthetic form of spiritualism also suggests sympathies with early twentieth-century occult movements such as Theosophy, the "most important neo-religious creation of the nineteenth century, . . . gather[ing] Europe's various 'occult' traditions," including Neoplatonism, gnosticism, kabbala, hermeticism, freemasonry, and esotericism into "a supra-confessional, universalistic, 'primitive' and 'world' religion, . . . contrast[ing] with the orthodoxies of Judaism and the Christian churches" and "'materialistic' Darwinism."[91] Theosophy was driven by the Ukrainian-born aristocrat Helena Petrovna Blavatsky, who cofounded the Theosophical Society in New York in 1875. Influenced by East Asian religions, Blavatsky's teachings and publications discussed "the evolution of the universe, . . . life, and humanity by the interaction of matter and consciousness from the first light through various 'root races' to its present state and beyond."[92] For Blavatsky, root races referred to human groups that existed on now-lost continents such as Atlantis and represented stages in human evolution. Vasconcelos's adoption of such theories can be seen in the following passage in *The Cosmic Race*: "The race that will come out of the forgotten Atlantis will no longer be a race of a single color or of particular features. . . . [It will be] . . . the definitive . . . synthetical . . . integral race, made up of the genius and the blood of all peoples and, for that reason, more capable of true brotherhood and of a truly universal vision."[93] Thus, Vasconcelos refers to Atlantis and universalist notions of God and humanity as a brotherhood — all common points of reference for Blavatsky.

Urzaiz also demonstrates an awareness and perhaps an identification with Theosophic thought, by pointing to neo-Theosophy, which he defines as "nothing more than ancient Theosophy, stripped of the Oriental myths and the remnants of Buddhism of other times, and reduced to a philosophical doctrine that recognized the existence of a Supreme Being, the immortality of the soul and its evolution toward superior worlds and planes through a series of reincarnations,"[94] as the major spiritual orientation of Villautopia.

Vasconcelos and Urzaiz were not alone among modernist intellectuals in their gravitation toward occult or esoteric belief systems. On the contrary, spiritualist movements and attention to the "occult sciences" were key features of modernism. Lay people practiced esoteric forms of spiritualism to personally cope with anxiety stimulated by dramatic changes associated with the ascent of the modern. Such changes included population growth, urbanization, migration, and a growing industrial consumer-based economy and gave rise to a number of new social problems or exacerbated preexisting ones. Medical professionals (including psychologists and psychiatrists) and applied and hard scientists studied the occult sciences in order to address and resolve specific problems and to scientifically examine "irrational" spiritual issues. For example, in Germany, the study of occult practices offered alternatives to nineteenth-century theories of physics, a means to systematically examine the human unconscious, and inspiration for "spiritual" artistic expression. Thus, intellectuals, professionals, and others struggling to reconcile the new opportunities of the modern age with the discomforting observation that their newfound material wealth had "impoverished them spiritually" found ways to address their needs in practicing and/or studying the occult.[95]

Despite the fact that Vasconcelos's interest in racial mixture was grounded in spiritual and aesthetic sensibilities, distancing him from peers who arrived at the same goal through "scientific" motivations, he used "scientific" language and eugenic theory to describe the inferior physical characteristics of certain "racial groups" and to explore the relationship between racial improvement and social development. For example, he writes that through racial mixing,

> the lower types of the species will be absorbed by the superior type. In this manner, for example, the Black can be redeemed, and step by step, by voluntary extinction, the uglier stocks will give way to the more handsome. Inferior races, upon being educated, will become less prolific, and the better specimens will go on ascending a scale of ethnic improvement, whose maximum type is not precisely the White, but that new race to which the White himself will have to aspire with the object of conquering the synthesis. . . . In a few decades of aesthetic eugenics, the Black may disappear, together with the types that a free instinct of beauty may go on signaling as fundamentally recessive and undeserving . . . of perpetuation. In this manner, a selection of taste would take effect, much more efficiently than the brutal Darwinist selection.[96]

Urzaiz articulates similar views. In addition to describing a state-regulated system based on "an organized scientific corporation," which is identical to that foreseen by Margaret Sanger in her pamphlet, distributed in the state of Yucatán through the birth control campaign in which Urzaiz collaborated, in *Eugenia* Urzaiz presents racial perfection as a prerequisite for modern, civilized advancement.[97] For example, Urzaiz describes Ernesto, an official reproducer, as "a figure worthy of posing for a Greek sculptor and a good example of what the progress in hygiene had achieved from a humanity that, hundreds of years before, is known all too well to have been rachitic, toxic, and sickly."[98]

Similarly, the government identifies Ernesto's "robustness, health, beauty, and other favorable conditions" as those making him qualified to act as an official breeder of the species.[99] Urzaiz's allusions to ancient Greece, which is often identified as the birthplace of western civilization, and to hygienic projects, which in postrevolutionary Mexico were conscious scientific efforts to modernize and civilize the populace, link racial perfection with modernity and civilization.

Such advancement is contrasted with an underdeveloped, inferior black race, represented by two African doctors who tour Villautopia's Institute of Eugenics with Ernesto and the institute's director. Urzaiz writes that when they smiled in greeting Ernesto, "the Africans displayed their pearly rows of formidable cannibal-like teeth. One young and the other old, they both were ugly" and the elder "looked like a domesticated chimpanzee."[100] In a conversation with the director, the director's daughter, and Ernesto, one of the Africans explains:

> the social state of our country is quite imperfect and lags behind by at least
> three centuries. . . . To avoid the evolutionary stagnation in which our country
> finds itself, we have tried to mix with superior races. But, given the excellent
> economic conditions of the white nations, and even the most advanced nations
> of Africa itself, so few are the incentives that we can offer immigrants that their
> only hope is the implementation of the system that has yielded such good results
> here and in all advanced countries.[101]

Thus, Urzaiz equates different races with different levels of development, suggesting that one avenue for African modernization would be to crossbreed black Africans with more developed, modern, and civilized white foreigners. Another option, Urzaiz states, is to adopt a eugenic system like Villautopia's to regulate reproduction, limiting procreation to selected representatives of certain racial groups.

Urzaiz and Vasconcelos also share a vision of mating and miscegenation as a product of free will, although Urzaiz limits the pool of *Eugenia*'s diverse population to selected breeders. In contrast, Vasconcelos predicts that "interbreeding will . . . [ultimately cease to] . . . obey reasons of simple proximity as occurred in the beginning when the white colonist took an Indian or black woman because there were no others at hand. In the future . . . the mixture of bloods will become gradually more spontaneous, to the point that interbreeding will no longer be the result of simple necessity but of personal taste."[102]

The descriptions of Ernesto as Greek-like suggest that he had white and European features. In contrast, Eugenia, Ernesto's new lover, appears to have qualities more indigenous to the Americas. In describing the meeting of Ernesto and Eugenia at a dance at the Institute of Eugenics, Urzaiz points to the superior physiology of both reproducers:

> In the turns of the waltz, Ernesto crossed paths several times with the young
> Dr. Suárez, who . . . signaled that they needed to talk. . . . "I've been looking for
> you for a while," said the doctor. "It's important that you know that tonight a
> precious young woman who has just been named an official reproducer will make
> her first public appearance. Her name is Eugenia and I guarantee you that she
> is a delicacy, an authentic innocent, and a splendid thing of beauty. Since she
> still is not aware of the responsibilities of her role, you will understand that there
> are more than four young men already lined up and determined to give her her

first practical lessons. But I want you, the pearl of our reproducers, the pride of the house, to be the zephyr in charge of opening the petals of that rosebud."[103]

After Ernesto accepts the proposition, Suárez takes Ernesto by the arm and crosses the room. Next, Urzaiz explains that Suárez's

> praises of the young woman were no exaggeration. A harmony of figure and proportions, youthful freshness and perfect health, all joined to make Eugenia an admirable example of the human species, a prototype of feminine beauty. There in a remote village in the interior of the region, in full and constant contact with nature, that lush flower of flesh had developed. . . . One might say that Ernesto was born at that moment, that he had never lived before and that the past didn't exist for him. . . . One would have seen Ernesto in a tight spot if someone had asked him if Eugenia was blonde or brunette. What color were her eyes? He wouldn't have been able to tell. Ernesto only knew that, surely tired of avoiding the stares of those annoying ladies' men, her eyes had met his with the calm and sincere happiness of one who, after an extended period, finally found a longed-for shelter, or of one who catches a glimpse of sunlight after a storm.[104]

Although Ernesto admits to not noticing the color of Eugenia's eyes or whether she is blonde or dark-haired, the references to her origins in a small village in the interior suggest that she poses a contrast to the urban and westernized Ernesto. Assuming that Eugenia is at least partially indigenous, one can conclude that Ernesto and Eugenia's pairing mimics the sexual unions (some consensual and some less so) of Spanish conquistadores such as Hernán Cortés with indigenous women such as Cortés's interpreter Malintzin (or Malinche, as she has been maliciously labeled in Mexican folklore). Likewise, the child that Ernesto and Eugenia soon conceive parallels the purported birth of the first mestizo to Cortés and Malintzin.

The union between Ernesto and Eugenia and the birth of their child can also be read as a manifestation of the "cosmic race" envisioned by Vasconcelos, which fuses the best racial and ethnic characteristics of the American and European peoples into the mestizo. In articulating his vision of the cosmic race, Vasconcelos explicitly mentions eugenic theories. He talks about the "crossing of opposites" as a component of Mendel's laws of heredity, arguing that through such interbreeding, "elective types will gradually multiply, while the recessive types will tend to disappear" and "in a very few generations, monstrosities will disappear; what today is normal will come to seem abominable."[105]

The Complex Relationship between the Specter of Depopulation and Eugenics in the Interwar Period and *Eugenia*

At the same time that *Eugenia* portrays a society that encourages only certain population groups to reproduce, the novel indicates a concern with depopulation. This concern is evident in the use of male pregnancy as a remedy for an "extreme depopulation crisis" caused by Malthusianism (an intellectual and social movement calling for population control to avoid disaster, in reference to Thomas Malthus's theory that if unregulated, population growth would surpass Earth's ability to support humankind) and *tocofobia*, the fear of childbirth.[106]

It is also important to consider that at the moment *Eugenia* was written, Sigmund Freud's ideas about "frigidity" might have influenced medical practitioners to interpret a fear of childbirth as related to a fear of sexual touch or sexual interaction, although Freud's writings on psychological impotence were still fairly recent.[107] Thus, tocofobia may be broader than the fear of childbirth — although this fear alone would have certainly been understandable in 1919, when, "for every 1000 live births, six to nine women in the United States died of pregnancy-related complications."[108] We have not been able to find any comparable statistics for Mexico. However, given its differential development experience, presumably Mexico would have had higher maternal mortality rates than the United States.

Many Mexicans shared Urzaiz's concern with depopulation; however, Urzaiz was unusual in pairing this sentiment with support for birth control. A much more common 1920s response (in Mexico and beyond) to the loss of life resulting from war was pronatalist (pro-reproductive) arguments. Thus, while some lauded family planning and eugenics as a way to ensure that poorer families would have fewer children, others, including governments in need of workers to increase industrial production and fight in wars with neighboring countries, criticized these ideologies and practices as promoting "race suicide."[109] In Europe and the United States, such pronatalist arguments were inspired by World War I. In Mexico, they were a response to this global discourse, as well as to the Mexican Revolution.[110]

In an article examining the relationship between fertility control and eugenics, Susanne Klausen and Alison Bashford have observed that although eugenicists' positions and approaches varied significantly, it is possible to identify a gradual shift over several generations from "a position of great wariness, if not outright antagonism to measures aimed at reducing fertility, to a point at which eugenics was defined by faith in them."[111] Early (late nineteenth-century) eugenicists rejected Malthusian calls for the need to restrict population growth and instead favored positive eugenic strategies to encourage population growth among certain social groups. Gradually, however, as they realized that the fittest groups were the ones most likely to use contraception and they therefore could not depend on the fit to out-reproduce the unfit, "eugenicists in Anglo-America— and many other modernizing countries in the non-Catholic world—began . . . to incorporate negative eugenics (and therefore fertility control) into theory and practice."[112] Thus, neo-Malthusian organizations, such as the British Malthusian League, founded in 1877, combined Malthusian ideas with calls to use contraception and inspired the creation of similar organizations in France, Belgium, the United States, and India, particularly in the context of international neo-Malthusian conferences. Margaret Sanger helped to connect neo-Malthusianism to eugenics by promoting birth control as a means to prevent social problems such as poverty and war.[113]

In advocating the use of birth control in the early 1920s, Esperanza Velázquez Bringas, Eduardo Urzaiz, and others were taking a controversial and uncommon position in a predominantly Catholic country that had just suffered a civil war contributing to the loss of at least a tenth of its population. *Eugenia* therefore serves as an excellent example of the complex relationship between concerns over national population numbers, fertility, and eugenic policies during these years. On the one hand, the depopulation crisis that Mexico faced at the time Urzaiz wrote *Eugenia* no doubt influenced Urzaiz in imagining that Villautopia had suffered an extreme depopulation crisis as a result of "Malthusianism" and "tocofobia." It would make sense, in such a context, for Urzaiz to embrace a pronatalist perspective favoring positive eugenic strategies only. However, Urzaiz calls for the sterilization of the majority of Villautopia's residents and for the euthanasia (mercy-killing) of any residents "condemned to spend the rest of their lives, or a large part of it, in a state of unconsciousness or among incurable sufferings," two classic examples of negative eugenic practices.[114] Urzaiz's participation in Yucatán's birth control campaign three years after the publication of *Eugenia* further demonstrates that he advocated blending negative and positive eugenic programs to discourage undesirables from reproducing (or over-reproducing), while encouraging desirables to reproduce.

The literary historian Robert McKee Irwin provides an alternative perspective on tocofobia and why Villautopian women were no longer allowed to carry children to term or bring them into the world through childbirth, which might explain Urzaiz's and others' willingness to limit reproduction among certain groups even in the face of depopulation. Since Villautopian "women who [bore] children ha[d] a maternal instinct that turn[ed] them into loving mothers (as opposed to productive workers or thinkers)," Irwin suggests, preventing

women from giving birth ensured that they would be productive socioeconomic contributors to Villautopian civilization.[115] Perhaps Sanger, Velázquez
Bringas, and others were concerned that potential female workers—and male
workers who earned a family wage—would be burdened by too many children
if reproduction was not strategically limited to those who could support children,
as well as those who had the most desirable traits for future humanity.

Mexicans besides Urzaiz were drawn to using negative eugenic techniques
and/or mixed positive and negative eugenic strategies to regulate reproduction.
The best documented example of this is found in 1932 in the state of Veracruz,
when Governor Adalberto Tejada put forth the "first and only eugenic sterilization law in the country."[116] The Veracruz law required potential parents to
apply to a state-administered board for permission to reproduce. The board
would inquire into whether the couple already had children, their health, and
their ability to provide for and educate their current and/or future children.
These factors would determine the board's authorization of new or continued
reproduction by the couple.[117] The law also authorized the state to perform
sterilization in "clear cases of idiocy . . . degenerate mad[ness], incurabl[e]
ill[ness], and delinquen[cy]"; legalized birth control; and called for sex education
in schools, the obligatory registration and treatment of venereal disease, and
the restriction of alcohol consumption.[118] However, despite his radical visions,
Tejada's eugenics experiment was short-lived; the eugenics law was forgotten
when Tejada was ousted in a conflict between radicals and conservatives over
land reform in the fall of 1932.[119]

Although there is no evidence of continued birth control advocacy in the
Yucatán after 1922 or of eugenics laws, policies, or institutions in Veracruz
after 1932, these brief experiments do illustrate the appeal that eugenic ideas
and policies had for postrevolutionary Mexican reformers, including Urzaiz,
who advocated racial mixture and lauded the mestizo as the symbol of Mexico's
rich heritage and exciting potential.

In addition to linking to contemporaneous approaches to racial uplift and
concerns with under-or overpopulation, Urzaiz's interest in eugenically inspired
reproductive systems was related to his interests in gendered—including
sexual—behavior, gynecology and obstetrics, and psychiatry. Sexuality played
a role in the specialized certification of professionals in many medical and
welfare-driven fields—including gynecology and obstetrics, psychiatry, anthropology, criminology, and social work—as sexual "deviants" and the consequences of sexual behavior, including pregnancy, gave rise to social problems
that demanded attention from eugenicists and other professionals.[120]

The Intersection of Medical Knowledge and
Eugenics Thought in *Eugenia*:
Obstetrician-Gynecologists, Sexologists, and Psychiatrists

Until the nineteenth century, Mexican childbirth was the domain of midwives (known as *parteras, comadres,* or *matronas*) and midwifery was considered a trade linked to experience with childbirth, home remedies, and folk practice rather than a profession relying on medical expertise. Following increased regulation of childbirth under the Real Tribunal del Protomedicato (Royal Tribunal of Medical Practice) and a rise in the publication of translated obstetric materials, by 1768 obstetrics was offered in Mexico's Real Escuela de Cirugía (Royal School of Surgery), which was part of the Real y Pontificia Universidad de México (Royal and Papal University of Mexico), created by royal decree in 1551. Midwives continued to teach physicians to deliver children, however, and surgeons and *parteras* both struggled to be considered legitimate birthers by the medical establishment until 1825, when the tribunal mandated equal consideration for both kinds of professionals. Thus, although the 1870 Ley de Instrucción Pública (Law of Public Instruction) required all medical students to accumulate practical experience in obstetrics, the public remained suspicious of male doctors (surgeons) treating women.[121]

During the Porfiriato, the successful performance of an abdominal hysterectomy helped to legitimize gynecology, while obstetricians linked the treatment of emotional and physiological health by studying feminine disorders.[122] For example, Dr. Manuel Guillén's 1903 thesis at the Escuela de Medicina, focusing on female adolescence, "offered a series of moral and hygienic suggestions to . . . [minimize] . . . the damaging effects of puberty on the reproductive capacity of women's bodies."[123]

Notably, Urzaiz received his medical degree with a specialization in surgery one year before Guillén (in 1902), exploring similar relationships as a gynecologist-obstetrician writing a thesis on "Mental Disequilibrium." Significantly, Urzaiz was not at the Escuela de Medicina in Mexico City; he matriculated in the Escuela de Cirugía y Medicina de la Universidad de Yucatán (the University of Yucatán's School of Surgery and Medicine). Guillén and Urzaiz both indicate that Mexicans were actively exploring medical and scientific issues under examination in other countries, and Urzaiz proves that such developments were not confined to major cities or national capitals.

Guillén and Urzaiz both indicate the reason for medical doctors' fascination and concern with female genitalia: to ensure healthy human reproduction.

Thus, at the same time that obstetrical literature exploring reproductive issues emerged, a related literature, written by social scientists and dedicated to defining and documenting "normal" copulation ("taking place between two individuals of a different sex, using the organs created by nature to propagate the species") and "abnormal" or "unnatural" sexual acts—such as anal or oral intercourse—also appeared.[124] This was as true in Mexico as anywhere else, as social scientific and "criminological investigation into sexual deviance was conducted" and strategies for rehabilitation were devised at the turn of the century.[125] Consequently, many of the doctors and professionals carrying out such investigations were eugenicists. Eugenicists constituted "professors in up to 75% of all courses offered at the national medical school during the 1920s and 1930s . . . [and] . . . dominated in the fields of obstetrics, gynecology and nursing."[126]

It was sexologists—doctors who focused on "the study of human sexuality in its physical, emotional, psychological, and cultural forms"—who dedicated themselves in particular to "demarcat[ing] sexual behaviors in terms of normality and deviancy" and "delineat[ing] . . . specific sexual identities," including "'the homosexual' and 'the pedophile' as categories of perversion" in the late nineteenth century.[127] Yet psychoanalysis competed with sexologists as another medical field focusing on sexual behavior. Freud believed that humans were "innately bisexual," but he "positioned his theory of homosexuality explicitly against sexological paradigms of sexual inversion, arguing that homosexuality was the manifestation of a choice of an object of desire of the same sex, reflecting deep-seated psychological causes."[128] In comparison, sexologists viewed "sexual inversion" as a biological fact related to endocrinological secretions. Individual psychiatrists and sexologists took different positions on the question of whether sexual disorders were "sicknesses" and to what degree such inclinations could be tempered or even reversed.

Medical professionals (including psychiatrists and sexologists) also took different approaches to applying evolutionary theories to sexual behavior. On the one hand, Darwin's writings suggested "that sex existed for the good of the species and . . . sexual selection was a key to evolution," making "sexual activity . . . natural and biologically inevitable"—something that sex radicals and sexologists could use to defend arguments in favor of sexual enjoyment.[129] On the other hand, Darwin warned that "the sexual instinct was beset by dangers that could only be countered or alleviated by social conventions, self-control, sanitary prescriptions, and sex education."[130] Sex drives needed to be kept within healthy limits, and "giving oneself up to uncontrolled impulse was considered dangerous for the health of the individual as well as that of society at large."[131]

Eugenia suggests that Urzaiz was influenced by theories emphasizing biological or "natural" causes for sexual behavior (favored by sexologists) as well as more social or "nurtured" tendencies explored by psychiatrists. Urzaiz promotes an ethic of free love that grants women an unprecedented degree of sexual enjoyment and expression and allows selected breeders to choose among one another, rather than assigning mates, although administrators at the Institute of Eugenics do recommend mates to new breeders. In this way, *Eugenia* is consistent with sexological uses of Darwin to defend sexual enjoyment, upholding Darwinist arguments that sex existed for the good of the species and sexual selection was key to evolution. Toward this end, Urzaiz promotes both a positive eugenic strategy relying on ideal breeders chosen to lead society toward gradual, racial improvement, and a complementary negative eugenic project of sterilizing unfit reproducers and administering euthanasia to people unfit to continue living. Urzaiz's claims that in Villautopia the injection of female hormones into male gestators results in the disappearance of "all erotic impulses" and that Ernesto intends to separate his "idealistic love" for Celiana from the "instinctive carnal possession" required in his work as an official reproducer also perpetuate sexological and conventional beliefs that biological forces (hormones) are the primary determinants of sexual behaviors and differentiations between male and female sex drives.[132] Different hormones, for example, explain why women's *natural* inclination to mother hampers their sex drive, whereas men's more spontaneous and demanding sexual needs allow them to more easily separate sex and love.

On the other hand, the troubled relationship between love and sexuality is at the center of *Eugenia*, and Celiana is clearly in a state of mental anguish related to her abandonment at the hands of Ernesto—her sexual and emotional life partner. It is not clear whether Celiana's psychological problems are solely related to losing Ernesto or are compounded by more general neuroses tracing back to deeper repressed origins, but regardless, they are related to emotional needs. Given Urzaiz's interest in psychiatry and that he has been described as a "Freud fanatic," it is interesting that Villautopian society does not offer Celiana the opportunity to talk about her problems with an analyst, a process that Freud was promoting at the time *Eugenia* was written.[133]

It is also notable that in *Eugenia*, Urzaiz never mentions homosexuality or crime, which were subjects of great interest and concern to psychiatrists, medical doctors, social workers, social scientists, and sexologists during this era. Doña

Candelaria Souza de Fernández reveals that Urzaiz used Freud's Oedipus
Theory to explain homosexuality.[134] Thus, perhaps the absence of such social
problems in *Eugenia* can be explained by Urzaiz's faith in psychological (including
Freudian) and social scientific efforts to uncover the causes for sexual neuroses
and crime and Villautopia's use of such techniques to successfully cure and
prevent these behaviors and problems from resurging (largely through the
elimination of nuclear families who bred neuroses). Perhaps Villautopia's use
of hormone supplements and replacements offers an additional, complementary
sexological approach to eliminating such undesirable characteristics from the
population. Such psychological and sexological means to fight sexual perversion
and crime were compatible with positive and negative eugenic theories and
practices.

Conclusion

Urzaiz's suggestion that racial perfection was a requirement for effective social,
political, and economic modernization (evident in descriptions of Ernesto as a
model of classical Greece—the birthplace of modern western civilization—
and the testimony presented by the two African doctors visiting Villautopia's
eugenics institute in hopes of learning how to overcome "evolutionary stagnation" and join the ranks of other "advanced nations") connects *Eugenia* to the
general postrevolutionary Mexican context in which it was written and to
specific eugenic initiatives that were part of that era. The visiting African
doctors' description of how their failure to attract immigrants allowing their
national natives to "mix with superior races" had convinced them of the need
to implement a system like Villautopia's refers to the relatively unsuccessful
attempts of nineteenth-century Mexican científicos to drive national development by attracting immigrants to Mexico and to the more productive turn to
educational programs designed to assimilate indigenous Mexicans into a more
modern, mestizo culture (defined by a mixture of the best of European and
indigenous influences and characteristics). In the postrevolutionary era, such
educational programs involved eugenically infused reform initiatives discussed
throughout this essay. These included child and maternal welfare programs;
the promotion of health and hygiene in schools; the collection of psychometric
and anthropometric data to track individual Mexican children's (and relatedly
national) development; prenuptial testing and marriage licenses as strategies to
encourage unions between those who were the most promising reproducers; a
child welfare conference resolution to sterilize criminals; a 1932 sterilization

law in the state of Veracruz; and a birth control campaign in the state of Yucatán that articulated a eugenic argument to discourage those with less desirable characteristics from reproducing, while encouraging the fit to be the ones to grow the population instead. Such negative eugenic strategies advocating the use of contraception and sterilization to achieve fertility control were unusual in the 1920s, particularly in a country that had recently lost a tenth of its population in war and had a strong Catholic tradition.

Urzaiz's involvement in the Yucatecan birth control campaign and Villautopia's reliance on medical and psychiatric evaluations and systematic sterilization to ensure the selection of the most fit as official breeders suggest that Urzaiz was familiar with, involved in, and curious about many of these initiatives. As a gynecologist-obstetrician with an interest in psychiatry, Urzaiz drew on sexological and psychological approaches to diagnosing and treating abnormal sexual and criminal behaviors and to designing eugenic strategies to discourage or prevent the unfit (including those displaying these problematic behaviors) from reproducing while encouraging the fit to reproduce instead.

All of these connections between the imaginary world that Urzaiz constructs in *Eugenia* and the real world of 1919 Yucatán in which Urzaiz carried this out suggest that Urzaiz promoted eugenics. Yet there are other ways in which *Eugenia* seems to be warning against the possible results of establishing an authoritarian state and society that takes eugenic programs too far. He does this first by providing certain checks against authoritarianism in Villautopia itself. For example, in Villautopia, selected breeders are allowed to choose one another as sexual partners (rather than being assigned a mate), while others form their own (non-procreating) family groups. Second, such sexual and familial freedom is supported by Villautopia's political economy, which supports children, the poor, the elderly, and the handicapped with stipends from the public services fund, counting on income from wealthy citizens since legacies and inheritance have been abolished.[135] In other words, Villautopia is not purely or extremely socialist or communist (with socialist, communist, and fascist political-economic formulations providing the major models of authoritarianism in Urzaiz's day), since Villautopians are able to earn a surplus and build up savings in the course of their lives. The final and most significant way that Urzaiz warns against and limits authoritarian extremes in Villautopia is by ending the novel with Ernesto and Eugenia's decision to abandon the eugenics institute, move to the countryside, and perhaps give birth to and raise their child outside the confines of Villautopia, thereby creating a nuclear family. By allowing the reader to imagine this ending to *Eugenia*'s plot, Urzaiz challenges the ethic of free love and the model of nonnuclear families that he has placed at the core of

Villautopian familial, love, and sexual relationships. In this way, Urzaiz may be voicing his rejection of authoritarianism and eugenic strategies to regulate human reproduction.

NOTES

1. Urzaiz, *Eugenia*, 7.

2. The term "interwar years" refers to the years between World War I and World War II (1919–39). For an excellent, recent introduction to the growing literature on global examples of eugenics in this and other periods, see Philippa Levine and Alison Bashford, eds., *The Oxford Handbook of the History of Eugenics* (New York: Oxford University Press, 2010).

3. Urzaiz, *Eugenia*, 30.

4. Ibid., 31–32.

5. Ibid., 30.

6. We are drawing on Alexandra Minna Stern's use of the term "mestizophilia" in "Responsible Mothers and Normal Children: Eugenics, Nationalism, and Welfare in Post-revolutionary Mexico, 1920–1940," *Journal of Historical Sociology* 12, no. 4 (December 1999): 372. Stern takes this term from Agustín Basave Benítez, *México mestizo: Análisis del nacionalismo mexicano en torno a la mestizofilia de Andrés Molina Enríquez* (Mexico City: Fondo de Cultura Económica, 1992).

7. Nancy Leys Stepan, *"The Hour of Eugenics": Race, Gender, and Nation in Latin America* (Ithaca, NY: Cornell University Press, 1991), 2; Alexandra Stern, "Eugenics," in *Encyclopedia of Mexico: History, Society & Culture*, ed. Michael S. Werner (Chicago: Fitzroy Dearborn Publishers, 1997), 1:462.

8. Sir Francis Galton coined the term "eugenics" in his work *Inquiries into Human Faculty and Its Development* (London: Macmillan, 1883) to refer to "the science of improving the stock" (Marius Turda, "Race, Science, and Eugenics in the Twentieth Century," in Levine and Bashford, *The Oxford Handbook of the History of Eugenics*, 64). Galton based the term on the Greek word *eugenes*, which is comprised of "eu . . . the Greek word for the adverb 'well,' and gen, which has its roots in the verb gignesthai, meaning 'to become'" (Nickolaus Knoepffler, "Eugenics," in *Encyclopedia of Anthropology*, ed. H. James Birx [Thousand Oaks, CA: Sage, 2006], 2:871), to mean "well-born" (Lynne Fallwell, "Eugenics," in *Encyclopedia of Genocide and Crimes Against Humanity*, ed. Dinah L. Shelton [Detroit: Macmillan Reference, 2005], 1:315). See also Garland E. Allen, "Eugenics," in *New Dictionary of the History of Ideas*, ed. Maryanne Cline Horowitz (Detroit: Scribner, 2005), 2:732.

9. Philippa Levine and Alison Bashford, "Introduction," in *The Oxford Handbook of the History of Eugenics*, 4.

10. Jean-Baptiste Lamarck, *Philosophie zoologique ou exposition des considérations relatives à l'histoire naturelle des animaux* (Paris: Germer Baillère, 1809).

11. Peter J. Bowler, *Theories of Human Evolution: A Century of Debate, 1844–1944* (Baltimore: Johns Hopkins University Press, 1986), 42.

12. For example, see Diane B. Paul and James Moore's discussion of how creationists have blamed Darwin "not just for the rise of eugenics, but for that movement's absolutely worst barbarities" ("The Darwinian Context: Evolution and Inheritance," in Levine and Bashford, *The Oxford Handbook of the History of Eugenics*, 27).

13. Paul and Moore, "The Darwinian Context," 34. Alexandra Stern explains that before the early twentieth century, genes were often called characters ("Gender and Sexuality: A Global Tour and Compass," in Levine and Bashford, *The Oxford Handbook of the History of Eugenics*, 182).

14. Paul and Moore, "The Darwinian Context," 28.

15. Spencer first used the expression "survival of the fittest" in the October 1864 installment of *Principles of Biology* (see note 5 of Letter 5140, from A. R. Wallace to C. R. Darwin, July 2, 1866 [Spencer 1864–67, 1:444–45], http://www.darwinproject.ac.uk /entry-5140). Galton first used the term "eugenics" in *Inquiries into Human Faculty and Its Development*, although he had researched the application of the "laws of inheritance" to humans for the previous twenty years, as is outlined above (see Knoepffler, "Eugenics," 2:871).

16. This was the last part of a *Synthetic Philosophy*, which Spencer began with *Principles of Psychology* in 1862 (*The New Encyclopedia Britannica: Ready Reference*, 15th ed., s.v. "Spencer, Herbert").

17. The term "social Darwinism" refers to the "theory that societies, classes, and races are subject to and a product of Darwinian laws of natural selection" (*Oxford English Dictionary*, s.v. "social Darwinism"). The first known quotation using the term is found in the *Transactions of the Royal Society* 5 (1877): 520: "I can find nothing in the Brehon laws to warrant this theory of social Darwinism." In the United States, the first reference is to "social Darwinists" in the *Harvard Quarterly Journal of Economics* 17 (1904): 448: "The master error of the social Darwinists is to see in the economic struggle a twin to the 'struggle for existence' that plays so fateful a part in the modification of species" (*Oxford English Dictionary*, s.v. "social Darwinist").

Years after the initial coining and use of these terms, the American historian Richard Hofstadter popularized the phrase and concept significantly in his *Social Darwinism in American Thought: 1860–1915* (Philadelphia: University of Pennsylvania Press, 1944), and ever since, according to Jon H. Roberts, "the nature and influence of 'social Darwinism' have dominated discussion of the relationship between evolution and American social theory. This is unfortunate, for while virtually all social thinkers after 1875 embraced the transmutation hypothesis and while many employed Darwinian vocabulary—'struggle,' 'selection,' 'survival,' and the like—in describing interactions among individuals, classes, nations, and races, the uses to which they put that rhetoric were so diverse that we are not well served by employing 'social Darwinism' as a descriptive term for a determinate set of ideas" (Jon H. Roberts, "The Struggle over Evolution," in *Encyclopedia of American Cultural & Intellectual History*, ed. Mary Kupiec Cayton and Peter W. Williams [New York: Scribner, 2001], 1:595). Thus, although the term itself was not necessarily used widely in the late nineteenth century, it "has become a universal catchword for late nineteenth-century social attitudes" (Charles A. Hale, *The Transformation of Liberalism in Late Nineteenth-Century Mexico* [Princeton, NJ: Princeton University Press, 1989], 205).

18. Adam Briggle, "Spencer, Herbert," in *Encyclopedia of Science, Technology, and Ethics*, ed. Carl Mitcham (Detroit: Macmillan Reference, 2005), 1848.

19. Oscar R. Martí, "Justo Sierra and the Forging of a Mexican Nation," in *Forging People: Race, Ethnicity, and Nationality in Hispanic American and Latino/a Thought*, ed. Jorge J. E. García (Notre Dame, IN: Notre Dame University Press, 2011), 156.

20. See John Hedley Brooke, "Darwin, Charles," in *Encyclopedia of Science and Religion*, ed. Wentzel Vreded van Huyssteen (New York: Macmillan Reference, 2003), 1:200. Malthus argued that population "increases in a geometrical ratio" whereas "subsistence increases . . . in an arithmetical ratio" making the "power of population . . . indefinitely greater than the power in the earth to produce subsistence to man." Consequently, if left unchecked, population would outstrip the food supply, leading to famine, disease, and social unrest. See "Malthus, Thomas Robert (1766–1834)," in *Encyclopedia of European Social History*, ed. Peter N. Stearns (Detroit: Scribner, 2001), 6:213.

21. Turda, "Race, Science, and Eugenics in the Twentieth Century," 64.

22. "Hereditary Talent and Character" was a two-part article published in the respected, popular, upper-middle-class *MacMillan's Magazine*. Four years later (in 1869), Galton revised the article into the book *Hereditary Genius*. See Nicholas Wright Gillham, "Galton, Francis," in Mitcham, *Encyclopedia of Science, Technology, and Ethics*, 2:817; and Paul and Moore, "The Darwinian Context," 29.

23. Paul and Moore, "The Darwinian Context," 29.

24. Richard Weikart, "Eugenics," in Mitcham, *Encyclopedia of Science, Technology, and Ethics*, 2:708.

25. See Levine and Bashford, "Introduction," 4; Paul and Moore, "The Darwinian Context," 32; and Peter Bowler, *Theories of Human Evolution*, 3.

26. Nils Rolls-Hansen, "Eugenics and the Science of Genetics," in Levine and Bashford, *The Oxford Handbook of the History of Eugenics*, 83.

27. Nathaniel Comfort, *The Science of Human Perfection: How Genes Became the Heart of American Medicine* (New Haven, CT: Yale University Press, 2012), 12.

28. Mark Wasserman, *Everyday Life and Politics in Nineteenth Century Mexico: Men, Women, and War* (Albuquerque: University of New Mexico Press, 2000), 9–10.

29. Colin M. MacLachlan and William H. Beezley, *El Gran Pueblo: A History of Greater Mexico*, 2nd ed. (Upper Saddle River, NJ: Prentice Hall, 1999), 47.

30. In 1866, Díaz led Juárez's liberal troops in a successful rally against the French, who had invaded Mexico in 1862 and installed Napoléon III's cousin, the Austrian Archduke Ferdinand Maximilian, as emperor in November 1864. Consequently, Juárez served his presidency from exile in various cities during these years.

31. James A. Garza, "Díaz, Porfirio," in Werner, *Encyclopedia of Mexico*, 1:406.

32. Martí, "Justo Sierra and the Forging of a Mexican Nation," 154. For a list of Comte's writings on positivism, including authoritative English translations, see Bruce

Mazlish, "Comte, Auguste," in *Encyclopedia of Philosophy*, 2nd ed., ed. Donald M. Borchert (Detroit: Macmillan Reference, 2006), 2:414.

33. Martí, "Justo Sierra and the Forging of a Mexican Nation," 154–55; Jürgen Buchenau, "Social Darwinism," in Werner, *Encyclopedia of Mexico*, 2:1351; Harold Kincaid, "Positivism in the Social Sciences," *Routledge Encyclopedia of Philosophy*, ed. Edward Craig (New York: Routledge, 1988), 7:558.

34. Margarita Vera Cuspinera, "Positivism," in Werner, *Encyclopedia of Mexico*, 2:1178.

35. Martí, "Justo Sierra and the Forging of a Mexican Nation," 155.

36. Organic Law of 1867 (see Martí, "Justo Sierra and the Forging of a Mexican Nation," 162).

37. See, for example, Gonzalo Aguirre Beltrán, *Obra polémica* (Mexico City: Instituto Nacional de Antropología e Historia, 1976), 35–40; Arnaldo Córdova, *La ideologia de la Revolución Mexicana: La formación del nuevo regimen* (Mexico City: Ediciones Era, 1973), 53–54, 63–64; and Moisés González Navarro, *Historia moderna de México: El Porfiriato, la vida social* (Mexico City: Editorial Hermes, 1970), 150–77, cited in Alan Knight, "Racism, Revolution, and *Indigenismo*: Mexico, 1910–1940," in *The Idea of Race in Latin America, 1870–1940*, ed. Richard Graham (Austin: University of Texas Press, 1990), 78 and 104n34.

38. Hale, *The Transformation of Liberalism in Late Nineteenth-Century Mexico*, 214. We have not found any citations in primary (journals and newspapers) or secondary sources indicating use of the term "Darwinismo social" (social Darwinism) in Mexico during the late nineteenth or early twentieth century.

39. Robert Moreno, "Mexico," in *The Comparative Reception of Darwinism*, ed. Thomas F. Glick (Chicago: University of Chicago Press, 1988), 346–74. Moreno's assertions regarding Mexican publications engaging with evolution and citing Darwin are based on a "laborious search of [Mexico's] nineteenth-century scientific and general press" (373). Santiago Serra's work translating *Descent of Man* is discussed by Moreno (351) and by Martí, "Justo Sierra and the Forging of a Mexican Nation," 175n17.

40. The term "científicos" was coined in reference to a particular group of Porfirian insiders by *El Siglo XIX*, a newspaper opposed to the científicos' reform, but was quickly adopted as a more general insult to Porfirian leaders (Jürgen Buchenau, "Científicos," in Werner, *Encyclopedia of Mexico*, 1:260–62).

41. See Alexandra Minna Stern, "From Mestizophilia to Biotypology," in *Race & Nation in Latin America*, ed. Nancy P. Appelbaum, Anne S. MacPherson, and Karin Alejandra Rosemblatt (Chapel Hill: University of North Carolina Press, 2003), 189, and Martí, "Justo Sierra and the Forging of a Mexican Nation," 166.

42. Knight, "Racism, Revolution, and *Indigenismo*," 73.

43. The citation for the historian is Enrique Krauze, *Porfirio Díaz* (Mexico City: Fondo de Cultura Económica, 1987), 8, and the contemporary was "an American who'd lived in Mexico for 24 years and whose views would have tallied with those of elite Mexicans" (both referenced, along with Alan Knight, *The Mexican Revolution*, vol. 1,

Porfirians, Liberals and Peasants [Cambridge: Cambridge University Press, 1986], 3–4, in Knight, "Racism, Revolution, and *Indigenismo*," 73).

44. Claudio Lomnitz-Adler, *Exits from the Labyrinth: Culture and Ideology in the Mexican National Space* (Berkeley: University of California Press, 1992), 292.

45. The quotation is from Stern, "From Mestizophilia to Biotypology," 190. Alan Knight discusses the thinkers that Molina Enríquez drew on in "Racism, Revolution, and *Indigenismo*," 85.

46. Levine and Bashford, "Introduction," 11.

47. Stern, "From Mestizophilia to Biotypology," 188–89. In discussing connections between ideas about race, medical and biological knowledge, state-building, and anti-clerical scientific reform in Mexico and beyond, Stern (205–6) cites Michel Foucault, *Ethics: Subjectivity and Truth*, ed. Paul Rabinow (New York: New Press, 1997); Michel Foucault, *The History of Sexuality*, vol. 1, *An Introduction*, trans. Robert Hurley (New York: Vintage Books, 1996); Sam Whimster and Scott Lash, eds., *Max Weber: Rationality and Modernity* (London: Allen and Unwin, 1987); Ann Laura Stoler, *Race and the Education of Desire: Foucault's "History of Sexuality" and the Colonial Order of Things* (Durham, NC: Duke University Press, 1995); Ann Laura Stoler, "Sexual Affronts and Racial Frontiers: European Identities and the Cultural Politics of Exclusion in Colonial Southeast Asia," in *Tensions of Empire: Colonial Cultures in a Bourgeois World*, ed. Frederic Cooper and Ann Laura Stoler (Berkeley: University of California Press, 1997), 198–237; Hannah Arendt, *The Origins of Totalitarianism* (New York: Harcourt Brace Jovanovich, 1973); and Patrick H. Hutton, "Foucault, Freud, and the Technologies of the Self," in *Technologies of the Self*, ed. Luther H. Martin, Huck Gutman, and Patrick H. Hutto (Amherst: University of Massachusetts Press, 1988), 121–44. In an examination of the late nineteenth-century relationship between the regulation of sexuality and the rise of racist thought ("in its modern, 'biologizing,' statist form, alternatively called the "thematics of blood""), Michel Foucault writes that "a eugenic ordering of society, with all that implied in the way of extension and intensification of micro-powers, in the guise of an unrestricted state control was accompanied by the oneiric exaltation of a superior blood; the latter implied both the systematic genocide of others and the risk of exposing oneself to a total sacrifice" (*The History of Sexuality*, 1:149–50).

48. Diego Von Vacano, "A Zarathustra Criollo: Vasconcelos on Race," in García, *Forging People*, 212. Von Vacano (225) cites Michael Omi and Howard Winant, *Racial Formation in the United States: From the 1960s to the 1990s* (New York: Routledge, 1994), 61–62.

49. Levine and Bashford, "Introduction," 14; Frank Dikötter, "Race Culture: Recent Perspectives on the History of Eugenics," *American Historical Review* 103, no. 2 (April 1998): 467.

50. Allen G. Roper, *Ancient Eugenics: The Arnold Prize Essay for 1913* (Oxford: Blackwell, 1913), cited in Levine and Bashford, "Introduction," 11.

51. In 1902, the English pediatrician Archibald Garrod, "who had been pointed in the right analytical direction by [the British naturalist William] Bateson, convincingly showed that certain 'inborn errors of metabolism'—notably alcaptonuria, a disease

signaled by a darkening of the urine after birth—were caused in a Mendelian manner by recessive genes" (Daniel J. Kevles, *In the Name of Eugenics: Genetics and the Uses of Human Heredity*, rev. ed. [Cambridge, MA: Harvard University Press, 1995], 44), thereby "describ[ing] the first Mendelian trait in human beings" (Comfort, *The Science of Human Perfection*, 2). Three years later, Bateson coined the term "genetics" while "applying unsuccessfully for a chair in the field he had helped to invent" (Comfort, *The Science of Human Perfection*, 17). Bateson was also the "first to use the term 'genetics' publicly (in 1906)" (Rolls-Hansen, "Eugenics and the Science of Genetics," 83). According to Kevles, "the likeliest reason" that it took so long for scientists to recognize Mendel's work was that "biologists were fastened on the problem of Darwinian evolution in a way that made them unripe for the advent of Mendelian genetics. Evolutionists of the day focused on the adaptation of species—on change. Mendel's theory accounted for the ongoing transmission of characters—for stability" (Kevles, *In the Name of Eugenics*, 42).

52. Patience A. Schell, "Nationalizing Children through Schools and Hygiene: Porfirian and Revolutionary Mexico City," *The Americas* 60, no. 4 (2004): 566–68.

53. Dr. Manuel Iturbide y Troncoso, "Informe de los Trabajos Ejecutados por el servicio Higiénico Escolar durante el Año Fiscal 1909–1910," *Anales de Higiene Escolar* 1, no. 2 (November 1911): 127, cited in Stern, "Responsible Mothers," 383 and 395n87.

54. Stern, "Responsible Mothers," 383. See also Francis Galton, *The Anthropometric Laboratory* (London: William Clowes and Sons, 1884), 3.

55. For the names and professions of many delegates to the conferences, see "Mañana se inaugura el congreso mexicano del niño a las 11 AM," *El Universal*, January 1, 1921, 1; "La inauguración del congreso del niño," *El Universal*, January 2, 1921, 1; "Todas las agrupaciones científicas y las dependencies educativas y sanitarias del Gobierno, representadas," *El Universal*, January 3, 1921, 1; "Hoy se inaugura el Segundo Congreso del Niño," *El Universal*, January 1, 1923, 10; "Ayer quedó instalado el Segundo Congreso Mexicano del Niño," *El Universal*, January 2, 1923, 1; "Eduquemos a los niños para una obra de amor, de fuerza, y de concordia," *El Universal*, January 3, 1923, 6; Buck, "Activists and Mothers," chap. 3, 242–46; Schell, "Nationalizing Children," 571–72; and Stern, "Responsible Mothers," 383.

56. The national daily newspaper *El Universal*, which sponsored the conferences, portrayed them as scientific explorations of ways to improve childhood and children to further Mexican social, political, and economic development ("Todas las agrupaciones científicas," *El Universal*, January 3, 1921, 1); on sterilization, see Alfredo Saavedra M., "Lo que México ha publicado acerca de eugenesia," in Ateneo Nacional de Ciencias y Artes, *Primero Congreso Bibliográfico Mexicano* (Mexico City: DAPP, 1937), 103–25, cited in Stepan, *"The Hour of Eugenics,"* 56.

57. See Stern, "Responsible Mothers," 369 and 373, and Patience A. Schell, "Eugenics Policy and Practice in Cuba, Puerto Rico, and Mexico," in Levine and Bashford, *The Oxford Handbook of the History of Eugenics*, 485. For Velázquez Bringas's and Ursúa's attendance at the child welfare conferences, see "Mañana se inaugura," *El Universal*, January 1, 1921, 1, and "Hoy se inaugura," *El Universal*, January 1, 1923, 10.

172 *Eugenia and Eugenics*

58. Schell, "Nationalizing Children," 576. Schell cites Secretaría de Educación Pública, *El esfuerzo educativo en México: La obra del gobierno federal en el ramo de educación pública durante la administración del presidente Plutarco Elías Calles (1924–1928); Memoria analítico-crítica de la organización actual de la Secretaría de Educación Pública, sus éxitos, sus fracasos, los derroteros que la experiencia señala; Presentada al H. Congreso de la Unión por el Dr. J. M. Puig Casauranc, secretario del ramo en obediencia al Artículo 93 constitucional* (Mexico City, 1928), 12.

59. Stern, "Responsible Mothers," 373, and Alexandra Stern, "Unraveling the History of Eugenics in Mexico," *The Mendel Newsletter*, n.s., 8 (February 1999): 1–10.

60. Stern, "Responsible Mothers, 373–74, and Schell, "Nationalizing Children," 576.

61. Schell, "Eugenics Policy and Practice in Cuba, Puerto Rico, and Mexico," 479.

62. Ibid.

63. Stern "Responsible Mothers," 372–75, and Schell, "Eugenics Policy and Practice in Cuba, Puerto Rico, and Mexico," 485. Espinosa de los Reyes's narrative history of the Child Hygiene Service ("Untitled," Archivo Historico de la Secretaría de Salubridad y Asistencia, Fondo: Salubridad Pública, Sección: Higiene Infantil, box 4, folder 21) is cited in Stern, "Responsible Mothers," 374.

64. Citing Alan Knight, Patience Schell writes that the "'new man' emerging from the [Mexican revolutionary] educational project was to be sober, industrious, patriotic, literate, and moral. He would dedicate his labor to capitalist gain for himself, his employers, and the nation" (Alan Knight, "Revolutionary Project, Recalcitrant People: Mexico, 1910–1940," in *The Revolutionary Process in Mexico: Essays on Political and Social Change, 1880–1940*, ed. Jaime E. Rodríguez O. [Los Angeles: UCLA Latin American Center Publications and Mexico/Chicano Program of the University of California, 1990], 242, cited in Schell, "Nationalizing Children," 563). Schell adds that "the new man needed, nay deserved, a new woman and new children. New women were to be educated, rational housewives and mothers, who creatively stretched husband's wages to design a domestic refuge, thus keeping the new man sober and productive" (Schell, "Nationalizing Children," 563). Beatriz Urías Horcasitas does an excellent job discussing the similarities between the new man and the importance of racial purification in reform and state consolidation in Mexico and other authoritarian case studies in her book *Historias secretas del racismo en México (1920–1950)* (Mexico City: Tusquets, 2007).

65. Urías Horcasitas, *Historias secretas del racismo*, 19.

66. Paul Eiss, "Deconstructing Indians, Reconstructing *Patria*: Indigenous Education in Yucatán from the *Porfiriato* to the Mexican Revolution," *Journal of Latin American Anthropology* 9, no. 1 (Spring 2004): 121.

67. Urías Horcasitas, *Historias secretas del racismo*, 17–18. In making this argument, Urías draws upon the work of Peter Gay, who, she writes, has shown how late nineteenth-century Europeans drew upon "racial theories derived from social Darwinism . . . to define codes of exclusion towards groups representing irreconcilable and unacceptable differences" (Peter Gay, *The Bourgeois Experience: Victoria to Freud*, vol. 3, *The Cultivation of Hatred* [New York: W. W. Norton, 1993]). Frank Dikötter discusses how eugenics used

race in this way as well, writing, "eugenics was not so much a clear set of scientific principles as a 'modern' way of talking about social problems in biologizing terms. . . . Eugenics gave scientific authority to social fears and moral panics, leant respectability to racial doctrines . . . [and] allowed modernizing elites to represent their prescriptive claims about social order as objective statements irrevocably grounded in the laws of nature" (Dikötter, "Race Culture," 467–68).

68. The emergent ruling faction of the revolution, the Constitutionalists, upheld the democratic, republican style of government inherited from the liberal reform era of the mid-nineteenth century. The 1917 constitution followed the 1857 constitution closely in establishing a division of powers between executive, legislative, and judicial branches, with a president and members of two congressional chambers elected by direct, popular vote. At the same time, Mexico stood out in a global context for its early and continued dedication to codifying populist labor and indigenous rights, as was reflected in the 1917 constitution, agrarian reform law, the 1928 civil code, and the 1931 labor code. Yet such popular laws also provided a basis for corporatist, co-optative, and at times authoritarian styles of rulership, defended particularly in constitutional articles 27 and 123. See, for example, Juan Felipe Leal, "Notas sobre el nuevo estado," in *Cien años de lucha de clases: Lecturas de historia de México (1876–1976)*, ed. Ismael Colmenares M., Miguel Angel Gallo T., Francisco González G., and Luis Hernández N. (Mexico City: Ediciones Quinto Sol, 1980), 1:307–10, and Kevin Middlebrook, *The Paradox of Revolution: Labor, the State, and Authoritarianism in Mexico* (Baltimore: Johns Hopkins University Press, 1995).

69. Stepan, *"The Hour of Eugenics,"* 8–9. Corporatism was an identifiable approach to social organization during these years in Mexico (particularly under the leadership of Lázaro Cárdenas in the 1930s), Brazil (particularly under the leadership of Getulio Vargas in the 1930s and early 1940s), and Argentina (particularly under the leadership of Juan Perón in the 1940s). Not insignificantly, these three countries (Mexico, Brazil, and Argentina) were Stepan's national case studies in *"The Hour of Eugenics,"* which she identifies as "exemplary [examples] of eugenics" in Latin America (Stepan, *"The Hour of Eugenics,"* 14).

70. Ibid., 111–12.

71. Ibid., 56.

72. Stern, "Responsible Mothers," 375.

73. Velázquez Bringas was born in 1899 in Orizaba, Veracruz, but spent much of her life until her 1968 death in Mexico City. In 1917, at the age of eighteen, she began writing for *El Pueblo*. She received her law degree in Mérida in 1924. She later became the children's editor for *El Universal*. She also wrote books on art, poetry, maternal and child welfare, Mexican law, Japanese and Russian culture, and women's involvement in the Pan American Round Table, and she attended the first child welfare congress. See Aurora Tovar Ramírez, *Mil quinientas mujeres en nuestra conciencia colectiva: Catálogo biográfico de mujeres de México* (Mexico City: Documentación y Estudios de Mujeres, A.C., 1996), 654.

74. "La limitación racional de la familia como mejoramiento de la raza," *El Popular*, March 1, 1922, 3.

75. Ibid.

76. Sanger, "La regulación de la natalidad," and Rico, *Congreso Obrero de Izamal*, 164.

77. Sanger, "La regulación de la natalidad," 4.

78. Velázquez Bringas acknowledged the works of the sexologist Havelock Ellis and the economists Thomas Malthus, Pierre-Joseph Proudhón, Adam Smith, and Karl Marx as influences on her ideas (see "La limitación racional de la familia"). See additional discussions of Malthus and Malthusianism in general, in postrevolutionary Mexico, and in *Eugenia* in the introduction and the essay "Social and Biological Reproduction in *Eugenia*" in this volume.

79. See notes 112 and 113 in "Social and Biological Reproduction in *Eugenia*."

80. See "Social and Biological Reproduction in *Eugenia*," 111–15, for a discussion of these articles and the genesis of Mother's Day celebrations in Yucatán and Mexico.

81. Secretary of the Government of the State of Querétaro to Governor Carrillo Puerto, March 24, 1922, AGEY RPE C 760.

82. "La circulacion del folleto aquel en V.Cruz: Una excitativa del diario 'El Dictamen,'" *La Revista de Yucatán*, April 1, 1922, 1.

83. José Vasconcelos, *The Cosmic Race/La raza cósmica*, trans. Didier T. Jaén, afterword by Joseba Gabilondo (Baltimore: Johns Hopkins University Press, 1997), 18.

84. Ibid.

85. Stern, "Responsible Mothers," 371. On the Mexican census, Stern (389n13) refers readers to Luis A. Astorga A., "La razón demográfica del Estado," *Revista Mexicana de Sociología* (January–March 1989): 193–210.

86. Arturo Erosa-Barbachano, "Historia de la Escuela de Medicina de Mérida, Yucatán, México," *Revista Biomédica* 3, no. 4 (October–December 1997): 267.

87. Vasconcelos, *The Cosmic Race/La raza cósmica*, 18, 23.

88. Ibid., 29. Diego Von Vacano shows that Vasconcelos's emphasis on a spiritual understanding of aesthetics draws heavily from the influence of Friedrich Nietzsche; for both Vasconcelos and Nietzsche, aesthetics is central to the metaphysics of life. Vasconcelos and Nietzsche also share concern with an over-reliance on science and attempt to restore spirituality; however, they do so in very different ways. Nietzsche struggles to reconcile his rejection of Judeo-Christian values and practices with a desire for a secular form of spirituality; Vasconcelos is a committed Catholic (Von Vacano, "A Zarathustra Criollo," 216).

89. Stern, "From Mestizophilia to Biotypology," 191.

90. Von Vacano, "A Zarathustra Criollo," 211, 213.

91. *The Brill Dictionary of Religion*, s.v. "Theosophical/Anthroposophical Society." According to Annie Besant, a key figure in the Theosophical movement, Theosophy was universalist in that it taught of "*the unity of God*, the universal one Existence which is the source of all existences actual and potential, the super-life and super-consciousness in which all lives and consciousnesses inhere" and of the "*universal brotherhood* . . . since there is but one life in all forms, all forms must be inter-related, linked together, and, however

unequal they may be in development, they none the less make one huge family, are 'of one blood'" (Annie Besant, "Theosophical Society," in *Encyclopaedia of Religion and Ethics*, ed. James Hastings [New York: Charles Scribner's Sons, 1924], 301).

92. Robert S. Ellwood, "Blavatsky, H. P." in *Encyclopedia of Religion*, 2nd ed., ed. Lindsey Jones (Detroit: Macmillan Reference, 2005), 977.

93. Vasconcelos, *The Cosmic Race/La raza cósmica*, 20.

94. Urzaiz, *Eugenia*, 73. Originally, the term "neo-Theosophy" was used to refer to ideas developed by Blavatsky's successors, Annie Besant and Charles Leadbeater.

95. Corinna Treitel, *A Science for the Soul: Occultism and the Genesis of the German Modern* (Baltimore: Johns Hopkins University Press, 2004), 19. I was introduced to Treitel by Thomas Laqueur in his excellent review essay "Why the Margins Matter: Occultism and the Making of Modernity," *Modern Intellectual History* 3, no. 1 (April 2006): 111–35, in which he also points to Alex Owen's work on similar historical phenomena in England (*The Place of Enchantment: British Occultism and the Culture of the Modern* [Chicago: University of Chicago Press, 2004]).

96. Vasconcelos, *The Cosmic Race/La raza cósmica*, 32.

97. Sanger, "La regulación de la natalidad," 4.

98. Urzaiz, *Eugenia*, 6.

99. Ibid., 7.

100. Ibid., 28.

101. Ibid., 42.

102. Vasconcelos, *The Cosmic Race/La raza cósmica*, 26–27.

103. Urzaiz, *Eugenia*, 79.

104. Ibid., 80.

105. Vasconcelos, *The Cosmic Race/La raza cósmica*, 31–32.

106. Urzaiz, *Eugenia*, 66. Dr. Castillo explains that the word "tocofobia" is a combination of the Greek terms *tocos* (*parto*, or birth) and *fobe* (*miedo*, or fear). This translation is borne out in the fact that today, one Spanish translation for gynecologist is *tocólogo*, suggesting that tocofobia is a fear of anything associated with touching genitalia or involving reproduction. *Ginecólogo* is another term for gynecologist that is commonly used.

The term "tocofobia" (*tokophobia* in German and *tocophobie* in French) was used in medical literature at least as early as 1897; see O. Knauer, *Urber puerperale Psychosen, für practische Aerzte*, cited in Singh Bhatia and Jhanjee, "Tokophobia: A Dread of Pregnancy," 158. Thus, given his interest and expertise in reproductive health and psychiatry, Urzaiz would certainly have been familiar with the term by 1919.

Doña Candelaria Souza de Fernández, who was close to Urzaiz and describes him as her mentor, suggests that Urzaiz was referring to a psychological fear of the responsibility of parenting with the term "tocofobia" (Sarah Buck Kachaluba, interview with Doña Candelaria Souza de Fernández, July 1, 2014, Mérida, Yucatán).

107. In his second paper on love, "On the Universal Tendency to Debasement in the Sphere of Love" (Contributions to the Psychology of Love II), published in 1912,

Freud suggested that one way to explain the behavior of "the immense number of frigid women" was to "compar[e] it with the more conspicuous disorder of psychical impotence in men" (*The Freud Reader*, ed. Peter Gay [New York: W. W. Norton, 1989], 394 and 399).

108. R. A. Meckel, *Save the Babies: American Public Health Reform and the Prevention of Infant Mortality, 1850–1929* (Baltimore: Johns Hopkins University Press, 1990), cited in Center for Disease Control, "Achievements in Public Health, 1900–1999: Healthier Mothers and Babies," *Morbidity and Mortality Weekly Report* (*MMWR Weekly*) 48, no. 38 (October 1, 1999): 849–58.

109. For discussions of population trends, see Dudley Kirk, *Europe's Population in the Interwar Years* (Geneva: League of Nations, 1946); R. R. Palmer and Joel Colton, *A History of the Modern World*, 8th ed. (New York: Alfred A. Knopf, 1995), 588; A. N. Carr-Sanders, *World Population* (Oxford: Oxford University Press, 1936); John D. Durand, "The Modern Expansion of the World Population," *Proceedings of the American Philosophical Society* 111, no. 3 (June 22, 1967): 136–59; United Nations, *United Nations Demographic Yearbook* (New York: United Nations 1989); and United Nations, *Population Prospects* (New York: United Nations, 1989). For discussions of population debates, see Linda Gordon, *Woman's Body, Woman's Right: Birth Control in America*, rev. ed. (New York: Penguin Books, 1990), 130, and Alisa Klaus, *Every Child a Lion: The Origins of Maternal and Infant Health Policy in the United States and France, 1890–1920* (Ithaca, NY: Cornell University Press, 1993), 19.

110. See the essay "Social and Biological Reproduction in *Eugenia*" (111–15) for an in-depth discussion of a Yucatecan case study on family planning and population debates (the Yucatecan birth-control campaign in which Urzaiz purportedly participated).

111. Susanne Klausen and Alison Bashford, "Fertility Control: Eugenics, Neo-Malthusianism, and Feminism," in Levine and Bashford, *The Oxford Handbook of the History of Eugenics*, 99.

112. Ibid., 100.

113. Ibid., 99–101.

114. Urzaiz, *Eugenia*, 32.

115. Irwin, *Mexican Masculinities*, 147.

116. Stepan, *"The Hour of Eugenics,"* 131.

117. "State of Veracruz to Draft Birth Control Law to Protect Future Children of the Proletariat," *New York Times*, October 30, 1932. See also "Veracruz to Adopt Birth Control Today: Radical Legislation is Designed to Benefit Working Class of Mexican State," *New York Times*, November 1, 1932.

118. Stepan, *"The Hour of Eugenics,"* 132.

119. Ibid. For an in-depth discussions of the ousting of Tejeda during his second term as governor (1928–32; he also served from 1920–24), see Andrew Wood, "Adalberto Tejeda of Veracruz," in *State Governors in the Mexican Revolution, 1910–1952: Portraits in Conflict, Courage, and Corruption*, ed. Jürgen Buchenau and William Beezley (Lanham, MD: Rowman & Littlefield, 2009), 90. Mary Kay Vaughan also mentions the ousting of Tejeda in *Cultural Politics in Revolution*, 66.

120. Foucault, *The History of Sexuality*, 1:30. See also Harry Oosterhuis's discussion of how treating sexual deviance allowed psychiatrists to "promote their specialty and . . . extend their professional domain" (*Stepchildren of Nature: Krafft-Ebing, Psychiatry, and the Making of Sexual Identity* [Chicago: University of Chicago Press, 2000], 13).

121. Cristina Rivera-Garza, "The Masters of the Streets: Bodies, Power and Modernity in Mexico, 1867–1930" (PhD diss., University of Houston, 1995), 183–90. For discussion of the Ley de Instrucción Pública and cooperation between the Escuela de Medicina and Hospital de Maternidad e Infancia, see Margarito Crispín Castellanos, "Hospital de maternidad e infancia: Perspectiva histórica de un centro de beneficencia pública de finales del siglo XIX," in *La atención materno-infantil: Apuntes para su historia* (Mexico City: Secretaría de Salubridad y Asistencia, 1993), 95–115, cited in Rivera-Garza, "The Masters of the Streets," 189. For indications in the national press of the public's hostility to surgeons performing obstetrical duties, see Crispín Castellanos, "Hospital de maternidad e infancia," cited in Rivera-Garza, "The Masters of the Streets," 190. In the nineteenth century, most Mexican doctors continued to study at the Royal and Papal University of Mexico (which was renamed the National University of Mexico in 1821). In 1833, the medical sciences were incorporated into the University as the Escuela de Medicina (School of Medicine). See "La Facultad de Medicina de la Universidad Nacional Autónoma de México (UNAM) Pionera en América Latina y Líder Regional en la Formación de Recurosos Humanos Para la Salud," http://www .facmed.unam.mx/fm/historia/evolucion.html.

122. Stern, "Responsible Mothers," 394n67.

123. Manuel E. Guillén, "Algunas reflexiones sobre la hygiene de la mujer durante su pubertad" (thesis, Facultad de Medicina, 1903), cited in Rivera-Garza, "The Masters of the Streets," 193. The bibliographic information in Guillén's thesis uses the word "Facultad" instead of "Escuela" to refer to the National University's School of Medicine. The word "Facultad" translates to academic department, program, or school.

124. Rivera-Garza, "The Masters of the Streets," 195.

125. Robert M. Buffington, *Criminal and Citizen in Modern Mexico* (Lincoln: University of Nebraska Press, 2000), 130.

126. Stern, "Responsible Mothers," 380.

127. Gail Hawke and R. Danielle Egan, "Sex, Popular Beliefs and Culture: Discourses on the Sexual Child," in *A Cultural History of Sexuality*, vol. 5, *In the Age of Empire*, ed. Chiara Beccalossi and Ivan Crozier (New York: Berg, 2011), 135; Louise A. Jackson, "Sex, Religion and the Law," in Beccalossi and Crozier, *A Cultural History of Sexuality*, vol. 5, *In the Age of Empire*, 98.

128. Freud, "An Autobiographical Study," in Gay, *The Freud Reader*, 22; Jay Prosser, "Transsexuals and the Transsexologists: Inversion and the Emergence of Transsexual Subjectivity," in *Sexology in Culture: Labelling Bodies and Desires*, ed. Lucy Bland and Laura Doan (Chicago: University of Chicago Press, 1998), 127. According to Freud, one's sexual object choice related to one's childhood. As Freud explained, "the first love-object in the case of both sexes is the mother. . . . Later, but still in the first years of infancy, the

relation known as the *Oedipus complex* becomes established: boys concentrate their sexual wishes upon their mother and develop hostile impulses against their father as being a rival, while girls adopt an analogous attitude. . . . Children do not become clear for quite a long time about the differences between the sexes" (Freud, "An Autobiographical Study," 22).

129. Hawke and Egan define sexology as "the study of human sexuality in its physical, emotional, psychological, and cultural forms" and explain that it was "established, but not necessarily adopted by the scientific community, by the last two decades of the nineteenth century" ("Sex, Popular Beliefs and Culture," 135). Sexologists joined other sex radicals to encourage men *and* women to explore and enjoy their sexual expression. Sexology complicated conventional medical discourses on sexuality with different streams of thought, including the ideas of John Stuart Mill, Marxist narratives of familial and economic structural oppression of women, and the work of psychiatrists and eugenicists. Some sexologists argued that free love and healthy sexual expression in both sexes would improve the race, for people would naturally choose the most fit and suitable partner for them and sexual enjoyment would produce healthy offspring; see Robb, "The Way of All Flesh," 591–93; see also Oosterhuis, *Stepchildren of Nature*, 32.

130. Oosterhuis, *Stepchildren of Nature*, 32.

131. Ibid., 32–33.

132. Urzaiz, *Eugenia*, 29, 49–50.

133. Although Urzaiz went to the United States to study psychiatry in 1904—five years before Freud's only visit to the United States in 1909, to lecture on psychoanalysis at Clark University ("Freud Comes to America," in *American Decades*, vol. 1, *1900–1909*, ed. Judith S. Baughman, Victor Bondi, Richard Layman, Tandy McConnell, and Vincent Tompkins [Detroit: Gale Research, 2001])—Freud had begun developing his "talking cure" (a term Freud took from the psychiatrist Josef Breur, who used it to refer to hypnosis-induced psychoanalytic sessions held with his patient "Anna O." [Bertha Pappenheim]) in the late nineteenth century. Anna O.'s case notes and Breur were both very influential in Freud's development as a practicing psychoanalyst and in his writings on psychology. For mention of the "talking cure" in Anna O.'s case notes, see Josef Breuer, "Anna O.," in Gay, *The Freud Reader*, 68. Given his interest in psychiatry and his own travels to the United States to study psychiatry in 1904, Urzaiz would have read Freud, others' responses to Freud, and followed the reactions of US psychiatrists to Freud's visit in 1909. It was Doña Candelaria Souza de Fernández, who considers Urzaiz to be her mentor, who described Urzaiz as a "Freud fanatic" (Sarah Buck Kachaluba, interview with Doña Candelaria Souza de Fernández, July 1, 2014, Mérida, Yucatán).

134. Sarah Buck Kachaluba, interview with Doña Candelaria Souza de Fernández, July 1, 2014, Mérida, Yucatán.

135. Urzaiz, *Eugenia*, 66, 65.

Eugenia's Literary Genesis and Genealogy

Eduardo Urzaiz's *Eugenia* describes life in the eugenically obsessed twenty-third-century society of Villautopia. Thirteen years before Aldous Huxley's *Brave New World* appeared, Urzaiz predicted a chilling Darwinian society of the future, where human reproduction would be guided by the scientific principles of eugenics, or the preservation of favorable traits and the elimination of the undesirable ones through selective reproduction. But *Eugenia* constitutes more than just a literary realization of what possibilities controlled human breeding could hold in terms of producing a genetically modified human race. Through *Eugenia* Urzaiz satirizes the prevailing faith in science as a way to systematically improve the overall quality of life while criticizing society for privileging eugenics over the free will of each individual. At the same time, the novel is framed by several simultaneous discourses, and it is the intersection of these discourses, especially in the character of Ernesto, that elevates Urzaiz's only novel to something more than a dystopian love story or satire of state-controlled human reproduction. First, there is the obvious scientific aspect, grounded in detailed discussions about human reproduction, eugenics, and race, and set in the seemingly utopic futuristic society. Second, *Eugenia* develops themes such as population control, education, and gender equality, thereby reflecting conversations that were taking place in response to the political unrest and social unease in Urzaiz's Mexico during and in the years that followed the revolution. Finally, that *Eugenia* should enjoy a place in the pantheon of groundbreaking early works of science fiction goes without saying.

A review of *Eugenia* provided by the *Revista de Yucatán* at the time of its publication indicates that contemporaries of Urzaiz were perplexed by the complexity of the novel and the multiplicity of themes it takes on. This review begins by asking: "Is Urzaiz's *Eugenia* a sketch of a novel of future habits? Or a serial exposition of dreams: half scientific, half fantastic—caressed by . . . that cultured writer. . . . Does *Eugenia* come from the imagination or is it the consequence of observations and studies? Is it a work of art or science?" It seems that the author (H.E.V.) was not particularly well versed in science fiction. The author went on to observe that "the life of the characters, imprecise and blurry, are not psychologically resolved; they are at the mercy of the author who follows his own reasoning and goes wherever he wants to." Later, H.E.V. explains that Urzaiz's descriptions of the eugenic advances and procedures characterizing Villautopia are central to understanding why the novel was written. H.E.V. writes:

> Minutely, [Urzaiz] describes the operations that will give rise to a superior SPECIMAN OF HUMANITY, blood, flesh, and spirit. . . . The maternal preoccupations that today form an unbreakable bond between she who gives LIFE and her child, will disappear. . . . Nature, then, will have lost her preeminence in the same hands of the most perfect work: destiny will conquer. It will be a fact that the sweet heights of FATHER and MOTHER won't exist and along with them, the duties that are implied will be happily erased. The state will take charge of the luck of the offspring and by them, if not with paternal anxiety and despair, with the frozen and rigid vigilance and stamp of national duty. They will not have hugs and kisses but will be healthy and well fed . . . receive a broad education, grow up strong . . . the world will be populated by Apollos and Sophocles.
>
> Such is the thesis, simply explained, that is the inspiring CRUX of *Eugenia*. And there is not in this, a script of a novel, but a light passionate intrigue, a psychological prejudice, I think, of the twentieth century. Or does it conclude in an about-face or contradiction? . . . Regardless, [the novel] exhales a subtle essence of administration, attraction, and optimism that will appeal to anyone who approaches social things with idealism and dreams, like Urzaiz, in "a humanity that is almost happy, free at last from the shackles and prejudices with which today's humanity willingly complicates and embitters life."[1]

Thus, if the *Revista de Yucatán* is any indication, readers of Urzaiz's era would have understood the novel to be more grounded in science than art, and been most moved and distressed by what they saw as an envisioning, forewarning, and perhaps condoning of the mechanization and dehumanization of human reproduction characterized by the removal of women from the practice of birthing and childrearing and a related sanitization of childhood socialization and education.

We offer another interpretation, based largely on close attention to previously overlooked yet important references to classical Greek imagery, enlightenment literary figures, and other allusions of recognizably high culture, which we believe constitute keys to uncovering Urzaiz's goals in writing *Eugenia*. Of particular importance are parallels between *Eugenia* itself and Rousseau's *Émile, or On Education* (1762) and Ernesto's relationship to Celiana and Rousseau's real-life love affair with Madame Warens. Such parallels suggest that *Eugenia* might very well be Urzaiz's attempt at a treatise on the inherent contradictions of a superficial society, governed by western scientific principles, in which man's natural tendencies, it seems, are tamed rather than nurtured. Attention and critique of western science and education in *Eugenia* is explained partly by Urzaiz's real-world role as a teacher, educational administrator, and obstetrician-gynecologist with great interest and accomplishments in psychiatry.

Scientific Discourse in *Eugenia*

Driven by more than an extensive academic and practical knowledge of gynecology and psychiatry, Urzaiz worked to promote reproductive health and hygiene as an integral part of social improvement, and these are subjects about which he thought and spoke prolifically. A fair number of his lectures, especially those from around the time that *Eugenia* was published, shed light on the scientific discourse that is one of the pillars of *Eugenia*. There is no doubt that Urzaiz actively engaged the medical community in enlightened dialogue in many areas that would provide fertile ground for his portrayal of Villautopian society as a laboratory in which he could test them. In perusing the titles of a series of publications by Urzaiz in *La Higiene: Órgano de la Dirección General de Salubridad e Higiene* (the official publication of the state of Yucatán's Department of Health and Hygiene), one quickly notices how remarkably similar their subjects seem to their fictional interpretation in *Eugenia*. And while stretching the imagination beyond the reality of his day, it is interesting to note that Urzaiz's lectures also provide a degree of scientific legitimacy to his novel. One of these articles, published by Urzaiz in September 1918 (one year before the published version of *Eugenia* was distributed), was "La especie, el género, las variedades y las razas: Herencia; Origen de las especies; Teoría de la evolución o del transformismo; Darwinismo; Lamarckismo; Neolamarckismo" ("The Species, Gender, Variations, and Races: Inheritance; The Origin of the Species; Theory of Evolution and Tranformism; Darwinism; Lamarckism; Neo-Lamarckism").[2] Racial differences and Darwinism were key components in conversations involving eugenics as a means to finding solutions to society's problems. As suggested by its title, *Eugenia* is a novel that examines the role of eugenics as the guiding ideology for social improvement. The term "eugenics" was coined by Francis Galton in *Inquiries into Human Faculty and Its Development* (1883). A cousin of Charles Darwin, whose own *On the Origin of Species* revolutionized the entire scientific community when it was published in 1859, Galton's pioneering work paved the way for understanding the science behind heredity. Galton's work in turn drew upon the work of the Austrian monk and amateur botanist Gregor Mendel, who deserves credit for having laid the foundation for the principles of modern genetics, and who observed through empirical experimentation the recurrence of certain physical traits from one generation of garden peas to the next.

Mendel's experiments (carried out in the 1860s) were based only on single traits. Under laboratory conditions, traits might be isolated and successfully passed from one generation to the next. However, half a century later (ca. 1908), geneticists realized that most traits were influenced by multiple genes, and that the environment also was a factor in determining if a predisposition to certain traits became manifest.[3] Thus, finding a way to isolate many traits in a single specimen, which, when crossed with another specimen, would pass those exact traits to the offspring, should have seemed next to impossible. Despite this high improbability, scientists speculated on the possibility of "breeding out" mental illnesses. Perhaps this development can be attributed to pressure from the psychiatric field, which, in turn, was a response to social problems resulting from increased urbanization related to migration and the consolidation of industrial and corporate capitalism in the late nineteenth century. At the same time that institutional psychiatry emerged as a tool to deal with the mental health needs of the urban poor and the higher crime rates accompanying urbanization, the profession had taken a turn from a clinical, hands-on approach to a more holistic, pathological approach in an attempt to better understand the genetics of mental disease. Thus, as institutions for the clinically insane became more and more crowded, psychiatrists began to search for ways to deal with mental illness from a preventative angle. Eugenics arose as a scientific response to the uncertainties surrounding the physical and mental health of human society in the late nineteenth and early twentieth centuries. These uncertainties were related to significant social changes, and the eugenic response to them was largely the result of advances in genetics and biology that allowed scientists to begin to understand the complexities of human heredity.

The degree to which the principles of eugenics were applied and social policies were developed as a result of the evolving schools of thought associated with the science of human reproduction reflected the almost desperate need of societies around the turn of the twentieth century to understand the human condition in relation to demographic shifts, new technologies, and responding changes in economic, political, and social systems that transformed daily life in just a few short years. The rapid advances in experimental and theoretical sciences outpaced humankind's ability to comprehend the possibilities for those sciences to shape the future, even on a genetic level. While European and North American scientists continued to develop sophisticated laboratory methods, conduct field experiments for the purposes of collecting data on physical and mental characteristics, and establish institutions to catalog and study that data, their biased views tended to influence their interpretations. Thus, while many of these scientists did much to advance the sciences of genetics and human heredity, many of their conclusions cannot be supported by scientific fact. For example, one of the leading pioneers in the study of eugenics in the United States was the biologist Charles B. Davenport. As prominent and well-trained as he was, Davenport was not alone in equating national identity with racial identity and in assuming that race determined behavior.[4] Edward M. East was a Harvard geneticist who "played a crucial role in convincing geneticists of the importance of Mendel's work."[5] Like Davenport, East also argued that public institutions had grown overcrowded with the genetically unfit. Many others followed suit. Thus, practically from its entrance onto the scientific scene, eugenics was motivated by a social agenda. And although approaches to eugenics varied in the degree of their reactions toward scientific tradition, race, and sterilization, generally all movements were united by a concern of preventing genetic degeneration and promoting measures to guarantee the reproductive health of society.

Although Mendel published his findings in 1866, his work had no immediate impact on the scientific community. His theories would not resurface until 1900, when three European botanists working independently from one another obtained similar results, validating the data and experiments that Mendel had collected more than three decades earlier.[6] What Mendel's experiments show is that careful observation of certain physical characteristics across several generations (in this case peas) suggest that some characteristics are dominant, while others are recessive. The frequency with which dominant and recessive traits were observed led Mendel to the conclusion that their appearance was governed by statistical laws.[7] By carefully controlling the patterns of breeding, Mendel discovered that he could accurately predict the physical characteristics of the offspring. Galton applied the theories of Mendel to human reproduction.

A practical extension into the social fabric of Galton's work can be found with the Fabian Society. Founded in 1900, the Fabians were a socialist organization that condemned capitalism. Lending their support to proponents of eugenics, the Fabians favored a planned economy and establishment of a guaranteed level of health, education, wages, and employment, what they called a "National Minimum."[8] Yet, even as a socialist organization, the Fabians envisioned a scientifically planned society that would empower not the workers, as might be expected, but rather experts, people like themselves who were middle-class professionals such as doctors, scientists, teachers, and social workers. The voice of Miajitas, the whimsically entertaining worker who first appears in chapter 3 of *Eugenia*, echoes this Fabian vision. Barging into the restaurant where Ernesto is dining with his friends, Miajitas is greeted sarcastically by one of the guests: "Welcome! . . . the false Spartacus, who comes to merrily drink with the privileged that those at the bottom have sweated to make!"[9] The hardened worker replies with revealing observation:

> "No sirs, . . . I have not come for that, but rather to exercise a sacred right; given that those on the bottom have fed me, I have come to demand from you, who call yourselves the *ones on top*, that you buy me coffee and pay me a bonus. It serves you well that I lack everything; and if the poor share with me the piece of bread that they earn with their work, I repay them fully with the sweet honey of my eloquence, which, in their tormented lives of wanting but never attaining, creates the golden mirage of an illusion, intangible, it's true, but for that very reason even more beautiful and seductive. What do you, who consume so much without producing anything, give them, you who get by on your good looks, supported by a man or a woman, like ladies' men? In spite of the countless evolutions and revolutions that humanity has suffered through, you continue to be as parasitic as your ancestors from semibarbaric centuries. Seeds of mistletoe, I curse you a thousand and one times!"[10]

Considering that *Eugenia* might be better understood as a pedagogical work rather than an entertaining novel, and given Urzaiz's tendency to mock the social institutions of Villautopia, it is doubtful that he himself was a Fabian. Rather, that Urzaiz worked toward advancing educational equality suggests that he would have favored an environment in which each individual reached his or her potential and so would have championed the working class as productive members of society. However, it is worth noting that the Fabian Society did attract a number of important literary figures, including ones engaged with eugenics, such as George Bernard Shaw and H. G. Wells, whose *Man and Superman* (1903) and *A Modern Utopia* (1905), respectively, "probably did more than any academic studies to popularize the concept of selective breeding."[11]

In other publications Urzaiz spoke on the differences between animals and vegetation, presumably in reference to their respective reproductive characteristics, since Urzaiz also spoke on the reproduction of phanerogamic (seed-bearing) plants (for example, in his February 1919 article "La reproducción en las plantas fanerógamas: Reproducción por estacas; Acodos e hijos, bulbos, rozomas, o tallos subterráneos; El ingerto y el cruce en las plantas; La simbiosis" ["The Reproduction of Flowering Plants: Reproduction by Stakes; Twists and Off-spring, Bulbs, Rhizomes, or Underground Stems; The Grafting and Crossing in Plants; Symbiosis"]).[12] The possibilities for generating synthetic life (simple cells to more complex vegetation) that could not be distinguished from natural life was introduced, as far as we have been able to determine, in the Cuban scientist Israel Castellanos's book *La plasmogenia* (1921).[13] Castellanos details a number of sophisticated laboratory experiments from the eighteenth to early twentieth centuries, in which synthetic tissues, shown to be almost indistinguishable from natural ones, were produced. The most noted Mexican scientist and founder of the school of plasmogenia was Alfonso L. Herrera, director of the Institute of Biological Studies in Mexico City. Even synthetic cells generated in test tubes behaved in a way that was similar to organic cells by dividing themselves and living for some time.[14]

But perhaps one of the more revealing articles—in terms of the significance of using human incubators rather than the biological mothers for human reproduction—that Urzaiz published in *La Higiene* during the time he would have been writing *Eugenia* was "El protoplasma: Su composición y propiedades; La célula; Los seres unicelulares y multicelulares; La vida de los seres y la vida celular independiente; Los seres coloniales" ("Protoplasm: Its Composition and Properties; The Cell; Unicellular and Multicellular Beings; The Life of Beings and Independent Cellular Life; Colonial Beings"), which demonstrates Urzaiz's knowledge of scientific, medical advances on this front.[15] In chapter 5 of *Eugenia*, Urzaiz articulates this knowledge when Dr. Remigio Pérez Serrato, director of Villautopia's Institute of Eugenics, explains in great detail not only the historical rationale for the institute's existence but also the scientific process that Villa-utopia has mastered for controlled human reproduction. When Dr. Pérez Serrato mentions that "illustrious fellow Earthling, whose statue you must have seen at the entrance of this building and whose name need not be spoken, since the entire world knows it, [who] demonstrated through experiment that the ovum of a mammal, once fertilized, can develop in the peritoneal cavity of another individual of the same species, even if that individual is of the male gender," he could have been referring to Walter Heape, who in 1890 conducted an experiment in which he transferred two fertilized ova from a female Angora rabbit to the uterus of a female Belgian hare.[16] However, while Heape does not speculate on the possibility of using a male specimen as the vehicle for gestation, Urzaiz might have, as noted by the title of a lecture he gave in December 1918, "La diferenciación de los sexos: Los seres asexuales; Hermafrodismo y pseudo-hermafrodismo; Caracteres sexuales secundarios; Reproducción asexual, sexual, y alternante" ("The Differentiation of the Sexes: Asexual Beings; Hermafrodism and Pseudohermafrodism; Secondary Sexual Characters; Asexual, Sexual, and Alternate Reproduction").[17] As far-fetched as it seems even by today's standards, Urzaiz's justification for using a male incubator in order to spare women the psychological suffering and physical pain of childbirth was based on what could be considered sound scientific evidence, giving at least an air of legitimacy to his portrayal of childbirth in the future.[18] Not unlike the procedure that Dr. Pérez Serrato describes to his African visitors and to Ernesto during their tour of the Institute of Eugenics in chapter 5 of *Eugenia*, in 1897, Walter Heape outlined the procedure used to transfer fertilized ova from one female rabbit to another:

> The operation is a very simple one. The Belgian Hare doe is put under anesthetics and stretched out on her stomach. A longitudinal incision, 2 in. long, is then made through the skin at a place 1½ to 3½ in. from the anterior edge of the pelvis, and on a level with the ventral border of the lumbar muscles. A smaller incision is then made through the body-wall just ventral to the lumbar muscles, and the anterior end of the fallopian tube is readily found and pulled out through the opening with the help of a pair of forceps. The foreign ova are then taken out of their maternal fallopian tube on the point of a spear-headed needle, the foster-mother's infundibulum is held open with a pair of forceps and the ova placed well within the anterior end of her fallopian tube; after pushing the latter gently back again and washing with some antiseptic solution, the wound is sewn up and dressed with collodion and cotton-wool.[19]

In chapter 5 of *Eugenia*, Pérez Serrato describes the procedure by which the fertilized human egg is removed from the female uterus and implanted into the male incubator, who has been "feminized" through hormone treatments:

> "Here," Dr. Serrato rushed to say, "we perform the removal of the ovum. . . . The operation, though delicate, is very simple. It comes down to delicately removing the fertilized egg when it has started to attach itself to the mucous of the uterus. . . .

> The egg is deposited into the peritoneal cavity as if it were a grain of wheat in a furrow, and, if the operation is successful—these days it is rare not to be so—exactly two hundred and eighty-one days later we perform a laparotomy and remove a perfectly developed and lively child. . . . I should warn you that, during the removal of the ovum and its grafting to the host uterus, it is crucial to keep the room at a constant temperature, which is approximately equal to that of the human body so that the elements aren't exposed to the smallest change or alteration.[20]

The detail with which Urzaiz describes the work conducted at the Institute of Eugenics seems to imply that he was at least familiar with Heape's work. The application of such knowledge to the program of controlled human reproduction depicted in *Eugenia* further suggests that Urzaiz was attempting to bridge the lacuna between experimental genetics and human heredity that prevented eugenics from becoming a cohesive science.

Political and Social Contexts

At the dawn of the twentieth century, Mexico was in a state of political, economic, and cultural chaos that would explode into a revolution by the second decade. The nation's president, Porfirio Díaz, had instituted a national policy of reform based on positivism that came to be associated with his term of rule—known as the Porfiriato (1876–1911)—and that was intended to lead Mexico once and for all out of the dark ages of colonialism and into the new century. Throughout the nineteenth century Mexico had struggled to create a national identity that reflected the rich historical and cultural realities of its people. But at the root of Mexico's identity crisis was the nature of the Mexican people. Centuries of interracial contact had produced a rich mixture of New World indigenous and Old World European heritages embodied in the mestizo. The nation's racial identity was further complicated by advances in the science of heredity in Europe, which began to speculate on the present state and the future fate of humanity as a race. In general, it was thought that eugenics could offer a solution to the degeneration of races that would be the eventual outcome if reproduction were allowed to continue unchecked.

Mexico's historical experience of racial, ethnic, and cultural blending, or mestizaje, had created a complex relationship among the people of Latin America. While Latin America's Creole upper class looked to Europe or the United States for cultural and political inspiration, the mestizo masses looked to create an identity out of their own history. Yet it was the mestizo that the Mexican philosopher José Vasconcelos would champion as the salvation of a future Latin American race in his *Cosmic Race* (1925). Nonetheless, the scientific community preached a different reality. Mexico's racial identity was further complicated by advances in the science of heredity in Europe and the United States, where speculation on the current state and the future fate of humanity as a race began to dominate scientific circles.

In the *Cosmic Race*, Vasconcelos responded to European and North American eugenicists' theories of racial hygiene with his suggestion that Latin America's mestizaje was a unique New World form of eugenics. That is, he argued that through hundreds of years of racial mixing, out of Latin America there would be born a highly evolved race that would be in essence a nonrace, since those barriers (both biological and cultural) that separate and divide one group of people from another would no longer exist. That is, eugenics as applied to Latin America's unique historical development was, through Vasconcelos's theory, the process of mestizaje that would culminate into the "cosmic race," the fifth and last great race of mankind who would characterize what he called the "aesthetic age." Vasconcelos applied the term "aesthetic age" to his cosmic race because he theorized that it would rise out of an evolved sense of beauty, where love would be the mutual attraction between two individuals of desirable qualities. There appears to be very little hard science in Vasconcelos's work; nonetheless, at the core of the *Cosmic Race* is a philosophical understanding that reproduction in a superior, utopian society will involve a certain degree of self-selection, and that breeding only between those individuals who possess a heightened sense of beauty will also possess those inherently desirable qualities that are favorable to a "cosmic race." It has often been argued that Vasconcelos's *Cosmic Race* is racist in the sense that it describes in part a process through which the "darker" indigenous races will become in essence "lighter." However, this is an oversimplification, evident in the fact that what Vasconcelos was proposing was a mechanism through which the most favorable qualities of each race would be preserved and propagated. For example, in the case of the indigenous peoples it would be their highly evolved sense of spirituality and aesthetic beauty (cultural rather than necessarily biological traits) that would blend into a single cultural expression.

Vasconcelos's approach to eugenics built in part upon neo-Lamarckian theories, which explained heredity as a function not only of genetic inheritance but also of the forces of the environment working on the molecular structures of organism. Decades before modern biology demystified the science of genetics, the neo-Lamarckians in Latin America believed that such diseases as alcoholism, tuberculosis, and syphilis—all social evils that plagued mankind—were as much products of poverty as they were causes of it. Thus, eugenics offered a solution to these and was applied toward their eradication rather than toward a "purification" of the race.

A Literary Contextualization of *Eugenia* from the Classical to the Modernist Era

While Urzaiz's story blends real medical knowledge with speculation, *Eugenia* was not the first literary piece to explore the science of eugenics in the context of a futuristic society. While the scientific term "eugenics" had been in existence for a little more than thirty years when Urzaiz published *Eugenia*, the concept of controlled reproduction to improve the human species predates even Mendel's experiments. Perhaps the first reference to regulating human reproduction for the purpose of obtaining favorable offspring can be found in Plato's *The Republic*. In this work, through a dialogue between Socrates and Glaucan, Plato introduces the guardians, who are men and women of like natures, obedient to the laws and trustworthy to carry them out, and who are appointed by the legislator of the republic to "live in common houses and meet at common meals."[21] The guardians will "be brought up together, and will associate at gymnastic exercises. And so they will be drawn by a necessity of their natures to have intercourse with each other."[22] Thus, Plato establishes a hierarchy, so to speak, of human traits, both intellectual and physical, in which those qualities that he considers to be favorable will be mutually attractive and thus be the most beneficial to the welfare of the republic. Making "matrimony sacred to the highest degree" will ensure the order and stability of this system, while at the same time preventing licentiousness, "an unholy thing which the rulers will forbid."[23] Another important point of contact between Urzaiz's novel and Plato's scheme is that after birth, children are taken to a separate place where they are cared for by nurses, such that no mother should recognize or have contact with her own child.[24] In Tommaso Campanella's *City of the Sun: A Poetical Dialogue* (1623), a similar group is charged with the responsibility to society of producing offspring with only desirable traits. In H. G. Wells's *A Modern Utopia* (1905), the order of the "samurai," or "voluntary nobleman," serves as both overseer of reproduction and comprises the pool from which the breeders are selected. Such works as Shaw's play "Man and Superman" (1903) and Wells's *A Modern Utopia* helped popularize the concept of selective breeding. While the relationship between all of these works merits further exploration, there is no doubt that Urzaiz read them and borrowed from their ideas in his portrait of Villautopia, the eugenically inspired society of *Eugenia*.

While not the first to integrate eugenics into its narrative structure, *Eugenia* does appear to be the first work of its kind written in Spanish. And this is important to note. A study of science and speculative fiction written between the late nineteenth and early twentieth centuries reveals that eugenics was a recurring theme of these early works. In his catalog of science fiction literature from the earliest years until 1932, Everett F. Bleiler describes forty-two works in which the authors emphasize aspects of eugenics with varying degrees of relevance in the telling of their stories. Of these, thirty-one develop concepts such as regulated marriages, selective breeding, and state-rearing of children, and therefore appear to offer additional examples of eugenics as a theme around which utopian and futuristic science fiction revolve.[25] Twenty-one of these thirty-one pieces were published before 1919, the year in which Urzaiz published *Eugenia*. Plato's *The Republic* (ca. 360 BC) and Campanella's *The City of the Sun* (1623)— both are included in Bleiler's catalog—are the earliest known works that deal with eugenic themes. The remaining nineteen works were published between 1871 and 1914. It is worth noting that not one of these works comes from a Spanish-speaking culture.

As a corpus of literature, these works—the majority having been published in England or the United States—provide the reader with a window into the social, political, and cultural milieu of their authors. Additionally, they are an invaluable resource for studying the varying attitudes toward eugenics in a period of rapid scientific advancement and social transformation. While eugenics is a main ingredient, other common themes not directly related to the subtexts of promiscuity or sexual equality that eugenic practice engenders add to the distinct flavor of these works and are also found within the pages of *Eugenia*. Among the more noticeable are the disappearance of the nation-state in favor of a single federation-style form of government, a satire of Darwinism and American democracy, a worship-like attitude toward women, highly advanced science and technology, and a denigration of non-Caucasian races. Thus, *Eugenia* is a product not just of its author's intimate knowledge of the potential medical and social applications of the science behind eugenics as outlined in the prologue but also of the literary tradition that eugenics spawned. When placed within its historical context, then, Urzaiz's speculative novel stands out as more than just a fanciful contribution to the literary experimentation of his day.

Eugenia might be considered an experimental novel of sorts. In addition to the fact that Eugenia is the only known novel dealing so thoroughly with these themes in Spanish, and although the late nineteenth and early twentieth centuries produced several literary works dealing with similar themes of eugenics, population control, and social engineering through euthanasia or sterilization, *Eugenia* is the only known work of fiction written by Eduardo Urzaiz. In contrast, canonical examples left by the likes of Aldous Huxley and H. G. Wells were part of a larger opus that these well-known authors produced, giving us a deeper understanding of their literary voices within the genre of speculative science fiction. But without other examples of Urzaiz's cosmovision against which *Eugenia* could be measured, we must rely on what biographical and other evidence we do have of Eduardo Urzaiz, while unfairly comparing *Eugenia* to other works of fiction to which this novel has often been measured. But in doing so we forfeit any chance of appreciating Urzaiz's work as an original literary interpretation of the theoretical scientific and social discourses that were occurring in his day and that would transform the landscape of twentieth-century Mexico.

The novel's title, a direct reference to the beautiful girl who becomes Ernesto's love interest in the later part of the novel, is derived from the very concepts of the science of eugenics that become the foundation upon which Urzaiz's Villautopia is built. Likewise, the name of the society crafted by Urzaiz is the laboratory for testing the theories of controlled human reproduction in a milieu of progressive social ideologies.

While a celebrated doctor and advocate for women's reproductive health and rights, with training in psychiatry that allowed him to serve as the director of Yucatán's asylum for the mentally ill, Urzaiz was not a prolific writer of fiction. He dabbled in painting, and the handful of sketches found within the pages of *Eugenia* are presumed to be his. He was a scholar of Cervantes and published articles on the subject. But *Eugenia* stands alone as Urzaiz's only known work of fiction. It is this point that can invite criticism and curiosity, as well as leave readers and scholars to speculate as to why Urzaiz even wrote it. There is plenty of evidence within *Eugenia* to suggest that its author was intimately knowledgeable about the science behind eugenics. But the novel is not just about science, and to privilege the theories exploring the practical or even ethical application of eugenics would diminish its value as an experimental work of speculative fiction with tinges of romance, historical analysis, and social critique. Urzaiz's style is a fanciful blend of scientific discourse and romanticism. Urzaiz explains the main points of eugenics in a language that could only come from the mouth of a scientist. It is in the same vein that he unleashes his descriptions of Celiana's deterioration from a woman who is beautiful for her intellect and mature beauty to a desperate and despondent victim of unrequited love. Did Urzaiz intend for his only novel to be taken seriously?

Polyclitus, Praxiteles, Rousseau, and Urzaiz:
Natural Man or Utopia?

The idea that *Eugenia* represents something more ambitious for Urzaiz than his depiction of a utopian society driven by an adherence to the principles of eugenics comes from two unique yet important comparisons that he makes in chapter 1. The first is when Ernesto recalls how he was when he met Celiana "thirteen years earlier in primary school, having just arrived from the farm-seedbed where his first years had elapsed in complete freedom. He was at that time a turbulent little boy of ten, full of health, who, like Rousseau's Emile, did not know his left hand from his right."[26] The second is when

> Ernesto remembered later that terrible crisis of puberty, which briefly alleviated the turbulence of his games and filled him with wandering anxieties and un-mentionable desires. The fresh color of his face and the youthful tonicity of his muscles gone, he turned sullen and solitary. He would have fallen hopelessly into a state of neurosis if Celiana—always she—had not reached out a lifesaving hand to him. Like Madame Warens to Jean-Jacques Rousseau, she opened for him the gates to the garden of Eros and was for him a complete woman: mother, teacher, sister, friend, and lover. And she was all of these to the degree that, in five years, his heart had not so much as sighed for other loves, nor had the countless beautiful girls that he would encounter along the way ignited the spark of desire in him.[27]

These comparisons are critical to our understanding of *Eugenia* in that they draw out the influence that Jean-Jacques Rousseau appears to have had on Eduardo Urzaiz's thinking, in particular with respect to the relationship between what could be considered the unadulterated, natural individual and the society in which that individual lives. These points represent a new area of inquiry with respect to *Eugenia*, and while many scholars describe Rousseau as a con-tradictory figure both in life and in his writings, his presence in Urzaiz's novel— partly because of the complexities and contradictions he evokes—provides clues to Urzaiz's intentions and argument to the extent that these exist. *Eugenia* is not without its own contradictions, and for this reason the question of whether Urzaiz intended Eugenia to be read as a utopia or a dystopia cannot be easily answered. But perhaps there are enough clues within the novel's narrative style and literary devices such as the references to Rousseau's life and works to point the reader more in one direction rather than the other. This question of the relationship of the individual to society becomes precarious when society needs to educate the individual in such a way as to conform with the norms that benefit and add to the progress of that society, even if that education results in the loss of certain natural rights and individual fulfillment, for example, fatherhood, a concept that Ernesto first begins to think about during his initial tour of the eugenics institute.[28]

Eugenia is a novel that relies not just on language but also on allusions and imagery to tell Ernesto's story. And because Urzaiz makes use of multiple forms of expression (written and visual, for example), his novel is in some ways a work of metafiction—self-referential text that relies on the reader's familiarity with the significance of symbols and images whose meanings are outside of the novel's structure, in order to make sense of their significance within the novel. This approach might allow the reader to connect in a multisensory way to the narrative voice, the characters, and the plot, uncovering clues as to how Urzaiz might have intended his novel to be read. *Eugenia*, therefore, should not be characterized by its similarities or differences to known works of utopian or dystopian fiction, but rather by how Urzaiz structured the novel around the images and references contained within.

The reader is initially drawn into *Eugenia* by the image on the front cover of a slender woman dressed in a toga-like dress that exposes her left breast. She reclines on a sofa chair; her hair is short and tucked under a hat. In her left hand she holds a cigarette, revealed by the long trail of smoke that ascends upward. The reader soon learns that this female figure is a mirror image of Celiana, not Eugenia. She is wearing what turns out to be standard attire for twenty-third-century Villautopian women—as depicted in chapter 12, "for women, style required Greek tunics, slit above the left thigh and leaving the right shoulder and breast exposed"—and the cigarette she smokes is not of tobacco but of cannabis.[29] The reader is given a glimpse of Celiana as she relaxes in her study:

> Sitting in front of a large desk covered with books and papers in disarray, Celiana lifted her hands from the keyboard of the tiny typewriter upon which she had been typing. She spun her chair around until she was facing the window, lit a *cannabis indica* cigarette perfumed with the essence of ambergris, threw back her elegant head, and contemplated with delight the verdant vastness of the heavens.[30]

In this way Urzaiz introduces Celiana first as an image of a women who is quite comfortable in her element, painting a visual narrative that frames how she will be depicted within the text of the novel. In a similar fashion Urzaiz introduces Ernesto as the visual embodiment of perfection:

His body was worthy of admiration. Taller than average, his proportions were exact, displaying the perfect muscular tone and the harmonious robustness of Doryphorus of Polyclitus, while his facial features greatly resembled those of Mercury of Praxiteles, but with that expression of high intellect that human physiognomy has acquired after many centuries of civilization. Add to all that the warm glow of healthy skin, perfect, silky and unblemished by superfluous hair, and you will have an idea of what Ernesto was like at twenty-three: a figure worthy of posing for a Greek sculptor and a good example of what the progress in hygiene had achieved from a humanity that, hundreds of years before, is known all too well to have been rachitic, toxic, and sickly.[31]

The references to Polyclitus and Praxiteles are important here in that Urzaiz uses them to contextualize, mainly for the benefit of his contemporary readership, Ernesto's chiseled and perfectly proportioned physique in such a way as to leave no doubt in the reader's mind of his eugenic perfection.

At the same time, however, the Celiana on the cover is not necessarily the same young woman that the reader comes to know initially in chapter 1, but instead the mature Celiana of chapter 2 whose youthful attractiveness is fading. Ernesto's flashback in chapter 1 conjures up the image of his current lover and former teacher thirteen years earlier as "a beautiful young woman of twenty-five."[32] In chapter 2 the reader catches a glimpse of an older Celiana who is perhaps becoming less comfortable in her skin:

Celiana was truly beautiful in a disturbing and unique way: tall, slender, and full figured, even if her breasts were not very pronounced. Her complexion was white and unpolished; her lips were fleshy and fiery. Her eyes were large and luminous, as if consumed by an internal fever, and intensely black, just like her short curly mop of hair and thin eyebrows, perfect outlines that extended toward her temples and almost came together above the bridge of her Greek nose. Her forehead was high and spacious, her arms admirable and she had hands that, just like her feet upon which she wore lightweight sandals, were as transparent as porcelain and graciously emerged from her loose, sensibly cut lilac robe detailed with a black pattern along the hem and square collar.

Paying close attention, a keen observer might notice a slight squint in Celiana's eyes, three fine wrinkles on her forehead, and a few gray threads in her hair. Next to the total whiteness of her face, her teeth, large and fine, appeared to be yellowing like old ivory.[33]

Unlike Ernesto's youthful perfection, Celiana's figure is not frozen in the statuesque eternity of chiseled marble and stone. And while Urzaiz is noticeably unkind to her body as the novel progresses, he does celebrate Celiana as a cerebral woman who "devoted herself to giving lectures on sociology and history, her favorite areas of study. As she gave one successful talk after another, her fame began to spread beyond the borders of her homeland. The financial reward was not insignificant either, more than providing for her needs and fancies."[34] In this sense one must wonder if Urzaiz created Celiana in his own image, as a female version of himself, a tireless intellect who sought fame and fortune as a respected scholar. Yet here is also one of the many contradictions found in *Eugenia*. That is, Celiana was sterilized in her youth to prevent her from reproducing because, as the reader learns through Dr. Pérez Serrato in chapter 5, high intelligence was deemed an undesirable trait among those selected for breeding. So her beauty, and not her scholarly achievements, it would seem, is also her curse, and by chapter 7 the reader finds Celiana coming to terms with, though not entirely accepting, the inevitable effect of passing time on her beauty. She sits at her piano, as she is frequently portrayed doing throughout *Eugenia*:

> And it was then that music became her salvation, suitable to translate the most delicate nuances of her feelings, with its universal and eternal language that, within its own vagueness, is the key to enormous strength of expression. . . . The piano was Celiana's favorite instrument and, ever since she overcame the technical difficulties of playing, she never played other people's music. She played only for herself, always improvising.[35]

While Celiana values experience over time as an invaluable teacher and a means to self-fulfillment, she still cannot come to grips with time's decaying effect on her outward appearance. Celiana's quickly fading beauty is further punctuated in chapter 11:

> When she returned to the dresser to comb her hair, the moon-shaped mirror accentuated with raw frankness the lines on her face left by her extreme inner turmoil. The sparkle and feverish passion in her eyes had now become intense dark shadows. The slight wrinkles of her forehead had become more pronounced. A stereotypical painful grin stretched across the corner of her mouth, and in the ebony of her hair, silver strands multiplied with alarming exuberance. Suddenly and without warning, as if she had all of a sudden reached the end of her rope, Celiana was tempted to dye her hair or tear out those insolent gray hairs, to restore her soft skin with powders, to color her faded lips.[36]

Of course, Celiana's outward decay is directly related to her internal suffering due to Ernesto's obligation to the state as official breeder, requiring him to impregnate younger women who themselves have been identified as acceptable mates. Ernesto discovers that his duty has given him a sense of fulfillment and self-worth that he never found with Celiana, and the process of her coming to terms with this means her downward spiral, for she was Ernesto's teacher and lover, roles that fulfilled her inner need for motherhood first, then teacher, and finally for passionate love as Ernesto passed from child, to adolescent, to manhood. It is in this relationship that Urzaiz underscores the possible importance of Rousseau's *Émile* as a metaphor for education as a natural, organic process that celebrates individualism, yet cannot reconcile an inherent innocence or goodness with the corrosive forces of society. Ernesto is not a bad person for leaving Celiana. She taught him everything she could, and his actions are a reflection of her influence on him. It was after all Miguel, the artist who becomes Celiana's confidant and a father figure to Ernesto, who used his contact in the Institute of Eugenics to speed up the young man's appointment as breeder. In this sense Miguel might be responsible for Celiana's deep depression at the end of the novel, for he gives Ernesto the following advice in chapter 4:

> Eternal fidelity is a beautiful utopia. When spring causes new flowers to bud and burst open, no one takes notice of the ones that dried up the previous spring. What foolish person ever thought of objecting to a falling star, the metamorphosis of an insect, or the budding of a plant? The natural law of the human heart is also the continual exchanging of old loves that wear out for new loves that blossom. And whoever chooses to go against this law will only cause their own misfortune and contribute to that of others, since simulated love is more tragic than oblivion and even more painful even than hate itself.[37]

Thus, not only does Urzaiz foreshadow the end of the novel here but he also poses for the first time the idea of natural laws that, seemingly contrary to the principles of eugenics, cannot or should not be ignored when it comes to the fulfillment of the soul. Or perhaps it could very well be that this contradiction is no mystery at all, but a carefully thought-out metaphor, an ambitious pronouncement of Urzaiz's thoughts on the relationship between free will and state-controlled reproduction. Interesting to note too is the misleading juxtaposition between the image on the cover of the novel and the novel's title. While one might expect a direct relationship between the two, Urzaiz does not introduce Eugenia, who by the end of the novel becomes Ernesto's lover and mother of his child, until chapter 12. One must ask, then: What was Urzaiz's strategy in this? While Eugenia might be considered a younger and therefore more beautiful though much less cultured version of Celiana, it is Celiana who nurtured Ernesto as a child, years before the novel even begins, first as a mother figure, then as his teacher, and finally as his lover. So devoted to Ernesto is Celiana that she even supports him to the degree that he enjoys a life of absolute leisure, not needing to work for his living. And while Villautopians in general enjoy the comforts of economic stability, Urzaiz points out that Ernesto is the only one among his friends to not be employed. Yet he still is not satisfied with his life, and when he observes the relationship of Pérez Serrato to his biological daughter, Athanasia, in chapter 6, he begins to understand that which is missing. The narrator gives the reader valuable insight into Ernesto's conscious awakening of the deeper meaning of paternity:

> Her name was Rosaura, but from the time she was very young Don Remigio had christened her with the name Athanasia, which for him represented the beauty of its etymological meaning (without death, immortal) and also reminded him of the circumstances through which she came under his care. She was his real daughter, since in his younger days and in his capacity as a healthy and strong man, he had fulfilled his quota as a reproducer. He was a surgeon in the same Institute for which he now served as Director, when the young Rosaura came into the world and, for scientific interest and out of paternal pride, he got used to frequently visiting his offspring and took pleasure in closely following their development. She was his favorite child, for her unique beauty, the spitting image of her mother, a woman with whom he had been madly in love and who had abandoned him early on, leaving him with the bitterness of unfulfilled love. When the little girl became gravely ill, Don Remigio arduously fought to save her from death's grip, something that he managed to do just when it seemed humanly impossible. The zeal of the battle and the happiness of the great triumph caused the paternal love in Don Remigio to be reborn with all the selfish force of the past. Ever since then he called the girl Athanasia and later, upon the completion of her education, he took her to live with him.[38]

This passage reveals a romantic bent to the novel, romantic as in the sense of paternal obligation that stands in stark contradiction to the laws of selective breeding that we saw in chapter 5. Urzaiz appears to have been a romantic in every sense of the word, and it makes sense that he would have injected his feelings of love, not just romantic love, but paternal love as well, into the story line.[39]

As the novel ends, we see Celiana hit rock bottom, having come to terms with the inevitable—that she had lost Ernesto completely and forever to his new lover, Eugenia. Ernesto is smitten with Eugenia, and upon learning in

chapter 13 that she is carrying his child, his reaction is one that the reader might
have come to expect:

> He who in the first years of his youth believed that he was completely happy
> and satisfied with a love that was sterile and later carried out his job as official
> reproducer with notable fervor and efficiency, but without dedicating a single
> thought to his offspring, upon learning that Eugenia's flesh was mixing with his
> to create the flesh and soul of another life that would be the soul and flesh of
> both of them, felt what he had never felt nor believed he could feel. Knowing
> that he would have an adorable child, who would also be the child of the
> woman he adored, he understood with exactitude the very purpose of his exis-
> tence; he saw clearly the motive of his life in the survival of his being through his
> life and death.
>
> For love to deserve being called complete, it is not enough for it to fulfill the
> physiological, aesthetic, and sentimental aspirations of a human couple. It also
> has to fulfill its first and natural purpose, which is the propagation of the species.
> When it does not fulfill each and every one of these purposes, it degenerates
> into an unconscious and brute act of breeding, or turns into a sterile sentimental-
> ism that almost borders on the pathological.
>
> The future began to exist once again for the young lovers. From that
> moment on, time became divided by months and days. The time that remained—
> and together they would count—up to the moment in which, leaning over the
> edge of an immaculate crib, time would be spent contemplating the rosy cheeks
> of a newborn, a baby like any other, but for them, different than the rest and
> the most beautiful of them all.[40]

The future, a new future, begins in humanity. The novel essentially ends here.
Ernesto and Eugenia run off to the chalet in the outskirts of Villautopia, much
like the young Rousseau and Madame Warens during their years living together.
And while Ernesto recalls with a sense of joy to Eugenia the procedure for
removing the fertilized egg and implanting into a male incubator, it is not clear
if they follow through with this act. Traditional scholarship has suggested that
as loyal employees and breeders for the state, Ernesto and Eugenia will return
when the time comes to submit to the procedure. However, given the nature of
Ernesto's transformation from a seemingly naïve, kept lover into a thoughtful
individual eager to experience the joys and personal fulfillment of fatherhood,
it seems likely that he and Eugenia will stay in their love nest, give birth to their
child, and live out the rest of their lives as a new, post-eugenic family of twenty-
third-century Villautopia. There are plenty of contradictions in *Eugenia*, but

there are also a number of clues that reveal that Urzaiz was grappling with the laws of nature against the backdrop of science, which appear to not always be compatible.

Conclusion

The idea of a utopian society anchored in the Latin America environment can be traced back to those first years following the discovery of a previously unknown continent—America—by weary fifteenth- and early sixteenth-century Spanish explorers who were ignorant of just how vast and complex the globe was. While such a discussion is beyond the scope of this essay, its relevance can shed light on the notion that Latin America has always been a place of enchantment, mystique, and endless imagination for those looking in from the outside, as first chronicled by those conquistadores and missionaries (Hernán Cortés, Bernal Díaz del Castillo, Fray Diego de Landa, and Fray Bernadino de Sahagún, among many others) seeking gold, glory, and God in return for risking life and limb to catalog the great unknown. But to those writing about Latin America from within, the depiction of Latin America as utopian has also provided an important source of identity, of belonging to a magical, elusive, and ever shifting reality. We mention this only to draw out the connection between pre-Columbian Mexico and Urzaiz's depiction of a future society deeply rooted in tradition vis-à-vis the neo-Mayan architecture that glosses the landscape of twenty-third-century Villautopia.

While four Spanish editions of *Eugenia* have appeared in Mexico since its original publication in 1919 (1947, 1976, 1982, and 2002), until now there has been no English translation. A work of this value deserves to be read by a wider audience and appreciated for its originality—five years before the publication of Yevgeny Zamyatin's *We* and over a decade before that of Huxley's *Brave New World*, which, similar to *Eugenia*, both depicted an artificial society governed by the laws of state-controlled genetic engineering, where the young are educated by hypnotic suggestion during sleep, where the family as an institution has been long dissolved, where the lack of any responsibility to other beings has alienated man from his origins and his destiny, and where euphoria is induced by drug use (although *We* does not rely on these last two practices to the extent that we find in *Brave New World*). As a literary response to the hard scientific speculations of the late nineteenth and early twentieth centuries, and as an examination into the validity and potential of those speculations, *Eugenia* demonstrates that without a doubt Latin American writers of science fiction have been just as creative as their American and European counterparts in their responses to the inquiries and advances that have defined the modern age.

NOTES

1. "Eugenia: Esbozo de Novela por Eduardo Urzaiz," *Revista de la Revolución*, October 25, 1919, 3.

2. *La Higiene: Organo de la Dirección General de Salubridad e Higiene* 1, no. 4 (September 1919): 156–57.

3. Diane B. Paul, *Controlling Human Heredity: 1865 to the Present* (Atlantic Highlands, NJ: Humanities Press International, 1995), 18.

4. Kevles, *In the Name of Eugenics*, 45–46. Kevles continues by stating that Davenport held that the Poles, the Irish, the Italians, and other national groups were all biologically different races; so, in his lexicon, were the "Hebrews." Davenport found the Poles "independent and self-reliant though clannish"; the Italians tending to "crimes of personal violence"; and the Hebrews "intermediate between the slovenly Servians and Greeks and the tidy Swedes, Germans, and Bohemians" and given to "thieving" though rarely to "personal violence." He conceded that "the great influx of blood from Southeastern Europe" was less prone than the native variety to burglary, drunkenness, and vagrancy, and "more attached to music and art." Some of the best professors of science with whom Davenport was acquainted came from a Hungarian family. Yet on the whole Davenport expected that the new blood would rapidly make the American population "darker in pigmentation, smaller in stature, more mercurial . . . more given to crimes of larceny, kidnapping, assault, murder, rape, and sex-immorality" (ibid., 46–47). With such statements made by prominent, well-established scientists, it is not hard to understand how racist thinking and tendencies came to be injected into, and in no small way justified by, the scientific establishment of the twentieth century. As the science that attempted to bring experimental genetics and human heredity closer together, eugenics was also swept up by the racist currents of scientific circles that were concerned with the fate of mankind.

5. Paul, *Controlling Human Heredity*, 18.

6. *The New Encyclopaedia Britannica: Ready Reference*, 15th ed., s.v. "Mendel, Gregor (Johann)."

7. Ibid.

8. Paul, *Controlling Human Heredity*, 75.

9. Urzaiz, *Eugenia*, 19.

10. Ibid.

11. Paul, *Controlling Human Heredity*, 75.

12. *La Higiene* 2, no. 2 (February 1919): 315–16.

13. See Stepan, *"The Hour of Eugenics,"* 56n49.

14. Ibid., 23, 76, 80.

15. *La Higiene* 1, no. 2 (July–August 1918): 80–82.

16. Urzaiz, *Eugenia*, 28–29; Heape, "Preliminary Note on the Transplantation and Growth," 457–58.

17. *La Higiene* 1, no. 7 (December 1918): 262–63.

18. See the discussion of tocofobia in chap. 10 of *Eugenia* and on page 158–60 of the essay "*Eugenia* and Eugenics" in this volume.

19. Heape, "Further Note on the Transplantation and Growth," 179.

20. Urzaiz, *Eugenia*, 34–35.

21. Plato, *Republic*, trans. Benjamin Jowett (New York: Modern Library, 1941), 180.

22. Ibid., 181.

23. Ibid.

24. Ibid., 183. For descriptions of the way this works in Villautopia, see chap. 5 of *Eugenia*.

25. Everett F. Bleiler, *Science-Fiction, the Early Years: A Full Description of More than 3,000 Science-Fiction Stories from the Earliest Times to the Appearance of the Genre Magazines in 1930* (Kent, OH: Kent State University Press, 1990).

26. Urzaiz, *Eugenia*, 8.

27. Ibid., 9.

28. Ibid., chap. 6.

29. Ibid., 78.

30. Ibid., 12.

31. Ibid., 5–6.

32. Ibid., 8.

33. Ibid., 12.

34. Ibid., 12–13.

35. Ibid., 45.

36. Ibid., 69.

37. Ibid., 23.

38. Ibid., 40.

39. Doña Candelaria Souza de Fernández, a close friend and admirer of Urzaiz, describes him as a hopeless romantic. For example, she explained, he hated the song "La Peregrina," written by Felipe Carrillo Puerto (with the assistance of musicians Ricardo Palmerin and Luis Vega) to express his love for the North American journalist Alma Reed, because it made him so sad that he cried (Sarah Buck Kachaluba, interview with Doña Candelaria Souza de Fernández, July 1, 2014, Mérida, Yucatán).

40. Urzaiz, *Eugenia*, 84–85.

Bibliography

ARCHIVES AND LIBRARY COLLECTIONS

Archivo General del Estado de Yucatán (AGEY)
    Ramo (R)
    Poder Ejecutivo (PE)
Archivo Histórico de la Secretaría de Salud (AHSSA), Mexico City
    Fondo Salubridad Pública, Sección Higiene Infantil
Biblioteca del Estado de Yucatán, Mérida, Yucatán
    Centro de Apoyo (CDA) a la Investigación Histórica del Estado de Yucatán
    Hemeroteca del Estado de Yucatán
Robert Redfield Papers, Special Collections, Joseph Regenstein Library, University of
    Chicago

PERIODICALS

Chispas (Mérida, Yucatán)
Diario de Debates (Mexico City)
Diario de Yucatán (Mérida, Yucatán)
Diario Oficial: Organo del Gobierno Constitucional de los Estados Unidos Mexicanos (Mexico City)
Diario Oficial de Yucatán (Mérida, Yucatán)
El Constitucionalista (Veracruz, Veracruz)
El Demócrata (Mexico City)
El Dictamen (Veracruz, Veracruz)
El Nacional (Mexico City)
El Popular (Mérida, Yucatán)
El Universal (Mexico City)
Excelsior (Mexico City)
La Higiene: Organo de la Dirección General de Salubridad e Higiene (Mérida, Yucatán)

La Revista de Yucatán (Mérida, Yucatán)
New York Times (New York)
Tierra (Mérida, Yucatán)

GOVERNMENT DECREES, INCLUDING LAWS

*Código Civil del Distrito Federal y Territorio de Baja California, con su parte expositiva e indices respeti-
vos.* Nueva ed. Mexico City: Imprenta Comercio de Dublan y Chavez, 1878.

*Código Civil del Distrito Federal y Territorios de Tepic y Baja California Promulgado en 31 de marzo
de 1884.* Edited by Antonio de J. Lozano. Ed. annotada. Mexico City: Librería de la
Vda. de C. Bouret, 1902.

Código Civil del Estado de Yucatán. Mérida, Yucatán: Gobierno del Estado, 1918.

"Código Civil para el Distrito y Territorios Federales en Material Comun y Para Toda
la Republica en material Federal." *Diario Oficial,* Mexico City. May 26, 1928.

"Ley de Divorcio, Reformas al Código del Registro Civil y al Código Civil del Estado."
Supplement to no. 7803 of the *Diario Oficial del Gobierno Socialista del Estado de Yucatán*
for April 3, 1923, Mérida, Yucatán.

"Ley Del Seguro Social." *Diario oficial de la Federación.* Mexico City. January 19, 1943.

"Ley Federal de Trabajo." *Diario oficial de la Federación.* Mexico City. August 18, 1931.

"Ley Orgánica de 1867." *Diario oficial de la Federación.* Mexico City. December 2, 1867.

"Ley Sobre el Divorcio." *El Constitucionalista.* Veracruz, Veracruz. January 2, 1915 (issued
on December 29, 1914).

"Ley Sobre el Divorcio." *Diario Oficial de Yucatán.* Mérida, Yucatán. May 27, 1915.

Ley sobre relaciones familiares expedida por el C. Venustiano Carranza. Mexico City: Imprenta
del Gobierno, 1917.

Plan de Guadalupe. Mexico City. March 26, 1913.

PUBLISHED SOURCES

Acevedo, Marta. *El 10 de Mayo.* Mexico City: Cultura/SEP, Martín Casillas Editores,
1982.

Aguirre Beltrán, Gonzalo. *Obra polémica.* Mexico City: Instituto Nacional de Antropología
e Historia, 1976.

Alba, Francisco. *La población de México: Evolución y dilema.* Mexico City: El Colegio de
México, 1977.

Alianza de Mujeres de México, ed. *La situación jurídica de la mujer mexicana.* Mexico City:
Alianza de Mujeres de México, 1953.

Allen, Garland E. "Eugenics." In *New Dictionary of the History of Ideas,* vol. 2, edited by
Maryanne Cline Horowitz, 732–37. Detroit: Scribner, 2005.

Alonso, Ana María. "Rationalizing Patriarchy: Gender, Domestic Violence, and Law in Mexico." *Identities: Global Studies in Culture and Power* 2, nos. 1–2 (September 1995): 29–47.

Alvarado, Salvador. *La reconstrucción de México: Un mensaje a los pueblos de América.* Mexico City: J. Ballesca y Cia., Sucs., 1919.

Anthias, Flora, and Nira Yuval-Davis. *Women, Nation and State.* New York: St. Martin's Press, 1989.

Arendt, Hannah. *The Origins of Totalitarianism.* New York: Harcourt Brace Jovanovich, 1973.

Arrom, Silvia M. "Changes in Mexican Family Law in the Nineteenth Century: The Civil Codes of 1870 and 1884." *Journal of Family History* 10, no. 3 (September 1985): 305–17.

Astorga A., Luis A. "La razón demográfica del Estado." *Revista Mexicana de Sociología* (January–March 1989): 193–210.

Basave Benítez, Agustín. *México mestizo: Análisis del nacionalismo mexicano en torno a la mestizofilia de Andrés Molina Enríquez.* Mexico City: Fondo de Cultura Económica, 1992.

Bennett Bean, R. "Human Types in Relation to Medicine." *The American Naturalist* 61, no. 673 (March–April 1927): 160–72.

Beezley, William. "Creating a Revolutionary Culture: Vasconcelos, Indians, Anthropologists, and Calendar Girls." In *A Companion to Mexican History and Culture,* edited by William H. Beezley, 420–38. Malden, MA: Wiley-Blackwell, 2011.

———. "Reflections on the Historiography of Twentieth-Century Mexico." *History Compass* 5, no. 3 (2007): 963–74.

Benjamin, Thomas, and Mark Wasserman, eds. *Provinces of the Revolution: Essays on Regional Mexican History, 1910–1929.* Albuquerque: University of New Mexico Press, 1990.

Besant, Annie. "Theosophical Society." In *Encyclopaedia of Religion and Ethics,* edited by James Hastings, 300–304. New York: Charles Scribner's Sons, 1924.

Birn, Anne-Emmanuelle. *Marriage of Convenience: Rockefeller International Health and Revolutionary Mexico.* Rochester, NY: University of Rochester Press, 2006.

Bleiler, Everett F. *Science-Fiction, the Early Years: A Full Description of More than 3,000 Science-Fiction Stories from the Earliest Times to the Appearance of the Genre Magazines in 1930.* Kent, OH: Kent State University Press, 1990.

Bliss, Katherine Elaine. "Social Reform and State-Building (Mexico)." In *Encyclopedia of Social Welfare History in North America,* edited by John M. Herrick and Paul H. Stuart, 342–45. Thousand Oaks, CA: Sage, 2005.

Blum, Ann S. *Domestic Economies: Family, Work, and Welfare in Mexico City, 1884–1943.* Lincoln: University of Nebraska Press, 2009.

Booker, M. Keith. *Dystopian Literature: A Theory and Research Guide.* Westport, CT: Greenwood Press, 1994.

Bowie, Ewen. "Longus." In *The Oxford Classical Dictionary,* 4th ed., edited by Simon Hornblower and Antony Spawforth, 858. Oxford: Oxford University Press, 2012.

Bowler, Peter J. *Theories of Human Evolution: A Century of Debate, 1844–1944*. Baltimore: Johns Hopkins University Press, 1986.

Boyer, Christopher. *Becoming Campesinos: Politics, Identity, and Agrarian Struggle in Postrevolutionary Michoacán, 1920–1935*. Stanford, CA: Stanford University Press, 2003.

Boylan, Kristina. "Mexican Catholic Women's Activism, 1929–1940." PhD diss., Oxford University, 2000.

Breuer, Josef. "Anna O." In *The Freud Reader*, edited by Peter Gay, 60–78. New York: W. W. Norton, 1989.

Briggle, Adam. "Spencer, Herbert." In *Encyclopedia of Science, Technology, and Ethics*, edited by Carl Mitcham, 1848–49. Detroit: Macmillan Reference, 2005.

The Brill Dictionary of Religion. Edited by Kocku von Stuckrad. Leiden: Brill, 2006.

Brooke, John Hedley. "Darwin, Charles." In *Encyclopedia of Science and Religion*, vol. 1, edited by Wentzel Vreded van Huyssteen, 200–203. New York: Macmillan Reference, 2003.

Broude, Gwen J. "Sexual Attitudes and Practices." In *Encyclopedia of Sex and Gender: Men and Women in the World's Cultures*, vol. 1, ed. Carol R. Ember and Melvin Ember, 177–86. New York: Kluwer Academic/Plenum Publishers, 2004.

Buchenau, Jürgen. "Científicos." In *Encyclopedia of Mexico: History, Society & Culture*, vol. 1, edited by Michael S. Werner, 260–62. Chicago: Fitzroy Dearborn, 1997.

———. "Social Darwinism." In *Encyclopedia of Mexico: History, Society & Culture*, vol. 2, edited by Michael S. Werner, 1350–52. Chicago: Fitzroy Dearborn, 1997.

Buck, Sarah A. "Activists and Mothers: Feminist and Maternalist Politics in Mexico, 1923–1953." PhD diss., Rutgers University, 2002.

———. "Women and Social Welfare (Mexico)." In *Encyclopedia of Social Welfare History in North America*, edited by John M. Herrick and Paul H. Stuart, 444–47. Thousand Oaks, CA: Sage, 2005.

Buffington, Robert M. *Criminal and Citizen in Modern Mexico*. Lincoln: University of Nebraska Press, 2000.

Burgos Nuñez, Santiago. "El Doctor Eduardo Urzaiz Rodríguez: Literato." *Gaceta Preparatoriana: Vocero Estudiantil de la Universidad Nacional del Sureste* 2, no. 12 (March 1955): 11–12.

Cámara-Vallejos, Rubén, and Marco Palma Solís. "Eduardo Urzaiz Rodríguez: Universitario ejemplar en Medicina, Psiquiatría, Educación, Artes y Cultura." *Revista Biomédica* 25, no. 2 (May–August 2014): 102–6.

Cano, Gabriela. "Congresos feministas en la historia de México." *FEM* 11, no. 58 (1987): 24–26.

———. "Las feministas en campaña: La primera mitad del Siglo XX." *Debate Feminista* 2, no. 4 (1991): 262–92.

———, ed. "México 1923: Primer Congreso Feminista Panamericano." *Debate Feminista*, no. 1 (March 1990): 303–18.

———. "The Porfiriato and the Mexican Revolution." In *Nation, Empire, Colony: Historicizing Gender and Race*, edited by Ruth Roach Pierson and Nupur Chaudhuri with the assistance of Beth McAuley, 106–20. Bloomington: Indiana University Press, 1998.

———. "Revolución, feminismo y ciudadanía en México (1915–1940)." In *Historia de las mujeres en Occidente*, edited by Georges Duby and Michelle Perrot, 301–11. Madrid: Taurus, 1993.

Carrillo Puerto, Acrelio. *La familia Carrillo Puerto de Motul, con la Revolución Mexicana.* Mérida, Yucatán, 1959.

Carr-Sanders, A. N. *World Population.* Oxford: Oxford University Press, 1936.

Center for Disease Control. "Achievements in Public Health, 1900–1999: Healthier Mothers and Babies." *Morbidity and Mortality Weekly Report (MMWR Weekly)* 48, no. 38 (October 1, 1999): 849–58.

Chávez Asencio, Manuel F. *La familia en el derecho.* Vol. 2, *Relaciones jurídicas conyugales.* 4th ed. Mexico City: Editorial Porrúa, 1997.

Chávez Padrón, Martha. *El derecho agrario en México.* Mexico City: Editorial Porrua, 1974.

Christianson, Stephen G., ed. *The American Book of Days.* 4th ed. New York: H. W. Wilson, 2000.

Comfort, Nathaniel. *The Science of Human Perfection: How Genes Became the Heart of American Medicine.* New Haven, CT: Yale University Press, 2012.

Córdova, Arnaldo. *La ideologia de la Revolución Mexicana: La formación del nuevo regimen.* Mexico City: Ediciones Era, 1973.

Crispín Castellanos, Margarito. "Hospital de maternidad e infancia: Perspectiva histórica de un centro de beneficencia pública de finales del siglo XIX." In *La atención materno infantil: Apuntes para su historia*, 95–115. Mexico City: Secretaría de Salubridad y Asistencia, 1993.

Cuspinera, Margarita Vera. "Positivism." In *Encyclopedia of Mexico: History, Society & Culture*, vol. 2, edited by Michael S. Werner, 1178–80. Chicago: Fitzroy Dearborn, 1997.

Darvill, Timothy. "Nebuchadnezzar." In *The Concise Oxford Dictionary of Archaeology*, 2nd ed., 305–6. Oxford: Oxford University Press, 2008.

Darwin, Charles. *The Descent of Man, and Selection in Relation to Sex.* 2 vols. London: John Murray, 1871.

———. *On the Origin of Species.* London: John Murray, 1859.

De Grazia, Victoria. *How Fascism Ruled Women: Italy, 1922–1945.* Berkeley: University of California Press, 1992.

Diccionario histórico y biográfico de la Revolución Mexicana. Edited and published by Instituto Nacional de Estudios Históricos de la Revolución Mexicana (INEHRM). CD ROM, 1994.

Dikötter, Frank. "Race Culture: Recent Perspectives on the History of Eugenics." *American Historical Review* 103, no. 2 (April 1998): 467–78.

Dore, Elizabeth. "One Step Forward, Two Steps Back: Gender and the State in the Long Nineteenth Century." In *Hidden Histories of Gender and the State in Latin America*, edited by Elizabeth Dore and Maxine Molyneux, 3–32. Durham, NC: Duke University Press, 2000.

Drummond, Andrew. "Pompilius, Numa." In *The Oxford Classical Dictionary*, 4th ed., edited by Simon Hornblower and Antony Spawforth, 1181. Oxford: Oxford University Press, 2012.

Durand, John D. "The Modern Expansion of the World Population." *Proceedings of the American Philosophical Society* 111, no. 3 (June 22, 1967): 136–59.

Dziubinskyj, Aaron. "The Birth of Science Fiction in Spanish America." *Science Fiction Studies* 30, no. 1 (2003): 21–32.

Ehrenberg, John. *Civil Society: The Critical History of an Idea*. New York: New York University Press, 1999.

Eiss, Paul K. "Deconstructing Indians, Reconstructing *Patria*: Indigenous Education in Yucatán from the *Porfiriato* to the Mexican Revolution." *Journal of Latin American Anthropology* 9, no. 1 (2004): 119–50.

———. *In the Name of El Pueblo: Place, Community, and the Politics of History in Yucatán*. Durham, NC: Duke University Press, 2010.

Ellwood, Robert S. "Blavatsky, H. P." In *Encyclopedia of Religion*, 2nd ed., edited by Lindsey Jones, 977–78. Detroit: Macmillan Reference, 2005.

Enciclopedia Yucatanense. Vol. 5. Mexico City: Edición Oficial del Gobierno de Yucatán, 1977.

Erosa-Barbachano, Arturo. "Historia de la Escuela de Medicina de Mérida, Yucatán, México." *Revista Biomédica* 8, no. 4 (October–December 1997): 266–73.

"Eugenia: Esbozo de Novela por Eduardo Urzaiz." *Revista de la Revolución*, October 25, 1919, 3.

Falcón, Romana. *El agrarismo en Veracruz: La etapa radical (1928–1935)*. Mexico City: El Colegio de México, 1977.

Fallaw, Ben. *Cárdenas Compromised: The Failure of Reform in Postrevolutionary Yucatán*. Durham, NC: Duke University Press, 2001.

Fallwell, Lynne. "Eugenics." In *Encyclopedia of Genocide and Crimes Against Humanity*, vol. 1, edited by Dinah L. Shelton, 315–16. Detroit: Macmillan Reference, 2005.

Fernández Delgado, Miguel Ángel. "Eduardo Urzaiz Rodríguez (1876–1955)." In *Latin American Science Fiction Writers: An A to Z Guide*, edited by Darrell B. Lockhart, 204–5. Westport, CT: Greenwood Press, 2004.

Ferrer, Adolfo. *El archivo de Felipe Carrillo: El callismo, la corrupción del regimen obregonista*. New York: Carlos Lopez Press, 1924.

Foucault, Michel. *Ethics: Subjectivity and Truth*. Edited by Paul Rabinow. New York: New Press, 1997.

———. *The History of Sexuality*. Vol. 1, *An Introduction*. Translated by Robert Hurley. New York: Vintage Books, 1996.

French, Laurence Armand, and Magdaleon Manzanárez. "Mexico." In *World Education Encyclopedia*, 2nd ed., vol. 2, edited by Rebecca Marlow-Ferguson, 879–90. Detroit: Gale, 2001.

French, William. "Prostitutes and Guardian Angels: Women, Work, and the Family in Porfirian Mexico." *Hispanic American Historical Review* 72, no. 4 (1992): 529–53.

Freud, Sigmund. "An Autobiographical Study." In *The Freud Reader*, edited by Peter Gay, 3–41. New York: W. W. Norton, 1989.

———. "On the Universal Tendency to Debasement in the Sphere of Love (Contributions to the Psychology of Love II)." In *The Freud Reader*, edited by Peter Gay, 394–400. New York: W. W. Norton, 1989.

"Freud Comes to America." In *American Decades*, vol. 1, edited by Judith S. Baughman, Victor Bondi, Richard Layman, Tandy McConnell, and Vincent Tompkins, 1900–1909. Detroit: Gale Research, 2001.

Galton, Francis. *The Anthropometric Laboratory*. London: William Clowes and Sons, 1884.

———. *Hereditary Genius*. London: Macmillan, 1869.

———. "Hereditary Talent and Character." *MacMillan's Magazine* 12 (1865): 157–66 and 318–27.

———. *Inquiries into Human Faculty and Its Development*. London: Macmillan, 1883.

Garagin, Michael. "Aeolus." In *The Oxford Classical Dictionary*, 2nd ed., edited by N. G. L. Hammond and H. H. Scullard, 15. Oxford: Clarendon Press, 1970.

Garza, James A. "Díaz, Porfirio." In *Encyclopedia of Mexico: History, Society & Culture*, vol. 1, edited by Michael S. Werner, 406–7. Chicago: Fitzroy Dearborn, 1997.

Gay, Peter. *The Bourgeois Experience: Victoria to Freud*. Vol. 3, *The Cultivation of Hatred*. New York: W. W. Norton, 1993.

———, ed. *The Freud Reader*. New York: W. W. Norton, 1989.

Gilderhaus, Mark T. "Many Mexicos: Traditions and Innovations in Recent Historiography." *Latin American Research Review* 22, no. 1 (1987): 204–13.

Gillham, Nicholas Wright. "Galton, Francis." In *Encyclopedia of Science, Technology, and Ethics*, vol. 2, edited by Carl Mitcham, 816–18. Detroit: Macmillan Reference, 2005.

González Navarro, Moisés. *Historia moderna de México: El Porfiriato, la vida social*. Mexico City: Editorial Hermes, 1970.

Gordon, Linda. *Woman's Body, Woman's Right: Birth Control in America*. Revised and Updated Edition. New York: Penguin Books, 1990.

Griffiths, Alan H. "Tantalus." In *The Oxford Classical Dictionary*, 4th ed., edited by Simon Hornblower and Antony Spawforth, 1430. Oxford: Oxford University Press, 2012.

Gruening, Ernest H. "Felipe Carrillo." *The Nation*, January 16, 1924, 61–62.

Guillén, Manuel E. "Algunas reflexiones sobre la hygiene de la mujer durante su pubertad." Thesis, Facultad de Medicina, 1903.

Guy, Donna. "White Slavery, Citizenship and Nationality in Argentina." In *Nationalisms and Sexualities*, edited by Andrew Parker, Mary Russo, Doris Sommer, and Patricia Yaeger, 201–17. New York: Routledge, 1992.

Haldane, J. B. S. *Daedalus; or, Science and the Future; A Paper Read to the Heretics, Cambridge, on February 4th, 1923*. 6th ed. London: K. Paul, Trench, Trubner, 1925.

Hale, Charles A. *The Transformation of Liberalism in Late Nineteenth-Century Mexico*. Princeton, NJ: Princeton University Press, 1989.

Hart, John Mason. *Anarchism and the Mexican Working Class, 1860–1931.* Austin: University of Texas Press, 1978.

Hausen, Karen. "Mother's Day in the Weimar Republic." In *When Biology Became Destiny: Women in Weimar and Nazi Germany,* edited by Atina Grossman, Renate Bridenthal, and Marion Kaplan, 131–71. New York: Monthly Review Press, 1984.

Hawke, Gail, and R. Danielle Egan. "Sex, Popular Beliefs and Culture: Discourses on the Sexual Child." In *A Cultural History of Sexuality,* vol. 5, *In the Age of Empire,* edited by Chiara Beccalossi and Ivan Crozier, 123–44. New York: Berg, 2011.

Haywood Ferreira, Rachel. *The Emergence of Latin American Science Fiction.* Middletown, CT: Wesleyan University Press, 2011.

H. Congreso de la Unión. *Las constituciones de México, 1814–1989.* Mexico City: Comité de Asuntos Editoriales, 1989.

Heape, Walter Further. "Note on the Transplantation and Growth of Mammalian Ova with a Uterine Foster Mother." *Proceedings of the Royal Society of London,* no. 62 (1897): 178–83.

———. "Preliminary Note on the Transplantation and Growth of Mammalian Ova within a Uterine FosterMother." *Proceedings of the Royal Society of London,* no. 48 (1890): 457–58.

Herrick, John M., and Paul H. Stuart. *Encyclopedia of Social Welfare History in North America.* Thousand Oaks, CA: Sage, 2005.

Hesiod. *Theogony.* In *Hesiod,* translated by Richard Lattimore. Ann Arbor: University of Michigan Press, 1991.

Hofstadter, Richard. *Social Darwinism in American Thought: 1860–1915.* Philadelphia: University of Pennsylvania Press, 1944.

Hutton, Patrick H. "Foucault, Freud, and the Technologies of the Self." In *Technologies of the Self,* edited by Luther H. Martin, Huck Gutman, and Patrick H. Hutto, 121–44. Amherst: University of Massachusetts Press, 1988.

Huxley, Aldous. *Brave New World.* New York: Harper & Row, 1932.

Ingle, Marjorie I. *The Mayan Revival Style: Art Deco Mayan Fantasy.* Albuquerque: University of New Mexico Press, 1989.

Instituto de Investigaciónes Jurídicas. *Diccionario Jurídico Mexicano.* 4th ed. Mexico City: Editorial Porrúa, 1991.

Instituto Nacional de Estadística, Geografía, e Informática (INEGI). *Estadísticas históricas de México.* Vol. 1. Mexico City: Instituto Nacional de Estadística, Geografía e Informática; Instituto Nacional de Antropología e Historia; SEP, 1985.

"Interesantes entrevistas entre la Señora Kennedy y nuestro 'leader' el ciudadano Felipe Carrillo Puerto, acerca del control de los nacimientos." *Tierra* 28 (November 4, 1923): 9 and 23.

Irwin, Robert McKee. *Mexican Masculinities.* Minneapolis: University of Minnesota Press, 2003.

Iturbide y Troncoso, Manuel. "Informe de los Trabajos Ejecutados por el servicio Higiénico Escolar durante el Año Fiscal 1909–1910." *Anales de Higiene Escolar* 1, no. 2 (November 1911).

Jackson, Louise A. "Sex, Religion and the Law." In *A Cultural History of Sexuality*, vol. 5, *In the Age of Empire*, edited by Chiara Beccalossi and Ivan Crozier, 83–100. New York: Berg, 2011.

Johnson, Lyman L., and Sonya Lipsett-Rivera, eds. *The Faces of Honor: Sex, Shame, and Violence in Colonial Latin America*. Albuquerque: University of New Mexico Press, 1998.

Jordan, Marc. "Watteau, Jean-Antoine." In *The Oxford Companion to Western Art*, 791–92. Oxford: Oxford University Press, 2001.

Joseph, Gilbert. *Revolution from Without: Yucatán, Mexico, and the United States, 1880–1924*. Durham, NC: Duke University Press, 1995.

Kerber, Linda K. "Separate Spheres, Female Worlds, Woman's Place: The Rhetoric of Women's History." *The Journal of American History* 75, no. 1 (1988): 9–40.

Kevles, Daniel J. *In the Name of Eugenics: Genetics and the Uses of Human Heredity*. Rev. ed. Cambridge, MA: Harvard University Press, 1995.

"Khoikhoi." In *The World Book Encyclopedia*, vol. 11, *J–K*, 309. Chicago: World Book, 2002.

Kincaid, Harold. "Positivism in the Social Sciences." In *Routledge Encyclopedia of Philosophy*, vol. 7, edited by Edward Craig, 558–61. New York: Routledge, 1988.

Kirk, Dudley. *Europe's Population in the Interwar Years*. Geneva: League of Nations, 1946.

Klaus, Alisa. *Every Child a Lion: The Origins of Maternal and Infant Health Policy in the United States and France, 1890–1920*. Ithaca, NY: Cornell University Press, 1993.

Klausen, Susanne, and Alison Bashford. "Fertility Control: Eugenics, Neo-Malthusianism, and Feminism." In *The Oxford Handbook of the History of Eugenics*, edited by Philippa Levine and Alison Bashford, 98–115. New York: Oxford University Press, 2010.

Knauer, O. *Urber puerperale Psychosen, für practische Aerzte*. Berlin: S. Karger, 1897.

Knight, Alan. *The Mexican Revolution*. Vol. 1, *Porfirians, Liberals and Peasants*. Cambridge: Cambridge University Press, 1986.

———. "Racism, Revolution, and *Indigenismo*: Mexico, 1910–1940." In *The Idea of Race in Latin America, 1870–1940*, edited by Richard Graham, 71–113. Austin: University of Texas Press, 1990.

———. "Revolutionary Project, Recalcitrant People: Mexico, 1910–1940." In *The Revolutionary Process in Mexico: Essays on Political and Social Change, 1880–1940*, edited by Jaime E. Rodríguez O., 227–64. Los Angeles: UCLA Latin American Center Publications and Mexico/Chicano Program of the University of California, 1990.

Knoepffler, Nickolaus. "Eugenics." In *Encyclopedia of Anthropology*, vol. 2, edited by H. James Birx, 871–73. Thousand Oaks, CA: Sage, 2006.

Krauze, Enrique. *Porfirio Díaz*. Mexico City: Fondo de Cultura Económica, 1987.

Kymlicka, Will, and Wayne Norman. "Return of the Citizen: A Survey of Recent Work on Citizenship Theory." *Ethics* 104 (1994): 352–81.

"La Criada de Moliere." *La Revista de Yucatán*, October 5, 1918, 3.

Lamarck, Jean-Baptiste. *Philosophie zoologique ou exposition des considérations relatives à l'histoire naturelle des animaux*. Paris: Germer Baillère, 1809.

Laqueur, Thomas. "Why the Margins Matter: Occultism and the Making of Modernity." *Modern Intellectual History* 3, no. 1 (April 2006): 111–35.

Lau, Ana. "Una experiencia feminista en Yucatán, 1922–1924." *FEM* 8, no. 30 (1983): 12–14.

Lavrin, Asunción, ed. *Sexuality and Marriage in Colonial Latin America.* Lincoln: University of Nebraska Press, 1989.

Leal, Juan Felipe. "Notas sobre el nuevo estado." In *Cien años de lucha de clases: Lecturas de historia de México (1876–1976),* edited by Ismael Colmenares M., Miguel Angel Gallo T., Francisco González G., and Luis Hernández N., 307–10. Mexico City: Ediciones Quinto Sol, 1980.

Lemaître, Monique J. *Elvia Carrillo Puerto: La monja roja del Mayab.* Monterrey, Nuevo León: Ediciónes Castillo, S.A. de C.V., 1998.

Levine, Philippa, and Alison Bashford. "Introduction: Eugenics and the Modern World." In *The Oxford Handbook of the History of Eugenics,* edited by Philippa Levine and Alison Bashford, 3–24. New York: Oxford University Press, 2010.

Liga de Acción Social. "Estatutos de la Liga de Acción Social: Reformados el 6 de noviembre de 1944." Mérida, Yucatán: Liga de Acción Social, 1944. Centro de Apoyo (CDA) a la Investigación Histórica del Estado de Yucatán, Biblioteca Yucatanense CXLVI 1944 1/2 14.

———. "Principales Sucesos de la Liga de Acción Social desde su fundación." Mérida, Yucatán: Liga de Acción Social, 1954. Centro de Apoyo (CDA) a la Investigación Histórica del Estado de Yucatán, Biblioteca Yucatanense CLXXII 1954 2/2 11.

Lomeli, Margarita. "La mujer en el derecho civil mexicano, primera parte." In *La situación jurídica de la mujer mexicana,* edited by Alianza de Mujeres de México, 45–46. Mexico City: Alianza de Mujeres de México, 1953.

Lomnitz-Adler, Claudio. *Exits from the Labyrinth: Culture and Ideology in the Mexican National Space.* Berkeley: University of California Press, 1992.

Longfellow, Henry Wadsworth. *Evangelina: Una historia de la Acadia.* Translated by Eduardo Urzaiz. Mérida, Yucatán: Talleres gráficas del sudeste, n.d.

López Rodríguez, Ramón. "El Doctor Eduardo Urzaiz Rodríguez: Su vida y su obra." *Gaceta Preparatoriana: Vocero Estudiantil de la Universidad Nacional del Sureste* 2, no. 12 (March 1955): 1, 13.

Macías, Anna. *Against All Odds: The Feminist Movement in Mexico to 1940.* Westport, CT: Greenwood Press, 1982.

———. "Felipe Carrillo Puerto and Women's Liberation in Mexico." In *Latin American Women: Historical Perspectives,* edited by Asunción Lavrin, 286–301. Westport, CT: Greenwood Press, 1978.

———. "The Mexican Revolution Was No Revolution for Women." In *Latin America: A Historical Reader,* edited by Lewis Hanke, 591–601. Boston: Little, Brown, 1974.

MacLachlan, Colin M., and William H. Beezley. *El Gran Pueblo: A History of Greater Mexico.* 2nd ed. Upper Saddle River, NJ: Prentice Hall, 1999.

"Malthus, Thomas Robert (1766–1834)." In *Encyclopedia of European Social History,* vol. 6,

Biographies / Contributors, edited by Peter N. Stearns, 212–13. Detroit: Scribner, 2001.

Marshall, T. H. *Citizenship and Social Class and Other Essays*. Cambridge: Cambridge University Press, 1950.

Martí, Oscar R. "Justo Sierra and the Forging of a Mexican Nation." In *Forging People: Race, Ethnicity, and Nationality in Hispanic American and Latino/a Thought*, edited by Jorge J. E. García, 152–78. Notre Dame, IN: Notre Dame University Press, 2011.

Martínez Assad, Carlos, ed. *Balance y perspectivas de los studios regionales en México*. Mexico City: Universidad Nacional Autónoma de México, 1990.

———. *El laboratorio de la revolución*. Mexico: Siglo Veintiuno Editores, 1979.

Mazlish, Bruce. "Comte, Auguste." In *Encyclopedia of Philosophy*, 2nd ed., edited by Donald M. Borchert, 2:409–14. Detroit: Macmillan Reference, 2006.

McCrea, Heather L. *Diseased Relations: Epidemics, Public Health, and State-Building in Yucatán, Mexico, 1847–1924*. Albuquerque: University of New Mexico Press, 2010.

Meckel, R. A. *Save the Babies: American Public Health Reform and the Prevention of Infant Mortality, 1850–1929*. Baltimore: Johns Hopkins University Press, 1990.

"Mendel, Gregor (Johann)." In *The New Encyclopaedia Britannica: Ready Reference*, 15th ed., 8:4. Chicago: Encyclopedia Britannica, 2002.

Menéndez Díaz, Conrado. "El Dr. Eduardo Urzaiz Rodríguez: Maestro Universitario." *Gaceta Preparatoriana: Vocero Estudiantil de la Universidad Nacional del Sureste* 2, no. 12 (March 1955): 10.

Meyer, Michael C., and William L. Sherman. *The Course of Mexican History*. 5th ed. New York: Oxford University Press, 1995.

Middlebrook, Kevin. *The Paradox of Revolution: Labor, the State, and Authoritarianism in Mexico*. Baltimore: Johns Hopkins University Press, 1995.

Mitchell, Stephanie, and Patience A. Schell, eds. *The Women's Revolution in Mexico: 1910–1953*. New York: Rowman & Littlefield, 2007.

Mohanty, Chandra Talpade, Ann Russo, and Lourdes Torres, eds. *Third World Women and the Politics of Feminism*. Bloomington: Indiana University Press, 1992.

Moreno, Robert. "Mexico." In *The Comparative Reception of Darwinism*, 2nd ed., edited by Thomas F. Glick, 346–74. Chicago: University of Chicago Press, 1988.

Morton, Ward. *Woman Suffrage in Mexico*. Gainesville: University of Florida Press, 1962.

Ochoa, Enrique C. "Constitution of 1917 (Mexico)." In *Encyclopedia of Social Welfare History in North America*, edited by John M. Herrick and Paul H. Stuart, 68–70. Thousand Oaks, CA: Sage, 2005.

Olcott, Jocelyn. *Revolutionary Women in Postrevolutionary Mexico*. Durham, NC: Duke University Press, 2005.

Olcott, Jocelyn, Mary Kay Vaughan, and Gabriela Cano, eds. *Sex in Revolution: Gender, Politics, and Power in Modern Mexico*. Foreword by Carlos Monsiváis. Durham, NC: Duke University Press, 2006.

Omi, Michael, and Howard Winant. *Racial Formation in the United States: From the 1960s to the 1990s*. New York: Routledge, 1994.

Oosterhuis, Harry. *Stepchildren of Nature: Krafft-Ebing, Psychiatry, and the Making of Sexual Identity*. Chicago: University of Chicago Press, 2000.

Orellana Trinidad, Laura. "'La mujer del porvenir': Raíces intelectuales y alcances del pensamiento feminista de Hermila Galindo, 1915–1919." *Signos Históricos* 5 (2001): 109–35.

Orloff, Ana Shola. "Gender and the Social Rights of Citizenship: The Comparative Analysis of Gender Relations and the Welfare States." *American Sociological Review* 58 (1993): 303–28.

Orosa Díaz, Jaime. *Breve historia de Yucatán*. Mérida, Yucatán: Universidad de Yucatán, 1981.

Owen, Alex. *The Place of Enchantment: British Occultism and the Culture of the Modern*. Chicago: University of Chicago Press, 2004.

Oxford English Reference Dictionary. Edited by Judy Pearsall and Bill Trumble. 2nd ed. Oxford: Oxford University Press, 2002.

Pallares, Eduardo, ed. *Leyes complementarias del Código Civil*. Mexico City: Herrero Hermanos Sucessores, 1920.

Palmer, R. R., and Joel Colton. *A History of the Modern World*. 8th ed. New York: Alfred A. Knopf, 1995.

Partido Revolucionario Institucional. *Presencia de la mujer en la vida cívica de México*. Mexico City: PRI, 1952.

Pateman, Carole. "Feminismo y democracia." *Debate Feminista* 1 (March 1990): 7–28.

———. *The Sexual Contract*. Palo Alto, CA: Stanford University Press, 1988.

Paul, Diane B. *Controlling Human Heredity: 1865 to the Present*. Atlantic Highlands, NJ: Humanities Press International, 1995.

Paul, Diane B., and James Moore. "The Darwinian Context: Evolution and Inheritance." In *The Oxford Handbook of the History of Eugenics*, edited by Philippa Levine and Alison Bashford, 28–42. New York: Oxford University Press, 2010.

Peniche, Piedad. "Las ligas feministas en la revolución." *Unicornio* (1996): 8–9.

Peniche Ponce, Carlos. "Introducción." In Eduardo Urzaiz, *Eugenia: Esbozo novelesco de costumbres futuras*, vii–xx. Mexico City: Universidad Nacional Autónoma de México, 2006.

———. "La infertilidad femenina en 'Eugenia,' de Eduardo Urzaiz." *Proceso* 1571 (December 10, 2006): 80–81.

Peniche Vallado, Leopoldo. "El mensaje de *Eugenia*." Preface to the 1955 edition. Reprinted in Eduardo Urzaiz, *Eugenia: Esbozo novelesco de costumbres futuras*, 19–30. Mérida, Yucatán: Universidad Autónoma de Yucatán, 2002.

Peniche Vallado, Luis. "La enseñanza secundaria en Yucatán, obra del Dr. Urzaiz." *Gaceta Preparatoriana: Vocero Estudiantil de la Universidad Nacional del Sureste* 2, no. 12 (March 1955): 3, 15.

Pérez, Emma. "Feminism-in-Nationalism: The Gendered Subaltern at the Yucatecan Feminist Congress of 1916." In *Between Woman and Nation: Nationalisms, Transnational*

Feminisms, and the State, edited by Caren Kaplen, Norma Alarcón, and Minoo Moallem, 219–39. Durham, NC: Duke University Press, 1999.

Plato. *The Republic.* Translated by Benjamin Jowett. New York: Modern Library, 1941.

Pollard, Miranda R. *Reign of Virtue: Mobilizing Gender in Vichy France.* Chicago: University of Chicago Press, 1998.

Porter, Susie. "The Apogee of Revolution, 1934–1946." In *A Companion to Mexican History and Culture,* edited by William H. Beezley, 453–67. Malden, MA: Wiley-Blackwell, 2011.

El primer congreso feminista de Yucatán: Anales de esa memorable asamblea. Mérida, Yucatán: Talleres Atenzo Popular, 1916.

Prosser, Jay. "Transsexuals and the Transsexologists: Inversion and the Emergence of Transsexual Subjectivity." In *Sexology in Culture: Labelling Bodies and Desires,* edited by Lucy Bland and Laura Doan, 116–31. Chicago: University of Chicago Press, 1998.

Radcliffe, Sarah, and Sallie Westwood, eds. *Remaking the Nation: Place, Identity and Politics in Latin America.* New York: Routledge, 1996.

Ramos, Carmen, and Ana Lau. *Mujeres y revolución, 1900–1917.* Mexico City: Instituto Nacional de Estudios Históricos, 1998.

Reed, James. *The Birth Control Movement and American Society: From Private Vice to Public Virtue.* Princeton, NJ: Princeton University Press, 1983.

Rico, Juan. *Congreso obrero de Izamal.* Mérida, Yucatán: n.p., 1922.

———. *La huelga de junio.* Mérida, Yucatán: n.p., 1922.

Rivera-Garza, Cristina. "General Insane Asylum: *La Castañeda* (Mexico)." In *Encyclopedia of Social Welfare History in North America,* edited by John M. Herrick and Paul H. Stuart, 148–50. Thousand Oaks, CA: Sage, 2005.

———. "The Masters of the Streets: Bodies, Power and Modernity in Mexico, 1867–1930." PhD diss., University of Houston, 1995.

Robb, George. "The Way of All Flesh: Degeneration, Eugenics, and the Gospel of Free Love." *Journal of the History of Sexuality* 6, no. 4 (1996): 589–603.

Roberts, Jon H. "The Struggle over Evolution." In *Encyclopedia of American Cultural & Intellectual History,* vol. 1, edited by Mary Kupiec Cayton and Peter W. Williams, 589–97. New York: Scribner, 2001.

Rojina Villegas, Rafael. "Capacidad de la mujer en el derecho civil y condición juridical de la mujer Mexicana." In *La situación jurídica de la mujer mexicana,* edited by Alianza de Mujeres de México, 11–23. Mexico City: Alianza de Mujeres de México, 1953.

———. *Compendio de derecho civil.* 7th ed. Vol. 1, *Introducción, personas y familia.* Mexico City: Editorial Porrúa, 1997.

Rolls-Hansen, Nils. "Eugenics and the Science of Genetics." In *The Oxford Handbook of the History of Eugenics,* edited by Philippa Levine and Alison Bashford, 80–97. New York: Oxford University Press, 2010.

Roper, Allen G. *Ancient Eugenics: The Arnold Prize Essay for 1913.* Oxford: Blackwell, 1913.

Ross, Edward Alsworth. "Recent Tendencies in Sociology." *Harvard Quarterly Journal of Economics* 17:3 (May 1903): 438–55.

Rousseau, Jean-Jacques. *The Confessions of Jean-Jacques Rousseau.* Translated by W. Conyngham Mallory. New York: Tudor Publishing, 1928.

———. *Émile, or Education.* Translated by Barbara Foxley. New York: E. P. Dutton, 1930.

"Rousseau, Jean Jacques (1712–1778)." In *Encyclopedia of European Social History,* vol. 6, edited by Peter N. Stearns, 301–5. Detroit: Scribner, 2001.

Saavedra M., Alfredo. "Lo que México ha publicado acerca de eugenesia." In Ateneo Nacional de Ciencias y Artes, *Primero Congreso Bibliográfico Mexicano,* 103–25. Mexico City: DAPP, 1937.

Salamini, Heather Fowler. *Agrarian Radicalism in Veracruz, 1920–1938.* Lincoln: University of Nebraska Press, 1978.

Sánchez Novelo, Faulo M. *José María Iturralde Traconis, "El Kanxoc": Ideología y política en un regimen socialista yucateco.* Mérida, Yucatán: Maldonado Editores, 1986.

Sanders, Nichole. "Mother and Family Programs (Mexico)." In *Encyclopedia of Social Welfare History in North America,* edited by John M. Herrick and Paul H. Stuart, 239–41. Thousand Oaks, CA: Sage, 2005.

Sanger, Margaret. "La regulación de la natalidad o la brujula del hogar: Medios seguros y científicos para evitar la concepción." Mérida, Yucatán: Centro de Apoyo CII, 1922.

Schell, Patience A. *Church and State Education in Revolutionary Mexico City.* Tucson: University of Arizona, 2003.

———. "Eugenics Policy and Practice in Cuba, Puerto Rico, and Mexico." In *The Oxford Handbook of the History of Eugenics,* edited by Philippa Levine and Alison Bashford, 477–92. New York: Oxford University Press, 2010.

———. "Nationalizing Children through Schools and Hygiene: Porfirian and Revolutionary Mexico City." *The Americas* 60, no. 4 (2004): 559–87.

Secretaría de Educación Pública. *El esfuerzo educativo en México: La obra del gobierno federal en el ramo de educación pública durante la administración del presidente Plutarco Elías Calles (1924–1928); Memoria analítico-crítica de la organización actual de la Secretaría de Educación Pública, sus éxitos, sus fracasos, los derroteros que la experiencia señala; Presentada al H. Congreso de la Unión por el Dr. J. M. Puig Casauranc, secretario del ramo en obediencia al Artículo 93 constitucional.* Mexico City, 1928.

Shaw, George Bernard. *Man and Superman.* New York: Brentano's, 1905.

Singh Bhatia, Manjeet, and Anurag Jhanjee. "Tokophobia: A Dread of Pregnancy." *Industrial Psychiatry Journal* 21, no. 2 (July–December 2012): 158–59.

Sloan, Kathryn. "Defiant Daughters and the Emancipation of Minors in Nineteenth-Century Mexico." In *Girlhood: A Global History,* edited by Jennifer Hengren and Colleen A. Vasconcellos, 363–81. New Brunswick, NJ: Rutgers University Press, 2010.

Smith, Stephanie J. *Gender and the Mexican Revolution: Yucatán Women and the Realities of Patriarchy.* Chapel Hill: University of North Carolina Press, 2006.

———. "'If Love Enslaves . . . Love Be Damned!' Divorce and Revolutionary State Formation in Yucatán." In *Sex in Revolution: Gender, Politics, and Power in Modern Mexico*, edited by Jocelyn Olcott, Mary Kay Vaughan, and Gabriela Cano, 99–111. Durham, NC: Duke University Press, 2006.

Soto, Shirlene Ann. *Emergence of the Modern Mexican Woman: Her Participation in the Revolution and Struggle for Equality, 1910–1940*. Denver: Arden Press, 1990.

———. *The Mexican Woman: A Study of Her Participation in the Revolution, 1910–1940*. Palo Alto, CA: R&E Research Associates, 1979.

Souza de Fernández, Candelaria. "Prólogo." In Carlos Urzaiz Jiménez, *Oficio de mentor: Biografía del Dr. Eduardo Urzaiz Rodríguez*, 9–13. Mérida, Yucatán: Ediciones de la Universidad Autónoma de Yucatán, 1996.

Spencer, Herbert. *Principles of Biology*. New York: D. Appleton and Co., 1864.

———. *Principles of Psychology*. New York: D. Appleton and Co., 1862.

———. *Synthetic Philosophy*. London: Williams & Norgate, 1862.

Stepan, Nancy Leys. *"The Hour of Eugenics": Race, Gender, and Nation in Latin America*. Ithaca, NY: Cornell University Press, 1991.

Stern, Alexandra Minna. "Eugenics." In *Encyclopedia of Mexico: History, Society & Culture*, vol. 1, edited by Michael S. Werner, 462–64. Chicago: Fitzroy Dearborn, 1997.

———. "Gender and Sexuality: A Global Tour and Compass." In *The Oxford Handbook of the History of Eugenics*, edited by Philippa Levine and Alison Bashford, 173–91. New York: Oxford University Press, 2010.

———. "From Mestizophilia to Biotypology." In *Race & Nation in Latin America*, edited by Nancy P. Appelbaum, Anne S. MacPherson, and Karin Alejandra Rosemblatt, 187–210. Chapel Hill: University of North Carolina Press, 2003.

———. "Responsible Mothers and Normal Children: Eugenics, Nationalism, and Welfare in Post-revolutionary Mexico, 1920–1940." *Journal of Historical Sociology* 12, no. 4 (December 1999): 369–97.

———. "Unraveling the History of Eugenics in Mexico." *The Mendel Newsletter*, n.s., 8 (February 1999): 1–10.

Stewart, Andrew. "Polyclitus." In *The Oxford Classical Dictionary*, 4th ed., edited by Simon Hornblower and Antony Spawforth, 1176. Oxford: Oxford University Press, 2012.

———. "Praxiteles." In *The Oxford Classical Dictionary*, 4th ed., edited by Simon Hornblower and Antony Spawforth, 1205. Oxford: Oxford University Press, 2012.

Stoler, Ann Laura. *Race and the Education of Desire: Foucault's "History of Sexuality" and the Colonial Order of Things*. Durham, NC: Duke University Press, 1995.

———. "Sexual Affronts and Racial Frontiers: European Identities and the Cultural Politics of Exclusion in Colonial Southeast Asia." In *Tensions of Empire: Colonial Cultures in a Bourgeois World*, edited by Frederic Cooper and Ann Laura Stoler, 198–237. Berkeley: University of California Press, 1997.

Summers, Lionel M. "The Divorce Laws of Mexico." *Law and Contemporary Problems* (1935): 310–31.

Tilly, Louise A. "Women, Work, and Citizenship." *International Labor and Working Class History* 52 (1997): 1–26.

Tovar Ramírez, Aurora. *Mil quinientas mujeres en nuestra conciencia colectiva: Catálogo biográfico de mujeres de México.* Mexico City: Documentación y Estudios de Mujeres, A.C., 1996.

Treitel, Corinna. *A Science for the Soul: Occultism and the Genesis of the German Modern.* Baltimore: Johns Hopkins University Press, 2004.

Turda, Marius. "Race, Science, and Eugenics in the Twentieth Century." In *The Oxford Handbook of the History of Eugenics*, edited by Philippa Levine and Alison Bashford, 62–79. New York: Oxford University Press, 2010.

United Nations. *Population Prospects.* New York: United Nations, 1989.

———. *United Nations Demographic Yearbook.* New York: United Nations, 1989.

Urías Horcasitas, Beatriz. *Historias secretas del racismo en México (1920–1950).* Mexico City: Tusquets, 2007.

Urzaiz, Eduardo. *Compendio de histología general y elementos de embriología.* Mérida, Yucatán: Universidad de Yucatán, n.d.

———. *Conferencias sobre biología.* Mérida, Yucatán: Talleres gráficos de "La revista de Yucatán," 1922.

———. *Conferencias sobre historia de las religiones.* Mérida, Yucatán: Imp. y Lin. El Porvenir, 1935.

———. *Conferencias sobre sociología.* Mérida, Yucatán: n.p., n.d.

———. *Del imperio a la revolución: 1865–1910.* Mérida, Yucatán: n.p., 1946.

———. *Don Quijote de la Mancha ante la psiquiatría.* Mérida, Yucatán: n.p., n.d. [Republished as *Don Quijote de la Mancha ante la psiquiatría: Tomado del Boletín de la Universidad Nacional del Sureste.* Mérida, Yucatán: Universidad Autónoma de Yucatán, 2002.]

———. "El hogar del porvenir: Amor, monogamia, y matrimonio." *Orbe*, no. 6 (April–May 1945): 5–8.

———. *El pintor Juan Gamboa Guzmán.* Mérida, Yucatán: n.p., n.d. Republished as *Juan Gamboa Guzmán.* Merida, Yucatán: Universidad Autónoma de Yucatán, 2002.

———. *El porvenir del caballo.* Mérida, Yucatán: n.p., n.d. Republished Mérida, Yucatán: Universidad Autónoma de Yucatán, 2002.

———. "El protoplasma: Su composición y propiedades; La célula; Los seres unicelulares y multicelulares; La vida de los seres y la vida celular independiente; Los seres coloniales." *La Higiene: Organo de la Dirección General de Salubridad e Higiene* 1, no. 2 (July–August 1918): 80–82.

———. *España es la misma.* Mérida, Yucatán: n.p., n.d.

———. *Estudio psicológico sobre el espíritu varonil de Sor Juana Inés de la Cruz.* Mérida, Yucatán: n.p., n.d.

———. *Eugenia: Esbozo novelesco de costumbres futuras.* Mérida, Yucatán: Talleres gráficos A. Manzanilla, 1919.

———. *Exégesis Cervantina.* Mérida, Yucatán: Universidad Autónoma de Yucatán, 1950.

———. "Historia de la educación pública y privada desde 1911." In *Enciclopedia Yucatense,* vol. 4. Mexico City: Gobierno de Estado, 1945.

———. "Historia del dibujo, la pintura y la escultura." In *Enciclopedia Yucatense,* vol. 4. Mexico City: Gobierno de Estado, 1945.

———. "La diferenciación de los sexos: Los seres asexuales; Hermafrodismo y pseudo-hermafrodismo; Caracteres sexuales secundarios; Reproducción asexual, sexual, y alternante." *La Higiene: Organo de la Dirección General de Salubridad e Higiene* 1, no. 7 (December 1918): 262–63.

———. *La emigración cubana en Yucatán.* Mérida, Yucatán: Editorial Club del Libro, 1949.

———. "La especie, el género, las variedades y las razas: Herencia; Origen de las especies; Teoria de la evolución o del transformismo; Darwinismo; Lamarckismo; Neo-lamarckismo." *La Higiene: Organo de la Dirección General de Salubridad e Higiene* 1, no. 4 (September 1918): 156–57.

———. *La familia, cruz del apóstol.* Mérida, Yucatán: Universidad Nacional del Sureste, 1953.

———. *Los hormones sexuales.* Mérida, Yucatán: n.p., 1922. Republished as *Los hormones sexuales: Tomado del Boletín de la Universidad Nacional del Sureste.* Mérida, Yucatán: Universidad Autónoma de Yucatán, 2002.

———. *La racha espiritualista contemporánea.* Mérida, Yucatán: n.p., n.d.

———. "La reproducción en las plantas fanerógamas: Reproducción por estacas; Acodos e hijos, bulbos, rozomas, o tallos subterráneos; El ingerto y el cruce en las plantas; La simbiosis." *La Higiene: Organo de la Dirección General de Salubridad e Higiene* 2, no. 2 (February 1919): 315–16.

———. *Las tribulaciones del maestro Buendía.* Mérida, Yucatán: n.p., n.d.

———. *Manual práctico de psiquiatría.* Mérida, Yucatán: n.p., 1936.

———. *Nociones de antropología pedagógica.* Mérida, Yucatán: n.p. n.d.

———. *Petite chose.* Mérida, Yucatán: n.p., n.d. Republished Mérida, Yucatán: Universidad Autónoma de Yucatán, 2002.

———. *¿Quién fue José Martí?* Mérida, Yucatán: Comité pro-centenario de Marti en Yucatán, 1953.

———. *Vidas tronchadas o Los dramas de la obstetricia.* Mérida, Yucatán: n.p., n.d.

Urzaiz, Eduardo [Claudio Meex, pseud.]. *Reconstrucción de hechos: Anécdotas yucatecas ilustradas.* Mérida: Ediciones de la Universidad Autónoma de Yucatán, 1992.

Urzáiz Jimenez, Carlos. *Oficio de mentor: Biografía del Dr. Eduardo Urzáiz Rodríguez.* Mérida, Yucatán: Ediciones de la Universidad Autónoma de Yucatán, 1996.

Vanderwood, Paul. "Building Blocs but Yet No Building: Regional History and the Mexican Revolution." *Mexican Studies/Estudios Mexicanos* 3, no. 2 (1987): 421–32.

Van Young, Eric. *Mexico's Regions: Comparative History and Development.* San Diego: Center for U.S.–Mexican Studies, 1992.

Vasconcelos, José. *The Cosmic Race/La raza cósmica.* Translated, with an introduction, by Didier T. Jaén. Afterword by Joseba Gabilondo. Baltimore: Johns Hopkins University Press, 1997.

Vaughan, Mary Kay. *Cultural Politics in Revolution: Teachers, Peasants, and Schools in Mexico, 1930–1940*. Tucson: University of Arizona Press, 1997.

———. "Education: 1889–1940." In *Encyclopedia of Mexico: History, Society & Culture*, vol. 1, edited by Michael S. Werner, 441–45. Chicago: Fitzroy Dearborn, 1997.

Vaughan, Mary Kay, and Stephen E. Lewis, eds. *The Eagle and the Virgin: Nation and Cultural Revolution in Mexico, 1920–1940*. Durham, NC: Duke University Press, 2006.

Von Vacano, Diego. "A Zarathustra Criollo: Vasconcelos on Race." In *Forging People: Race, Ethnicity, and Nationality in Hispanic American and Latino/a Thought*, edited by Jorge J. E. García, 203–27. Notre Dame: Notre Dame University Press, 2011.

Wasserman, Mark. *Everyday Life and Politics in Nineteenth Century Mexico: Men, Women, and War*. Albuquerque: University of New Mexico, 2000.

———. "You Can Teach an Old Revolutionary Historiography New Tricks: Regions, Popular Movements, Culture, and Gender in Mexico, 1820–1940." *Latin American Research Review* 43, no. 2 (2008): 260–71.

Weikart, Richard. "Eugenics." In *Encyclopedia of Science, Technology, and Ethics*, vol. 2, edited by Carl Mitcham, 707–10. Detroit: Macmillan Reference, 2005.

Wells, Allen. *Yucatán's Gilded Age: Haciendas, Henequen, and International Harvester, 1860–1915*. Albuquerque: University of New Mexico Press, 1985.

Welter, Barbara. "The Cult of True Womanhood: 1820–1860." *American Quarterly* 18 (1966): 151–74.

Whimster, Sam, and Scott Lash, eds. *Max Weber: Rationality and Modernity*. London: Allen and Unwin, 1987.

Woloson, Wendy. "Mother's Day." In *St. James Encyclopedia of Popular Culture*, vol. 3, edited by Sarah Pendergast and Tom Pendergast, 417–18. Woodbridge, CT: St. James Press, 2000.

Wood, Andrew. "Adalberto Tejeda of Veracruz." In *State Governors in the Mexican Revolution, 1910–1952: Portraits in Conflict, Courage, and Corruption*, edited by Jürgen Buchenau and William Beezley, 77–94. Lanham, MD: Rowman & Littlefield, 2009.

Zamyatin, Yevgeny Ivanovich. *We*. New York: E. P. Dutton, 1924.

Index

abortion: as negative eugenic strategy, 143

activist. *See* feminist; Marvini, León; Mexican Revolution; Urzaiz Rodríguez, Eduardo

adultery: in Mexican laws, 99, 103

Aeolus and Aeolian harp, 11, 11N6

aesthetics/aestheticism. *See* Vasconcelos, José; Von Vacano, Diego

African American. *See* black (people)

Africans: doctors visiting Institute of Eugenics in *Eugenia*, 155–156. *See also* Hottentot

age. *See* citizenship; education; Mexican Revolution

agrarian law: effect on women in postrevolutionary Mexico, 125–126NN66–67

Alba, Francisco: on influenza as cause for population decline following Mexican Revolution, 132N125

alcohol: anti-alcohol or temperance campaigns/initiatives, xxvii, 108–109, 130N116, 147, 160; use restricted in Eugenic Sterilization Law, 160

Alianza de Mujeres: on Mexican women's legal status, 105, 125N65

Alvarado, Salvador: and anarchism, xxvii; and anti-alcohol and anti-drug campaigns, xxvii; and capitalism, xxvii; and coeducation, xxvi; and divorce, xxvii, 99; and educational reforms, xxvii; and family law, xxvii, 99–100; and feminist conferences/congresses, xxvii, 105; and feminist organizations, xxvii, 109–111; and labor law (including for female domestic servants), xxvii, 106; and Mexican Revolution/postrevolutionary reform, xxiv, xxvi–xxviii, 109–111; and program to revitalize Yucatecan henequen industry, xxvi–xxvii; and socialism, xxvii–xviii; and women's suffrage, 105

American Birth Control League, 112. *See also* Kennedy, Ann; Sanger, Margaret

anarchism, xxvii–xxviii. *See also* Hart, John Mason; rationalist education and schools

anarcho-syndicalism, xxviii

angels of the house, 106, 117, 117N1

anthropology, xxx, 160

anthropometric testing and data, 144–146, 164

anticlericism, xxv–xxvii, 97, 111, 138–139, 147

Argentina: and eugenics under Perón, 173N69

Arrigunaga, Maritza: on Urzaiz Rodríguez, xxiii, xxxivN32

artificial (human, as opposed to natural) selection: in *Eugenia*, 134–136

Asilo Ayala. *See* Ayala Asylum

Ateneo Peninsular (Asociación Científica y Artística Ateneo Peninsular/Peninsular Scientific and Artistic Association), xxiv, xxxvN37

authoritarian/authoritarianism: Mexican postrevolutionary state as, 146, 148, 173N68; Mexican postrevolutionary state compared with other national authoritarian states, 146; Urzaiz Rodríguez warning against the extremes of, in *Eugenia*, 165–166. *See also* Beezley, Bill; Urías Horcasitas, Beatriz

authoritarian bureaucracy, 148

City of the Sun (Campanella). *See under* Campanella, Tommaso
ciudadana/ciudadanía, 95–96, 118N6
ciudadano, 96, 119N6
civil citizenship rights, 94–104, 110, 175–176, 185; ability to inherit and bequeath property as, 110; acquisition and defense of property as, 94; freedom of expression/speech as, 94, 121N14; freedom of religion as, 94, 121N15; freedom to decide when to have children as, 110; opportunity to divorce as, 110; opportunity to enter or end a contract, including labor and marriage, as, 94; opportunity to pursue education as, 94, 121N14; opportunity to serve as guardian to children as, 110; opportunity to work as, 94; responsibilities and prerogatives of, 118–120N6
civil codes. *See* Mexican civil codes
civilization: ancient Greece as birthplace of modern western, 155, 164; pre-Colombian American, 12N7; Villautopia as, 160
civilizing mission: goal of Mexican Revolution, xxvi, xxix, 155; racial improvement as prerequisite for, xxix, 155–156
civil registry: in Mexico, 188; in Yucatán, 112; Yucatecan civil registry's involvement in birth control campaign, 112
civil society (including Church organizations), 95, 120N9. *See also* Ehrenberg, John; public sphere
coeducation. *See* Alvarado, Salvador; Urzaiz Rodríguez, Eduardo
Coeducational Teachers' College (Escuela Normal Mixta, Yucatán), xxiv
comadres. *See* gynecologists; gynecology; midwives/midwifery; obstetricians; obstetrics
Comfort, Nathaniel: on Bateson and Mendel's theories of inheritance and genetics, 170–171N51
Committee on Education, State of Yucatán, 150
communism: in *Eugenia*, 165
compulsory primary education in Mexico, 144
Comte, Auguste, 139–140, 142, 153
conferences/congresses. *See* child welfare conferences/congresses; conferences/congresses

on pedagogy in Yucatán; feminist; National Educational Conference; National Pedagogic Hygiene Conference; Pan American Eugenics and Homiculture Conference; Pan American Women's Conference; Urzaiz Rodríguez, Eduardo
conferences/congresses on pedagogy in Yucatán (1915 and 1916), xxiv
conquest of Americas, 142
conquistadores, 157, 199
Consejo Superior de Salubridad (Health Council, Porfirian), 109
conservatives (in nineteenth-century Mexico), 138
Constitution. *See* Mexican Constitution
consumerism, 154
contraception/contraceptives. *See* birth control
cooperative kitchens, xxvii, 110
cooperativism, xxviii
corporatism/corporatist and corporatist-populism, 146, 148, 173N69; Latin American case studies of, 173N69; linked to eugenics and race ideology, 148; in Mexico, 148
Cortés, Hernán, 157, 199
cosa pública. *See* civil society; public sphere
The Cosmic Race. *See under* Vasconcelos, José
courtship: as a goal of the Mexican Revolution, 147. *See also* Ellis, Havelock
crime: lack of, in *Eugenia*, 163
criminology: and eugenics, xxx; and sexuality, 160
Cuba: Guanabacoa, birthplace of Urzaiz Rodríguez, xx, xxii; Havana, xx, xxii, 145; La Vibora, Havana, xxii. *See also* Pan American Eugenics and Homiculture Conference
cult of true womanhood, 117N1. *See also* Welter, Barbara

Daedelus. *See under* Haldane, J. B. S.
dance: rigadoon, 76, 76N29
Daphnis and Chloe, 25, 25N12
Darvill, Timothy: on Nebuchadnezzar, 19N8
Darwin, Charles: *The Descent of Man and Selection in Relation to Sex* (1871), 137, 140; influence

homosexuality (*continued*)
  study of, by various medical and welfare professions, 162. *See also* Freud, Sigmund; Urzaiz Rodríguez, Eduardo
honor codes (colonial era), 99, 123N35
hormones: feminization with hormone therapy of gestators in *Eugenia*, 107, 163, 164, 186
hospital. *See* La Castañeda; Hospital Divino Salvador; Hospital General; Hospital Morelos; Hospital O'Horan; Hospital San Hipólito
Hospital Divino Salvador (Divine Savior Hospital), 109
Hospital General (General Hospital, Mexico City), 109
Hospital Morelos (Morelos Hospital, for syphilitics, Mexico City), 109
Hospital O'Horan (O'Horan Hospital, Mérida, Yucatán): Urzaiz Rodríguez's contributions to, xxiv
Hospital San Hipólito (Saint Hipolito Hospital, Catholic, Mexico City), 109
Hottentot, 27N13. *See also* Africans
Howe, Julia Ward: as advocate for Mother's Day in the United States, 132N131
Huxley, Aldous: *Brave New World* (1932) compared to *Eugenia*, xxxiiN3, 179, 191, 199
hygiene: as focus of eugenics in Mexico, 143, 148; as goal of Revolution, xxvi–xxvii, 111; Mexican revolutionary programs promoting, xxvi–xxvii. *See also* child hygiene centers; Child Hygiene Service; Department of Psychopedagogy and Hygiene; Inspección Médica e Higiénica (Medical and Hygienic Inspection Service); National Pedagogic Hygiene Conference; School Hygiene Service; Secretariat of Justice and Public Instruction; Urzaiz Rodríguez, Eduardo
hysterectomy: performed in nineteenth-century Mexico, 161

immigration: as strategy to whiten (eugenically improve) population, 141, 164. *See also* migration
incubators. *See* gestators

independence, of Mexico (from Spain), 138, 177
India: Malthusian/neo-Malthusian organizations in, 159
Indian. *See* indigenous people
indigenismo and *indigenistas*, 152–157; defined, 135. *See also* mestizophilia
indigenous people: becoming mestizos or "whitening" through education, migration, and occupational shifts, 141; dispossession of land from, 97, 141; Porfirian projects to assimilate, 141; viewed as degenerate by Porfirian *científicos*, 141
industrialization in Mexico, 139, 141, 142, 154, 182
influenza: as case for population decline in Mexico, 132N125
Ingle, Marjorie I.: on neo-Mayan architecture, 12N7
inheritance (genetic, related to evolution): Darwin and theories of, 167NN12–13; intellectual history/theories of, 135, 170–171N51. *See also* Darwin, Charles; Galton, Francis; Lamarck, Jean-Baptiste Pierre Antoine de Monet; Lamarckism; neo-Lamarckian/neo-Lamarckism; Mendel, Gregor; Spencer, Herbert; Wallace, Alfred Russell
Inquiries into Human Faculty and Its Development (1883). *See under* Galton, Francis
insanity: *Eugenia* described by author as work of madman, xix–xx. *See also* Urzaiz Rodríguez, Eduardo
Inspección Médica e Higiénica (Medical and Hygienic Inspection Service), 144
Institute of Eugenics in *Eugenia*, 105, 106, 107, 134, 185, 186, 187, 193, 196, 197
Instituto Nacional de Estadística, Geografía, e Informatíca (INEGI): on population decline following the Mexican Revolution, 132N124
interwar years: defined, 166N2; depopulation and eugenics in, 158–159; eugenics in, 134; pronatalism in, 113
Irwin, Robert McKee: on economic motivations for male pregnancy in *Eugenia*, 159–160, 176N115; on *Eugenia* and the Mexican Revolution, xxv; on *Eugenia* as a dystopia

Vasconcelos, José (*continued*)
153–155, 174N88; and black (people), 152, 155–156; and Catholic Church/Christianity, 174N88; as critic of Comte and Darwin, 153; and Darwinism, 155; and eugenic theory, 155, 157, 188; as *indigenista*, 152; and Mendel, 157; and *mestizaje*, 152, 188; and miscegenation, 156; as national minister of education, xxiv; and occult, 154; and positivism, 153; *La Raza Cósmica/The Cosmic Race* (1925), xxiv, 152–154, 157, 188; and spiritualism, 154; and Theosophy, 154

Vaughan, Mary Kay: on ousting of Governor Adalberto Tejada, 176N119

Vega, Luis: coauthor and co-composer of the song "La Peregrina," 201N39

Velázquez Bringas, Esperanza: biography, 172N73; on distribution of Sanger's pamphlet for birth control campaign, 131N120; intellectual influences on, 174N78; involvement in birth control campaign, 145, 149, 159; presented at the child welfare conference/congress (1921), 145

venereal disease: addressed by Eugenic Sterilization Law, 160

Venus, 11. *See also* Citeres

Veracruz, Mexico: Eugenic Sterilization Law, 160

Vichy regime. *See* France

Villautopia: as futuristic, xvii; key characteristics of, xvii; socioeconomic organization of, 105. *See also* civilization; *Eugenia*; population; utopia

violence: following Mexican Revolution, 147

virginity: production of blood-stained nuptial cloth as proof of, 77, 77N31

Voltaire: Miguel (character in *Eugenia*) compared to, 16

Von Vacano, Diego: on Vasconcelos and aesthetics, 174N88; on Vasconcelos and Christianity/Catholic Church, 174N88; on Vasconcelos and Nietzsche, 174N88

vote/voting. *See* citizenship; Mexican Constitution; political citizenship rights; suffrage

Wallace, Alfred Russell, 140

war. *See* interwar years; World War I; World War II

Warens, Madame: as mother, 192; role for Jean-Jacques Rousseau compared with Celiana's role for Ernesto, 9, 9N59, 181, 192, 198

Wasserman, Mark: on regions as laboratories of the Mexican Revolution, xxxviiN46, 118N2

Watteau, Jean-Antoine, 24, 24N11

We (1924). *See under* Zamyatin, Yevgeny

Weismann, August, 143

welfare services: and/for children, 108–109; Church-administered in Mexico, 108–109; as focus of eugenics in Latin America, 148; in *Eugenia*, xxviii, 66, 105, 165; and Mexican Revolution, 108–110; in Mexico (federal), 108–109; and/for mothers, 93–94, 109, 116; poorhouses, 142; in Yucatán (provincial), 93–94. *See also* Child Hygiene Centers; Child Hygiene Service; child welfare conferences/congresses; Espinosa de los Reyes, Isidro; Ochoa, Enrique; Public Services Fund

Wells, Allen: on henequen production and industry in Yucatán, xxxviiiN47

Wells, H. G., 102, 125N60, 184, 189, 191; *A Modern Utopia* (1905), 184, 189

Werther (character in Goethe, *The Sorrows of Young Werther*), 90, 90N34

women: and citizenship, 94–106; election to office in Yucatán, 105; legal rights, responsibilities, and status in *Eugenia*, 97; legal rights, responsibilities, and status in nineteenth- and twentieth-century Mexico, 93–100, 103–106; legal rights, responsibilities, and status in twentieth-century Yucatán, 99–100, 105; and mothering/parenting in *Eugenia*, xviii, 106, 107, 115, 117, 180, 185, 189, 197; and mothering/parenting in late nineteenth- and early twentieth-century Mexico, 110, 116, 143, 163, 172; roles in *Eugenia*, xxix, 106–107, 117, 183; roles in late nineteenth-century

Mexico, 93–94, 96, 99, 103, 106, 109 115–
117, 117N1, 183–184, 195; roles in Mexican
Revolution, 109; and welfare, 109, 115–
116; worship of, as key feature in science
and speculative fiction, 190. *See also* angels
of the house; Irwin, Robert McKee;
maternalism

Wood, Andrew: on Tejada, 175N119

workers: in *Eugenia*, xxix, 106–107; houses (*casas
del obrero*), xviii; organizing into leagues
and syndicates, xxvii; rights, 105–106. *See
also* labor law

World War I, 113, 132
World War II, xxxvN35

Yucatán Civil Code, 100
Yucatán's School of Medicine and Surgery. *See*
School of Medicine and Surgery
Yucatecan Society of Obstetrics and Gynecol-
ogy: Urzaiz Rodríguez as president of,
xxiv

Zamyatin, Yevgeny: *We* (1924) compared to
Eugenia, xxxiiN3, 199